The Tears of Jihad

Sean Emerson

Cover design by Aaron Hover

ISBN: 1 494 33862 9
ISBN-13 978-1 494 33862 6

To my family,
for letting me write it

To Dawn,
for making me write it.

1. Eastern Syria
June 8, 634

Khalid bin Al Waleed shifted uncomfortably in the saddle. He resisted the temptation to lick his lips, knowing that it would do no good. His mouth was as dry as cotton; his tongue felt swollen. His camel hung its head, slowly sniffing the ground. Khalid worked his mouth, trying to summon enough spit to speak. When he did, his voice came out as a hoarse croak. "Raafe, if you cannot find the water you promised, we're all dead men."

Raafe bin Umeira turned his head towards Khalid's voice. The intense Syrian sun reflecting off the sand had taken his sight, and he'd covered his eyes with his turban against the pain. His voice was barely a whisper. "Are we in a large wadi?"

Khalid nodded, then remembered that Raafe couldn't see him. "Yes," he said and craned forward to hear the whispered response.

"Look for two hillocks," Raafe gagged and swallowed drily. "Like the breasts of a woman." Khalid sat upright and jerked the reins to get his camel moving. The head of the long column wearily begin moving up the wide wadi.

Raafe was too weary, too thirsty to be scared. He clung to the saddle of his camel and wondered if his sight would ever return, or if he'd be forever doomed to be a beggar, living on the handouts of the more fortunate. Perhaps it's Allâh's blessing that he die here of thirst.

He felt the hot wind tug at his beard, not cooling or soothing, but like a breath from Hell. This expedition was insanity itself. Only a madman would have ventured to force march four thousand men across a trackless, waterless desert for five days. Had it been only five days since they left the wide banks of the Euphrates? For what? Syria would always be here. An extra two weeks to trek north and follow a more reasonable route wouldn't have hurt anything. Khalid's eagerness to find a fight had surely doomed them all. Raafe was beyond caring about that. After all, it was his fault for telling Khalid that such a desert crossing could even be done.

The column rounded a slight bend in the wadi, heading west, and two gentle hills came into view. The guide leading his camel tugged at Raafe's cloak. "I see the hills!"

Raafe dared to hope. 'Has Allâh shown mercy on us?' He raised his whisper as loud as he could. "Look for a thorn tree shaped like a man in a sitting posture." The guide passed along his instruction to Khalid.

Khalid had been saving a last swallow of water for this moment, when he would need to be heard. He halted his camel and waved the column forward. As the first hundred or so of the hardiest men gathered around him, he raised his parched voice as loud as he dared and repeated the instruction. Using hand gestures, he made assignments for his men to search.

Khalid dismounted and squatted in the shadow of his animal. An hour passed and the column slowly filtered in from the desert and filled the wadi. The men who'd been sent to search returned with no news. They could find no thorn tree. Khalid's anger was tempered by the sympathy he felt for the blind Raafe. "Raafe, there is no tree! Our lives are in your hands! You need to find the water you promised!"

Raafe spoke wearily. "Our lives are in the hands of Allâh. We belong to him and indeed to him we shall return. If you can't find the tree, then we've perished." The realization became something of a relief to him. The struggle was over; now he could relax and wait for death. "Look again, if you will."

Khalid heard the resignation in Raafe's voice, his usefulness clearly at an end. He rose and set his mouth in determination. "Pass the word. Spread out. Form a grid, ten cubits to a man, and dig." He didn't tell them what to dig for. These men had all grown up in the rocks and sand of Arabia. They knew that wood or damp sand would lead to water.

When a cry went up at the edge of the wadi, Raafe struggled to his feet in excitement. A messenger reported, "We've found the trunk of a tree!"

"Dig under the roots!" Raafe cried. Across the wadi, men abandoned the holes they'd been digging and gravitated towards the source of the excitement.

The hole was enlarged and deepened, then the bottom suddenly bubbled and the men sank knee deep in saturated sand. A trench was quickly dug down the hill and the water flowed like a small river.

Dhiraar bin Al Azwar was holding back the men and horses from the flowing water when Khalid walked up. Arabs would always test an unknown water source with a single horse or a camel, in case it was poisoned. "Let them drink, Dhiraar. If it's poisonous, we will die either way."

Khalid took a cup of water to Raafe. "My friend, you've saved us. Allâh's blessings on you. Praise be to Allâh!"

Men were still filtering in out of the desert. Hundreds had still not arrived. Khalid directed some of them to fill water skins and work their way back along their route, refreshing the stragglers. As the animals were led to the water and the shadows began to lengthen, he sat to rest and reflected on his mission. He felt a great weight lift from his shoulders. Indeed, he'd commanded that his men have faith in Allâh, and he showed no outward doubt that the forced march across the Syrian desert would be successful. Inside, however, the doubt had grown daily. He'd used every trick of desert survival he knew. He'd even kept the camels from water before they set out and on the last day allowed them to drink their fill, so they could be butchered as walking water tanks as needed. When Raafe had lost his sight, when they couldn't find the thorn tree, the knot in his stomach had tightened and made him almost physically ill. How close had he come to dooming four thousand elite soldiers? Was Allâh really watching over him, or was he just lucky – again?

Ubaidah was in charge of the four Muslim armies attacking Syria. He would soon get word that Khalid was to relinquish command of the attack on Persia and assume command of the Syrian campaign. He wouldn't expect Khalid for another month and would be doing his best to capture as much territory as he could in the meantime. Allâh only knew how many mujahideen would die under his inept leadership. Khalid smiled, anticipating the look on Ubaidah's face when he arrived two weeks ahead of time.

2. Tadmur, Syrian High Desert June 9, 634

Imad bin Najib turned to Bashour and Marid and inspected his students one last time. The boys' cloaks were a bit threadbare, but clean. It would have to do. In an outpost town like Tadmur one could hardly be expected to have fine clothes at hand for every occasion; especially when you've been growing as fast as these two had done. "Don't be shy towards our guest, but do be polite. A good impression will go a long way towards securing a recommendation for you to study under one of the Patriarchs in the west. And don't forget to speak Greek. Our guest doesn't understand Arabic, and it's impolite to speak a tongue that someone in the room doesn't understand."

"Yes, Mudarres!" Bashour patiently replied. He looked at his best friend, Marid, who rolled his eyes when Imad wasn't looking. Bashour suppressed a smile. Imad was clearly more excited about this meeting than they were.

Imad turned and faced them and placed his hands on their shoulders. He was surprised to realize that he was looking up at the boys. Even Bashour, the shorter of the two, was several inches taller than their teacher. When did that happen? He smiled proudly and then gathered himself. "Right, then, here we go."

The visiting priest, Marcian Kalekas, was seated in Imad's dining room. He rose to greet them when they entered. Imad greeted him with a hug, and introduced the boys. "Father Kalekas, may I present two of my most promising students, Bashour bin Ghalib and Marid bin al-Asad."

The priest was a spare man with hair curled in ringlets and a neat beard. "Gentlemen," he said as he shook their hands. They murmured greetings in return as they sat. Imad poured wine as his wife served the meal, then retired to the adjacent kitchen.

Father Kalekas pronounced a blessing over the meal, and some inconsequential talk followed for several minutes as they began to eat. Bashour tried to relax, knowing he didn't have to contribute to such a discussion. He felt nervous excitement in his stomach, for he knew that he might be called upon to discourse and he feared he'd make a fool of himself. He wished for a moment that he had the confidence that seemed to ooze from Marid.

Kalekas studied the young men as they ate. Bashour was on the tall side. He had broad shoulders that had yet to develop the bulk of a man. He had the normal prominent nose of his people, but it was softened somehow, seeming to fit his face more than highlight it. His chin was strong but not too prominent, and a lock of straight black hair arched over his forehead. The boy had a polite smile, but when prompted he burst into a broad grin, showing straight white teeth. The boy's voice was gathering the deepness of manhood and he had a soft, clear way of speaking. Kalekas kept coming back to the young man's eyes. They were dark, nearly black, and quick, like a hawk's. When he looked at you, you felt that he was studying you. After a few minutes, he decided that the young man could best be described as intense.

Marid was even taller than Bashour, with a lanky frame. His hands were huge and strong, but his eyes were empty compared to his friend's. He was quick to speak, quicker to laugh, and his voice carried when he spoke. Something about his apparent confidence suggested that he was overcompensating. Kalekas thought that Bashour's quiet intensity was more sincere than Marid's bravado, but he reserved judgment; his first impressions had been in error before.

When the meal was finished, Imad leaned back and took up his wine goblet. "So, Marcian, tell us the news of your travels."

"Well, what concerns most people these days is the Arab stirring to the south. There's an army moving near the southern borders. I've heard news that they've captured some of our outposts on the southern frontier. Some say they're massing for an invasion, but that hardly seems possible. The news from Persia is that they've been overrunning cities there. If that's true - and I have no reason to believe one way or another - then I don't think they'd have enough forces to mount much of an invasion of Syria."

Imad said, " I heard there was a civil war going on in Arabia."

"Yes. They had a chief there, Muhammad was his name; who forged an alliance among many of the tribes. He did it by threats and coercion; probably bribery as well. Some say he was some sort of prophet; that he claimed to talk to God. But he died a couple years ago with no heir, and the alliance shattered. Now it seems they've worked out a line of succession and are on the move."

"I wouldn't think you could mount much of an army from the desert. There can't be that many people there."

"Oh, there are more than you would imagine. There's much more rain than there used to be; the desert is blooming. My grandfather remarked on it, that Arabia never used to see such rain. The population there has no doubt exploded as a result."

Bashour imagined garden plants growing out of the cliffs in the desert mountains, a forest of green with crystal waterfalls in what had once been a barren, sun-blasted landscape.

Imad seemed thoughtful. "How much of a threat do these Arabs really pose?"

Kalekas waved his hand dismissively. "I don't think the Emperor takes them very seriously. Word is that his son-in-law, Thomas, has moved to Damascus. I doubt Heraclius would let his daughter accompany her husband like that, if he felt the Arabs posed any threat."

Imad leaned forward, interested. Bashour started paying more attention, not sure why his mentor felt this was important. "Really? That is news. Has Azrail fallen out of favor with Heraclius, then?" Bashour wondered who Azrail was and decided he must be some sort of official in Damascus. He shot a questioning look at Marid, who raised his eyebrows and gave a subtle shrug of his shoulders in return.

"Makes one wonder, doesn't it? Thomas claims he's in Damascus on private business, but no one that close to the Emperor moves without everyone taking note. Tongues are wagging, but as usual they have nothing useful to say."

Imad's face formed a look of disgust. "It's been my unfortunate experience that you won't go far wrong distrusting the Emperor's court." He shifted his weight and gathered his thoughts for a moment. "It was a great day when the Persians left Syria, and we rejoiced that we were once again under the government of Christians. But what has that gained us? Ruinous taxation and troops stationed in our cities, consuming our supplies. An Emperor who fornicates with his own kin. And they deign to instruct us in a ridiculous theology and spread lies about the true nature of the Christ. By God, we were better off under the Sassanids, who at least left us alone to practice our faith as we wished."

Bashour and Marid nodded their emphatic agreement. They were too young to remember much about the Persian occupation, and what they did remember didn't seem important. But they'd listened to Imad and their fathers criticizing the Emperor throughout their teen years and could recite their arguments almost verbatim.

The two men fell into a discussion about the nature of Christ, the controversy that seemed to consume the Christian world since the Sassanids had been defeated. Some believed that Jesus was all man and all god at the same time. Others believed that they were two distinct natures in one body. Both sides were accusing the others of heresy. The Emperor Heraclius was offering a compromise, that the human and divine natures of Christ were separate, but acted with one will, a position that didn't set well with either camp. It all seemed terribly trivial to the boys, and their minds wandered while the two men debated the positions at great length. They had heard it all before, and were quite bored with the controversy.

"This Arab invasion," Imad said, sitting back, "I'm telling you, Father, God's punishing this Emperor. Rome can still be saved, but Heraclius will have to annul his incestuous marriage and renounce heretical compromises. God will cleanse this land of his stain, if he doesn't do it himself."

Kalekas raised his goblet. "God will do as he will, old friend." He turned to the two boys. "Now, young men. I assume you're tired of herding sheep on the edge of nowhere?"

Bashour ducked his head in agreement. "Yes, Father. I want to study in the city."

Marid thumped his chest. "I want to be an officer in the army."

"A soldier's life can be hard, boy. But a head for numbers and a literary education can get you out of a lot of formation drill and into contact with people who'll teach you to lead. And it's a ticket to see the world. A soldier today is likely to serve along the Danube, keeping an eye on the Huns. I can make some inquiries."

Marid's eyes sparkled. He'd heard tales of the lands beyond the Bosphorus that were green as far as the eye could see.

Kalekas turned to Bashour. "And what will you study, boy? Do you wish to be a priest?" Bashour flushed crimson. He didn't want to insinuate an insult by declining the priesthood too vigorously, but he had no intention of following that path.

Before he could formulate a response, Marid rescued him. “He likes girls too much,” he said with laughter. The older men laughed as well.

“Don’t be shy about it. Holy orders aren’t for everybody, young man. Trust in God to show the way he’s prepared for you.”

Imad spoke up. “I’ve taught them all I can, Father. Mathematics, history, logic, theology. I could do more, but I haven’t the books with which to do it. The boys have promise and they need a better mentor than I can provide.”

“You’ve done well. Their Greek is excellent, almost without accent.”

The boys looked at each other and they seemed to swell with pride. Imad said, “I have a theory that if you begin teaching them at a young enough age, they can speak a language as well as a native, with no accent at all. Their brains are very adept when they’re young.”

“I said they have hardly any accent. In fact, they have exactly the same accent as you, you old fraud.” Kalekas laughed and Imad joined him. The boys smiled politely, not quite sure what was funny, thinking maybe it was an inside joke. Kalekas went on. “The world has a place for someone who can think and speak his mind. No doubt a student of Imad can do that. The rest is a matter of training. I’ll make inquiries and find positions for you.”

The late night air was still warm and the stars dominated the desert sky as Bashour and Marid made their way home from Imad’s house. When he was sure they couldn’t be heard, Marid said, "They sure love to carry on about the nature of Christ, don't they?"

"I'm so tired of that subject," said Bashour, "They might as well argue about how many angels can dance on the head of a pin, for all the difference it will make."

"I know. It sounds like they're arguing over how to say the same thing, sometimes."

"If I were a patriarch, I would direct them to throw both arguments away and start over from scratch. These kinds of discussions suggest make me think there's been a mistake in our initial assumptions somewhere.”

"Stay with fundamentals, right?" They grinned at the lesson their teacher was fond of repeating

Bashour went to bed that night happy. He felt that he'd been tested somehow, and that he'd passed. The future was looking up. He allowed himself to dream of being in the court of a patriarch in Damascus or Jerusalem. Maybe Constantinople! Every time his imagination ascended to a new level of achievement, he longed for even greater honor, until he was serving at the office of the Patriarch of Rome himself.

He also felt a current of unease. As bored as the discussion over the nature of Christ made him, he couldn't help by try to sort it out in his mind. The thing that bothered him was that God couldn't suffer and die, and that made the concept of the Trinity seem illogical. When he tried to ask a priest about it, he always got stonewalled, told that, "It's a mystery." You couldn't dismiss such fundamental issues. There had to be an answer and you had to keep exploring it until you found it.

3. Emessa, Syria
June 8, 634

Heraclius, the Emperor of the Roman Byzantine Empire, felt like death. A dull, throbbing ache was centered behind his eyes, and his stomach was threatening to reject his breakfast. He swallowed hard and leaned forward over the map table. "Speak to me!"

Caloiis, Commander of the Imperial Cavalry, did his best to ignore the obvious distress of Heraclius. The old man wouldn't tolerate sympathy. He'd served in enough campaigns under him to know that it was killing Heraclius to be here in Emessa, instead of joining his troops in the field. "We know of four main bodies of Arabs attacking. One has advanced towards Gaza on the west side of the Dead Sea. The other three are advancing abreast into Jordan. We've encountered some of their scouts and the columns appear to be slowing. These Arabs appear to have very little information about the land beyond the established trade routes."

Heraclius looked grim. "How many?"

"It's hard to say. It's difficult to get close to the main bodies, and we don't know how many are fighters and how many are camp followers. Call it perhaps five thousand effective soldiers in each column."

Heraclius massaged his temples. "I thought you said this was just a raid. Twenty thousand soldiers is hardly a raid, Merarch." The generals shifted uncomfortably around the map table. "How did the Arabs get reorganized so quickly? The last I heard, they were fighting a religious civil war, because that cult leader of theirs had died."

"Arabs grow up fighting. They've been fighting each other for centuries. This cult of 'Allâh' has somehow transcended tribal divisions and brought them together. They're fierce warriors, but undisciplined. I don't think they pose an effective threat unless they find a general who can organize them. I expect they'll melt away when they meet a professional army."

"I wish I shared your optimism, Merarch. I don't favor excessive caution, but I think it's a mistake to underestimate this opponent. We fought the Persians long enough, and I hear alarming things about what these Arabs have done there."

Turmarch Psellus spoke up. "Reports from Persia suggest that the Arabs' main advantage is superior mobility. They can choose the fight, fade away if things go badly and reappear somewhere else, faster than you can react. They hold the initiative."

Caloiis spoke dismissively. "They're not the only ones with cavalry you know, Psellus."

Psellus ignored the condescending tone. "Your cataphracts are no faster than the baggage train that accompanies them, Merarch. These Arabs can ride and fight all day on a handful of dates, and their camels can go a week without water. How many camels do you have?"

"That's enough!" Heraclius barked. Then, in a calmer tone, "They hold the initiative while they're attacking in the open field. How will they fare when they encounter walled cities? What if they're forced to defend?" The advisors maintained a respectful silence as the Emperor studied the map. "We're better off attacking their strongholds than defending ours." He jabbed his finger down on Jerusalem. "There. They will attack Jerusalem. They can't afford to leave it in their rear."

Caloiis said, "They couldn't take Jerusalem with a hundred thousand men."

"Exactly. But they don't know that. When they place Jerusalem under siege, I want to be ready for them. How many men can we muster to Palestine in a month's time?"

Psellus hesitated. This was a loaded question. He chose to be conservative. "I can have fifty thousand in a month's time, seventy-five thousand in six weeks. But that will place a tremendous strain on the supplies Jerusalem holds against a possible siege."

Heraclius smiled. "That's why we won't station them in Jerusalem. Encamp them a day's march from the city. If the enemy lays a siege, we'll break them and send the Arab back to the desert with his tail between his legs."

Many men would have stayed silent, but Psellus and Heraclius had seen too many campaigns together. He felt it was his duty to play devil's advocate. "And if the Arabs bypass Jerusalem and strike north on the east side of the Jordan River?"

"Even better. We screen to the east to cut his lines of communication." His left hand traced an arc through Bosra.

"Then our main force drives due south." The right hand drove forward, deep into the Arabian Peninsula. "We strike at their heart. Medina is their center. That's where their fat leader sits, like a spider in its web. Without Medina, the Arabs will be reduced to chaos. We bypass a direct confrontation and eliminate their capitol, exactly the way we defeated the Persians."

The commanders nodded in silent admiration. The old man was ill, but they knew of no other man who could plan contingencies the way Heraclius could. "Psellus, take a message to Andrew at Antioch. Notify him that I've promoted him to Strategos. He's to assemble a themata of six turma and bivouac a day's march from Jerusalem. He's authorized to use naval assets as necessary to move his forces. Then you remain in Antioch. I may need you there.

"Caloiis, bring your cataphracts up to battle readiness. When the time comes, I'll ride south with you on the Damascus road.

"Libanius, take a fast ship to Constantinople and assess the situation in Thrace. The Avars and Bulgars have been at each other for several years now. Let's hope they still are and will leave us alone. If it looks quiet enough, strip ten or fifteen thousand cavalry off the front and bring them back here."

"Shall we alert the city governors, advise them to prepare for an Arab attack?" asked Psellus, still acting as favored advocate. Psellus admired Caloiis' accomplishments in battle, but the man was a dullard when it came to planning. Caloiis was a warhorse, but his vision was narrow, as if he were wearing a warhorse's blinders.

Heraclius thought for a moment. "Send the governors an advisory communiqué only. Apprise them of the situation, but give no instructions. Let them decide what's appropriate. I don't want to start a widespread panic. I intend to defeat these brigands before they become a problem.

"Questions? No? Very well then. Dismissed."

Psellus and Caloiis left together. When they were out of earshot Psellus asked, "Do you think he was serious about riding with you?"

Caloiis snorted. "Yes, he was serious. But there's not a chance in hell. He won't admit how sick he is. Have you noticed how he never sits?"

"I worry about him. We need his leadership when we go into battle."

"The old lion's teeth are dull, but his mind is still sharp." They walked in silence until Caloiis spoke again. "A mere half-dozen years of peace and now this. I was hoping to die a landed gentleman on a peaceful farm, Psellus. Do you think there'll ever be a lasting peace?"

Psellus shrugged noncommittally. In his years close to court, one lesson Caloiis had never fully learned was when to keep his mouth shut. "It's in God's hands."

"Yes, it is and I'll tell you what's happening. This is God's punishment. It's because our Emperor – oh, excuse me, our *Basileus* – took his niece for a wife! Until he renounces her and puts her away, along with their idiot children, God will withhold his blessings from the whole empire."

Psellus wasn't prone to displays of anger. Caloiis was going to dig his own grave with his loose mouth. He stopped and faced Caloiis. "I believe you're thinking far above your station, Merarch. Be careful who hears you voice such opinions. You've no shortage of enemies here."

Caloiis' jaw worked in anger as he tried to stare down the shorter Psellus. He was checkmated, caught out, and he knew it. He wheeled and changed the subject. "What drives these Arabs? What do they want? Land? Power?"

Psellus released the breath he'd been half holding. "That's an easy one. Gold. They're operating an extortion racket. I've heard tales from Persia that they overrun a town and tell the inhabitants to pay them a gold coin for every person. They say that pays for safety and protection. But if you ask what people need safety and protection from, they won't admit that they're buying protection from the protectors."

"Criminal bastards."

"Indeed."

4. Eastern Syria
June 9, 634

Sameer Al-Ziyad rose from the morning prayers with his companions and rolled his prayer rug into a tight bundle. He adjusted the water skins slung over his shoulders and followed his companions as they set out in the cool predawn. They climbed out of the wadi and joined the rest of the army across the desert again. As the sun peeked over the horizon, Sameer began to hum quietly.

The five men had said little in the last few days. They'd been too thirsty and too tired to do more than trudge through the desert. Even the evil-tempered she-camel who carried their possessions lacked the energy for her customary attempts to maim whoever was nearby. No one had dared suggest the possibility that they might not find the water; especially when Raafe' bin Umeira had lost his sight. Now Rashad Al-Hamza noticed his friend humming ahead of him and could no longer contain himself, "Sameer, the longer we walk, the more cheerful you seem. Why are you in such good spirits?"

Sameer looked happily enigmatic and continued to walk without answering.

Jabir Bin Adham Al-Ansari leaned across Sameer as they walked and answered, "Haven't you noticed, Rashad? Ever since Khalid dismissed the baggage train to return to Medina, every step has taken us further away from our women."

Rashad took a couple of faster steps so he could see his companions better. "I understand that, Jabir. If I hadn't been so tired and thirsty, I'd have been increasingly distressed by it." he jerked his thumb at Sameer, "How come he's grinning like a monkey?"

Qutayba Bin Faruq spoke up from the other side of Rashad. "Because every step carries him that much farther from his beloved Dimah!" He spoke the last words in a mocking falsetto.

Rashad shot a puzzled look at Sameer for an explanation. At the mention of his wife's name Sameer's face darkened. "That woman is evil. She's a punishment from Allâh. For what, I don't know."

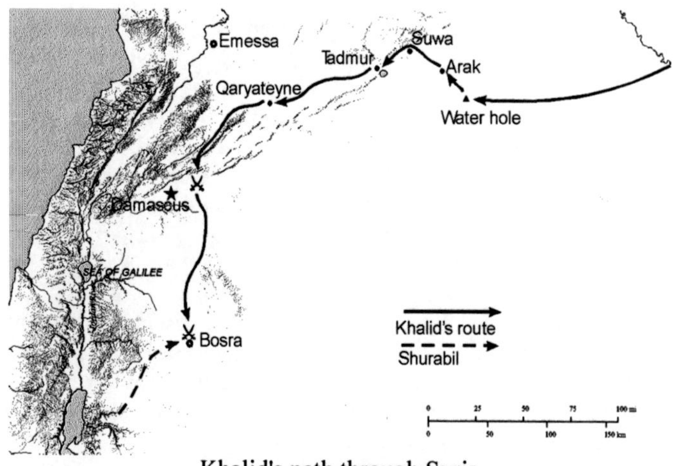

Khalid's path through Syria

Qutayba laughed. “She’s a punishment for your lust and greed, Sameer!”

Rashad had been meaning to ask for a long time but had refrained out of politeness. “Why did you marry such a . . .ah. . . prodigious woman, anyway?”

“Had I known I was, I would have run, believe me! I’d still be running!”

“I don’t understand, how could you not know who you’re marrying?”

Now it was Jabir’s turn to laugh. “He thought he was marrying Bahiya, Dimah’s little sister.”

Sameer developed a wistful look on his face. “Bahiya. By Allâh, her face was shaped like a heart. Her skin was perfect and smooth. Her slender legs, long and brown. . . .Her lips small and perfect and her laughter . . .the sound of a sparkling waterfall! She could smile at you and melt your heart!”

Qutayba continued, “So our love-struck hero goes to their father and says ‘May I have your daughter’s hand in marriage?’ The old man was cunning and he knew damn well that it was Bahiya that Sameer was after. But oh, he was crafty! He made Sameer give promises.” He winked at Rashad and started counting on his fingers. “He would never divorce her. He would never marry another. He’d support her forever. He would never lay with any of their slave girls. A dozen other unreasonable demands. And Sameer cheerfully agreed to every one, because he was so in love with Bahiya and thinking only with his small head!"

Jabir could hardly contain himself. "They held a great wedding and the bride was decked in the finest clothes in Medina – like a princess! Huge veils, bangles on her ankles and wrists. They even brought her in on a sedan chair. She was so covered up, her own mother wouldn't have recognized her!"

"I should have known from the way the chair bearers were staggering under her weight!" said Sameer sourly.

"So Sameer was hopping from foot to foot with excitement all through the wedding, and when he finally got her to his tent and took off the veils. . ." Jabir was grinning from ear to ear.

Qutayba interjected, "I heard a scream of anguish that sounded like a camel's throat being cut!"

Jabir pointed to himself. "I thought he'd found out that Bahiya wasn't even a girl!"

Sameer rolled his eyes. "Better that, than being Dimah. At least I would have married a beautiful boy!"

Jabir could barely contain himself. "Sameer doesn't care what he sticks it in, as long as it looks good, right?" He stuck an elbow in Sameer's side.

"Well, what did he do?" pressed Rashad.

"He screamed, 'Yasser bin Sami, by Allâh what have you done to me!'" Jabir continued. "He came boiling out of that tent and it took four people to hold him from killing Yasser!"

Sameer looked disgusted. "That bastard was ready for me. He had all his brothers there to protect him, because he knew what was going to happen!"

Rashad was enjoying the story. "But surely you could have divorced her right then. The marriage was made under false pretenses."

"Yes," said Jabir. "That was his first thought. He even said that to her father, Yasser. But Yasser was ready for him and suggested they take it to the Prophet, peace be upon him, to adjudicate."

Rashad looked at Sameer for confirmation, but Sameer just scowled. Jabir continued, "So they went that very night to Allâh's Messenger, peace be upon him, and each presented his case. And afterwards the Prophet, may Allâh be pleased with him, said . . ."

"After he'd stopped laughing!" rumbled the huge Wahid Bin Aswad Al-Ansari, who'd been keeping quiet, as he normally did.

"Well, he never laughed, but was smiling so hard that he couldn't talk! When he finally spoke, he said the marriage contract would stand and that Sameer would have to honor all his promises to Yasser."

"May Allâh, Subhanahu wa Ta'ala, grant Yasser an early and painful death!" cursed Sameer. "And all those promises will die with him."

"Tsk tsk. That's no way to talk about your Father-in-Law," chided Qutayba. "One must be respectful!"

Jabir smacked Sameer on the shoulder, sending him stumbling. "You're destined to die on Jihad, brother, and you'll have your choice of virgins in Paradise for the sacrifice you've made here!" The others laughed in agreement.

"But. . . She is your wife. . . .have you laid with her?" asked Rashad, smiling expectantly.

Sameer shrugged noncommittally. "Either that or have her make accusations that would make me a laughing stock."

Jabir was beside himself with glee. "We offered to tie a rope to his ankle, so we could pull him out if he got lost!"

"But. . . by Allâh, how could you go through with it?"

"Desperate times call for desperate measures." observed Qutayba sagely.

Sameer drew himself erect, with all the dignity he could muster. "I'm no fool. I brought her a big dish of dates and took her while her mouth was full, so I didn't have to listen to her screech or experience her foul breath." With that, the other four howled with laughter, so long and hard that they could hardly breathe.

As they slogged through the desert, Rashad smiled for a long time at the story. When Sameer began humming again, his smile grew wider.

That afternoon, the stark brown of the desert gave way to a green tint. They crested a ridge and saw the first signs of life since they'd left the Euphrates. Word spread through the column that this place was called Suwa. An oasis was surrounded by a small patch of impoverished pastureland. A few dilapidated mud huts housed several families who tended large herds of sheep and cattle.

With very few words and some quick hand gestures, Khalid directed several mounted soldiers to round up all the animals but a few, and drive them with the army. The locals gathered near their huts and glared balefully at the Muslims but did nothing. Khalid's son, Abdur-Rahman rode up to him. "Father, what of the settlers?"

"If they offer no resistance, let them be. They're of no consequence to us. Leave a few animals for them, but take the rest. The animals will be their Jizyah."

As the sun neared the horizon, the soldiers made camp near the oasis. Khalid studied the horizon to the west. This was Syria! Who would have expected him to enter it from the east? All his life, Syria and north had seemed like the same thing. Now he was eager to see what this country had to offer. The yearly caravans of Ramadan had carried riches from the Roman Empire to Mecca for trade during the Hajj. Now, instead of a few camel loads of goods, he was near the source of those riches. He'd heard tales from the traders about the bazaars of Syria - mountains of cloth, streets of metal wares. And gold, flowing like water through the markets in an endless stream, all waiting for him to put out his hand and fill it.

There was much to be done and he couldn't wait to do it!

5. Arak, Eastern Syrian Desert
June 10, 634

Abdul Ferran, mayor of Arak, reclined in the shade of his porch in the heat of the late afternoon. He enjoyed a relaxing nap when it was too hot to do anything else. Most people in this small settlement felt the same way, and there was little noise or activity to bother him.

He grimaced as a clatter of hooves ended the respite. He shifted, wiped his brow, and tried to return to his dreams, when loud footsteps were followed by an urgent call. "Mayor! Mayor Ferran!"

He opened a baleful eye and regarded the soldier who'd disturbed him. "What is it, Tetrarch?"

"Kentarch Sidonius' regards, sir. An army is approaching!"

Ferran laid his head back. "How does this concern me, Tetrarch? Isn't this the concern of the garrison?"

"They approach from the east, mayor."

Ferran sat bolt upright, sleep forgotten. "The hell you say!" He stood, adjusting his tunic and gathering his thoughts. He pointed at the young officer. "Go fetch old Gemistos and have him meet us at the watchtower." He winced as he stepped into the bright sun.

Sidonious, commander of the garrison, was at the town watchtower when Ferran got there. Chaos reigned among the soldiers in the nearby barracks. Garrison duty in a godforsaken desert outpost like Arak wasn't supposed to require formation drills. Sidonious looked grim as Ferran ascended the ladder. Without a word, Sidonious nodded to the east, where a line of riders shimmered in the heat waves.

"I sent a rider out to meet them and learn who they are and what they want," said Sidonious.

Ferran remained silent, his apprehension rising. How could such an army be coming from the east? Sidonious continued, "They met our messenger and sent back a reply, 'In the name of Allâh, the most merciful, surrender the city. You may accept Islam, pay the Jizyah, or submit to the sword.'"

Ferran shook himself out of his reverie. "What? What the hell is that supposed to mean?"

Sidonious shrugged. "I have no idea. My rider speaks Arabic; he's sure he repeated their message verbatim."

"It means the Arabs are here!" called a voice from below. They looked down at a tall old man at the base of the watchtower.

"Gemistos!" cried Ferran. "I'm glad you're here. Come on up!"

"I'll stay on the ground thank you. I'm not as young as I used to be."

"I don't think there's anything more for us to see here," murmured Sidonious. He began to descend the ladder.

When they were all on the ground, Ferran addressed Gemistos. "What can you tell us, teacher?"

"These Arabs have been giving the Persians hell for months. I'd say that it's our turn now."

"Did you hear the message they sent?" asked Sidonious. "What does it mean?"

"Allâh is their God. Islam is their religion; it means submission. I don't know what Jizyah is, but I suspect it's something like a tribute."

Ferran looked expectantly at Sidonious, whose eyes darted around as though he were looking for an escape. Old Gemistos asked for the messenger to be brought. When the young rider appeared, he commanded him, "The leader of this army. Describe him."

"He's very tall. Huge shoulders. His face is almost completely hidden by his great beard, and his cheeks have pockmarks. He wears a black turban and a tunic of chain mail."

"Any banners, flags?"

"Yes, they have a banner with a black eagle on it."

Gemistos turned to the centurion. "Beware of fighting this army, Kentarch. I believe this is the commander they call Khalid. He's ruthless and they say he and his men are unbeatable in battle. He's been campaigning in Persia and somehow he's come across the desert for us."

Sidonious was apologetic to Ferran. "I can't hold them, Mayor. They have four thousand men or more. I only have a century."

Ferran shook his head and started to say something, then stopped. His lips pulled tight until they turned white and he snarled, "Son of a bitch!" He waved his hand in dismissal.

"Stand down, Kentarch. There's nothing you can do. We'll surrender the town. We have no choice."

Sidonious turned to a nearby sergeant. "Send a rider to Tadmur. Pass the word that we've surrendered to a meros of Arabs, commanded by Khalid. Send the warning on to Damascus."

"Do you think they'll fight, father?" Abdur-Rahman rode easily beside Khalid.

"These Christians love life too much. A village like this won't have much of a garrison. They'll surrender."

"What if they can't pay the Jizyah? What then?"

"Have you ever squeezed a handful of sand and gotten water? There's nothing in a place like this to loot. These are subsistence farmers, herdsmen. We'll take what animals we need and call it good. We lose nothing by being generous. Look! Riders! They're coming to surrender."

Khalid halted as the two riders pulled up to him. One wore some sort of uniform, the other just a light tunic and breeches. The latter spoke. "I am Ferran, Mayor of Arak. This is the garrison commander. We wish to negotiate a surrender."

Khalid eyed Sidonious, who glared back at him coldly. "The commander does not speak?"

"He does not speak Arabic."

"I see. Very well. We will require one heifer or two sheep for every person in town. You may continue your lives and worship as you require. We will not billet in your town and will be gone come morning. You are now under the rule of the Caliph, Abu Bakr." He never took his eyes off Sidonious, who returned his gaze with a burning intensity.

Ferran was holding his breath, waiting for the rest of the demands. After a tension filled moment as the two commanders struggled in silence, he asked, "Is that all?"

"How many men-at-arms are in the garrison?"

"One hundred in all."

"The garrison will surrender all weapons. Each man may retain one knife not longer than a hand."

The Mayor spoke to the commander in Greek. Without dropping his eyes from Khalid, he spoke a single word. "We agree," Ferran said.

"It is done then. Go in peace. Allâh is merciful!"

Ferran let out his breath. Surely, it wouldn't be that easy? He was amazed that the terms were so generous. The two men turned their horses toward the town. Sidonious never dropped eye contact with Khalid until his horse began to canter.

Abdur-Rahman spoke up when they were gone. "I wouldn't trust that one, Father. He's a dangerous man to leave in our rear."

"He has a fire in his belly, but he's no fool. Even the most ferocious lion is just a pussycat when you take his teeth and his claws. This man is harmless."

The army encamped on the outskirts of Arak. Beyond some meetings near the town well, they had no interaction with the townsfolk. Rashad returned to the small cook fire laden with full water skins and nearly collapsed. "Oh, you should have seen the beauty I saw at the well! She had stunning eyes, perfect skin; her hair was shiny and just glowed!" His four friends looked up with interest. "She smiled at me. I think I'm in love!"

Qutayba threw himself back on his bedroll. "I'm too damned tired to think about women right now. If I had an houri to do my bidding, I'd just have her rub my feet."

Jabir grumbled, "I just wish one of these places would put up a fight. I want to loot something. It's been more than two weeks since I had a woman; even Wahid is starting to look good to me!" He ducked as Wahid aimed a stone at his head.

Rashad saw his chance to take a shot. "What about you Sameer? Ready to claim a slave girl?"

"Sameer's sworn off women," Jabir said. "His last encounter didn't work out so well."

Sameer took one of the water skins and rinsed some dust off his face. "Women are a curse from Allâh!"

Wahid broke his silence with his deep voice, rarely heard, "May Allâh curse us so, frequently and well!" Their laughter, seeming to reach to the stars, echoed across the camp as the light faded.

6. Damascus
June 10, 634

The last light of the sun had faded over Damascus, unnoticed by the guests crowding the home of the merchant Nicetas. The sounds of the party filtered into the small office where Nicetas had led Thomas. Nicetas lit a lamp and retrieved a cloth-covered object from a cabinet. "You know, we'll make a fine living brokering the usual goods, but if you've got some spare funds to invest, there are opportunities waiting to make us rich. Take this, for example. . ." With a flourish, he removed the cloth and revealed a hefty block of nearly flawless turquoise.

Thomas whistled as he took the stone and examined it close to the lamp. Nicetas went on, "I can buy that by the cartload. We could sell it raw, or we could ship it to Athens, get it carved and sell it for ten times as much. The problem is getting it to market."

"Where does it come from?"

"A place called Mahd al Dhahab in Arabia. About a thousand millarium from here."

Thomas snorted, "It might as well be at the bottom of the sea."

"But think! In the proper markets, one wagon load of this could make us rich!"

"Sure. All we have to do is transport it for six weeks across a waterless desert infested by bandits. And there's the Arab civil war to consider, not to mention the recent Arab attacks we've been suffering in the south."

"Well, we'd have to wait for the current problems to die down, but don't worry about bandits. I have that figured out. You see. . . .we paint the ore! Who would attack a wagon load of rocks?"

"Someone who's wondering what kind of idiot would transport rocks across a desert." Thomas laughed. "I don't suppose you can find any of this turquoise in Persia? At least we're not at war with them. Maybe some trading would strengthen the peace."

"As a matter of fact," Nicetas said thoughtfully, "I've heard rumors that Persia is rich with turquoise. But, Thomas, that's the problem - they're sophisticated! They know what this stuff's worth. The Arabs – if they find a pretty rock, they just build an altar and start worshiping it."

Thomas chuckled. "Keep thinking, my friend. One day one of your schemes may actually work. But for now, I think your guests are missing you."

As they returned to the main room, Nicetas' wife hurried up to him. "Where have you been? The guests are all here and the wine is flowing. You have to make the announcement, before people start to get drunk."

"Yes, woman. Where's the young couple? Bring them!" In a few moments she returned with his daughter and her young man in tow. Nicetas stood on a nearby chair. He whistled for attention and the crowd grew quiet.

Nicetas savored the silence for a long moment, then asked, "How's the wine?" A short cheer answered him. "Well, the reason I've brought you all here is to make a formal announcement. Most of you already know this, but tonight we make it official." He stopped and took a long look at the two youths standing next him, then continued. "Last month, Jonas and his father came to me and very solemnly requested that I consider the advantages of him taking my daughter Eudocea's hand in marriage." He waited for the applause to fade. "Well, we had a long period of negotiation. I mean, we're talking a commodity of inestimable value here. . ." General laughter and knowing smiles showed that everyone in the room knew of Nicetas' ruthless mercantile nature. "Unable to reach an equitable assessment, I finally consulted Bishop Peter," he gestured towards the honored cleric, who bowed his head in acknowledgment. "Who advised me that, in the interests of propriety, I part with my treasure at a loss.

"Therefore, my dear friends, it's my great pleasure and honor to announce the betrothal of my beautiful daughter, Eudocea, to Jonas Tournikes!" He raised his wine goblet. "To the happy couple!"

He clambered down from the chair amid deafening applause, hugged his daughter and shook Jonas' hand. He made his way through the press of the crowd, shaking hands and receiving backslaps, until he arrived at the side of Thomas, who stood unobtrusively in a corner with his wine goblet. Thomas shook his hand. "Well done. Congratulations!"

"We'll see. I'm going to put the lad to work and see what he's made of. He's a good kid, but I fear he's lived too long in luxury. He's not hungry. He has a fine education, but now I plan to teach him something. I have no sons, Thomas; he'll have to take over when I'm gone."

Thomas winked at him. "He'll do fine. There's no better teacher than you."

Nicetas ran a hand through his thinning hair. "Ah, I have a head for commerce, but I couldn't do anything without your organizational skills. When are you going to have a son to teach?"

Thomas smiled. "Making a grandson for the Emperor isn't something to be undertaken lightly. Besides, any kentarch can organize better than I can." Thomas was being too modest. They both knew that few could match his abilities to organize logistics and move men and goods long distances. Heraclius had put this skill to good use in his campaigns against Persia.

"Come on. I need to introduce you to the Governor." Nicetas turned to Thomas and put a finger to his lips, "Tread lightly. No one believes you're here as my business partner, and the rumors are flying that you're spying for Heraclius."

He led Thomas through the crowd to a group gathered around Bishop Peter. "Gentlemen, I'd like to introduce Thomas of Antioch; Chiliarc, retired; and son-in-law to the Emperor. Thomas, Bishop Peter."

Thomas bowed deeply and kissed the offered hand. "Your Grace."

"Governor Azrail, and Abbot Lecanepus from the monastery east of the city." Thomas shook the hands of each.

"I believe we campaigned together," said Lecanepus. "I was a young priest, ministering to the army."

"Of course. What has it been, five years now?" Thomas had only a vague recollection of the man and couldn't honestly remember if it was him at all, but he smiled and pretended recognition.

"Time is a merciless master. More like seven."

"So the Emperor has sent you here to keep an eye on me, eh?" Azrail said with a polite smile. He kept a confident game face, but secretly worried that he was under scrutiny.

"I assure you, governor, I'm here of my own accord. I'm no spy." He tipped his goblet and the two men exchanged a toast. "Besides, Heraclius would never be so obvious. His spies are those you would least suspect."

Nicetas chimed in, "I distrust that half-wit stable-boy of yours, Azrail. I suspect he hears more than you think." The men laughed as Azrail adopted an exaggerated look of surprise and concern.

The Abbot spoke up, "What does bring you to Damascus, Thomas?"

"Well, our friend Nicetas had need of my abilities to collect horses and set men into straight lines. And Damascus seemed like a good choice for one who wishes to be as far as possible from the Emperor's court."

"The court appears to be attracted to you," observed Azrail. "I understand Heraclius has relocated to Emessa."

"This whole territory is still being consolidated since we took it back from the Sassanids. You know Heraclius, he's never been the kind to issue orders from afar and trust that they'll be carried out. Wherever the action is, you can be sure that Heraclius is near. He always leads from the front."

"You served under him, I understand?"

Nicetas cut in. "Thomas was the chief of logistics for the army during the march on Nineveh."

Azrail cocked his head slightly, a polite smile on his face. "A quartermaster, then?"

"You might say that." Thomas bowed his head with an air of humility.

Lecanepus, who'd marched as a young priest with Heraclius himself, detected the condescension in the governor's tone and couldn't contain himself. "Thomas wasn't a mere quartermaster, Governor. He distinguished himself several times in combat, both at Nineveh and Dastigard, and helped negotiate the treaty with Kavadh."

Azrail regarded Thomas with renewed respect. Thomas, for his part, seemed absorbed in the contents of his wine goblet.

Bishop Peter broke the uneasy pause. "Thomas, we were just discussing something and I'd be interested in your opinion on the matter. Tell me, sir, what is your opinion on the divine nature of our Savior?"

Thomas' face remained calm and neutral. "In what regard, your grace?"

"Of course," Azrail said. "The Christ can only be divine. As the son of God, he is in essence, God himself!"

Lecanepus spoke up, "But does not the opening of the Gospel of Matthew identify Jesus as a Son of David, a Son of Abraham? How can God be the son of a man? Jesus had human aspects: he ate, he drank, he suffered."

"But when asked to show them the Father, Jesus replied, 'I am in the Father and the Father is in me,'" responded Azrail.

"Yes, he responded that the Father is in him. Not that the Father is him."

The Bishop placed his hands on the shoulders of the two men and addressed Thomas. "So you see, Thomas, the pressing question is how much – and what parts – of Jesus were human and how much was divine. Surely you have an opinion on the subject?"

"To tell the truth," Thomas said. "I've never given it much thought."

Azrail scoffed, "Of course you have. The lowest of my servants debate the issue endlessly. I practically have to gag them on the subject to get any work done at all. Stop anyone on the street and merely ask and you'll get a half-hour of discourse from them. Everyone has an opinion on the subject."

"I'm curious," said Bishop Peter, "Since you're connected to the Emperor's court, if you subscribe to the compromise philosophy that Heraclius is proposing, that Christ had both a divine and a human nature, but only one will?"

"I assure you, your Grace, that I've not considered the matter. However, were I pressed on the subject. . ." He gazed into his wine cup and spoke slowly, as if in deep thought. "With regard to my faith . . . I don't suppose it matters to me what the nature of the Christ was. Was he a man? Or God? Or some combination of each? Certainly not just a man; his miracles prove that. Would the nature of his divinity change what he taught? What he did? I follow the teachings of Christ, the example of Christ. What he *was* affects neither of those things. I wouldn't believe any less, have any less faith in Him, no matter what the outcome of your argument is.

"I believe that all this controversy is straining at so many gnats. I don't think it really matters in the end, does it?"

Outside the reception, Jonas and Eudocia finally managed to break free. Holding hands, they jogged to the edge of the rooftop balcony and embraced, laughing. The soft lights of torch lamps throughout the city stretched below them. They spent several minutes embracing and murmuring endearments. Jonas' hands found their way lower and lower. Eudocia removed them with a laugh when they went below her hips.

"Let's get married as soon as possible!" Jonas said.

"Silly! There's so much to do yet! Planning, invitations, the food! And besides, where would we live? You haven't even got your own house yet!"

"We can live at my Father's house at the olive plantation."

She laughed and kissed him again. "I know what you want. But my Father wants you to start learning the business. How will you do that from the olive plantation?" Again, she removed his hand from her buttock, this time more firmly.

"But I have an apartment."

"That hovel? And shall my servants then sleep in the same room as us?" She playfully rubbed the front of his trousers. "You're doing too much of your thinking with this!" They kissed again. "Mmm, in time, Jonas, in time, I'll be yours every night!"

"But I want you now."

"Mmmmm. Silly boy. Of course you do. Wait!" His hands became more insistent and she broke free. "Come on, people will start asking where we went."

7. Tadmur, Eastern Syrian Desert
June 11, 634

After feeding and watering the herds, Bashour and Marid arrived at Imad's house for their lesson at midmorning. They carried buckets of drinking water from the town well, as was their habit. They walked into a scene of confusion. Several floorboards were lifted and Imad was carrying buckets of dirt and spreading them behind the house, where some younger students were raking it into the soil. On one side of the room, Imad's wife was packing scrolls and books into small wooden crates.

"What are you doing, Mudarres?" Bashour said, aghast.

Imad stopped and wiped the sweat and dirt from his forehead. "A messenger arrived last night from Arak. An Arab army several thousand strong is heading this way from the east."

The two boys looked at each other in astonishment. Marid asked, "But why are you tearing up the floor of your house?"

"Think, boy! Armies pillage, rape and burn. My treasure isn't in gold, it's in books. These aren't the Sassanids, and by the stories I've heard from Persia, I've no reason to expect civilized behavior from them. So I'm burying my books under the floor. Even if they should burn the house, I can rebuild, then dig down to recover my treasure. For all I'd expect, they'll use some of these priceless manuscripts to light their fires."

"What do you want us to do?" Bashour asked, but Marid tugged insistently at his sleeve. "Come on!" Marid urged, and turned to go. Bashour started to follow, but looked back at their teacher. Imad just looked resigned and waved him on.

"Go on, I can't keep you from such exciting experiences."

The two boys ran through the streets to the eastern wall, which was fully manned by the soldiers of the garrison. They mounted the wall and took up watch between a couple of guards. From the wall they could see over the orchards and palms that stretched for several miles in every direction. The horizon to the east was lifeless. The guards looked at their enthusiasm and smiled.

They watched and enthusiastically speculated about what the invading army would be like, what would happen, what the soldiers would be riding. Tadmur had once been occupied by the Sassanid Persians, but they'd left without fanfare before the boys wore shoes, and Bashour remembered little of it. Nothing this exciting had happened in years. The desert remained still, and the watching soon became tedious under the blazing summer sun. It took less than an hour for them to give up the watch and return to Imad's house.

When they arrived, the house was again in order. The floorboards were back in place and it looked as if nothing had been disturbed. Imad was putting on his formal cloak. "Ah, there you are. Had enough of guard duty? Come with me. I may have use for you." He led the boys down the Decumanus, the long, column-lined street that ran through town to the ancient pagan temple that now served as a meeting hall. When they arrived, the town Sheik and the garrison commander were there with several senior townsfolk. Imad waved the boys to a seat on the wall and enjoined them with a look to be quiet.

The commander was speaking. "I know Sidonious. If he could have mounted a resistance, he would have. Instead, he gave up Arak without a fight. I'll wait to see it with my own eyes, but we have to plan as if this army is overwhelming."

One of the townsfolk spoke up. "So you're going to do the same? Just surrender to an Arab rabble?"

The commander drew himself straight and glared at the man who spoke. "No. I intend to evaluate the situation as it develops and take the appropriate action as it presents itself. If there's no hope of successfully defending this town, I suggest you beg for mercy and don't antagonize your new masters.

"Sidonious only had a century of men. I have five centuries and might offer a fight where Sidonious would've been hopelessly outnumbered."

The Sheik raised his hands for order, "Callinicus is right, gentlemen. We've lived under occupation before. We'll do it again, if necessary. Quite frankly, I don't think it matters much who we pay our taxes to." This brought a murmur of assent. The Sheik turned to Imad. "Imad, you probably have the best grasp of both Greek and Arabic in the town. Should it become necessary, can I ask you to mediate between the garrison and the invaders?"

"Of course. I've brought two of my senior students who can help if necessary." Bashour grinned and nudged Marid. They would be right in the thick of negotiations.

The Sheik looked at Bashour and Marid and nodded silent assent, and turned back to the men. "An army like this moves across the land like locusts. I suggest you instruct the townsfolk to hoard food where it cannot be easily found, but leave some out to make it look like. . . "

The boys' excitement waned as the meeting dragged on. Bashour could never understand how adults carried on so intently about the most mundane details. Didn't they see that there were things to do? But they just gathered here and talked all day. Noon came and went, and the boys were whispering plans of a getaway when a church bell began to ring. The meeting immediately broke up in confusion, and the boys escaped to return to the walls. They were there when the Sheik and Commander Callinicus arrived.

Through rippling heat waves across the desert, a dark line was visible under a cloud of dust. Below the walls, children were herding the last of the animals through the town gates as the soldiers began to close them. The dust faded as the column entered the green area surrounding the oasis. The boys caught glimpses through gaps in the trees as the line resolved itself into individual horses and camels. At the head was a rider bearing a banner. The column was huge, bigger than the two boys had dreamed it would be. Bashour wasn't far from Callinicus and heard him suck in his breath and mutter a sharp curse. This was no rabble of bandits. As they approached the wall through the orchards, a gesture from the head of the column caused two wings to split off and envelop the town with military precision.

Callinicus called out to his archers, "Hold! Cease shooting!" Resistance would be pointless.

Khalid brought his horse up a hundred paces short of the town gate. He would have stopped further back, but he'd seen the archers stand back from the edge of the fortress wall. The commander of this garrison had apparently made the wise decision. Standing here in easy arrow range was foolhardy and his companions shifted nervously. Khalid kept an eye on the wall for signs of a trap, but he was confident there would be none. This display of fearlessness would simply add to his legend.

He waited patiently, unwilling to lower himself to hail the guards at the gate. Let them come and seek favor from him. He didn't have to wait long. The gate opened slightly, and a single man in brown desert robes came towards them. When he'd crossed half the distance, Khalid moved forward to meet him.

"I'm the Sheik of this town. What do you want?"

"This town is now subject to the Caliph, Abu Bakr. All inhabitants will submit to Islam, or pay the Jizyah. Anyone who resists will be put to the sword."

"And the town? The people, their goods?"

"You are under Islam now. If you pay the Jizyah, you will be under the protection of Islam. You will be protected from harm and none will take your goods, so long as you offer food and shelter to any passing Muslim."

The Sheik cocked his head to the side. "What is a Muslim?"

"A Muslim is one who submits to Allâh, who professes that there is no God but Allâh, and that Muhammad is his messenger."

The Sheik thought about that for a moment. "Your. . . Allâh. Will we be required to worship him?"

"Your people are Christian?"

"They are."

"Then your god is Allâh. They are the same."

That seemed strange to the chief, but it was reassuring. "Very well. I formally surrender the town of Tadmur to you, according to the conditions you have proposed. As a sign of this, I present you with a gift." He turned and waved a hand towards the gate, which opened and a man leading a magnificent horse came out.

Khalid struggled to keep the expression off his face at the sight of the horse. The animal was large, black and powerful, with excellent lines. It pranced impatiently as it was led forward, full of spirit. One of the men behind him whistled in appreciation. Khalid resisted the urge to rebuke the man for breaking discipline in front of their new subject. The Sheik took the reins from the handler and stepped forward to pass them to Khalid, who decided to be gracious.

"You have an excellent eye for animals. Your gift is appreciated. Now, my army needs water. I will send deputies to collect the Jizyah, in the form of livestock." He ran his eyes across the line of men surrounding the city. They'd been marching nonstop for nearly two weeks. Turning back to the town Sheik, he said, "Tell your people to feed my men. Butcher a hundred cattle and declare a feast. I'll send helpers to assist. We're all Arab brothers after all, are we not?" The Sheik bowed his head in assent and Khalid turned and rode back to his lines, one eye on his new prize.

As he rode, Dhiraar fell in beside him. "They've surrendered?"

"Did you expect anything else? They can count as well as you or I."

"The men are grumbling. They've marched this long for loot and women, but all they've gotten is mutton and beef. We could have stayed home for that."

"In time, Dhiraar. We've got days yet before we encounter the wealth of the Romans. Tonight, this town will feed us. Pick two hundred men and have them report to the town chief. No weapons. Tell him that they are the kitchen help I promised. Instruct the army that there will be no cooking or cook fires tonight."

Bashour was preparing a fire pit in front of his house when the Sheik came by and dropped off two of the Arab soldiers with him. His father had to donate four head of cattle for the feast to honor the conquering army, and he wasn't happy about it. But the Sheik said that they were here to help him, for which he was grateful. The younger of the two, about Bashour's age, introduced them, "I am Rashad. This is Jabir."

"Bashour."

"What can we do to help?"

Bashour put them to work in the shade of the house, erecting a series of planks into a rough table on which they would carve the meat. He'd started the fire when his father arrived with the cattle. The two Muslim men worked efficiently and without speaking very much, which was fine with Bashour. They'd slaughtered the first heifer and placed it on the table for further cutting when a horn sounded in the distance followed by a far-off voice crying, "Hasten to prayers! Hasten to prayers!"

Bashour turned to ask his father what was happening when the man named Jabir asked him if they had any water. He indicated a nearby cistern and the two men proceeded to ladle water out and wash their hands and their feet. They huddled and whispered while glancing at the sun. One of them pointed slightly west of south. They then produced small rugs and placed them on the ground facing south. They knelt on the rugs, prostrated themselves and began a recitation. Bashour was fascinated by the musical quality of it, the way their voices rose and fell as one.

"In the name of Allâh, most gracious, most merciful. Praise be to Allâh, the cherisher and sustainer of the worlds; most gracious, most merciful. Master of the Day of Judgment. You do we worship and your aid we seek. Show us the straight way. The way of those on whom you have bestowed your grace, those whose portion is not wrath and who go not astray."

Bashour whispered, "What are they doing?"

His father just stared at them. "I think they're praying."

"They seem very devoted."

"Perhaps what we've heard of these people is wrong."

The spectacle continued for some time and after a while Bashour and his father returned to carving the beef. When the praying had finished, the two Muslims rolled their rugs up and returned to their meat cutting. Bashour was cutting meat opposite from Rashad and asked, "Do you do that often?"

"We pray five times a day, as Allâh commanded us."

"Allâh is one of your gods?"

"There is no God but Allâh, and Muhammad is his messenger!"

"Who is Muhammad?"

"Muhammad, peace be upon him, is the Prophet, the messenger of Allâh. He was the perfect man, the one we all try to emulate."

"Was? He's dead then?

Rashad bowed his head. "Yes, he died two years ago."

Bashour said to his father, "Kalekas the priest told us about this man. He united the Arabs."

"Not all of us, son," murmured his father. He turned towards the two Muslim men. "I don't know your God, but we worship the God of Abraham and his son Jesus, the Christ."

The one named Jabir dumped a handful of chopped meat into the large cauldron to boil and said, "Abraham is our father, too. He built the Ka'aba. Allâh is the God of Abraham."

This had Bashour's attention. "But we also worship Jesus."

Rashad looked to Jabir with a puzzled expression. They mumbled to each other for a moment and Bashour caught the words "Jesus" and "Isa." Comprehension dawned on Rashad's face, "Ah, Isa, your . . . Jesus. Yes, he was a great prophet. We have great respect for him."

Bashour's mind was on what the traveling priest and Imad had discussed a few nights before. Perhaps these strangers could offer a fresh view of things. "Then what is your interpretation of the trinity?"

Again, the two Muslims huddled and discussed it. Jabir stood and began to count on his fingers. His mouth moved as if he were working through the words of a song to himself. Then in the same singsong fashion in which they'd prayed, he recited, "O People of the Book! Commit no excesses in your religion: nor say of Allâh aught but truth. Christ Jesus the son of Mary was no more than a messenger of Allâh, and his word, which He bestowed on Mary, and a spirit proceeding from Him: so believe in Allâh and his messengers. Say not 'Trinity': desist: it will be better for you: for Allâh is One Allâh: glory be to Him: for exalted is He above having a son. To Him belong all things in the heavens and on Earth. And enough is Allâh as a Disposer of affairs!"

Bashour was taken aback at the enormity of what he'd heard. Jesus wasn't God? "Where do these words come from? How do they sing so well, yet still convey the message?"

"These are the words of the Holy Qur'án, which was given to Muhammad, peace be upon him, to teach to all Muslims, as the Gospel was given to Jesus. These are the words of Allâh, written before the universe was formed. The angel Gabriel was sent to teach them to Muhammad, who in turn taught them to us."

Bashour was fascinated by this idea. He spent the rest of the afternoon quizzing the Muslim men about Muhammad. Could it be possible that another prophet had arisen in his lifetime? It made sense, as Christianity was tearing itself apart trying to agree on what the nature of Jesus was. But these fellows came with a message from God that solved the whole problem. Maybe it was all a big mistake, that Jesus was just a prophet and not the Son of God at all. That made everything that he'd been trying to understand seem to fall into place.

Muhammad seemed a likely prophet as well. Every time they quoted from Muhammad's Qur'án, they did so in a hypnotic rhythm that seemed to lull his consciousness and soothe his questions. The stories he heard, that Muhammad took care of the poor and infirm, always made sure the widows had enough to eat. He'd distributed all his wealth to help others and died penniless. These stories seemed to confirm to Bashour that Muhammad was a man that he would want to follow.

As the sun slipped below the horizon, a call to prayer sounded again and he watched as the two men again washed and prostrated themselves in prayer to the south. Then the Arabs from Khalid's army arrived and began feasting on the meat that they'd cooked. With the situation well in hand, Bashour went to find his friend Marid and discuss what he'd learned. The town was teeming with Arab soldiers. He found Marid gathering more firewood and picked up an armload himself to help.

"Have you heard of the Muhammad that these soldiers follow?"

"Heard about him? Hah! It's all these men talked about! I couldn't get them to shut up about him."

"What do you think? Do you think he's a real prophet?"

"I think it's possible. It makes sense, in a way."

"I want to know more about him."

"I know this, it sounds like a lot more fun to be a Muslim. They don't have priests, and did you know they're allowed to have as many as four wives at once?"

"You're joking!" That subject had never arisen with Jabir and Rashad.

"On my honor. One of the Muslims working with us had two already and was making plans for a third."

They dropped the firewood at Marid's cook fire. Marid has a thoughtful look on his face. "What are you thinking, Marid?" Bashour asked suspiciously.

"I'm thinking about becoming a Muslim. They seem very devout, they profess to the same God we do. And I like the idea of four wives."

"You're not serious."

"Why not? What if this Muhammad really is a prophet? Did they talk to you about what he said about Jesus?"

"Yes, they said he was a great Prophet, like Muhammad."

"Well, think about it. We've been getting twisted around this debate over whether Christ could be human or divine or both, and no one, not even the Patriarchs or the Emperor can agree. Maybe the answer is that Muhammad was right and there's nothing to discuss."

"It makes sense." Bashour admitted.

"It makes all the sense in the world. I want to learn more, but they told me I have to become a Muslim before they will teach me the Qur'án."

"Yeah, what is that? They said it was the words of Allâh or something?"

"They told me it was the book that Allâh wrote before he created the universe, that he made Muhammad memorize and teach to all Muslims."

"And they told me that Allâh was the same as our God, the God of Abraham."

"So what have we got to lose? I'm going to do it."

Bashour wasn't as confident, but he kept his doubts to himself as they approached Bashour's house.

They found Rashad and Jabir sitting with three other Muslims, eating the stew that had been cooked. Bashour made quick introductions, then Marid said, "We want to become Muslims!"

Rashad smiled and Jabir said, "Excellent! All you have to do is to profess that there is no God but Allâh and that Muhammad is his messenger."

Bashour and Marid repeated the formula and were congratulated by all those present. They scooped up bowls of meat and joined the Muslims. The large, dark one named Wahid said in his rumbling voice, "You'll need to learn the Qur'án. Jabir and Rashad will teach it to you. You must memorize it, for it is not something to be written down."

The two boys looked at each other in surprise. "But you're in an army on the march," Marid said, "Won't you be gone tomorrow?"

Wahid contemplated the boys from underneath his thick brows. "Well, you'll just have to come with us, won't you?"

It took a moment for this to sink in. The boys realized that they'd just gotten invited to join one of the most momentous events in recent history. Adventure beckoned, and they grinned broadly at one another. "I guess we will," Bashour said. "I guess we will."

8. Antioch
June 12, 634

The main parade ground of Antioch had turned brown. Scores of hobnailed sandals had crushed everything that might have grown on the flat field and ground the soil into a fine powder. It hadn't rained in months. When it did, the powder would turn into a quagmire of mud. But for now it was kicked up under the summer sun by endless footsteps of drilling soldiers, until it was hard to tell where the earth ended and the air began.

Komes Taticus wasn't happy. Four centuries of recruits were under his supervision. None of them, in his opinion, had reached an acceptable level of training in the two months he'd been working with them. The endless drills, combat training, and strengthening exercises had had an effect, but with very few exceptions the young men still treated military life less than seriously. Their attitude was lackadaisical; they didn't seem sincere about learning the vital skills that could save their lives in battle. Taticus had enough of using the textbook to train these men. Today he'd elected to work directly with an allaghia of fifty men on close combat tactics.

They were given wooden weapons and paired off in a line to practice their sword work. For hours that morning, they'd practiced fighting moves by the numbers, with their Pentecontarch calling the drill. "Thrust! Parry! Yield! Strike! Sweep!" Now they were allowed to practice freestyle, honing their reactions. Taticus strode along the lines, observing the drill. They were making so many mistakes, he saw so many flaws; it was a struggle to remember that he'd once been so inept and that it had taken years of constant drill to develop his skill. Nevertheless. . . .

"Halt! Gather 'round! Make a circle!" He strode to the nearest recruit and relieved him of his sword. He pointed at the biggest man in the unit. "You! Come here!" The man looked both ways at his companions and tentatively advanced. He was a good head above Taticus, who looked up at him with some contempt. "Attack me!"

Taticus stood with his sword held loosely at his side. The big man looked confused and Taticus motioned impatiently with his left hand. The recruit took a step forward and swung his wooden sword backhanded at him. Just as the blade was about to hit, he pulled it up short. Taticus hadn't moved.

In a blur, the flat of Taticus' sword struck him across the wrist. He yelped as he dropped his sword and his hand went numb. "This is not a fucking game! I told you to attack me!" Taticus yelled, "Now pick up your weapon!"

Tension seemed to crackle in the ranks. The men were surprised. Before this, everything they'd endured over the previous eight weeks had been impersonal and expected. Suddenly danger was in the air, and they were uncomfortable.

Not taking his eyes off Taticus, the big recruit in the center of the circle rubbed his wrist as he bent to pick up the weapon. The Komes gestured again. This time he lunged straight for the older man's ribs in a direct thrust. Taticus' sword never moved, but at the last instant, he slid sideways and pivoted on his left foot, grasping the big man's sword elbow and driving it down and forward. The man stumbled and the flat of Taticus' sword struck him at the base of the neck, driving him to the ground.

"When you lunge, don't overextend yourself!" Taticus walked slowly around the center of the circle, pitching his voice to carry in the way only an experienced sergeant can. "When your head is no longer above your hips, you're off balance and easy to kill! Strike hard, but don't commit yourself completely! If you lose your balance, you'll be unable to move if your strike doesn't succeed. Pair up and practice!"

Again he walked up and down the line, occasionally stopping to correct a man's stance or adjust how he held the sword. Almost every man was fighting right-handed and was using his free hand for balance. After correcting several men to get their left hands higher and in front of them, he called them back into a circle. "You have two hands! Stop thinking that just because you have a sword in one that the other is useless. We're not carrying shields today. You may not have a shield in combat. If your hand is free, use it!" He motioned another recruit. "You, attack me!"

The young man visibly swallowed. This time Taticus did not even have a sword to defend himself. He stepped forward, took a deep breath and charged Taticus with a roundhouse swing to the neck. Instead of ducking, Taticus stepped inside the blow and turned so the man's sword arm was coming over his right shoulder. Grabbing the man's sword wrist with his left hand, he wrapped the man tight around his chest, twisted and dropped to his right knee. The recruit sailed over his shoulder and landed on his back with a heavy thump. Taticus got up and kicked him lightly. "Get back in ranks." Then he picked another soldier. "You!"

This time the recruit attacked with a straight downward chop to the head. Taticus shifted his weight and slid towards the man, just off the line of attack. He met the sword arm of the attack with his own as he stepped in and used his left hand to drive a solid punch against the man's rib cage. The recruit collapsed towards his left, the air driven out of him. Before he lost his footing, Taticus had reached around his neck and grabbed a handful of tunic, twisting it so his knuckles sank deep into the man's jugular. Taticus dropped to his right knee, the other planted in the recruit's back, still holding the man's sword wrist. He rolled him over so he was kneeling on the man's back, then pulled up with both hands, cutting off blood to the man's brain. The sword slipped out of his fingers and Taticus released him, scooping up the sword. As the recruit gasped and retched in the dust, Taticus paced and addressed the unit. "This sword does not make you super-human! It does not imbue you with supernatural powers! It does not make you invulnerable to the unarmed man! It's a tool for killing. If you respect it for what it is, you can use it. If you rely on it to substitute for skill, you will die! A trained man will kill you just as quickly with his bare hands as with a sword! Go into combat with the attitude of an unarmed man! Recognize that your opponent is dangerous and that you have to be more dangerous if you expect to live!"

Tacitus returned to his normal composure. "Form for column march," he said. He reached down and lifted the soldier from his knees and returned his sword, saying quietly, "Good job. Get back in ranks."

He turned to the Pentecontarch in charge of the company. "Run five laps around the parade ground. Have them hold their swords over their heads with their right hands for all five laps. Go!"

As the men ran, Taticus approached another platoon of soldiers who were drilling with wooden swords. "Pente Doukas, I'd like to borrow your allaghia for a while." He had the fifty soldiers get a drink and rest. As the running allaghia were starting their fifth lap, he formed them up in a combat drill line. They were fresh and confident looking when the runners stumbled up, gasping, short of breath, dusty and sweating.

"Drop your weapons and give me fifty push-ups!" The men rolled their eyes and did as they were told. As they exercised, Taticus walked among them. "You will fight tired! You will fight thirsty! You will fight sick! You will kill waves of enemies and you will be exhausted! You will face new waves who are fresh and just as eager to kill you! Everyone up! Pair up against that allaghia. Fight!"

The wooden swords felt like lead in the hands of the exhausted soldiers. They raised them wearily and moved onto the line, doing their best to hold the fresh platoon at bay as the rested recruits cheerfully pressed their attack.

Taticus walked the drill line. He noticed a group of high-ranking officers on the edge of the field, watching the training. He wasn't the only one. The recruits had seen them and many began to secretly hope that someone would intervene. The training had been hard, but since Taticus had started working directly with the men, it had become inhuman. Barracks lawyers were already plotting ways to relieve themselves of the sudden discipline.

Taticus lightly smacked the back of one of the fresh recruits. "Stop going easy on him. Press your attack!" Down the line, one of the exhausted men stumbled and fell. His training partner stopped his attack and offered a hand to help him up. Both men were smiling at one another. Taticus decided it was a good time to stage a complete loss of control. "What the fuck is going on here!" He ran up to the two men. "Soldier, what the fuck do you think you're doing? Do you think this is some fucking game? Did I just see you being sportsmanlike?"

The men were shocked and stood silently at attention. Taticus pushed his face into that of the one who'd helped his opponent up. "Soldier, why the fuck did you help that man up? He is your enemy! When your enemy stumbles, you kill him! Do you think the enemy is going to help you up when you slip?"

"No, sir!"

"You're damn well told! And you!" He turned and put his face into that of the man who'd fallen. "Did I see you fucking smiling? Do you think this is fun?"

"No, sir!"

Taticus moved in a blur and smashed his fist into the recruit's face, just below his nose. Blood exploded. "Are you having fun now, godammit?"

"Komes!" A sharp voice brought Taticus to attention. The officer who'd been watching from the edge of the field was striding towards the men. Recruits whispered and nudged each other. Taticus had gone too far this time and now it was his turn.

Turmarch Psellus faced Taticus and addressed him loudly enough to be heard by everyone present. "Komes, is this an example of the discipline these men are getting under your command?" Unseen by all but Taticus, he quickly winked.

"Yes sir!" Taticus responded loudly. The recruits were beside themselves. Taticus was in serious trouble now!

"Komes, I am tired of you mollycoddling these men! I'm not running a girl's school here; I'm trying to build an army! I would appreciate it if you would stop screwing around and start training these men to be real soldiers! Do you understand me?"

"Yes, sir!" Taticus bellowed.

The men looked surreptitiously at each other in disbelief. Had the whole army gone insane?

Psellus ran his eyes over the century. "Pentecontarchs, drill your men! Dismissed! Komes, you're with me."

Taticus and Psellus watched silently as the platoon leaders formed their men up and marched them away. Psellus then turned to Taticus and the two men gripped hands. "Taticus, it's damn good to see you again. Walk with me."

As they walked, Psellus asked, "How are the men, Taticus? Are they ready to go to war?"

"They're weak and undisciplined, sir. Give me a year or two and I could turn them into a fighting force. Right now, they're little more than an armed rabble. They're too green to know fear, so of course they don't know how to control it. In a fight, at the first sight of blood, ninety percent of them will drop their weapons and run like hell."

"Are they really that bad?"

"There's too many recruits and not enough veterans. If we had more seasoned troops, we could use them as a cadre to bolster the ranks and add some backbone. But most of the veterans mustered out when the war ended. These pups think this is some sort of game."

Psellus stopped and turned to Taticus. "I haven't got any veterans to give you and I'm afraid you haven't got a year. Your turma has been activated. You and your men will board a ship to take you south to Joppa, where you'll march to join with a themata being assembled southwest of Jerusalem."

"And the reason for this, sir?"

"The Arabs are invading. They have four armies advancing into Palestine and Syria. Heraclius wants a strike force to relieve Jerusalem if they besiege it, or to strike at their capitol if they get engaged in Syria."

"Will you be leading us, sir?"

"I will not. You'll march under Andrew Kymineianus. Your themata will become the anvil. I'm charged with raising another army, which will be part of the hammer that will crush these invaders."

"Pray to God they run from the threat. I can't guarantee these men in battle."

"They're just Arabs, Taticus. They wouldn't dare engage a professional army in a pitched battle."

9. Tadmur, Eastern Syrian Desert
June 12, 634

The pack had seemed light when they left Tadmur, but now Bashour was shifting his shoulders uncomfortably under its weight. As the straps cut into him, he regarded the camel placidly carrying the gear of the others, and he resolved to transfer his pack the next time they stopped.

The Muslims with him had set a brutal pace and didn't seem affected. It was all he could do to keep from panting. Conversation was completely out of the question while they traveled this fast.

He reflected on his departure that morning. His mother had been upset at the sudden news that her son was leaving to seek his fortune with the Muslims. His father had been silent, but there had been a faint air of disapproval in his eyes. His younger siblings looked up at him with something like hero worship, and they expressed regrets that they couldn't have an adventure such as he was embarking upon. He thought of Fariha, the girl who'd been occupying his thoughts for months. He imagined her giving him a farewell kiss and escorting him to the edge of the town, then watching him disappear to the west, a tear on her face, pledging to wait for his return. Alas, he hadn't seen her. He didn't dwell on the fact that she'd hardly talked to him in the months that he'd been besotted with her.

Only Imad had taken the news with any sort of equanimity. As they were preparing to leave, he met the boys and pressed a heavy object into Bashour's hand. "Take this. It may come in handy." As he shook the young man's hand, his free hand on Bashour's shoulder, he looked straight into Bashour's eyes and said cryptically, "Remember. Not everything is as it seems." Moments later, Bashour unwrapped the cloth to reveal a small lead cross, barely the length of his palm, with very little ornamentation. It was a strange gift after the many years that they'd been under his tutelage. He rewrapped the cross and buried it in his pack.

He and Marid had found Rashad, Jabir and their companions in the Muslim column as it had assembled along the Decumanus, the mile-long thoroughfare that ran the length of

Tadmur. They'd been met with smiles and the greeting, "Peace be upon you." which Bashour began to realize was some sort of formula for the Muslims. Rashad had suggested that they load their packs on the she-camel that appeared to be asleep in the shade of one of the massive fluted Grecian columns lining the Decumanus. Marid moved to do so when Rashad warned, "Be careful, she bites!" He ducked aside just as the camel's teeth snapped closed where his ear had been, then danced as she attempted to stomp his foot while he was off balance. The group laughed. Bashour demurred and chose to carry his pack himself.

The town had turned out to watch as the Muslims marched out of Tadmur. The Decumanus was lined with people, and Bashour's chest swelled. The columns on either side of the street cast long morning shadows across their way. The street was alive with eight centuries of history. As he passed under the arch at the Damascus gate he felt himself part of that history.

His sense of history deserted him once they were in the desert. The unchanging sand mocked him. History had no effect on the sand. It remain unchanged long after any human trace had fallen into dust. His grandiose feelings forgotten, his world collapsed to putting one weary foot in front of another.

He'd made the journey to Qaryateyn twice before with his father. Normally it took five or six days, but at the pace they were traveling, they would get there before the end of the third day. They stopped to pray at midmorning and again when the sun was highest. Bashour and Marid followed the prayers as best they could. It wasn't difficult after the first few times. The rhyming sequence helped Bashour predict the next words in each sura. If he lagged just a heartbeat behind his companions, he could recite with a fair amount of authority.

By the time the sun touched the horizon, they'd covered twenty miles. Bashour was exhausted and could barely rise after the evening prayers. He was asleep as soon as he stretched out under his cloak.

10. Qaryateyn, Syrian High Desert
June 14, 634

Tamara bint Waqar felt a little embarrassed by the bold stares of the Byzantine soldiers as she and her cousin, Jamila, carried their laundry to the town square for washing. Jamila nudged her. "I think that one likes you!" she said playfully.

"Which one?"

Jamila laughed, her voice tinkling off the walls along the street. "Does it matter? They're all staring!" She feigned a slight stumble and as she recovered, she hitched her dress higher, exposing her legs almost to the knees. One of the soldiers milling about the front of the market whistled appreciatively.

"Jamila!" Tamara scolded in a loud whisper, but she was amused at her cousin's boldness. It wasn't often so many young men were in town, and Jamila had always been a bold spirit.

Jamila shrugged. "What? It'll give them something to think about. If they're here to defend us, they should know what they're defending, right?" She winked at Tamara, who smiled. They'd grown up together in Qaryateyn and were more than cousins – Jamila was her best friend.

The soldiers had arrived late the previous evening, force-marched from Damascus on the rumor that a huge force of Arabs was prowling the surrounding desert. The mayor of the town was wringing his hands in worry, trying to billet three thousand weary soldiers. With most of the able-bodied townsmen taking the herds to their summer grazing, most families were temporarily without fathers and brothers. To billet a soldier in a family home without the man of the house present would be scandalous. Runners had been sent to bring some men back, but they could be days returning.

When Tamara and Jamila arrived at the open pool in the town square with their laundry, they joined the many women already there. Someone had rigged a canopy over the brick-lined pool to keep the worst of the morning sun off the women. Clothes were drying rapidly on open lines in the sun. One of their aunts spotted Jamila and scolded her. "Jamila! Cover your legs, child! What kind of trouble are you trying to cause?"

Jamila smiled at Tamara as she shook out her dress and they set to work. The older women were full of gossip. "Did you hear that young widow last night? I heard she invited a half-dozen officers to stay with her. You could hear them all night long, drinking and laughing."

"That woman will have a lot of explaining to do come Sunday Mass, before the priest will give her communion."

"Tsk. If she's not careful, the soldiers will all leave here and all she'll have to show for their passing is a big belly."

Jamila muttered in a voice loud enough for only Tamara to hear. "Good for her. If she can snare a husband to take her away from this pit, more power to her."

Zuhayr, the subject of this conversation, was a few years older than Tamara. Shortly after she'd married, her husband had caught a fever and died. "Yes," said Tamara, "but she shouldn't be giving free samples like some common merchant."

Jamila's eyes flashed. "She should do whatever it takes. What future does she have here? No one our age wants her. All these boys want a virgin. Her only hope is some old man whose teeth are loose, who doesn't care as long as she's warm in his bed. If I were her, I'd do whatever I could to get out of here and start anew. I doubt the men are so picky in Damascus. Zuhayr would make any man a good wife. Virginity is overrated."

Tamara said in mock horror, "Don't let your father hear you say that. You won't be able to sit for a month!"

The two girls laughed. They were almost twin sisters. They had long black hair that flowed and shone like silk, and their thick eyebrows highlighted their dark oval eyes. Tamara's chin was finer than Jamila's and her nose not quite as prominent. The last few years had seen the baby fat melt away, revealing fine cheekbones. A line of hopeful suitors had begun to form for each of them, but their fathers had guarded them jealously. Tamara had her eye on a couple of potential husbands, but was in no hurry to decide. Her father and Jamila's father were brothers, and they believed in treating their baby girls very well, with the understanding that any suitor would have to be ready to treat them at least as well, if not better, to be noticed. The sudden appearance of thousands of soldiers in town added a new perspective to the idea of marriage.

After the laundry was done and they shared a midday meal of flatbread with the other townswomen, they made their way home with their baskets filled with folded clothes. The marketplace entrance was still crowded with soldiers. Someone had placed some tables and produced several bottles of wine. As the two girls passed they heard more whistles and catcalls from the soldiers, some of whom had also been there that morning.

One of the men rose and fell in behind them. He smiled as his companions urged him on with hand motions. He touched Jamila's shoulder. "Excuse me, miss." Tamara frowned and they both picked up their pace as Jamila shrugged away from the contact. He looked helplessly at his friends, who motioned him to try again. "I'm sorry, miss?" He laid his hand on her shoulder this time.

Jamila stopped and put her basket down and whirled on him. "What do you want?"

He gave her a great smile and said, "Well, you're very attractive and I was wondering if you and your little friend here would be interested in joining us for a glass. . ."

"What do you think I am, some whore here to entertain you? Is that it?" Jamila interrupted angrily.

He shrugged comically and grinned at his friends. "Well, I was hoping you weren't, because you see, my friends and I haven't got much money and we hoped we wouldn't have to pay for anything. . ." He never got to finish, as Jamila struck him with such force that the slap could be heard well down the street. His face clouded with anger and she stood glaring defiantly at him. Several of his friends came towards them, concern on their faces. They took his arms while he was still recovering from the shock of the unexpected blow. Tamara tugged on her friend's sleeve. "Let's go!" she hissed.

11. The Syrian Desert, East of Qaryateyn

As Bashour and Marid prepared themselves for the noon prayers, Jabir caught Bashour's arm. "Your cloak. Take it off for prayer."

Bashour looked confused and motioned to everyone around them as they washed their arms from a communal bucket "What? Why? Everyone's wearing a cloak."

Jabir caught the hem of Bashour's cloak and held it up to him. "Yes, but yours is embroidered with a pattern." Bashour's cloak had a three-inch strip on his cloak with a complex lattice pattern. Bashour looked at him in confusion, so Jabir elaborated, "The Prophet traded his garment with that of Abu Jahm, because his garment had a pattern on it that diverted his attention from the prayer."

Bashour fought to hide the frustration and disgust at the request. They practiced so many minute details and rules regarding prayer. The day before he'd been unceremoniously hauled to his feet and left the prayer area to perform ablutions with a half-dozen others, because they'd all heard and smelled someone passing gas near them. Kneeling and bending over in prostration tended to compress the intestines and promote flatulence.

When the prayer finished, they resumed their march. Marid fell into step beside him. On the second day, Bashour had summoned his courage and loaded his pack on the camel with only a grazing kick to his thigh to show for it; so they walked with just a small shoulder bag containing some dates, bread and a water skin.

After the usual complaints of how tired and footsore they were, the talk generally drifted to the subject of women. Bashour asked, "Did you get to see Rudaba before you left?" Marid and Rudaba had been conducting a quiet romance for several months.

Marid shrugged. "Yeah. She sneaked out and we spent most of the night together."

Bashour raised his eyebrows. He never could tell when Marid was boasting or telling the truth or both. Under most circumstances an angry father would be ready to kill a young man who tempted his daughter out of the house in the night, but Marid lived a charmed life. Rudaba's parents thought he was wonderful and would overlook a great deal of misbehavior on his part. Bashour couldn't understand it. "So what did she say about you leaving?"

"Oh, she cried. She offered herself to me."

"Did you. . . ?"

Marid simply grinned at him. Bashour was frustrated by his lack of a straight answer. He seriously doubted that Marid would do anything with Rudaba, even if she offered, but he wondered if he knew his friend as well as he thought he did.

An hour of sunlight remained when the word came to stop and make camp. No campfires were to be lit. Scouts had spotted the outskirts of Qaryateyn, and they were to spend the night here, complete the march after morning prayers, and strike well before midday. Going further today would invite a sneak attack during the night.

12. Qaryateyn
June 15, 634

Tamara was awakened before dawn by the ringing of the bell in the church. She could hear shouting in the streets and the tramp of hobnailed sandals. Tamara and her mother stood in the door and watched as troops of soldiers trotted down the street, heading east. Neighbors gathered on rooftops and passed the news: an Arab army had been spotted not far to the east and the soldiers were deploying in the orchards to repel them.

After they'd marched for an hour, Bashour could see the low trees of Qaryateyn ahead. The word came to mount up. With few exceptions, the Arab soldiers led their horses when on the march, mounting them only for battle. Bashour's group was without a mount except the camel they called Shai-tan. As the mounted forces deployed in both directions, the dismounted warriors continued straight ahead, forming the center.

A horn sounded ahead to their right. Wahid Bin Aswad turned to him and said, "They've chosen to fight. You two have no weapons. Stay here and mind the camel. We will signal you to bring her forward with the horn. Two, then three, then two. Got it?" The boys nodded.

They tied the camel to a small shrub and squatted in its shade. "Well, I guess we need to get some swords." said Marid.

Bashour agreed, and they consoled themselves with tales of the glory they'd garner in battle, each secretly relieved that he didn't have to fight this day. They could hear the sounds of shouting and horns west of them, and once a bloodcurdling scream was abruptly cut short. The boys looked at each other with concern.

Bashour hadn't expected there to be a fight over Qaryateyn, which was a quarter the size of Tadmur. How could it possibly hope to defeat the Arabs? He began to worry about what might happen to them if the Arabs were defeated. He decided that he and Marid could claim they were merchants or pilgrims following the Muslim army. They had no weapons and their accents were local; no one would have reason to disbelieve them. A few residents even knew him, although it had been several years since Bashour had been here.

Khalid gathered his senior officers. "Dhiraar, tell me what your scouts see."

Dhiraar picked up a stone and traced in the dirt as he spoke. "We've had intermittent contact since late last night, when mounted Roman scouts encountered our western camp in the darkness. One of our men infiltrated the town and returned. He reports a large number of soldiers in the town, sleeping in tents. This isn't a permanent garrison. There's no wall to speak of. The city is on a slight rise to the northwest of the oasis. Orchards start just north of the road we're on and extend in a southwest line east and south of the town. Low walls separate the orchards. Our column has been spotted. We've heard bells from the town and seen a lot of movement in the orchards."

Khalid grunted, "There have been no messengers from the town?" He looked around. All were shaking their heads. "Our messenger. Did he make contact?"

"He was cut down by archers as he approached the orchards along the roads."

Khalid's eyes blazed with fury. "They're going to make a stand in the orchard. Abdur-Rahman, take five hundred horses and go right between the orchards and the ridge to the north. Pull up short of the city and await a signal. Dhiraar, take fifteen hundred horses and follow the orchards south until you've flanked their line, then attack their right flank. Sound a horn when you begin your attack. I'll send the dismounts forward up the middle to keep their attention and hold a thousand horses in reserve. When you hear Dhiraar's horn, everyone attacks. We'll take them from three sides. Questions?"

No one spoke. "Allâh will give us victory. Let's ride!"

As the foot soldiers passed him, Khalid enjoined them to move on the orchard, but to use the sparse cover to avoid arrows. Make the trees and cause a lot of noise, to mask Dhiraar's approach.

It was almost too easy. His foot soldiers had formed a ragged skirmish line and were leapfrogging across the open desert down to where the land turned green, when Dhiraar's horn sounded from the left. They jumped up and ran in a full assault for the orchards, easily dodging the uncoordinated barrage of arrows from the orchard. As they made the trees, the mounted soldiers crashed into the Roman lines from both sides. The Arabs scythed through the defenders with ease and the Roman lines collapsed in chaos. The dismounted soldiers had to run through the orchards to catch the fleeing Romans, who were butchered piecemeal by the Arabs. Khalid kneed his horse forward at a leisurely walk, followed by his reserve forces.

Wahid gasped for air, slowing to a trot. Qutayba was behind him and prodded him with the butt of his sword. "Come on, big man! We're going to miss some of them!" The others slowed to allow Wahid to keep up with them.

"I'm built for fighting, not running!" Wahid proclaimed through gulps of air. "Let the horses run down the cowards as they flee!"

Sameer laughed. "They took one look at you and started running. They think you're Shai-tan. If you want one of these girl-men to fight you, you should go into battle wearing a veil."

"I'd pay good gold to see that," said Jabir. "A veil on Wahid's hairy face. Hah!" He reached up and plucked a low hanging clump of dates from a nearby tree.

Rashad smiled, but kept silent. He was earnestly scanning the lines of trees, making sure that no one was waiting in ambush. Ahead, they could hear the carnage as the cavalry rampaged among the fleeing Romans.

They slowed to a walk. Before long, they were walking through an abattoir. First a few, then dozens, then hundreds of Roman bodies littered the ground of the orchard. The ground was well tended and clean, and the ranked lines of trees didn't impede the horsemen as they swept the Roman lines. After a quarter of a mile, they broke out of the orchard and faced the bare ground that separated the small town from the orchard. Arab cavalry milled about in confusion, waiting for orders. No Roman soldiers were in sight. Wahid turned to Qutayba. "You better send for the boys." Qutayba lifted his horn to his lips.

Tamara was apprehensive. Rumors from the fighting swept through the neighborhood. The Arabs had been beaten. The armies were locked in fierce battle. Someone said they'd seen horses coming out of the orchard, but someone else said that was preposterous. The idea that men were locked in a life-and-death struggle so close by didn't seem real to Tamara. Then a boy ran shouting through the street and ice gripped her gut when she heard what he was saying. "The Arabs have won! The soldiers have fled! The city has fallen!"

Someone down the street cheered. The town was mostly Ghassanid Arabs, and many people had no great love for the heavy-handed Roman rule since they'd defeated the Persians six years before. Tamara looked to her mother in fear, but her mother remained calm. "So now we're Arabs again." She shrugged. "We lived under the Sassanids, we lived under the Romans. We'll live under the Arab empire now. Is there really any difference?"

"What should we do?"

Her mother shrugged. "Wait and see. God willing, everything will be all right. Remember, no matter what king owns this or that, the animals have to be tended, the crops have to be harvested. Nothing really changes."

Khalid sat implacably astride his horse in the town square, waiting for his lieutenants to report. Dhiraar broke a consultation with his men and reported to him. "Sahib, there are no men in the town whatsoever. They've all left with the livestock for summer pastures to the north, leaving only old men and a few others. Their Mayor wishes to speak to you."

Khalid turned his head to the north and glowered under his shaggy eyebrows at the low hills a mile distant. "That doesn't make me happy, Dhiraar. Detail a hundred riders to screen north a half-day's ride. I don't want to be taken in the flank by a tribe of angry husbands and fathers." He turned back to Dhiraar. "And tell that mayor that the time to see me was before we were attacked by the Roman soldiers. I'm not interested in anything he has to say. If I see him, I may well kill him."

"Will we plunder the town, Sahib? The men fought well, they expect a reward."

Khalid looked thoughtful. The men's bloodlust was up after the battle. They were going to find an outlet for that, whether he agreed to it or not. "Dispatch to Medina that we encountered a military force east of the town, but that the town surrendered without a fight." He paused and Dhiraar grinned. If the town didn't resist, then there would be no official plunder and they wouldn't have to make a formal accounting to send Medina the fifth part. Dhiraar raised an eyebrow questioningly and Khalid continued, "I don't want to be loaded down with a baggage train. Tell the men to take only the valuables they can easily carry –

gold and jewels. There can't be that much in this hole. Any captives taken must be able to keep up, or we'll leave them. Understood?" Dhiraar nodded in assent and turned to go, but Khalid stopped him. "And Dhiraar, tell the men that any women they enjoy but don't take with us must be compensated. Even whores deserve to make a living."

Wahid found the boys leading Shai-tan into the orchard and directed them to the southern edge of the orchard, where water from the oasis pooled into a wide, sluggish stream. Soldiers were gathering with their horses and camels. The horses were wet with sweat. The men were laughing and jubilant. Those with camels staked their animals near the water, while the horses were tied to trees in the shade of the orchard. The horses stamped their hooves and snorted at the smell of the water.

"Do you know about horses?" the big man asked.

The boys looked at each other, then Marid hesitantly said, "Yes?"

"Each of you take a couple of horses at a time to drink. Don't let them drink too much. Then tie them back to the trees. Horses are stupid, and they'll kill themselves if you leave them alone with water when they're thirsty." Bashour relaxed with relief. Everyone knew that.

"What of the camels?"

"Just make sure they don't get free. Camels can drink all they want."

"Where will you be?"

"We're going to make sure Sameer doesn't meet the girl of his dreams and disappoint Dimah," laughed Wahid. "And to look for the girl of our dreams in the process," he said with a wink.

A commotion at the edge of the orchard silenced them as a big man in black dismounted his horse. Some men cheered him and all treated him deferentially. He strode to the water and addressed Wahid, "You have arranged care for the animals?" Bashour studied the man; he was huge, with pockmarks on his cheeks above a rough, full black beard. His eyes appeared small on his broad face and he spoke like a man accustomed to being obeyed. Bashour felt intimidated as the man's gaze passed carelessly across him.

Wahid ducked his head reflexively. "Yes, Sahib! These two will help care for the horses."

Khalid scrutinized the boys. “Who are these?”

The boys stood out because of their sparse beards among the crowd of Arabs. Wahid tried to hide the nervousness he felt. “They joined us in Tadmur. They have accepted Islam.”

The boys nodded silently in affirmation.

The man drew himself up and addressed them directly. “I am Khalid. Your loyalty is to Allâh, then to the Caliph, then to me. Do you understand?” The boys nodded mutely. “Have you no tongues? Do you understand Arabic?”

The boys blurted at once, “No, Sahib! I mean yes, Sahib. Ah, no. I mean. . . ”

“Enough!” Khalid said with a slight smile. He turned back to Wahid. “Pair each of them with a mentor. See that they learn the Qur’án.”

“It shall be done, Sahib.”

Khalid grasped Wahid’s cloak and drew him along as he walked back towards the orchard. When they were out of earshot, Khalid said, “Split them up.”

“Sahib?”

“They don’t look like spies. Even so, boys together can cause mischief. Split them and teach them separately. I’m holding you responsible for their behavior.”

“Yes, Sahib!”

“Well, this stinks.” Marid proclaimed.

They’d been watering the horses for several hours, going back and forth from the water to the orchard, escorting the animals in pairs to drink.

Bashour shrugged philosophically. “Someone has to do it.” The horses he was holding began to drink. He sat under one of them for some shade. “What do you think of Islam?”

“The more I learn about it, the more sense it seems to make. It answers a lot of questions that I’ve always struggled with.”

That got Bashour’s attention. While watching the flocks, he and Marid had often dissected old Imad’s teachings, and often found themselves asking more questions than they were answering. “Such as?”

“Well, the whole trinity thing. The empire is splitting itself apart how Jesus and God are connected, what the nature of Jesus is. Islam solves this.”

“How so?”

"The problem is that we say Jesus is God, yet he prayed to God. Why would God pray to himself? The Muslims say that Jesus is just a prophet. They revere him, but he was just a man."

"But the resurrection? He rose from the dead."

"Ah, that's what Paul told us to believe. How could God die? No, Jesus was never crucified. Allâh told Muhammad that people had been fooled into thinking that another was Jesus, and that they crucified him instead of Jesus. Then Jesus was raised into heaven."

"But why did they lie about it to us? Why have they taught that Jesus was God?"

"That's easy," Marid said. "Power. Look at the church, how rich it is. You want to know where the gold in a town is, you go to the church. It's all about money and power. It always was."

Bashour thought about this. It neatly answered many of the mysteries that had plagued him about Christianity. Yes, of course, if Jesus wasn't God, if they crucified someone else thinking it was Jesus, yes, that would explain a lot. He was eager to learn more. It seemed Islam held all the answers. Maybe Islam was the answer?

Tamara's mother had put her to work baking bread. "The conquerors will be hungry. If we have something with which to placate them, it will be easier." Tamara wasn't sure about her mother's logic and her heart sat in her throat. Occasionally she'd hear something in the streets – an altercation, a shout, a scream, laughter – and the cold hand in her belly would squeeze tighter.

Then she heard shouts and the banging of doors growing closer to their house. She'd picked up a water jar to rinse her hands of flour so she could see what was happening when the door burst open. The sudden brilliant light was blocked by a massive form as a man in armor entered, followed by two companions. Tamara's mother came into the kitchen from the back door and screamed. Then she started shouting, "Get out! Out!"

The first man looked closely at her and dismissed her, then pointed at Tamara. "Take that one." They grabbed her arms and easily lifted her off her feet towards the door. Tamara tried to fight. She kicked and screamed, but they were impervious to her efforts in their battle armor. Their hands were like steel vises that crushed her skin. Once outside in the sunlight, the man on her right grunted, "You've got her?"

The other man twisted his right hand through her hair, gripping her head tight at the base of her head. "Yeah, I got her." She was dragged towards the town square, unable to resist. Her captor held her head at an odd angle and she had to watch out the corner of her eyes to see where she was going.

A cluster of nearly a hundred girls lined the square, under guard by a dozen or so soldiers. Tears streaked their cheeks and a low wail rose and fell among the young women. Some of them sported darkening bruises. Tamara was twenty years old and experienced enough to realize what was happening. She saw her nine-year-old cousin, Miriam, crying and looking confused and thought, *Oh, My God, no! Not Miriam! She's just a child!* She recognized Jamila and the two girls fell into each other's arms in tears.

"Jamila, what's going on?"

Jamila held her by the shoulders and locked eyes with her. "Remember, you have to let them get close enough so you can get to their eyes."

Tamara blinked in confusion. "Wha. . . what?"

"Their eyes. When they get close enough, put your hands on their face like this." She cupped Tamara's face tenderly in her hands, her thumbs resting beside her eyes. "Then take your thumbs and jab hard and dig!"

"I don't know if I can do that!"

Jamila looked fierce. "Your only other choice is to give in and let them take what they want." Tamara could hardly breathe. The fear in her belly seized her and squeezed her chest. Her eyes darted left and right looking for an escape.

A growing mass of Arab warriors was filling the square, inspecting the group of girls appreciatively. A large man, naked from the waist up, paced back and forth between them and the girls, a large smile on his face. "Who among you distinguished themselves in battle today?"

A voice from the front shouted, "Get on with it, Dhiraar. I'd like to get to know my new wife before evening prayers!" The crowd of sweating men laughed and murmured their assent.

One man stepped up. "I was riding at the left side of Jawhar Abd-Fattah, and I saw him slay two dozen Romans." A man was pushed forward among scattered applause and ululating yells from the ranks.

Dhiraar smiled and called out, "Has anyone a greater achievement than Jawhar Abd-Fattah this day? No?" He made a grand gesture at the crowd of girls. "Then, exalted warrior, you may have first pick of the fruits of our labor today. Choose wisely!"

The man sauntered forward. The other men gave him good-natured boos, catcalls and advice. He strode up to one girl and lifted her chin and examined her. Then he moved on to another and turned her head from side to side. He leered at his companions; they cheered and shouted encouragement. He shook his head with a smile and moved down the group. He stopped at Tamara and Jamila. Tamara turned her head and tried to bury it in Jamila's shoulder. Jamila glared at him.

"Oh, you're a fiery one. I like you!" He grabbed Jamila by the arm and tore her out of Tamara's grasp. Tamara shrieked and reached for her, but was restrained by several other women, who held her as she wept. The man dragged Jamila to a nearby house and entered it. Moments later, the woman who owned the house was forcibly ejected from the doorway and the door barred from within.

The auction of merit went on. The one they called Dhiraar would choose men who would take a woman from the group and disappear down a street, looking for a house that could be commandeered. This had gone on for some twenty minutes when the air was rent by a coarse shriek from the house where Jamila had been taken. That scream came from no woman, and everyone in the square turned towards it with a start. Moments later, the door opened and the soldier came out, screaming. He was naked to the waist, clothed only in a breechcloth. His hand was over his left eye and his face was covered in blood.

Dhiraar reached him with several quick strides, a grim look on his face. He pulled the man's hand away and examined the ruined eyeball. Tamara was horrified. "Oh God, Jamila, no!" Dhiraar strode into the house and returned in a moment, Jamila in tow. He threw her on the ground and motioned for two men to pick her up and carry her to a place in front of the rest of the women. His face was red with fury. He went to one of the men in the crowd and snatched an evil looking scimitar from him.

Jamila had been forced to kneel in front of the women. Standing beside her, he addressed them loudly. "This is the penalty for resisting that which Allâh has ordained! Allâhu Akbar!" Without elaborating, he turned to Jamila. With a motion of his head, the men holding her let go and jumped away. His sword flashed.

Time slowed to a stop. Jamila appeared to be looking right at Tamara, as her head slowly fell away from her body. The body remained kneeling for what seemed an eternity, and a fountain of blood shot skyward to an impossible height. The head hit the ground with an awful thud. The body slowly toppled forward and began twitching horribly, its limbs jerking without any coordination in a macabre dance.

Time slowly started again. Tamara heard an earsplitting wail that would never end, before she realized that it was her own voice. She screamed and screamed, unable tear her eyes from the body of her best friend. She uttered no words; her mind was numb. This wasn't happening. This couldn't be happening. Oh, God, Jamila!

An awful silence descended on the square except for Tamara's weeping. Dhiraar motioned the men to take the body away. He returned the sword to its owner and angrily strode from the street. The men mixed uncomfortably, unsure what to do next. After a few moments, a young man stepped forward and addressed the men. "I am Abdur-Rahman bin Khalid. Who objects to my authority to allocate the spoils?" His question was met with silence and after a few moments he began striding among the crowd of men, quietly selecting those who could choose a woman.

Tamara was one of the last ones taken. Her cries caused most of the men to pass her by. Her throat was raw and it hurt to breathe. A man with angular features and a ragged beard studied her closely. His long nose was bent slightly to one side and a ragged pink scar ran down his cheek to his neck. He smiled and his fetid breath assaulted Tamara's nose. "By Allâh, aren't you the pretty one?" Without another word, he took her and led her stumbling through the streets. She went without protest. She couldn't see where she was, all she could see was Jamila's body kneeling, headless, over and over again. Everything was a blur to her and she didn't know whose house they entered.

She offered no resistance when he threw her on the bed. He took a moment to slow down and remove her garments without damaging them. She lay limp and unresponsive, but as she was laid bare, her hands instinctively went to her groin and across her breasts. He stood and stared at her in appreciation, then quickly stripped himself. He pulled her hands away and one coarse, thorny hand grabbed her breast roughly. A scream tried to rise in her throat, but never made it past her lips. She closed her eyes tightly and bit her lip, turning her head away from his kisses as he forced himself on her. She retched at the smell of his stale sweat, mixed with the metallic tang of blood. The room was silent except for his animal-like growls, and the silence seemed to crush her. The pain she felt was nothing compared to the horror she'd already experienced. She felt completely detached from what was happening to her, as her mind continually replayed Jamila's headless body falling into the dust.

He was finished in a merciful few minutes. The man calmly dressed himself and arranged his clothing as Tamara curled up into a fetal position on her side and cried silently. Her throat was raw and had a huge, painful lump in the back of it. She didn't move to clean the blood between her legs. She cried endlessly for all she'd lost that day — her best friend, her dignity, her security, her maidenhood, herself.

Hours later, Tamara squeezed her eyes shut against the darkness. A dog barked in the distance. The bark was abruptly replaced by a yelp of pain that quickly turned into a series of agonized cries, then cut short. Terror walked the streets that night, cutting down anything that challenged it.

The man sleeping next to her shifted his weight and she sidled away from him on the thin mattress to avoid his touch. She was hungry and cold. The desert night air chilled her and the man – his name was Mus'ad – had pulled the cover off her in his sleep. Should she pull it back? Could she do it without touching him? What if he woke up? No. He'd raped her twice more that evening. She'd rather freeze than face that again.

A woman was sobbing quietly somewhere nearby. Tamara wished she'd be quiet. Her cries only amplified the despair Tamara felt. She thought of her empty stomach, but as soon as she did, she felt nausea rise in her throat. If she ate anything now, she'd throw up.

She could get up, get away. It would be easy. Just slide off the end of the bed and creep away. She could do it. She moved her weight slightly and the bed creaked. Mus'ad shifted restlessly and she was paralyzed, the fear gripping her in an icy fist. Was he waking up? No. She turned her head to the stone wall, just inches away. What if she did get away, what then? Where were her clothes? Could she find them in the dark without waking him? What was happening in the streets? Where could she hide?

As if to answer her, a woman screamed in the distance. All her muscles tensed, as she suppressed the urge to scream in response. The streets were no safer than where she was, perhaps less so.

She willed herself to be calm, to clear her mind. Then, unbidden, the image of Jamila, headless, blood everywhere, invaded her mind's eye. *No! Anything but that, God, please!* She knew that if she dwelt on the death of her friend that she'd lose her already tenuous grip on sanity. She thrust the image aside and it was replaced by the memory of Mus'ad, his weight heavy on her, thrusting into her, his foul breath and the acrid smell of his sweat making her gasp as he emptied himself into her.

The night seemed like an eternity, an endless, agonizing procession of horror, as her mind struggled to make sense of everything that had happened. She closed her eyes tightly and prayed to die as tears squeezed past her eyelids.

13. Damascus
June 15, 634

"Thomas, let me put you at ease. I'm sure you're aware that my invitation to come here this morning is more than a social call."

Thomas adopted a patient expression and regarded Governor Azrail. Since he'd arrived in Damascus, the rumors had been flying about his presence. Because he was the son-in-law of the Emperor, everyone assumed that his presence had some imperial sanction, an ulterior motive that had yet to be revealed. He'd hoped that after some time the fact that he was here as a private citizen, on private business matters, would put an end to the rumors; but the intrigue was irresistible and the rumors had, if anything, grown.

Azrail had invited him to dine at mid-morning with Harbis, the general in charge of the region, and Bishop Peter. They met on the roof of the governor's mansion, shielded from the sun by a cloth awning. As they were served an excellent dish of rice and chicken garnished with cherries, Thomas waited patiently for Azrail to declare what was on his mind.

Azrail glanced at Harbis, who cleared his throat before speaking. "Have you any communication from Basileus Heraclius recently?"

Thomas raised an eyebrow. He didn't like being outnumbered and at a disadvantage. This felt like more intrigue, which he detested. "No."

"Several days ago we received a dispatch from the east. A large Arab force, possibly as many as five thousand strong, has marched through several towns in the highlands beyond the mountains." He gestured to the northeast, where the anti-Lebanon mountains faded in the distance. "They're apparently heading this way. If our reports are right, we may see them in this valley within a week."

Thomas leaned forward with interest. This was surprising news. Arabs from the south were to be expected, but he couldn't fathom how such a force had braved the inhospitable desert of eastern Syria to arrive from Persia. Once a soldier, he was always interested in military matters.

Harbis continued, "We force-marched three thousand light infantry to reinforce Qaryateyn, which is the last town before they have to cross the mountains. We have no idea if they managed to stop the invaders yet."

Azrail leaned in towards Thomas. "If the Arabs cross those mountains, Damascus may be placed under siege for a time. We have a garrison strong enough to withstand a siege, but not to meet them in the open. Emessa has promised that they'll send Caloiis with a themata of cavalry to relieve us if we're placed under siege. They could be here now, but that would leave Emessa wide open, should these Arabs strike north instead of crossing the mountains."

Thomas contemplated the geography. "They'll cross the mountains; Emessa's too far north. They're going to try to link up with the Arab armies to the south."

Harbis regarded Thomas critically. "Why do you say that?"

"Where are the Arab armies in the south?"

"They're encamped on the east bank of the Dead Sea," Azrail said. "One army is milling around Gaza, raiding towns, without any pattern."

Thomas nodded his head. "You see, someone isn't happy with their lack of progress. The reports I heard from Persia say that they sliced through the Sassanids like a sword. They moved fast and defeated the Persian army before they could regain their balance in action after action. They were led by this black-hearted devil called Khalid. It's not like the Arabs to take a slow, methodical approach to an invasion. My guess is that Khalid has been transferred to Syria to put some life into this invasion. He's coming south to take command of the army."

Harbis and Azrail regarded each other in surprise. What Thomas said made almost too much sense. The Bishop spoke up. "Thomas, I fear the Emperor wasted your talents placing you in charge of logistics. You would make a fine commander of intelligence."

Azrail shifted his weight and regarded Thomas. "Yes, I certainly see the logic of your analysis. But I was wondering, Thomas, if we could impose upon your extensive experience to help us prepare for a siege?"

Thomas breathed a sigh of relief to himself. The intrigue he assumed to be there had not materialized. Instead of trying to discern some hidden motive, or currying him for some imperial favor, these men were honestly petitioning him for something that he could provide. He immediately regarded his companions with considerably more charity. He raised his glass. "Governor, you have but to ask. I'll be happy to provide whatever assistance you require."

Eudocia's steps were light as she ascended the steps to the wide porch in front of Jonas' apartment. She addressed the young man lounging in the shade on the balustrade. "Narses, have you seen Jonas?"

Narses shrugged noncommittally. "No. I've been looking for him myself. We were supposed to look at some horses this morning."

Eudocia lips pursed angrily. "Well, if you see him, tell him my father wants him as soon as possible. He was supposed to oversee a warehouse inventory today. My father is starting to get angry!"

Narses smiled and flicked a salute towards her. "I'll be sure to tell him if I see him."

"See that you do. He's got to start taking things seriously, and not running around like a playboy horse trader!" She whirled and strode back down the street with determination, trying to hide her anger and frustration. Her father was definitely unhappy at the lackadaisical attitude that Jonas took towards business.

Narses waited in the shade until Eudocia had turned the corner and was gone for some minutes, then rapped on the door. A minute later, Jonas opened it, a linen towel wrapped around his waist. "What is it?"

"Your bride-to-be was looking for you. Said you're supposed to be at some audit of a warehouse."

"Shit." He opened the door wider and turned to the girl in his bed, covering herself with a thin sheet. "Time for you to go." He scrabbled on a table and tossed a few coins at Narses. "Thanks, I owe you one. Can you take care of her?" He jerked his thumb at the girl.

Narses licked his lips, an evil grin crossed his face. "I'd love to. Do you mind?" He looked pointedly at the girl and raised an eyebrow.

Jonas waved a dismissive hand, concentrating on donning his clothes. "Whatever you like. Just have her out of here before I get back." Narses smiled at the girl, who smiled shyly back at him.

Nicetas regarded the list that Thomas had presented him and whistled. "This is quite an order."

"That's just the start. The Governor will subsidize whatever we can lay our hands on until Damascus is up to its knees in food."

Nicetas reached for his cloak. "Walk with me. I need to go down to warehouse three to supervise an audit."

"Nicetas, you have to learn to delegate. You can't run this kind of enterprise and still get your hands dirty with accounting like that."

"I did delegate. I told that Tournikes kid to be there an hour after dawn and it's almost midday and he's not there. I tell you, Thomas, I'm going to have to put my boot in that boy's ass pretty soon and he's not going to like it! I'm really starting to question Eudocia's judgment here."

As they walked, Nicetas studied the request and observed, "Most of the harvest from Lebanon is being shipped to Palestine. I've heard that Heraclius is assembling a huge army there to face these Arabs. Prices are going through the roof. I hope Azrail is aware of that."

"He's given me an unlimited line of credit. He said that money's no object. So send your messengers to the markets; anything that's not commandeered by the army, have it sent here."

"Money is no object? This could be the mother lode we've been waiting for!" Nicetas smiled slyly.

Thomas stopped and turned seriously to Nicetas. "Not this time. Look, there's going to be food shortages across the country for the common folk. Let's not compound that crime with profiteering at the expense of the government. You know the Emperor will just raise taxes to pay for it and cause more misery for the commoners. We'll charge a modest, but fair, markup for services, nothing more. I want to be able to look at myself in the mirror."

Nicetas slapped him on the shoulder and resumed walking. "You're never going to get rich if you stay so honest, my friend, but if I stay close to you, I might just get into heaven by association."

14. West of Qaryateyn, Syrian High Desert June 16, 634

Bashour fanned the cloak he'd drawn over his head to protect himself from the brutal sun. They'd been on the march for several hours since morning prayers. Rashad was walking alongside him, reciting the Qur'án from memory, teaching Bashour as they walked. Bashour had a quick mind, but he was beginning to despair that he'd ever be able to memorize the whole Qur'án. It seemed to go on forever. Rashad was reciting one of the shorter parts, one called Al Ma'arij. Bashour listened carefully and tried his best not to interrupt his serious young companion, because if Rashad stopped, he'd get lost and have to start all over. The verse was hypnotic and Bashour would get lost in the rise and fall of the rhythm, making it a pleasant distraction while they were walking. Rashad's voice took on a soothing, comfortable tone as he recited, and the cadence of the poetry was beautiful and unpredictable.

"Truly man was created very impatient –

"Fretful when evil touches him;

"And niggardly when good reaches him --

"Not so those devoted to Prayer --

"Those who remain steadfast to their prayer;

"And those in whose wealth is a recognized right

"For the needy who asks and him who is prevented from asking;

"And those who believe in the Day of Judgment;

"And those who fear the displeasure of their Lord --

"For their Lord's displeasure is the opposite of Peace and Tranquility --

"And those who guard their chastity,

"Except with their wives and the slaves whom their right hands possess -- for then they are not to be blamed. . ."

"Hold on, you got that wrong." said Qutayba, walking on the other side of Rashad. Bashour rolled his eyes. Not again! These Muslims were constantly bickering over what Muhammad had taught them.

"I did not!" said Rashad, "I recited it exactly the way Abu Sa'id Al-Khudri taught it to me."

"Well, he was a fool then, because the verse as you recite it is very, um, passive. The verse that Muhammad recited showed Allâh's anger more. Like this:

"And those who believe in the Day of Judgment,

"And those who are fearful of their Lord's doom -

"Lo! the doom of their Lord is that before which none can feel secure. . ."

Qutayba smiled, "You see? Allâh isn't displeased, he's threatening doom. That shows his real power!"

Rashad shook his head in derision. "That doesn't even rhyme. It's awkward and breaks the cadence."

Jabir, leading the camel behind them, quickened his step to come closer. "I agree with Qutayba. If there's ever a question about Muhammad's words, you can generally count on the recitation that speaks of doom! I bet old Abu Sa'id changed the verse so he could remember it easier."

"Well, it says basically the same thing, so if it's easier to remember, I think that's important. I'd rather remember it the way Abu Sa'id taught me, than forget it the way you recite it."

Qutayba's face grew dark and he roughly shoved Rashad. Bashour danced out of the way as Rashad stumbled. "Look, you little shit! The Qur'án was written in heaven before Allâh even created the Earth. You recite it the way Muhammad taught. The likes of you has no business changing the perfect word of Allâh!"

Wahid moved between the two Muslims, his bulk separating them like a mountain. "You two stop. Like as not Muhammad taught it both ways. Didn't he say the Qur'án has been revealed in seven different ways, so recite it in the way that's easier for you?"

Qutayba grumbled, "I never heard that. You're making that up, Wahid."

"No, it's true!" said Jabir. "I was there when Umar bin Al-Khattab hauled Hisham bin Hakim bin Hizam in front of Allâh's Apostle and charged him with reciting al-Furqan incorrectly. That's exactly what the Prophet told him."

Bashour spoke up, "If there's a question of what the Prophet said, why doesn't someone just write it down?"

Sameer, walking on the other side of Bashour, hooked his thumb at Rashad. "Then we'd all have to rely on him to tell us what the Qur'án says."

"I'm the only one of us who can read," said Rashad. "Can you read?"

Bashour was a little surprised. Couldn't everyone read? "Uh, yes. I read Greek and some Latin."

Sameer said in derision, "Well, that doesn't help anyone. Allâh revealed the Qur'án in Arabic. Nobody speaks Greek!"

Bashour raised his eyebrows at that statement, but remained silent in surprise. Then he remembered something that occurred to him while Rashad was reciting. "That line about guarding chastity – except wives and slaves? Allâh allows you to do that with slaves?"

Qutayba shrugged. "Why not? They're only slaves."

"I need to get a horse," said Sameer. "So I can fight with the cavalry. They always get the first choice of the slave girls when we fight to capture a city."

Jabir laughed. "Keep dreaming, Sameer. If Dimah catches you with a slave girl, she's going to cut your manhood off."

Sameer's face fell. "You don't have to rub it in." Then he brightened. "How long do you think they'll be in Medina before they allow the camp followers to join us? Maybe I can get a slave girl at the next town and be done with her before Dimah finds out."

Bashour was thinking about the women who'd joined the column at Qaryateyn. The road out of the town had been lined with older women. Girls from the column had tried to break free to embrace their mothers, causing many emotional scenes. They'd been roughly cuffed back into the line. It bothered him, somehow. The people of Qaryateyn weren't enemies of his. "What will happen to the girls taken from Qaryateyn?"

Rashad shrugged. "Some will be sold. If their men like them and they accept Islam, they may be allowed to marry."

Bashour was pondering the merits of marrying a slave when Jabir pointed northwest at a rising cloud of dust. "We have company."

A horn sounded in the column ahead and the men scrambled to retrieve their weapons from the camel's pack. The sword that Bashour had acquired at Qaryateyn was shorter than the scimitars of his companions, and he felt inadequate by comparison. They left the track and began angling across the desert. Other foot soldiers formed a line on either side of them.

Nearly a mile ahead, at the head of the column, Khalid merely had to point and his cavalry commanders wheeled right and headed off to flanking positions against the force coming from the north. On the track ahead was a low-lying depression with a small oasis able to support some grass. A medium sized herd of cattle grazed there. Khalid had sent scouts forth to see if there were any defenders when the attackers from the north were sighted. Riding to intercept them was a motley collection of horsemen, with some even riding donkeys. Khalid twisted in his saddle and examined the column behind him. The cavalry ranged ahead while the foot soldiers were leaving the desert track and forming a line abreast. He smiled at how well his men responded to a threat. His army was like an extension of his will, as if he had to merely think of a movement and they did it without further bidding.

His cavalry outnumbered the attackers by three to one. They encircled the force and rode in a ring about them. The men trapped in the wheeling circle turned in confusion. Then the first foot archers arrived and began picking off targets inside the circle. The attackers had no archers. After many of them fell, the rest dismounted and collapsed onto their faces in the dust. Their mounts, riderless, ran out to the circling Arab cavalry. Except that they tried to attack the Arab column, it hardly qualified as a military engagement.

Dhiraar cantered up to Khalid, who sat observing the action from the desert road. "Nearly two hundred men have surrendered, Sahib. What shall I have done with them?"

"Where are they from?"

"These are the men from Qaryateyn, those who had mounts to chase us, and Bedouins from the desert who have joined them. They were trying to reinforce the ranchers ahead."

"We haven't got the time or men to tend prisoners. Slay them all, take what's valuable."

"As you desire, Sahib."

Tamara's heart leapt when she saw the column being attacked. She recognized the red and black cloaks of men from Qaryateyn and knew that they'd rushed from the summer pastures to rescue her. But her hopes were soon dashed when the confusion was resolved and she could see the same men kneeling in the dirt, their hands bound. They'd been made to discard their cloaks into a pile and were bare to the waist. They were too far off for her to identify any of them. She saw Muslims arrange themselves behind the men and her heart caught in her throat when she realized what was about to happen. She turned away with a sob. The tears came unbidden as she covered her head with her cloak. She tried to reassure herself that her father wasn't one of the men. He'd gone north. He was too far away to have made it in such a short time. He was still with the flocks. She kept telling herself this, trying to control the panic that threatened to engulf her. She kept her face in her cloak for hours, as the column resumed its march across the desert, looking only at the ground at her feet.

15. Near the Dead Sea, Jordan
June 17, 634

Abū 'Ubaidah ibn al-Jarrāh felt like a weight had been lifted from his shoulders. He smiled gently as he shifted on the cushions in his tent and beamed at his commanders. A slave poured hot coffee into the cups of his two visitors.

Yazeed ibn Abu Sufyan and Shurahbil bin Hasanah could sense that Ubaidah's mood had changed. For several weeks, an air of defeatism had been slowly growing around Ubaidah. Scouts had been returning with descriptions of the defenses at Jerusalem. He'd grown increasingly uncertain as each report arrived. The armies had been milling about in southern Syria for nearly a month. Ubaidah claimed that he was waiting for Amr ibn al-Ās and his 9,000 troops to make contact from southern Palestine and the Gaza region, where they'd been sweeping through villages and rural areas. But that excuse was growing thin, as Ubaidah made no attempt to send messengers to order Amr to link up.

Shurahbil was fond of Ubaidah, but was beginning to chafe under his command. The older man was far too thoughtful to lead an army such as this. He was a sound and brave tactician and known for his mercy in conquest, but lacked the organizational skills to effectively control the large force he led into Syria. Shurahbil waited for Ubaidah to open the meeting as they sipped their coffee and honey.

Ubaidah savored the sweet taste with his eyes closed, then put the cup down. "Yazeed, what news of Amr and his army?"

"Sahib, my men have scouted a day's ride west from the great salt sea, without contacting his army."

"Detail a force to find him and order him to assemble his army where the river Jordan flows into the salt sea."

Shurahbil leaned forward. "We're to attack then? May I ask where? Are we going to Jerusalem?"

Ubaidah smiled and the gap where his front teeth were missing reinforced the image of a harmless old man. "That's not for me to say." He took a deep sip of coffee, enjoying the suspense he was placing on his commanders as they waited politely for him to explain himself. Shurahbil shuddered at the image of Ubaidah as harmless. He knew himself that the man was anything but. He was courageous and could be merciless in battle. How many men would have killed their own father in battle, as Ubaidah had done at Badr?

Ubaidah broke the suspense. “I have received a message from Medina. Abu Bakr has commanded Khalid to leave Persia and take command of our four armies.”

Shurahbil looked at Yazeed, whose eyebrows were crawling into his hairline, then back at Ubaidah. Hesitantly, he said, “You’re taking it. . .well.”

Ubaidah raised his hands in a gesture for them to drink. “Abu Bakr is Caliph and I serve at his pleasure. Truth to tell, I’m happy that Khalid will be the one to dash our armies against the walls of Jerusalem and not I.” He leaned forward and lowered his voice conspiratorially. “We know well that in victory all the glory goes to Allâh, but in defeat, the blame goes to those in charge, eh?”

Yazeed said, “Surely it will take Khalid weeks to get here. What shall we do until then? The army is growing restless.”

Ubaidah looked smugly relaxed. “Jerusalem is the prize, my friends, the diamond for Allâh’s crown. But that’s Khalid’s problem now.” He paused for a moment. “Shurahbil, you’ve been to that city to the east, Bosra. Is it worth the taking?”

“Oh, yes, Sahib. It’s a crossroads of trade routes and has buildings the likes of which I’d never imagined. Why, they have a theater where fifteen thousand people can sit at once and you can hear the speakers on the platform from the highest seats, as if you were standing right beside them.”

Ubaidah’s brows crossed in a brief expression of irritation and Shurahbil fell quiet. Ubaidah was a simple man of the desert and scorned the majesty of human engineering, except when it was militarily significant. Ubaidah knew well the power of treasure and booty for keeping the morale of his army intact, but disdained it himself, leading a nearly monastic life free of material distractions. He looked sideways at Shurahbil. “Perhaps then, you would like to take your army and invest Bosra while we wait for Khalid?”

Shurahbil realized that he’d been led into a trap. Hesitation now would indicate cowardice. As fear and uncertainty suddenly squeezed his innards, he looked Ubaidah in the eye and said confidently, “Of course, Sahib. I shall assemble the men at once!”

Ubaidah closed his eyes in pleasure. Impetuosity was a common trait among his people. It was a blessing – and a curse. He'd just taught Shurahbil a valuable lesson. He made a small gesture with his hand and said softly, "Take your time."

Yazeed asked, "When Khalid takes over, will you return to Medina?"

"No. Khalid is coming with half his army. I shall remain and retain command of my army, under Khalid."

"Won't that be . . . uncomfortable for you?"

"Not at all. Khalid is a sword among knives. Allâh knows best who should command the army here and Abu Bakr is Caliph for a reason. I'm happy to share in the successes that Khalid will bring us. The man simply cannot be defeated."

From any other man, Shurahbil suspected that these would be just words, but Ubaidah was genuinely selfless. He knew that he'd accept Khalid's command with no resentment and be happy to do so. Shurahbil wasn't so sure he'd be as sanguine if it were him, but Ubaidah disdained glory like no other man he'd ever met.

A campaign under Khalid would certainly be free of boredom.

16. Syrian High Desert
June 17, 634

Tamara lay in the tent, curled in a blanket against the evening cold. She was exhausted from the day's walk. They'd left the oasis at Huwareen that morning. Tamara had kept telling herself all day that her father hadn't been in the group that had attacked the Muslim army at Huwareen, that he was too far away, that he was still alive. She occasionally forgot it for a few moments, then the memory returned, unbidden, and the horror and hopelessness welled up within her. As exhausted as she was from the walking and the crying, every time sleep overcame her, the dreams came — Jamila's head flying through the air, her body jerking like a beheaded chicken, and the blood, the blood, the blood! Then Mus'ad on top of her, his weight and stink, and the pain and humiliation. She would jerk awake with a cry and vow never to sleep again.

Beside her, Mus'ad slept soundly, his blanket rising and falling with his slow, relaxed breathing. The moon was full and bright, so she could make out shapes clearly in the light that filtered through the tent fabric.

She was considering the idea of sneaking out. She could get away from camp, hide and make her way back to Qaryateyn. It was only two day's walk. A day back to Huwareen, where she would no doubt meet some of her townsfolk watering animals there. She could do it. All she had to do was sneak out and start walking. In the moonlight it would be easy, almost like walking in daylight. She would hide at sunup and wait until the Muslims had moved on to the west until she was sure no one was following her.

She began to shift the blanket noiselessly off her body and slowly rise. She heard voices talking softly nearby. She relaxed back to the ground and lay motionless, scarcely breathing. Oh, God, what if she was caught? The vision of Jamila's head on the ground reminded her of what punishment could await her.

She lay under her blanket, staring up as the night continued like an eternity. The moon was well past its peak when her body told her she needed to go. Her bladder was full. This could be an opportunity! Yes, she would make her way to the edge of the camp and if anyone stopped her, she'd simply tell them she was going to urinate. If anyone saw her, she would return to the tent and no one would be the wiser. It was perfect. She didn't even have to try to be that quiet, because she had a legitimate reason to leave the tent. She slowly rose, found her sandals and cloak and slipped out of the tent.

Bashour pulled his cloak around him and admired the sky. He'd spent many nights like this on the desert with his father and Marid, tending the animals, keeping night sentry over the sheep. Tonight was no different, except he'd been detailed to keep sentry over the camp, to raise an alarm if he saw anyone approaching. He knew that even with the full moon making things seem almost like daylight that his vision would be ruined by fires, so he'd made his way well north of the camp and parked himself with his back to a rock, facing his sector to the northeast. If he turned his head, he could just make out the tail end of the camp, several hundred yards away. Above him the stars wheeled in a frozen burst of fire that made him feel small. He loved the stillness, the quiet of the night, when not even a breeze disturbed the silence.

A motion to his right caught his eye and he turned his head. Someone was coming towards him. Not silently, but almost furtively. It wasn't the confident stride of a man. Khalid was known to walk the sentry lines checking the guards, but this wasn't him. Bashour enjoyed this game. He knew he was nearly invisible if he didn't move. As bright as the moon was, everything was still black and white. He knew the human eye reacted first to motion, then to color and finally to shapes.

He watched as the figure drew closer, then smiled as it squatted and he heard the distinctive sound of liquid. Marid and he had played this game for years, hiding outside at night, hoping to catch one of their female cousins in the call of nature. This was one of the women they'd picked up at Qaryateyn. Bashour had seen them from afar and was curious, but not curious enough to break his cover.

She finished her business and stood, then looked for a long time back at camp. That was odd. She turned her head to the desert and examined the emptiness, then back at the camp. Then she crouched and began moving quickly and quietly away from the camp.

Bashour's pulse quickened. He was supposed to watch for attackers. Nothing in his instructions covered deserters. What should he do? After a moment's thought, he decided he wouldn't get in trouble if no one escaped. It wasn't worthwhile raising an alarm. What could a woman do? He rose and silently began shadowing her.

The ground dipped into a shallow gully not far north and the camp was out of sight when he finally overtook her. He had plenty of experience sneaking through the night, playing with Marid. She jumped when he touched her and asked quietly, "Where are you going?"

The woman looked wildly at him as she jerked away and fell to her knees, covering her head. She didn't cry out, but he could hear her choking, as if she couldn't breathe. He began to be alarmed after several moments when she still couldn't seem to draw a breath. He knelt beside her and put his arm on her. "Are you all right?" She flinched at his touch, but didn't move further. He gently patted her back for several minutes while she fought to get her breathing under control. She finally looked at him, but her eyes were no less wary. She looked like a caged feral animal. He reached up and drew her cloak back off her head. Even in the moonlight, he was surprised. She was extremely beautiful. "What's your name?"

She looked at the ground, away from him. "Tamara."

He didn't know what to say for a moment, then asked, "Are you trying to run away?" She didn't respond, she just kept looking at the ground. He reached out and lifted her chin, so she would look at him. "Do you have water? Did you bring food?"

She shook her head. He moved around so he was in front of her. "How far do you think you can get without water?"

She shrugged. Bashour regarded the moon, halfway down in the western sky. "The sun will be coming up in a few hours. What do you think will happen when they wake up and you're not there? You know they'll look for you." Bashour wasn't sure of this, himself, but he guessed they would perform a perfunctory search, at least. "What if you can't find a place to hide?"

She looked at him and clutched his arm. "No! They can't find me. They'll kill me!"

The vision of Jamila's death raced through Tamara's mind again. She regarded the young man talking to her in the moonlight. He was different from the rest, his beard was wispy, and his accent was like a local. He didn't have the stink of death surrounding him that the rest did. "I can't go back there. I'd rather die."

"Sister, if you go out in the desert, they'll find you. If they don't find you, the sun will kill you. You can't live for a day without water this time of year. Not while you're walking. It'll take you a day to get back to Huwareen."

She thought about Mus'ad, about him raping her for the last three nights and started to cry. "You don't understand!"

Bashour was torn. He really wanted to help this beautiful girl, but he didn't want to get in trouble. His gut tightened when he thought of what Khalid would do if he heard that someone escaped through Bashour's sentry. For that matter, Khalid could be checking the guard any minute and he was away from his sector. He had to convince this girl to go back, now, however much he empathized with her desire to get away. He feigned a firmness in his voice. "Look, if you don't turn around and go back, right now, I'll have no choice but to raise an alarm."

He stood and lifted her to her feet. She fell against him and clung to him, crying, "Noooo!" He felt her ample breasts against his body and the warmth of the skin on her arms as they clung to his. She didn't resist when he turned her towards the camp and she continued to stumble towards the tents when he resumed his guard position.

Silence returned to the night and Bashour contemplated the moon hanging low in the west. It didn't seem as bright as it should for being full. He wasn't sure, but it seemed dim, as if thin clouds or smoke were in the way, but the sky was crisp and clear. He pulled his cloak about him. Even in summer, it got cool at night in the high desert.

A short time later, Bashour was fascinated to see that a bite had been taken out of the bottom of the moon. He'd never seen such a thing before and he involuntarily crossed himself. He wondered if he should raise an alarm, tell somebody, but he didn't want to look foolish. As he watched, the phenomenon slowly cleared and the moon began to brighten again. He relaxed and wondered what had caused that darkness to cross the moon.

The rest of the night was quiet, but it wasn't peaceful. Bashour's thoughts were still on a lovely girl with tears running down her face when the sun began to peek over the horizon and the camp started stirring to life.

After Tamara had returned to Mus'ad's tent, exhaustion and despair swept over her and she fell into a deep, dreamless sleep. Sunrise came too quickly and she was jolted awake by Mus'ad sticking a toe into her side. For a second she was irritated, then the reality of her situation returned to her, along with the fear and despair.

Above the normal bustle of the camp stirring to life and preparing for the day's march, she heard a commotion not far away. It started with a man cursing loudly, then cries of surprise. Then women started wailing, first one, then more joined in. Tamara was finishing rolling the tent and Mus'ad was preparing to hoist it onto his horse. He jerked his head toward the noise. "Go see what's wrong."

For the two days since they'd left Qaryateyn, Tamara hadn't talked with any of the other women. Mus'ad had kept her close to him the entire time. As she came close to where several women were crying, one saw her and called, "Tamara!"

"Nathifa!" She was Tamara's older cousin, married just the previous year. The two girls embraced. "What's wrong?"

Nathifa wiped tears from her face. "Do you remember Yarah bint Ratib?" She cast her eyes down. "She took her own life last night."

Tamara knew the girl, but not well. She crossed herself. "How? How did she do it?"

"I'm not sure, but there's blood everywhere."

The man who had been cursing yelled at the women, "You! Take her away! Get her out of here!" His face was red with fury. The knot of women parted and several of them came bearing a body. Tamara saw the face, ashen and blue, the eyes were closed, and she looked peaceful. Her cloak was covered in blood.

A Muslim on horseback rode up. "What's going on here? Get moving!"

The man who'd been cursing wheeled towards him. "My slave girl cut her wrists last night!"

The rider shrugged. "What is that to me? Leave the body. Get ready to march."

Several women wailed at this and Nathifa stepped forward, her eyes on the ground, but speaking with a tone of authority, "Please Sahib, give us time to bury her. It won't take long."

The horseman regarded her for a moment, then turned to the man. "Take two other men and watch over these women. See that it is done quickly, then hurry to rejoin the column. We won't wait."

The ground was hard and the women unaccustomed to digging, so they buried Yarah under a stone cairn on the side of the path. They wanted to place a cross on the grave, but the Muslim men refused to allow it. They rejoined the column by midday.

Tamara and Nathifa walked together in the afternoon. They hadn't spoken during the morning. They'd been pushed so hard to catch up with the column that they had no breath to spare.

"How are you faring, cousin?" asked Nathifa.

"Oh, Nathifa . . ." Tamara couldn't find words. Too much had happened. She was afraid that if she started talking, it would all come out and she'd break down. She couldn't afford that.

Nathifa touched her hand. "Hush, child. It's all right, I know." After they'd walked in silence for some minutes, she asked, "How are you sleeping?"

"I can't sleep. I have dreams."

There was another long pause. "Your man," Nathifa asked, "Does he beat you?"

Tamara felt a stab of anger penetrate her despair. "He's not my man. I want nothing to do with him. He's my tormentor, my. . . . my rapist!" She spat on the ground.

Nathifa patted her gently. "You're right, I spoke poorly. Does he hit you?"

"No," Tamara said in a faint voice. She hated saying anything that mitigated the evil that she felt Mus'ad personified.

"Be glad for that. Some of these men," her eyes cast around the column, "They enjoy hurting women as much as they like to lay with them."

"Why, Nathifa? Why?"

"I don't know." The older woman shrugged. "Maybe they're upset because they have small penises?" She smiled wryly, looking sideways at her cousin.

"Nathifa, how can you joke about this?"

Nathifa's face grew hard. "Look, Tamara, you'd better learn to joke about it. Get this through your head, girl: You and I, we're dead. We're never going to see home again and you don't know when the sun comes up if you're going to live to see it set. You need to learn to find laughter wherever you can, because you won't have to look for the tears!" As she said this, her eyes welled up and tears ran down her face.

Tamara was shocked by the words and even more by the tears. She realized that she'd been thinking only of herself, that everyone else was suffering at least as much as she was. "Nathifa, I'm so sorry. You're right. You're right!"

Nathifa leaned on Tamara's shoulder as they walked and the tears turned into sobs. Tamara held on to her quietly. After some minutes, Nathifa looked up and between sobs cried, "He's dead, Tamara. Hani's dead!"

Tamara consoled her, "No, no. I'm sure he escaped. He's fine!"

Nathifa shook her head. "I saw him. He was at Huwareen. They killed him!"

Tamara walked in silence, supporting her widowed cousin until the tears stopped.

Khalid drove the column mercilessly after Qaryateyn. The night before, very few people even had the energy to seek fuel to make fires for cooking. They contented themselves with dried dates and salted meat. Those on foot had virtually collapsed where they stopped, while the horsemen had it no easier. Most of them walked to preserve their mounts, and at the end of the day they had to feed and care for the animals.

For the last two days they'd been moving along a mountain range to their left, slowly growing closer to it. Now the dawn sunlight reflected off the mountains, almost near enough to touch.

Since they only had the one camel to care for, Bashour's group had started before the mounted soldiers,. They were near the head of the column when the road began ascending into the mountains. Khalid was a short way ahead, leading a black stallion at the front of the column.

Qutayba studied the mountains and pronounced: "On the other side of these mountains are rich fields and Jerusalem."

"Do you think we'll attack Jerusalem?" Rashad asked.

Wahid snorted. "The walls of Jerusalem will laugh at a puny force such as this. It takes nearly two hours to walk all the way around the walls, and they're twenty cubits high, with archers along the entire way. The ground is rough and uneven, with no place to assemble an army for an assault. On the south and east sides, the ground falls away from the city walls almost like a cliff. No, attacking Jerusalem wouldn't be an easy thing."

"Of course, we won't attack it ourselves," said Jabir, "We'll link up with Ubaidah's army first. With thirty thousand men, we'll be able to take the city easily."

Wahid shook his head. "This is no desert encampment, Jabir. Nothing the Persians have can prepare you for the height and thickness of those walls. I remember trading there years ago and wondering how anyone could assault such fortifications. The walls are so huge, you would think they'd taken a mountain and built a city inside. I can't imagine any way to assault such a thing."

"You've been to Jerusalem?" Bashour asked. "What's it like?"

"There's a marketplace there as big as all Mecca and you can't throw a stone without hitting a church or holy place. It has a well inside the city with plentiful water and could withstand a siege for years. The buildings have many levels and the space between the houses is so narrow the sunlight sometimes doesn't reach the street. There's a place they call Abraham's rock that the Jews say is where Father Abraham was to sacrifice his son, before Allâh stayed his hand. When I was last there the Romans had just retaken the city from Persia and much destruction and rebuilding was going on."

Rashad didn't seem bothered by the descriptions of the defenses. "I can't wait to get to Jerusalem, so I can kill some Jews!" Jabir enthusiastically nodded in agreement.

"What do you have against Jews?" asked Bashour.

Jabir spoke up. "They mocked Allâh's apostle, peace be upon him, and said he was foolish. They said the Qur'án was in error."

Qutayba adopted an authoritative tone. "Allâh's apostle, peace be upon him, said, 'The Hour will not be established until you fight with the Jews and the stone behind which a Jew will be hiding will say, "Oh Muslim! A Jew is hiding behind me, so kill him."'"

Bashour thought for a moment on that. Something wasn't right; then he realized what it was. "But there are no Jews in Jerusalem. If you want to kill Jews, you'll have to find them elsewhere."

Rashad looked at him skeptically. "What are you talking about? Of course there are Jews in Jerusalem. Where do you think Jews come from?"

"No. An army of Jewish traitors helped the Persians take the city, and when he'd taken it back, Heraclius ordered them out of Jerusalem. The city is empty of them."

He stumbled forward and nearly fell as Jabir slammed into his back. Jabir's face was dark. "You don't know what you're talking about, boy. Why don't you keep quiet?"

Wahid spoke quietly, his voice carrying like far-off thunder. "Leave the boy alone, Jabir! He speaks the truth. I was there four years ago, and in all of Jerusalem, I did not see a single Jew. They're all Christians there."

Bashour felt emboldened by the support. "It's the holy city for both the Jews and the Christians, but the Jews couldn't accept that, since they don't believe in the Christ. They kept having riots against the Christian churches, so Heraclius ordered them all to leave."

"Jerusalem is a holy city for us, as well," Qutayba stated. "We used to pray facing Jerusalem, until Allâh directed his Apostle to change the direction of our prayer towards the Qibla in Mecca."

Rashad said, "Abu Bakr says that it was from the grand mosque in Jerusalem that Muhammad, peace be upon him, ascended to heaven on the winged horse."

Qutayba corrected him, "He didn't go to heaven on the Al-Buraq; it took him to the Al-Aqsa and from there he ascended by a ladder."

Bashour had never heard of there being a mosque in Jerusalem. "I didn't know Muhammad had traveled to Jerusalem."

Jabir pushed him again. "Do not mention the prophet's name without blessing him!" Bashour glared at him.

"It was a night journey," Rashad continued, "The Al-Buraq carried Allâh's Apostle to the Al-Aqsa, the farthest mosque, and from there he ascended to heaven on a great ladder. Gabriel escorted him to the seven levels of heaven and he met with Adam, Abraham, Moses, Jesus and Allâh himself."

"The Al-Aqsa is the mosque at al-Gi'ranah," said Qutayba, "Muhammad, peace be upon him, never said it was in Jerusalem."

Rashad retorted, "Then why when people questioned him about it, did he start describing Jerusalem as if from above? I think Abu Bakr is right, that he went to Jerusalem, not al-Gi'ranah."

"He did all this in one night? Maybe he was dreaming?" Bashour had never heard of such a tale as a prophet going to heaven.

"That's what many people thought, but when questioned, he could tell us about Jerusalem as if he were right there looking down on it from above. Those who'd been there were astonished by his descriptions."

Wahid snorted, "Allâh's apostle was overseer for Khadija's caravans for many years. I'd be surprised if he hadn't been to Jerusalem. I'm not that impressed."

The conversation fell into an awkward silence. Wahid had the authority of being one of the first Ansari to follow Muhammad and no one wanted to challenge the big man on what he said, but they were all uncomfortable at his skepticism, save Bashour, who didn't know any better.

Near midday, they stopped near a small well with a handful of buildings beside it along the road. Khalid dismounted his horse and accepted a bucket that Dhiraar had drawn from the well.

Being near the front of the column for the day, Bashour was one of the first to the well and sought shade against a nearby hut. He could clearly see Khalid from where he sat. He tried to ignore his complaining feet and dug out some hard bread and a goatskin full of water.

Two men who lived near the well came out to greet Khalid. Bashour was close enough to hear the conversation. The older one hailed Khalid, "Salaam, Sahib! Are you the Arab conqueror of whom we've heard?"

The big dark man looked sideways at them and simply said, "I am Khalid bin Al-Waleed."

"I have heard tales that you follow a prophet of God, Sahib. Is this true?"

"I am a follower of Muhammad, peace be upon him, the Prophet of Allâh, the One God." Something in Khalid's tone told Bashour that he wished these people would go away.

"Ah! We believe in the One God, too. We'd like to follow your prophet."

Khalid's gaze focused on them like a hawk and his voice adopted a tone of authority. "Then profess your faith and become Muslims." His hand casually dropped to his sword.

The two men looked at each other and exchanged a whispered question, then the older man stated, "We believe in the one God almighty, Creator of Heaven and Earth, of all that is visible and invisible."

He took a breath to go on, but never finished. Khalid's sword flashed and the man's head separated from his shoulders. His companion looked stunned and before he could recover, Khalid had run him through. Khalid wiped his sword on the old man's garments and said, "That is incorrect."

Bashour was rooted in shock. The words, "There is no God but Allâh and Muhammad is his Prophet!" echoed in his head like a chorus. Were these words so important that you would die if you got them wrong?

Nathifa and Tamara drew water from the well and filled their water skins. Black flies covered a red stain in the dirt not far from the well. Tamara was terrified of asking what had happened there.

The grade grew steeper as they struggled on that afternoon. To their left was a series of dun-colored bluffs that drew closer to the road. Tamara's feet were sore and burning. Her hair was dry and full of dust. Every night Mus'ad raped her, but at least by day she could walk with the women now. She was sore between her legs, but it was nothing compared to the weight in her soul that crushed her spirit.

The road leveled out and she couldn't see it rising before her anymore. Had they reached the top? On an elevated table to the right of the road ahead, a knot of mounted barbarians had gathered, watching the column pass. One was holding a standard with a black eagle emblazoned on a red background. One horseman stood ahead of the rest and the others seemed deferential to him. Tamara studied him as she drew closer. He was powerfully built, with huge shoulders. His bare arms bore innumerable scars and his thick beard reached halfway down his chest. Above his beard, his skin was pitted and cratered with pockmarks and small, pig-like eyes glowered from under thick, bushy brows. He wore a suit of black chain mail with a broad leather belt that held a vicious looking sword. He had an iron helmet over a leather headpiece and a bright-red turban wound around the helmet.. When he shifted in his saddle, the bulk of his weight forced his horse to take a step to adjust. This must be the one they called Khalid, the chief of these barbarians, she thought.

17. Bosra, Southern Syria
June 20, 634

"I have twelve thousand men and no cavalry. I can't possibly do battle with thirty thousand Arab cavalry. If they attack us, we have no choice but to surrender the city and pay tribute." Romanus, the military commander of the city of Bosra had no intention of dying to gain time for Heraclius. When word of the great Arab army from the south had reached him, he'd implored Heraclius by messenger to send 50,000 troops to reinforce his garrison. The request had been denied. Heraclius apparently felt that the fertile hills of Palestine were more important than the ancient trade city of Bosra.

In truth, he'd already made plans to evacuate his force from the city. As far as he was concerned, if 30,000 screaming Arabs wanted Bosra, they could have it. Born and raised in Constantinople, Romanus resented this assignment, commanding the garrison of what he considered a backwater outpost of the empire, well away from the court of Heraclius. While he rotted here out of sight, others were climbing the slippery path to success in the halls of power surrounding the Emperor.

Romanus had instructed his quartermaster to begin gathering supplies and assembling the necessary logistics for a march to Damascus or Jerusalem. The city fathers had become suspicious of his preparations and his quartermaster was being slow-rolled. Everything took much longer than expected, supplies were mysteriously unavailable and prices for the army were exorbitant.

The assembly hall held the Mayor and the town council on one side of the table, Romanus and his lieutenants on the other. Sideways looks passed between the councilmen at his statement. The Mayor said, "Turmarch, the walls of the city are strong. If the Arabs send their entire force we can defend the city from within and wait for the army from Jerusalem to relieve us."

One of his lieutenants spoke. "Sir, they have no siege weaponry. No battering rams or ballista. What can they do, but wait outside the walls and starve, faster than we can starve?"

Romanus glared at the fresh-faced young man. His father was well connected at court, which gave the boy courage to be less than circumspect with his superior. *Very well, you little shit,* thought Romanus. *The next scut job I find goes to you!*

One of the councilmen spoke, addressing Romanus, but his words were directed at the whole audience. “I think we’ve all had enough of foreign domination under the Sassanids. I have no wish to pay tribute to another foreign king. These are only Arabs, after all. It’s not like we’re dealing with an empire. When they get tired of waiting, they’ll flee to their desert.”

The rest of the council nodded their agreement.

Romanus asked, “What difference does it make who you send your tribute to? If you send it to Persia, or to some Arab in a tent down south, or to Constantinople, what is the difference? None of it comes back here. Do you know how long it’s been since Heraclius has paid my men?”

“The difference, my dear Turmarch, is that we prefer to be ruled by Christians. The freedom to worship our Lord and Savior can be taken away from us under a foreign power. We should be prepared to fight to preserve that freedom.”

Rather my freedom than my life, thought Romanus, but he said nothing. After much continued posturing, by evening they’d decided that the city would be defended under siege from within the walls, should they be outnumbered on the field of battle. Romanus remained against the idea in principle, but too much stubborn resistance would be reported to Heraclius. Even here, the spies of court were alert for dissension and weakness. Romanus shuddered at the thought. He could think of even worse assignments than Bosra.

18. Twenty Miles East of Damascus June 21, 634

People from miles around had converged on Marj Rahit, at the base of the eastern pass through the Anti-Lebanon Mountains. They came to celebrate the midsummer's festival during the summer solstice, the longest day of the year. The small town was bursting at the seams. The market had overflowed its normal confines as merchants sought advantageous positions to hawk their wares to the travelers who'd come to join the festivities. The entertainment was plentiful. Wine flowed freely in the streets. Music, dancing and theatrical performances would continue until it was too dark to see. Magicians and street performers filled the streets, and ladies of negotiable virtue tempted the men with promises of unforgettable afternoons of sin and pleasure.

No one paid attention to the rumors of unrest in the high desert to the east. That was a different world, and most thought the rumors were merely exaggerations of a raiding band of itinerant Bedouins. Nevertheless, as a precaution the local commander had placed his garrison in a screen to the east of the town, guarding the base of the pass.

Khalid was in the vanguard of his army when it first encountered the infantry in the road at the foot of the pass. The defenders were scrambling to fighting positions. Horns were blowing and frantic flags were waving to alert those stationed to either side of the roadblock.

Khalid saw no mounts, just foot infantry. With an unspoken look and a gesture, he directed his well-trained cavalry to move into position on the flanks. He stood fast in the center of the road, just out of arrowshot from the roadblock, as his army deployed for battle.

As word spread quickly through the advancing Muslim column, the soldiers prepared themselves for battle. Cloaks were exchanged for weapons. Bashour observed the orderly confusion as he nervously handled the unfamiliar sword he carried. He hoped his nervousness didn't show. Everyone around him was businesslike, they were all veterans of the Muslim invasion of

Persia and many of them had also fought in the Arab Civil War – what they called the Riddah Wars.

When Bashour had accepted Islam, he hadn't considered that it would involve fighting. But in the last week he'd been taught that Jihad was the highest calling of a Muslim; to fight in Allâh's cause. He'd found out that if you're killed in Jihad, then all your sins were forgiven. Bashour considered that in the 600 years since Christ, humanity hadn't spread the word as it should have. Now Allâh was angry and Islam was spreading His word through force, where Christianity had failed to do so through charity.

They left the camel and moved forward. As they passed a group of women, Bashour searched in vain for the girl he'd spoken to several nights before. She'd been on his mind since then and she seemed to become more beautiful in his memory every day. He wanted to see her, speak to her again.

As they got closer to the head of the column, they were joined by other foot soldiers. Bashour found himself swept along at a fast lope in the surging crowd. He thought going into battle would be something done with foresight and precision; that the soldiers would have prescribed places and roles to play and everyone would know his place. The reality shocked him. In the confusion and noise he couldn't see more than a few yards into the crush of bodies and the choking dust that they kicked up. He had no idea where the enemy was or even where he was; he just blindly followed the person in front of him as they trotted and tried not to stumble. If he did, he wasn't sure that he'd be able to get up again before being trampled.

Suddenly they turned right, and the crowd thinned quickly. He found himself in a line of soldiers, facing the enemy across empty ground. The army facing them sported a forest of spears and lances that glittered in the harsh summer sun. The men around him were waving their swords and shouting, "Allâhu Akhbar! Allâhu Akhbar!" Some were in such a frenzy that words escaped them and they just ululated. Fear left Bashour and he found himself baring his teeth and yelling himself, buoyed by the enthusiasm of those around him.

If there was a signal, Bashour never saw it, but the line he was in surged forward in a slow trot toward the opposing soldiers. A few desultory arrows fell among them, but no one paid any notice. To his right Bashour saw the Muslim cavalry in a full charge. As the horsemen crashed into the enemy line, those in front of him seemed to step back, hesitantly. Bashour raised his sword and braced himself for the impact when the lines met, but just before they did, the line facing them dissolved, their morale shattered by the ferocity of the charge. A great shout went up around him and any semblance of organization dissolved and they all began running as fast as they could after the fleeing enemy. Bashour started sprinting late, and a few seconds later stumbled over a body. He raised himself and could hear screams as the opposing soldiers were run down and executed.

The fight was over almost as soon as it had started. The blocking force had simply ceased to exist. The ground was littered with dropped weapons and bodies. Some were writhing in agony and Muslims walked among them, cutting the throats of the Christian wounded.

Bashour looked for Wahid. The huge man was easy to spot on the battlefield. He joined his companions as they waited for instructions. Wahid looked at Bashour's bloodless sword and said nothing. Word came soon enough to form a line of skirmish and continue a marching advance. They walked for ten minutes before it became apparent that they were approaching a village. Trees and vegetation were replacing the dust and sand. It puzzled Bashour, but he seemed to hear faint music coming from the town.

"Do you think Khalid will negotiate with them?" asked Rashad.

Qutayba snorted. "Not likely. They fought us. Everything they have is forfeit."

"I wish all our battles were like that," Jabir said, "Why, if all Christians fight like these we shall become very rich indeed, with very little effort."

"You call marching from one end of the earth to the other effortless?" asked Wahid.

"If I'm to walk to the end of the earth, it would be nicer if I didn't have to fight when I get there." replied Jabir.

"I don't care where I walk or how much I have to fight, as long as it takes me farther from Dimah!" said Sameer.

When they quit laughing, Rashad asked seriously, "Do you think we'll stop to count the booty? It'd be nice if we could rest awhile."

"I doubt it," said Jabir. "Khalid is driven to link up with Ubaidah's army. We won't stop until that happens. We'll sack the town and divide it tonight."

Sameer groaned, "There goes my sleep for the night."

"Look at the bright side," said Jabir. "We're done for the day and it's not even noon. You have all afternoon to rest. Maybe you'll get a slave girl here to marry."

Sameer brightened at the thought, then frowned again. "Not unless the town is fabulously wealthy. I dare not let Dimah catch me with a second wife and I can't afford Mut'ah right now."

Bashour was puzzled at the unfamiliar term. "What is Mut'ah?"

"If you want to marry a woman for a fixed period," explained Jabir, "you agree on a dowry for her and when the time is passed, your marriage is over."

"This is allowed?" Bashour wasn't sure if they weren't pulling his leg.

"Absolutely. The Prophet himself, Peace be upon him, specifically allowed it."

"You need not pay her Mut'ah, Sameer," said Qutayba. "How happy would Dimah be if you presented her with a slave girl to clean the house? And didn't the prophet say that you could bed those whom your right hand possesses?"

"If I were to have a slave," said Sameer, "Dimah would allow only the ugliest crone imaginable."

Qutayba said, "Well, maybe you'll get lucky and Khalid will permit you a slave girl, then you can sell her before you reunite with Dimah."

Sameer contemplated that for a moment, then shook his head. "No, that could go bad a thousand different ways. I don't dare!"

Wahid let out a rumbling laugh and slapped Sameer's back hard enough to make him stumble. "Young man, I think you love Dimah too much."

Everyone howled with laughter as Sameer turned red.

After a few minutes, Wahid said thoughtfully, "We may be spared a night of counting loot." They looked at him expectantly and he, in turn, looked at Bashour. "Can you write? Can you do sums?"

Bashour raised his eyebrows. Couldn't everybody? "Of course."

Wahid stood straighter. "Friends, I present our new accountant."

They regarded Bashour with new respect, except Qutayba. "Are you kidding me? You trust him? For all we know, he's just bragging. You expect a whelp like him to know how to read and do sums?"

Bashour bridled, but realized before he said anything that to refute Qutayba wouldn't help his cause. Wahid saw the flare in his eyes and smiled. "Ah, Qutayba bin Faruq, I think the boy will surprise you. I'd be careful. If you make him mad, he might shortchange you, and how would you know? You can neither write nor do sums."

Qutayba's lips grew tight with anger. "You'd better be able to do what you claim, boy. And if I find out you're shortchanging me. . ."

"Don't worry about me," spat Bashour. He was beginning to realize that Qutayba was a bully and he wasn't going to give him the idea that he could be bullied.

The Muslim army was bivouacked outside Marj Rahit by mid-afternoon. Bashour's companions had commandeered a cart and a donkey and had filled it with loot from the town: Cloths, tents, wares, food and trinkets. They'd spread a tent on the ground and sorted the spoils into piles. Bashour was busy counting and inventorying them, as Jabir instructed him. "Divide everything into five equal parts and set one part aside for the caliph. Then divide the rest into six for each of us."

"Why does the Caliph get a fifth?"

"Allâh directed in his Qur'án, in the Spoils of War: 'And know that out of all the booty that you may acquire in war, a fifth share is assigned to Allâh, and to the Apostle and to near relatives, orphans, the needy and the wayfarer; if you do believe in Allâh and in the revelation We sent down to Our servant on the Day of Testing, the Day of the meeting of the two forces. For Allâh has power over all things.'"

"I don't see why he should get a share. I saw no blood on his sword," grumbled Qutayba.

Bashour's face flushed red and Rashad came to his defense. "Would you preferred to have held the camel at Qaryateyn? He's done his share of cooking and now he's doing your sums for you, faster than I ever saw you do it. He was in the charge, I was right there beside him. Not every sword gets bloodied when the enemy's outnumbered, Qutayba bin Faruq."

Bashour completed the division of the spoils while it was still light. Each man bundled his share of nonfood items in a large cloth and identified it with his mark. The largest bundle was marked for Abu Bakr, the Caliph. Bashour was uncertain what to do with his share. He was assured that it would be well taken care of in Medina for him and he could reclaim it when the campaign was over. The next morning as they set out, their cart joined a train of similar carts and a line of slaves bound for Medina.

19. Damascus
June 24, 634

Thomas had invited Governor Azrail and Abbott Lecanepus to dine with himself and Nicetas. Thomas greeted his guests and led them to the open veranda on the back of his house, where a meal had been prepared. A canvas awning protected the balcony, but it was mid evening and the sun was slipping under the canopy. Thomas had arranged the table so no one was facing west and squinting into the sunset.

After the food was served and the Abbot said the blessing, Azrail remarked, “Thomas, you amaze me.”

“Why is that, Governor?”

“I’m quite surprised that you haven’t brought house servants from Antioch with you. It appears your domestic help is all local.”

“Ah, the problem with bringing an entourage from Antioch or Constantinople is that you can never be sure how many spies you’re bringing with it. Being married to the Emperor’s eldest daughter tends to attract some . . . unwanted attention.”

Azrail cocked his head inquiringly. “Does such attention bother you?”

“Not as such, not in the way you would think. But my wife and I are private citizens and have no interest in being the objects of such scrutiny.”

“But is that even possible? Has your wife renounced her birthright? Has the Emperor, sorry, the Basileus, renounced her? If not, then her very being is a matter of imperial concern. What if she were threatened by forces hostile to the court?”

Thomas smiled wryly. “Your point is well taken, governor. My only defense is that there’s security in anonymity. We’d prefer that the details of her family be held as a private matter. I’m a private businessman, and I take pride that I can prosper without connections I have at court. I don’t dabble in politics. Abbot, may I tempt you with more roast?”

“My old friend thinks that politics and honest men mix like oil and water,” said Nicetas.

Thomas shot him a sideways glare, but Azrail just laughed. "Perhaps the problem with politics is that it has too few honest men to support its reputation, Thomas."

Thomas smiled at him diplomatically. "Indeed, Governor, it would be an admirable thing if more men like you were to aspire to public office. I feel that my skills allow me to serve the community far more effectively as an arbiter of commodities than as a maker of laws."

The Abbot smiled and raised his glass. "Well spoken. But Thomas, how far must you flee to escape the shadow of your wife's birthright?"

Thomas smiled. "Not far enough, I fear. But this is the crossroads of the frontier. There's commerce to be developed through Damascus. A virtual river of money is flowing here and one has but to know where to dip his hand to partake of the bounty. We considered relocating to Carthage. Heraclius' family still has strong connections there, but we decided this is more appropriate. I know the local markets and I think it's a more vibrant commercial climate."

Azrail swallowed a mouthful he'd been chewing. "Reward and risk go hand in glove. Does the Arab uprising concern you?"

Thomas spoke slowly, deliberately choosing his words. "In the long term I don't think the Arab problems are much of a concern. We've had profitable dealings with the Arab traders in the past. In the short term, I think it's obvious we'll have to fight. The Arabs are far too bold from their conquests in Persia to run from a show of force now."

Azrail nodded his head. "I'm relieved to hear you agree with my thoughts on this. So far, your analysis has been insightful. Let me bring you up to date on the latest developments." All the men leaned imperceptibly forward at this. "This afternoon I received reports from several scouts I sent eastward. The Arab army did indeed cross the mountains and looted Marj Rahit during their Solstice festival. We had a garrison there; some two thousand soldiers who were routed and killed in a matter of minutes. They invested the city, killed a number of men in the town square and took many captives. Their disposition is unclear, but as near as I can tell the main body of their force departed on the road to Bosra yesterday morning. Mounted raiding parties are attacking in this direction, looting the smaller settlements as they go, but there's no column coming this way. I don't think they'll come as far as the city. It appears your analysis was correct. They're trying to join the main force in Jordan."

Servants began clearing the table and lighting lamps around the porch, as the last rays of the sun faded from the sky.

"This Khalid fellow worries me," said Thomas. "I think the Arabs are normally pretty much ineffective, but they've enjoyed some pretty impressive victories under his banner."

Abbot Lecanepus spoke up, "I'm worried about more than one man with these Arabs, I'm afraid."

Azrail regarded the priest. "Why is that, Father?"

"There's an Arab merchant who emigrated here a couple years ago, a Christian. He tells stories of this 'prophet', one Muhammad, that gained power over the last few years. He claims to have been relatively well-acquainted with the man from long before he claimed to be a prophet.

"This Muhammad apparently had quite a gift of speaking and his followers memorized huge tracts of poetic scripture that he taught. According to my source, much of what he taught was drawn from Christian and Jewish scripture, but it was mixed up with fables and pagan legends."

The other men around the table regarded each other. "Forgive me, Father," said Nicetas. "But why is this a concern?"

"Well, it's much more than a religion. Muhammad seems to have built the religion about himself and demanded absolute fealty. Anyone who didn't swear allegiance was executed. He was quite ruthless in demanding faithfulness. His followers all believe that he speaks with the authority of their god. Soon they began to come to him to arbitrate all of their problems and questions. Over time he built a political system of absolute obedience, enforced by the threat of death. I'm wondering if, after his death, his followers still use the system he developed to motivate and organize their armies. If so, we're not facing an ordinary band of Arab brigands. We're facing a fanatical group of believers, who'll subordinate themselves to a greater cause and die for a leader who claims that his mandate comes from heaven.

"From what I've heard from the tales of the civil war that occurred across Arabia after his death, I'm afraid this is the case."

The men digested this new piece of information in an uneasy silence. Azrail snapped his fingers. "This explains something that's been confusing me. The stories coming from eastern Syria say that Khalid requests that the towns 'accept Islam, pay some sort of tribute, or die.' I've been wondering what this Islam is. Isn't that the name for their religion?"

The Abbot nodded. "Quite so. In Arabic, it means 'submission.'"

Thomas was still unimpressed. "I still don't see it. What does this have to do with the armies attacking us?"

"According to my source," said the Abbot, "one of the tenets of Muhammad's religion is that all who follow him are to wage a holy war to spread this 'Islam' by force if necessary. Their god promises them riches in the form of booty from conquered foes if they survive, and automatic paradise if they die. We all know the Arab penchant for brigandry and raiding, it seems to be their national pastime. But if they become united under this 'Islam' and are given a holy authority to systematically do that which they so enjoy doing . . ."

Thomas nodded. "Yes, I see now." He turned to Azrail, "Governor, I think this insight is exceedingly important. May I suggest that you draft a summary of what the good Father has just told us, and pass it to Heraclius as soon as possible? I'm afraid we might be underestimating our enemy. If what the good father says is true, these pirates may not go back to their desert when they get tired."

"I'll pass this along," said Azrail. "But I think Heraclius is taking this seriously. I've gotten word that he's assembling a force of some ninety thousand soldiers outside of Jerusalem. If I know Heraclius, he'll outmaneuver the Arabs, engage and hold them while he strikes at their lines of communication, or even drive on their capital. Even if we meet them directly in battle, we outnumber them three to one."

Thomas raised his eyebrows. "Has Heraclius taken the field then?"

"No, I understand he's too ill to travel. He's still in Emessa, last I heard." Thomas pursed his lips, without saying anything. "This bothers you?" asked Azrail.

"Heraclius is a brilliant commander. I campaigned with him. He's better than any three generals put together. He has a nimble mind and intuitively reads the battlefield and the strategic situation. His decision-making process is lightening fast, but I'm afraid that he won't be able to make timely decisions and communicate them to his commanders from Emessa. His commanders are necessarily going to need a certain amount of autonomy and freedom of action. I'm just afraid that the commanders aren't up to the task. I can't think of anyone who can fill the shoes of Heraclius. Psellus comes the closest. I'd feel better if Heraclius would take the field."

The Abbot smiled. "Gentlemen, you'll have to forgive Thomas. He's always the eternal pessimist. He's tried to find the worst side of every situation as long as I've known him."

Thomas raised his cup to the Abbot. "Guilty as charged! In the army I wasn't paid to be an optimist. My job was to think of the absolute worst thing that could possibly happen and be ready with an answer when my commander wanted to know what to do when it happened."

Azrail asked, "Thomas, forgive me for discussing business, but how goes the provisioning of the city?"

"Nicetas can provide the boring details, but I believe we've laid in enough dry goods to support the city for up to eight weeks of siege. I'd be happier if we could double that. We could probably do so with severe rationing, but doing that may impact our combat capability. We could also evacuate non-combatants. Fewer mouths to feed. Beyond twelve weeks we're going to start losing people to illness, after our fresh vegetables run out."

"I'm not going to authorize, or even suggest an evacuation right now. The first wheat crops are going to be harvested in a couple of weeks. We simply cannot shut down this city in preparation for an event that may never happen."

"Agreed. But if we wait for a siege to become imminent, we may be unable to evacuate noncombatants by that time. The road to Emessa is closed. We have no idea what kind of force might be waiting for us up the pass. A refugee column would be too exposed."

"That's a risk I'm prepared to take."

"Well, Governor, I've always found that if you're going to try to beat the odds, you should be sure you can survive the odds beating you."

Everyone smiled politely at this wisdom. After his guests had left that evening, Thomas and Nicetas burned lamp oil deep into the night, poring over inventories, planning storage facilities and wondering if they'd overlooked any markets.

20. Ten Miles North of Bosra, Southeastern Syria July 1, 634

The Muslim camp surrounded the tiny town of Soweida and its small church. The town had surrendered without a fight, agreeing to pay the Jizyah head tax of a gold drachma per person. The night was quiet compared to the previous nights, which had been filled with the wailing of the women taken by the Muslim column at Marj Rahit. A camp as large as this always had a background noise, the crackling fire, the low murmur of voices, the throaty coughs of the camels. Cattle lowed softly ear the edge of the camp in bovine confusion at being made to travel so far so fast.

Every night Tamara hoped in vain that Mus'ad would be too fatigued, too tired after the day's travel to force himself on her. She didn't understand how anyone could tolerate the punishing pace they set and still have energy to rut in the moonlight.

This night after he grunted to his climax and lifted himself off her, he hovered over her. She could just make out his shape in the gloom. "You might at least try moving a little," he slurred in his southern accent. "You could at least act like you enjoy it." To her these southern Arabs all sounded as if they had a mouth full of rocks when they spoke. He leaned down as if to kiss her and she hurriedly turned her head away. He was rough, but he'd never yet actually hit her. She dreaded finding out what it would take to provoke him. She'd seen how little life meant to these barbarians.

She said nothing, but inside her head she screamed. *Enjoy it? You bastard! You're raping me! You sadistic, inhuman savage! You expect me to enjoy you?* As he shifted his weight away, she curled into a fetal ball, pulled the thin blanket tight around her and squeezed her eyes tight against the tears. Her anger replaced the despair that was her constant companion and she welcomed it. It was all she had that was truly hers; it was her touchstone to sanity and the only promise that she had that she was still alive.

The next morning, while preparing Mus'ad's tea, she satisfied herself with a small act of rebellion, as she discreetly spit in the drink while he wasn't looking. It wasn't much, but it was fighting back. She began to look for other small ways to fight back.

Romanus was on the walls before dawn, examining the Muslim army encamped around Bosra. They'd arrived two days previously and surrounded the city. They stayed a respectful distance from the walls, after quickly learning the range of the Byzantine archers.

Romanus pursed his lips in irritation. No other Arabs had arrived to reinforce the siege in the night. The previous evening he'd been called to task for not attacking the Arab army. No more than 4000 Arabs surrounded the city. His garrison outnumbered them three to one. Of course, Romanus would cheerfully attack at such odds, but he sensed a trap. He didn't believe that they'd try to take the city with such a paltry force. No military commander was that incompetent. Just over the horizon could be 25,000 more Arabs, just waiting for him to open his gates to pounce.

Lacking any evidence of a larger force of Arabs, the city council had pressured him to attack and throw off the invaders. A bloody nose here would send the Arabs reeling back into the desert. Perhaps the reports of a larger force were just exaggerations, and this was all there was. Romanus was running out of options. If he didn't attack soon, reports would fly to Heraclius. Some in the Emperor's court would interpret his lack of recklessness as cowardice.

Romanus bit back a wave of anger. He didn't know what he'd done – or failed to do – that had earned him this shit assignment in the armpit of the empire. He was sure it was his lack of political acumen. He'd done nothing wrong except refuse to play the political games in court. Now, exiled to Bosra, well outside the notice of the power brokers that surrounded the Emperor, he was sure that he'd taken on the stink of failure. Now his abilities could be endorsed by Christ and three other responsible witnesses, and he would still be thought of as tainted, no matter what he did.

He turned to the aide who'd maintained a discrete distance in the predawn gloom. "Rally the Turma. We sortie at sunrise."

The Muslim army woke as one and prayed facing south when it was bright enough to see. After the prayers, the army burst into activity, hauling water, making fire and preparing breakfast. Shurahbil's bladder had been near bursting when the prayers began. He thankfully relieved himself towards the sunrise when he was disturbed. "Sahib! The gates of the city are opening and soldiers are forming up under the city walls."

The morning lethargy left him immediately and he started striding towards the city main gate. "Fetch my sword and armor. Sound the alarm. Alert the archers to stand ready. Breakfast is canceled. Damn you! Why are you still here! Go!"

He reached the edge of the siege line opposite the main gate on the west wall of the city. The gates were open and he'd never seen the like. Rank after rank of soldiers marched forth and formed up in the morning shadow of the great wall. A line of archers had formed a screen in front of the formation of soldiers and had driven the Muslim line back to a more respectful distance.

Shurahbil knew that the time to strike was now, before they were fully deployed, but his army was strung out over three miles surrounding the city. "Send out runners. Gather the army here. Abandon the siege. We'll concentrate here."

Nearly a half-hour later, the city gate was still disgorging troops. They were well drilled, forming neat ranks facing the Muslims. Shurahbil had never seen such discipline. By comparison, the Arab force was a chaotic mess. Three men bearing a banner separated themselves from the army and marched towards the Muslim line. Shurahbil motioned his aides and strode out to meet them. In the no-man's land between the lines, with archers on both sides ready to rain death on them, they stopped about ten feet apart and regarded each other. Shurahbil examined his counterpart. He was dressed in fine armor, with an inlaid cross on the breastplate. He had a large, protruding forehead and a slightly crooked mouth and overly large teeth. He was clean shaven, in the Greek fashion. To Shurahbil, this seemed effete. He idly wondered if this man were a lover of boys.

Romanus broke the silence. "In the name of the Emperor Heraclius, I command you to return to your lands. We have no quarrel with you."

An aide began translating, but Shurahbil made a curt gesture. "I speak Greek." He regarded the other for a dramatic moment, locking gazes with the man and making it clear that he wasn't considering the other's words at all.

"In the name of Allâh, the most magnificent, the merciful, I command you: Surrender your city. You may accept Islam, or pay the Jizyah. Or my army will put your city to the sword."

Romanus broke eye contact and cast his eyes about the Muslim lines. Arab soldiers were frantically gathering from the south and east, forming up opposite the Byzantine garrison. He looked back at Shurahbil and grinned. "You will do that with this army?"

Shurahbil knew the weakness of his position and fought an urge to lick his lips nervously. He raised his bluff. "Allâh marches with this army and will deliver victory!"

Romanus again regarded the Arab army to either side, then condescendingly informed him, "I'm under instructions not to pay any tribute, or to accept Islam."

The two men regarded each other silently for a long moment. Then Shurahbil shrugged. "Such is the will of Allâh." Then he spun on his heel and marched back to his lines. Romanus cast a questioning look at his aides and did the same thing.

The Byzantine formations unfolded themselves like some giant living origami army, neatly expanding in both directions as they marched methodically towards the Arabs. The Arabs held their line and encouraged their enemies forward with ululating yells. Arab archers shot ineffectively into the Byzantine ranks. The second rank used their shields to protect the front rank from plunging fire, while the front rank held their shields to defend against direct arrows.

Romanus had organized his lieutenants and given them their orders before the battle had started. He forbade a heroic charge; no risks were to be taken. The front of the Byzantines was to engage the Arabs, hold their attention and fight a conservative battle, concentrating more on avoiding friendly casualties than inflicting them. With the Arabs engaged to the front, his superior numbers would execute a precise envelopment to both sides and surround the Arabs.

Romanus had the main line followed by a chiliarchy, or battalion, of archers. When they'd advanced into range, they loosed a concerted barrage of arrows into the Arab rear, causing a great deal of carnage. Individual arrows could be watched and avoided, but when it rained arrows like that, stepping away from one would move right into another. Panic began to rise in the Muslim ranks.

By virtue of his superior numbers, Romanus controlled the pace and initiative in the battle from the beginning. He desired a precise victory and he had the luxury of executing his plan with leisure. It took nearly two hours from the first contact with the enemy before his wings had positioned themselves for an encirclement. The battle in the center was indecisive, with the Byzantines content to hold position rather than inflict injury.

Romanus stood in the stirrups of his saddle to get a better view of how his envelopment maneuver was proceeding. He glanced longingly at the walls behind him. He would command a much better view of the battle from there, but what would his men say if he commanded the battle behind the safety of the city walls? The banners on the left wing had been raised for some time, indicating that they were in position. Romanus was about to send a runner to find out what the holdup was on the right when he saw the banners there lift skyward. He turned to his signal men. "Send the execute!" The banners surrounding him dropped simultaneously. The banners on his wings dipped in acknowledgment and the roar of the battle intensified as the two wings surged forth to flank the enemy from both sides.

Shurahbil's command post was littered with dead and dying. The Byzantine arrows had taken a terrible toll. When he heard the charge on his flanks, he realized what had happened. If the enemy wings closed the circle, all was lost. He issued desperate orders, "Tell the center to begin falling back! Reinforce the flanks! Archers, draw swords and protect the rear! Don't let them get behind us!"

But it wasn't enough. The Byzantines had the initiative and controlled the battle. The Muslim soldiers could sense the encirclement and doubled their efforts, flailing in vain against the impenetrable crush of well-disciplined Byzantine soldiers who were pushing them into a killing circle.

Khalid was at the head of his column when they clambered out of the wadi, their thirst slaked by the narrow stream below. The walls of Bosra became visible when a strange sound carried to him on the wind. He'd signaled a halt when a breathless scout galloped up. "Sahib! There's a battle on the west wall of the city!"

The report confirmed what his ears had told him. Khalid didn't wait for details, he moved instantly. "Charge!"

Bashour was in the middle of the small stream at the bottom of the wadi, washing the dust from his face, when the trumpets sounded from the embankment above them. The reaction of those around him wasn't quite panic, but would have looked like it to the untrained eye. Men dropped their water skins and leaped for their weapons. Those with mounts charged up the high embankment, the foot soldiers following as quickly as they could. When Bashour made the top of the bank and looked across the flat desert scrub, all he could see of the cavalry was a dwindling dust cloud to the southwest. Wahid emerged behind him, puffing heavily. Then he looked towards the disappearing cavalry and took a deep breath. Clapping Bashour on the shoulder, he grunted, "Come on! Sounds like there's enough for everybody." The big man broke into an easy trot.

"But what about the camel and our goods?" cried Bashour after him.

"It's Sameer's turn to take care of her today. Come on!" Bashour followed him, easily keeping up with the bigger man.

Romanus was organizing in his mind the dispatch he would send to Emessa, detailing the drama and brilliance of his victory. The trap was almost closed on the remaining Muslims. Anytime now they would see the hopelessness of their situation and lay down their arms and bargain for peace. One advantage of his methodical approach to the battle was that his men operated with disciplined efficiency and their bloodlust wasn't too high. He'd have no problem controlling his men if a surrender were offered. His attention was on the battle, not wanting to miss the climax of his victory, when one of his aides gasped and cried, "Turmarch!"

Romanus turned and his heart sank at the sight of a disorganized mob of cavalry descending on them from the north. Where had these come from? The main Arab forces were supposed to be west of Bosra. Their shouts preceded them, "Allâhu Akbar! Allâhu Akbar!"

Romanus broke out of his shock. "It's the main force. I was right, this was a trap. Sound the retreat! Bring up the archers to cover! Everyone get back inside the city!"

Before the order could go out, the Arab cavalry smashed into the right wing of his forces. The horsemen waded among the infantry, causing mass confusion as they laid about with their swords. As the rest of the army broke contact and fled toward the city gates, the Arabs let them go, too exhausted from their near defeat to pursue. Part of his right wing was engaged and couldn't break contact with the newly arrived cavalry. Romanus watched the chaos and hardened his face to the decision he knew he had to make, "Archers! Aim for the enemy cavalry!"

"But sir! Our men. . .!"

"They're dead anyway if we can't break up that cavalry! Do as I said, damn you!"

The skies blackened with arrows. Horses and riders fell screaming. As they hit the ground, they were dispatched by the remaining Byzantines, but friendly soldiers had suffered under the arrows as well. Still more horsemen were arriving from the north, and Romanus could see infantry behind them. He watched helplessly as a quarter of his army was butchered. When the last of his men had made the shelter of the gates, he turned and followed them, avoiding their eyes.

Khalid was in the front of the charge, leaning into the wind with a smile on his face. Nothing was better than charging into battle on a swift horse. He glanced back over both shoulders to make sure the vanguard of his cavalry accompanied him. Their battle cry reached his ears and his smile grew even wider.

They crashed into the Romans, who'd just realized the threat in their rear. The precise maneuver formations of the Romans shattered into confusion. Khalid swung about with his scimitar, the curved blade guaranteed to make contact wherever he swung. After a few moments Dhiraar appeared on his left, facing the other way. Together they formed a swirling whirlpool of death among the Roman formation. Dhiraar, as was his custom, had removed his shirt and fought bare-chested.

The Romans closest to the city gates broke off the engagement and retreated towards the city. Several of Khalid's men moved to pursue, but he called, "Let them go!" There was plenty of fighting to be done among those who'd been cut off.

Khalid kept an eye on the city as he fought; trying to stay aware of the tactical situation as well has his personal combat. He became alarmed when a cloud of arrows rose from the Roman ranks. He shouted a warning and turned so his side and back were towards the barrage, his head down and covering his neck with his arm. Dhiraar flung himself low on the side of his horse away from the barrage. Khalid felt an arrow glance off his back at an oblique angle and hazarded a glance to see if any more were coming. Miraculously, his horse was spared. Men were screaming all around him, both Romans and Muslims.

The foot soldiers in his column were catching up now and sweeping to the right, overwhelming the remaining Roman soldiers in the field. Khalid broke out of the melee and worked his way around the battlefield to the left, looking for the other Muslim commander.

He came across a group of Arabs sitting exhausted on the ground, surrounded by dead and wounded, their weapons bloodied. "You! Who's your commander?"

One looked up, no sign of recognition in his eyes. "Shurahbil bin Hasanah leads us."

Anger flashed across Khalid's face and he urged his horse into a trot. He spied a banner and jumped off the horse as they pulled up to Shurahbil's command post. Shurahbil recognized him and rushed to greet him. "As-Salāmu Alaykum, Khalid! Allâh be praised!"

Khalid's face remained dark. "Again I have to rescue you from your folly, Shurahbil? You didn't learn your lesson at Yamamah?" He looked around, gauging the size of Shurahbil's force, "What are you thinking, trying to lay siege to a city with stone walls with so small a force? Have you no sense at all?"

Shurahbil took a step back from the big man. "Khalid, I was only following the orders of Ubaidah. He told me to take Bosra while they remained to guard against a Roman incursion from Palestine."

Khalid snorted in derision. "Ubaidah is a worthy man and a tremendous warrior, but beyond the end of his sword my horse knows more of warfare than he does."

Khalid strode towards the banner, then whirled back. "Very well. I command now, by orders of Abu Bakr. Form a perimeter around this point. Gather the wounded and tend them. Station archers around the city and put scouts out to monitor the other gates. How many defenders are in there?"

"I think more than ten thousand marched out today. Perhaps six or seven thousand remain."

"We're evenly matched on the open field, then. But they're behind walls. We'll camp here and hope they sortie again. If they don't, then when my men are ready to travel again, we'll rendezvous with Ubaidah."

Khalid surveyed the battlefield for a moment, then collected his horse and rode off. Shurahbil turned to an aide and ordered,

"Send your fastest rider to notify Ubaidah that Khalid has taken command. Tell him not to stop through the night until he reaches Ubaidah."

Tamara was used to the routine of pitching camp. Since she'd been taken, Mus'ad had used her as a valet when he wasn't using her to slake his lust. She wrestled the tent off the camel and soon had it pegged and set up. Normally Mus'ad supervised her efforts, but this day the men were all mopping up after the fight. She moved woodenly, not caring about the battle or its outcome. When finished, she sat and rubbed her feet and waited for Mus'ad to return.

She was shocked when he did return. Four men carried him to the tent and dropped him. Two arrows protruded from him, in his thigh and shoulder. A ragged tear had removed most of his throat and his tongue lolled out as his head rolled limply to his side. Tamara was shocked for a moment. Then, as she realized what had happened to him, a small smile crept across her face.

Several men around her were discussing Mus'ad. "Does he have family?"

"I'm not sure where he came from."

"I think his family is in As Suwaydirah. I remember him talking about his mother there."

"His belongings should be sent back to his family."

"He got these weapons and armor in Persia. I know he has no brothers that would use them. We should auction them and send the money to his mother."

One of the men gathered leered at Tamara. Fear raced through her body and settled as a cold lump in her stomach. "What about the girl? He was awarded her at Qaryateyn."

She dropped her head and tried to hide behind her hair as they regarded her. "By Allâh," one said. "I'd give six hundred dirhams to make her mine."

"She belongs to Mus'ad's family. Maybe they can auction her as well and send the price to his mother." The was a general murmur of assent.

"Someone find an Imam," one of the men said and a couple of men trotted off.

Another man squatted in front of Tamara and brushed her hair away from her face. She flinched from the touch. "Gather all of Mus'ad's belongings," he said. "Do it now."

Tamara became confused and cast her eyes around. The man looked at her quizzically. "Are you his wife, or his slave girl?" Tamara's eyes grew wider and she just looked at him in confusion. She was a rape victim! How could she be his wife? The man asked patiently, "Do you speak Arabic?"

She nodded. She was starting to panic at the unknown situation she found herself in. A simple yes-or-no question was welcome.

"When you joined us, did the two of you present yourself before an Imam? Did you wed?" Tamara had no idea what an Imam was. She'd heard the term used since she'd been taken. But a wedding? There'd been nothing remotely resembling a wedding. She shook her head. He smiled and Tamara thought she could sense hunger in his eyes. The fear rose even higher in her chest and threatened to choke off her breathing. "Take his tent down and pack it. Gather his weapons with the tent. We have to deliver it all to his family. You might go with it. We'll figure that out later."

As the light faded, Romanus stood atop the battlements of the city wall and surveyed the cook fires springing up in the Arab encampment below, mocking him. A sick feeling in the pit of his stomach had formed, as he imagined what the consequences of his defeat this day would bring. A runner approached him. "Turmarch, the city council has requested you." The young man – a boy, really – seemed reluctant to elaborate. Romanus didn't need much of an imagination to figure out what they wanted.

He muttered a terse, "Very well," and whirled to descend from the wall.

The city elders looked grim when he entered. Romanus was determined not to be intimidated by these civilians, not be placed in a position of defending his actions this day. When he entered the chamber, he angrily announced, "I told you the main Arab force was waiting to draw us out today. Thanks to your interference in military matters, I lost nearly four thousand men because you insisted I walk into a trap."

The mayor, a corpulent man in his mid-fifties, rose and answered Romanus, "Turmarch, don't you dare make this assembly responsible for your battlefield failure!"

"My failure? I told you we were better off holding the city walls. It was your. . . "

"You were defeated and forced to retreat by a smaller, less organized force!" The two men were attempting to shout over one another.

"We were ambushed by the main body of Arabs, which I told you would happen if we left the city!"

One of the other councilmen spoke up, "Turmarch, as near as we can tell, that wasn't the main body of the Arab force. They came from the north, not the west, and by our estimates there are only six thousand enemy around the city now. Hardly the twenty-five thousand you were expecting."

Romanus moved to address the entire group. "Who here expected Arabs to attack from the north?" Silence met his question. "Anyone?" He turned to the Mayor. "You know we couldn't reconnoiter the perimeter because we were under siege. I was ordered to engage and defeat the besieging forces, which I did successfully. If any of you think yourselves a military genius and can look me in the eye and tell me you would have expected an ambush from the north, I will surrender my commission to your superiority."

The council shifted uneasily in their seats and avoided eye contact with Romanus, who now dominated the room in his sweat-stained battle dress.

The mayor adopted a respectful look. "Turmarch, I applaud your success today. Indeed, your victory was brilliant. We watched from the walls. We thank you for taking the time to come and brief us on the situation." He looked directly at Romanus. The trap was primed. "Given that you still outnumber the invaders by some two thousand men, I'm sure you're busy planning how to defeat them tomorrow. We shall not keep you any longer. Thank you for your service, Turmarch." He bowed and the rest of the assembly rose and quietly applauded him.

Romanus' face grew purple with rage. These imbeciles had outmaneuvered him again. He could not deny he had the numerical advantage, but what did these political seat-warmers know of battle, the plight of foot soldiers against cavalry, or the effects that today's demoralizing retreat would have on the willingness of his men to attack again? Yet any suggestion that he was unwilling to reengage the enemy when he had the advantage would be reported as cowardice to the imperial court. Realizing he'd been outmaneuvered, he nodded and whirled on his heel and stormed from the room.

Bashour and his companions were gathered around Qutayba, who displayed a clean gash down his right forearm. Sameer helped press the skin together on either side of the cut, trying to hang on through the blood. An apothecary was preparing a silk thread to close the wound. "Hold him still," he commanded Wahid. The huge man grasped Qutayba's hand and elbow firmly.

Qutayba didn't look at the arm. His eyes were dull and he stared at the distance to his left, studiously ignoring his injured arm. "Can you move your fingers?" asked Wahid, in his deep, rumbling voice. Qutayba flexed all his fingers one by one and Wahid grunted, "Allâh be praised, you're lucky. You won't have to learn to swing a sword left-handed."

Rashad craned his neck to examine the wound and advised the apothecary, "Don't make it too neat. The man needs something worthy of bragging about."

Qutayba's skin was turning gray and a light sweat popped from his forehead. As the apothecary's needle slipped quickly along the wound, he barely flinched. "By Allâh," Sameer said, "that will teach you to hack at the infidel without a sword." Qutayba smiled weakly at the lame joke.

When the wound was sealed, they lay Qutayba down to rest and elevated his arm. A commotion not far off caught Bashour's attention. Rashad pulled at his arm. "Come on. There's going to be an auction." Bashour quickly tied off Shai-tan to the stake he'd driven into the ground, being careful not to turn his back on the camel.

Bashour asked questions as he followed Rashad. "What is the auction? I thought spoils were divided evenly?"

"This isn't spoils. One of the men who was killed, they've decided to send money to his family instead of his goods. They're selling his belongings."

A crowd had gathered already by the time they arrived. Most of the belongings had already been disposed of, all that was left was some armor and a sword. . . and a girl. Bashour realized with a cold shock that it was the same girl he'd encountered trying to escape in the desert two weeks previously. His heart leapt at the sight of her. Her head was bowed, but she watched the crowd warily from under her eyebrows. He could see both fear and defiance in her manner. He longed to talk to her.

Rashad noticed his attention and nudged him. "You like that one? You could have her tonight if you bought her."

Bashour glared at him. He had some money that had been given him from the conquest of Marj Rahit, but it wouldn't be enough. "What do you mean I could have her 'tonight'?"

"As your slave girl, she'd be yours to do with as you wished. You have needs and she'd be your slave."

"No, you would have to be married to do that." The idea of marrying such a creature intrigued Bashour well enough.

Rashad shrugged. "You could do that if you liked, but it's not necessary. For the Prophet, peace be upon him, taught us in the 'Allies': 'We have made lawful unto you your wives unto whom you have paid their dowries and those whom your right hand possesses of those whom Allâh has given you as spoils of war.'"

" 'Your right hand possesses?' What does that mean?"

Rashad held up his right hand. "The right hand is the powerful hand. It's the hand that holds the sword. It's the hand that you eat with and the hand that you take things with. If you hold something with your right hand, then it's yours; you own it."

Bashour cocked his head at the idea. To own such a girl? It would remove the uncertainty of a failure-prone courtship. . . but. . . "I don't have any money to speak of." said Bashour.

The weapons and armor were gone and the Imam addressed the gathered crowd. "I will begin this sale at five hundred Dirhams. Raise your hands if you'll give five hundred for this lovely addition to your household!" Several men raised their hands. Rashad elbowed Bashour, who glared at him and hissed, "No!"

"Go on, the rest of us will loan you the money. This will be a glorious campaign."

"Six hundred!" Some of the hands dropped. Bashour kept his at his side.

"Go on, Bashour! You know you want her." Bashour's eyes had never left her. He did want her. She was so beautiful. . .

Marid elbowed his way to their side as the Imam called, "Six fifty!"

"What's going on?"

Rashad grinned. "Bashour wants the girl, but he's too cheap."

Marid looked at her and whistled softly. "By Allâh, she's delightful. I'd buy her if I were you." Bashour looked sideways at him for adopting the Muslim manner of speech. It still sounded forced to Bashour.

"Seven hundred fifty!" All hands dropped save one, a tall, dark man with a thin beard, who grinned and looked around before stepping forward. "Nu'man, do you have seven hundred and fifty dirhams?" asked the Imam.

The man gave a short laugh. "You know I do, Dhiraar. I'll fetch it for you come morning."

"Will this woman be your slave, or will you marry her?" This caused pandemonium among the assembled men, voices recommending either choice.

Nu'man let his eyes roam over Tamara. He cupped her chin in his hand and raised her head. She jerked at the touch and glared at him. "Do you speak Arabic?" he asked.

"And if I do?" she spat back. He laughed and his hand fell to her breast, which he squeezed roughly, then both hands traced the outline of her hips.

"Yes, you would give me many fine sons," He growled, then turned to the crowd. "I will marry this one!"

The Imam announced, "You bid seven hundred and fifty dirhams of gold, which will be delivered to the mother of Mus'ad. That is your mahr, which you have paid in honor." He then look looked at Nu'man sternly. "Nu'man, you know that this woman has belonged to the right hand of Mus'ad. Will you delay your marriage by the prescribed one month to make sure she does not carry Mus'ad's child?"

Nu'man looked taken aback. "By Allâh, I will not!" He leered in Tamara's direction and the crowd cheered.

"Then you agree that any issue shall be raised as your legitimate child, regardless of the date of birth." He turned to Tamara. "Girl, what is your name?"

"Tamara," she said softly. Bashour barely heard it, but the name was etched in his heart. *It's hopeless*, he thought, *she's going to be married.*

"Tamara, do you give your permission to be married to Nu'man?"

Tamara was terrified, realizing what was happening. She looked at Nu'man, his lean features and sparse beard looked cruel to her. She couldn't bring herself to say anything, terrified of what might happen if she said no.

"Her silence indicates her permission!" announced the Imam. "Nu'man, Tamara, you are married. We're in a combat encampment, so Nu'man, you'll have to postpone your wedding banquet."

Nu'man leered at Tamara again and said loudly, "I will eat my banquet tonight, alone!" Laughter followed him as he seized Tamara by the arm and led her through the crowd.

Rashad shook his head at Bashour, still smiling, "Tsk, tsk. A soldier should be more decisive. Allâh knows best!"

Bashour shot a quick glare at Rashad then, searching, caught a last glimpse of Tamara's head-scarf as the crowd closed behind her.

As the sun was setting, Khalid roamed the perimeter of the siege encampment. The men were exhausted; his men from the weeks of forced marching and Shurahbil's men recovering from the shock of their near-defeat that day. Khalid wasn't satisfied with the minimal watch that had been set against another possible sortie from the city, but he said nothing, knowing that part of his authority lay in knowing how far he could push these men. They were near their limit. He reasoned that the Romans were probably licking their wounds as well and had no stomach for another field battle.

He didn't seek acknowledgment from the men as he drifted, wraithlike, among the tents and campfires. Eavesdropping on casual conversation often gave him a better feel for the mood of the men than did guarded conversations when he approached them overtly. These men were unusually quiet, save from the agonized cries of the wounded.

One conversation caught his attention and he stopped just inside earshot. "I'm just saying that the truth should be obvious to anyone who hears it." The crisp, clipped northern accent sounded like one of the converts that had joined in Northern Syria.

Jabir leaned forward to look closely at Bashour. "No, that's up to Allâh. For the Qur'án says, 'when you recite the Qur'án, we place between you and those who do not believe in the Hereafter a hidden barrier; and We place upon their hearts veils lest they should understand it and in their ears a deafness; and when you make mention of Allâh alone in the Qur'án, they turn their backs in aversion.'"

Bashour thought about that for a second, puzzled. “So how can someone believe, if Allâh obscures the truth from them because they don’t believe?”

“It’s not up to you, if you are to believe or not,” said Qutayba. “That has been decided by Allâh. I remember a funeral procession in Baqi Al-Gharqad; Allâh's Apostle, peace be upon him, said, ‘there is none among you and no created soul but has his place written for him either in Paradise or in the Hell-Fire and also has his happy or miserable fate in the Hereafter written for him.’”

“But then,” said Bashour, “why would one seek to do good deeds at all, if his fate is sealed by Allâh?”

Qutayba smiled and, pointed his finger at Bashour. “An excellent question, and one which was posed to the Prophet, peace be upon him. Allâh’s messenger replied, ‘those who are destined to be happy will find it easy and pleasant to do the deeds characteristic of those destined to happiness, while those who are to be among the miserable, will find it easy to do the deeds characteristic of those destined to misery.’”

“So, if Allâh has decided that you are to be a disbeliever, doesn’t he want some people to disbelieve? Shouldn’t that be respected?”

“We do respect that,” Jabir answered. “We don’t require that you believe in Allâh, blessed be his name. That’s between you and Allâh. But whether you believe or not, all must submit to Allâh. This is his commandment; that idolaters be brought to submission. In ‘Repentance’, the Qur’án says, ‘when the sacred months have passed, slay the idolaters wherever you find them and take them captive and besiege them and prepare for them each ambush. But if they repent and establish worship and pay the poor-due, then leave their way free. Lo! Allâh is Forgiving, Merciful!’”

Sameer spoke up. “There’s a difference between believing and submitting. For the wandering Arabs say, ‘We believe.’ But Allâh commanded Muhammad, peace be upon him, to say, ‘You believe not, but rather say, "We submit," for the faith hath not yet entered into your hearts. Yet, if you obey Allâh and his messenger, He will not withhold from you aught of the reward of your deeds. Lo! Allâh is Forgiving, Merciful.’”

Bashour could tell Sameer was quoting another passage from the Qur’án, because of the lilting quality in Sameer’s recital. “But,” he asked, “if Christians and Jews all worship the same God, the God of Abraham, as we do, aren't they already submitting?"

Jabir answered him, "Fight those who believe not in Allâh nor the Last Day, nor hold that forbidden which hath been forbidden by Allâh and his Messenger, nor acknowledge the religion of Truth, even if they are of the People of the Book, until they pay the Jizyah with willing submission and feel themselves subdued."

Sameer elaborated on this. "The Christians have strayed from the Book that Allâh gave Isa and the Jews have strayed from the book that Allâh gave Moses. They must pay the Jizyah and submit themselves to Allâh."

Bashour was still troubled by the violent intent his companions had towards spreading their faith. "But doesn't that mean you'll be forever at war? There will always be more lands to conquer, more people who don't believe."

"There will always be two houses," said Sameer. "The House of Islam and the House of War."

"It's good, is it not?" said Rashad. "There will always be Jihad, as Allâh desires. And there will always be a chance to be a martyr for Islam."

Bashour was taken aback. "You want to be a martyr?"

"Oh yes," said Rashad brightly. "A martyr is guaranteed a place in paradise if he dies in Allâh's cause. Jihad for Allâh's cause is the greatest calling one can answer. The Prophet, peace be upon him, said, 'the person who participates in Jihad in Allâh's cause and nothing compels him to do so except belief in Allâh and his Apostles, will be recompensed by Allâh either with a reward, or booty if he survives, or will be admitted to Paradise if he is killed in the battle as a martyr. Had I not found it difficult for my followers, then I would not remain behind any sariya going for Jihad and I would have loved to be martyred in Allâh's cause and then made alive and then martyred and then made alive and then again martyred in his cause.'"

"Nothing is greater than Jihad," added Jabir. "When asked what deed equaled Jihad in reward, Allâh's apostle, peace be upon him, replied that he did not find such a deed."

Khalid nodded to himself and smiled. He resumed moving among the army, satisfied that even in the pause of battle that his new mujahideen were being properly instructed.

Nu'man thrust Tamara into his tent, pitched next to his horse, which was grazing on one of the sparse tufts of dried grass that dotted the desert landscape. He followed her in and started removing his armor. She turned her back to him and didn't move. Panic rose in her and paralyzed her. Oh, God, was this happening again? His hand roughly grasped her shoulder and turned her. "What are you waiting for? Take these off!" He tugged at her shawl and cloak. She seemed to collapse into herself and turned away again.

This time he spun her to face him. "I said take these off!" He hit her hard across the face with his fist.

She cried out and sank to her knees. She saw stars in her left eye and could taste blood. Her hand went to her cheek where he'd hit her. Tears erupted and she wept bitterly.

Nu'man grabbed a handful of her cloak and dragged her to her feet. She cried in terror as he did so. "You're going to learn to do as I say, wife!" He hit her another crushing blow with the back of his hand on the right side of her face. Tamara swore she heard something click in her head when he hit her. The tent swam as she collapsed at his feet. She lay there, crying hysterically. He kicked her a couple of times to prompt her to get up and undress, but she was paralyzed with pain and fear. He finally stopped and she wondered if he'd given up, when he roughly grabbed her hips from behind and hoisted her to her knees. He pulled her cloak up to expose her legs and backside and roughly took her from behind as she lay there on her knees, her cries of pain and fear muffled by the bedding that she was face-down in. As he grunted and rutted, she cried in misery and disgust. A detached part of her brain actually regretted the death of Mus'ad, who'd never treated her so.

21. Bosra, Syria July 2, 634

Bashour was deep asleep when the haunting cry of the Muezzin pierced his rest. "Allâhu Akbar! I testify that there is no God but Allâh and that Muhammad is his messenger! Make haste towards the prayer! Make haste towards the reward! Prayer is better than sleep! Allâhu Akbar! There is no God but Allâh!"

Bashour had heard this five times a day since he'd joined the Muslims three weeks before. The songlike call was etched into his brain and he sometimes found himself reciting it under his breath as the Muezzin chanted. But not this morning. The previous night had been filled with camaraderie well past sunset as they'd greeted the army of Shurahbil. He flung back his bed roll and regarded the lightening sky, just growing bright in the east.

Someone had provided a large bowl of water, thankfully. Sometimes on their journey no water had been available to wash, yet they'd still performed the washing ritual with sand, which Bashour detested. He gathered with Sameer, Rashad and Jabir and began washing his hands. He cupped some water and rinsed his mouth, spat on the ground, then inhaled some water into his nose and blew out. Then he washed his arms to the elbow, scrubbed his face and ears and wiped his wet hands through his hair. Then he wet his hands again and rubbed them over his feet. He repeated this twice more, then moved out of the way quickly to allow Qutayba access to the water. He took his place in a line facing south, arranging his prayer rug in front of him.

When everyone had gathered they raised their hands and declared: "Allâhu Akbar! In the name of Allâh, the Most Beneficent, the Most Merciful. Praise be to Allâh, Lord of the Worlds, the Most Beneficent, the Most Merciful Master of the Day of Judgment. To you we worship and to you we turn to in help. Show us the straight path, the path of those who you have favored; not the path of those who earn your anger nor of those who go astray." Bashour followed along easily, as it was a standard prayer, repeated every time they were called to pray. Then the Imam began reciting a sura that Bashour was unfamiliar with. Like a person who knows the tune but not the words, Bashour followed along as best he could, mouthing the verse just a half second behind the rest, not really paying attention to the words, which were sometimes unintelligible to him.

Then as one, the congregation placed their hands on their knees in a half-bow. They stood upright, then knelt on their rugs. Bashour bent forward and touched his forehead and nose to the ground in submission to Allâh. As one, they sat upright on their knees, then bent forward to prostrate themselves again. Then they recited: "All worships are for Allâh. Allâh's peace be upon you, O Prophet, and His mercy and blessings. Peace be on us and on all righteous servants of Allâh. I bear witness that there is none worthy of worship except Allâh, and I bear witness that Muhammad is his servant and messenger." Then Bashour turned to either side and greeted his companions with, "Peace be upon you and Allâh's blessing."

They stood and repeated the whole process. Then they rolled up their rugs, their prayers for the morning completed. "Is it so important that we do this before dawn?" asked Bashour. "Surely Allâh is patient and can wait a little."

Jabir gave him a dirty look. "There are angels who take turns in visiting you by night and by day, and they all assemble at the dawn and the afternoon prayers. Those who have spent the night with you, ascend to the heavens and Allâh, who knows better about them, asks: 'In what condition did you leave my slaves?' They reply: 'We left them while they were performing salat and we went to them while they were performing salat.'"

Rashad smiled and winked at Bashour and he felt better, knowing that the angels would be able to give a positive report on this day.

Breakfast was a cold, hurried affair. The shadows were still long and the air was just starting to warm from the crisp desert night. Rashad had just stoked a small fire to boil some barley when trumpets began to sound. They stood for a better view and saw the gates of the city were open. Roman soldiers pouring out and forming up. Wahid opened a pack full of dried meat, cut a large hunk for himself and tossed it to Jabir. "Eat quickly and well. Allâh's work will soon be at hand."

Shurahbil was impressed by the calm efficiency with which Khalid's lieutenants handled the news that the Bosra garrison was coming out. There was no shouting or excitement, just cool efficiency as runners relayed orders to deploy the forces. Khalid commanded a tight circle of confidants. "Abdullah bin Umar, take fifteen hundred cavalry on the right. Dhiraar, take the rest of the cavalry on the left. Abdur-Rahman, you'll command the foot soldiers in the center. Shurahbil, your forces will stand behind Abdur-Rahman as a rapid reserve. The wings will not engage first. They outnumber us, so I want the wings to harass and keep them off balance until they commit, then seek their flanks and turn them. Try to get between them and the city walls, but don't take unnecessary chances if they leave archers on the walls."

The bulk of Khalid's forces had encamped to the west of the city and quickly assembled into ranks. Shurahbil's forces had resumed their siege positions and were streaming in from the east and north to form up behind the front rank.

Romanus shifted in his saddle, looking behind him at the progress his men were making at forming up in the shadow of the city walls. He knew their morale was shaken from yesterday's debacle, but was pleased to see it didn't seem to affect the precision of their formations. Handling this many men on a battlefield required an unthinking ability to respond to orders and maintain formation. The army that maintained cohesion in the heat of battle was the one most likely to emerge victorious.

Through the gates he could see the tail of the turma approaching the city gates. He then examined the Arab forces that had formed up facing him. Horses and camels of their cavalry were on either side, with the center formed of foot soldiers. He was nervous about his flanks. He'd raided the stores of Bosra and found enough heavy pikes to outfit two numeri of menavlatoi, or heavy pikemen. These six hundred men weren't enough and he was uneasy about their training on the unfamiliar heavy pikes. Still, it was the only chance he had to slow the cavalry. The Arab general had done as he'd expected and set the mounted soldiers on the flanks. Romanus had deployed his menavlatoi accordingly. He wondered if it might have been better to keep his force together; at least then he could secure one flank completely. It was too late to worry about that now.

His standard bearer and translator were looking at him expectantly. "Let's go," he said as he kicked his horse forward. When they'd moved fifty paces, a contingent of three Arabs separated from the force in front to meet them. As they approached, Romanus observed that their leader was a different man than he'd spoken with the previous day. They pulled up short a few paces apart and regarded each other silently. Romanus opened the dialogue. "You are in command of this army?" The question hung in the air, followed by silence and no sign of understanding among the Arabs. The translator interpreted the request.

"Khalid bin Al Waleed commands this army."

"I wish to speak with him."

"Khalid does not wish to speak to you."

"Who are you?"

"I am Abdur-Rahman bin Khalid." Even through the translator, he said it so that Romanus felt he was supposed to be impressed. The name meant nothing to Romanus. The Arab, irritated, continued, "Your city will accept Islam, submit and pay the Jizyah, or you will all die!"

Romanus snorted. Is this the only negotiation tactic these barbarians had? "Your forces are outnumbered. Leave this place and return to the desert from whence you came."

Instead of a retort, the Arab surprised Romanus by producing a wicked looking scimitar and lunging his horse towards him, shouting, "Allâhu Akhbar!" Romanus barely avoided the attack, reining his horse to the side as he fumbled for his sword.

The horses circled one another and it was all Romanus could do to counter the endless storm of blows delivered by the Arab. Romanus' sword was unwieldy compared to the light scimitar and the Arab seemed inexhaustible. Romanus concentrated on fending off blows, but tried to keep track of those around him out of the corner of his eye. Thankfully, the other Arabs were preoccupied chasing after his companions. He didn't have to worry about being taken from behind.

He pivoted his horse out of reach, earning him a moment's respite, and studied his opponent. Black eyes peered from under a heavy brow. Underneath a thick beard he could see the man was smiling evilly, as he pressed his horse to circle him back in range. *My God*, thought Romanus, *this barbarian is actually enjoying this!*

The next flurry of blows came in low, then a sudden swipe to his shoulder opened a gash just below the leather armor that protected the joint. Romanus felt the blow, but didn't think he'd been cut until he glanced at it and saw blood pouring furiously.

His hand suddenly felt heavy and he knew any advantage he might have had was long gone. He turned his horse to stay outside the Arab's reach and when he had a clear path to his army, he kicked hard into a gallop. He leaned into the neck of the horse, urging speed, not looking behind him to see if he was being pursued. His men opened a hole in their line that he plunged through. He reigned to a halt and turned to look behind. The entire Arab front line was rushing forward to engage. Aides were rushing to him, alarmed by the amount of blood coming from his arm. He ignored them, shouting, "Archers! Shoot!"

The sky blackened with arrows, but most of the barrage fell long, as the Arab army rushed forward faster than expected.

Khalid was fighting in the center, with the dismounted soldiers. The first volley of arrows fell behind them as they advanced at a dead run. He smiled, seeing that they would crash into the Roman lines in the shadow of the city wall before there would be time for a second volley. Realizing that a solitary mount would present a lucrative target for short-range archers, he pulled his horse up short, dismounted, slapped the horse to send it back and proceeded on foot. He was a big man and carried a Persian broadsword, which he used to lay about him. He disdained a shield, preferring to use two hands to swing his sword like an axe. His men avoided getting in front of him, allowing him to take point and protecting his flanks from slightly behind him, to allow him to swing away at the enemy. Caught up in the joy and excitement of battle, he began reciting the sura Al-Fatiha, using the rhyme to time his swing. Those closest to him smiled at how their commander relished his bloody work.

The Roman lines held firm after the initial shock of contact dissipated, repulsing the Arab assault with shields and short stabbing swords. Khalid relinquished his place in the line and worked his way back. Archers from the walls were picking off Arabs in the rear of the crush, but his archers were working in pairs to clean off the walls. One archer would hold a large shield to cover them, while the other would pop from behind it to target an enemy. Khalid signaled Shurahbil's troops to join the battle on the left side.

The July desert air quickly grew hot as the searing sun climbed higher. Because they had no formation discipline, Arab soldiers were free to disengage from the front and make their way back for a drink of water. Plentiful volunteers would always take their place.

Khalid observed the lines, examining the fight. The battle was set piece, with a clear line and no need for any maneuvering. He could see the horsemen milling about to either side, working like a grinder on the Roman flanks.

Khalid paced behind the battle line, exhorting here, adjusting there. His men were holding the pressure on the Romans, though relatively little blood had been shed. Khalid directed aid stations for the wounded be set up beyond the range of the dwindling archers on the walls. Water was brought forward for the weary fighters. For three hours the fighting went on, and the sun reached its zenith.

The end came suddenly. The Romans couldn't cycle their fighters efficiently nor make any maneuvers against the mobile cavalry on the flanks. Fatigue started to take a toll on the Romans. They started losing people as fresh Arabs were committed from the reserves. Romanus called a retreat and the formations maintained their discipline as they efficiently withdrew into the city. The menavlatoi with their huge pikes were the last, keeping the Arabs at bay at the gate until the doors were closed in their face.

Dhiraar rode up to Khalid, a broad grin on his bearded face. Khalid was shocked by his appearance. "Dhiraar bin Al Azwar, where is your tunic and armor?" The man was naked from the waist up, save for blood spatters across his body.

"By Allâh, Khalid! I was compelled to remove my armor, lest I collapse from the heat. That made me so light and happy, I removed my tunic. That let the sweat cool me and made me feel even happier and lighter. I slew a score or more of these infidels! Allâh be praised, this is a great day!"

Khalid laughed at the fearless warrior. "Direct the foot soldiers to spread out along the walls and hold the siege. I don't think they'll come out again. Keep the cavalry in reserve to the west." Khalid turned and spied a yellow banner in the west, a rider and three companions making their way through the ranks of Arabs. Khalid began to walk towards them. The tall man in the front saw him and smiled a toothless smile. As they neared, he moved to dismount and Khalid called to him, "Stay on your horse!" As they drew together, Khalid reached up and they grasped hands.

"O Father of Sulaiman," said Ubaidah, "I received with gladness the letter of Abu Bakr appointing you commander over me. I have no resentment, for your skill in matters of war is greater than mine."

"By Allâh," replied Khalid, "were it not an order from the Caliph, I would never have accepted command over you. You are much higher than I in Islam. I was a companion of the Prophet, peace be upon him, but you are one whom the Messenger of Allâh had called 'The Trusted One' of Islam."

Ubaidah smiled genially. "I received word of your presence after the mid-watch last night and immediately set out and rode all night. I see you haven't been idle."

Khalid hawked and spat towards the city. "The Romans tested our siege this morning, for the second time. I don't think they'll do it again. Now the question is how we're going to break into the city? Have you brought reinforcements?"

Ubaidah's smile never wavered as he delivered the bad news. "Yazeed is still south of the River Yarmuk; Amr bin Al Aas is raiding the Valley of Araba; and there are several detachments spread over the District of Hauran. But I've ordered something better. Coming behind me is a herd of sheep, enough to feed your army for a fortnight, and behind that I've ordered cattle. Unless they've been hoarding food for months, the city will starve while we grow fat outside their walls."

Khalid despised a static siege, but he had no idea how to penetrate the walls of Bosra. He considered Ubaidah's suggestion. "There's water in a wadi just north of here," He mused. "But we'd be in trouble if a relief force is sent to break the siege."

"Oh, I shouldn't worry about that." said Ubaidah. "My scouts have reported that all the forces in Syria have been ordered to Palestine, just southwest of Jerusalem. The Romans are building a huge army there, presumably to crush us from the left flank, should we venture further north."

22. Port of Jaffa, Palestine
July 5, 634

The ship cleared the line of reefs and turned starboard, approaching the entrance to the breakwater of the harbor. To port, the beach gave way to a low hill that guarded the harbor entrance. Men groaned with relief as the ship steadied itself in the relatively calm water behind the reefs, no longer subject to the pitch and heave of the open sea. The crew grinned at each other at the weakness of their passengers, then returned to work. It took all hands at the stays to react as needed in the tight confines of the Jaffa harbor, made even tighter by a plethora of ships clogging the docks.

Taticus stood at the gunwale, studying the scene, bewildered at the differences of the ships around him. Rowboats made their way around the port, fishing boats came and went with a reckless speed born of years of experience. Huge, round bottomed scows like the one they were in heaved at their hawsers around the harbor.

The ship's captain ordered the sails to be furled except a few tiny scraps that allowed him steerage. He sought Taticus and conferred with him quietly for a second. Taticus turned to the men, who began gathering their belongings and struggling to their feet in hopeful expectation of leaving the floating hell that they had been trapped in for three days.

"As you were, men. The docks are full, it may be hours before they clear a spot for us to put in." This produced groans of dismay and despair.

"Hurry up and wait! That's all the army's about." complained one sergeant. Taticus grinned. That complaint had probably been a staple of armies since the dawn of antiquity.

The men suffered under the baking sun without relief for several hours, without even the satisfaction of a stiff breeze to cool them. The water of the harbor was foul and putrid, clogged with waste and garbage that didn't get flushed out to sea. The air was thick with humidity that made it difficult to breathe.

Finally, near mid-afternoon, the captain ordered more sail and lifted the mushroom anchor they'd dropped. Aided by four large oars at bow and stern, they put in at an empty stretch of dock and a gangplank was rigged. The men went ashore, then helped unload the small two-man pull-wagons that carried their heavy gear.

Men stumbled as they hit the shore, unused to standing on a surface that wasn't heaving and pitching. Taticus formed them up on the dock. He looked for a dock master to tell them where they were to go, but found nobody in charge. "Typical," he muttered under his breath. He motioned one of his flankers out of formation. "Leave your weapons and run down the docks and find the best place for us to march out of here." The young man took off down the docks and soon reported a gap in the warehouses that led to wide streets behind. Taticus wheeled the formation in place and began marching them in the indicated direction. As they turned off the docks, they were met by a harried looking lochaghos. "Who are you?" he asked with an air of exasperation.

"Komes Taticus with four centuries!"

The lochaghos gave him a look filled with contempt. "That doesn't tell me anything. Unit?"

"Twenty-seventh training Numeri. We've been activated, but I never received a themata assignment."

The lochaghos shuffled through a sheaf of papers he was holding. After several minutes of examination, he gave up. "You're not on my manifest, but it doesn't matter. Everyone's heading the same way anyway. Here's a map. Your destination is the valley of Elah, about two day's march from here. They'll sort you out there. Are your men provisioned?"

"No."

The lochaghos took back the map and scribbled a quick sketch on the back. "The Quartermaster's warehouse is here. You should pull four days rations, you'll probably run into delays on the march. Now get these men out of the city. There's a river about one and a half millarium down the main road. You can form up there while you resupply."

Israel – Palestine, since the Romans destroyed Israel 560 years before – had been inhabited for so long that many cities were built on the refuse of their earlier incarnations, forming mound-shaped tells. Such a tel dominated the dock area of Joppa. The road followed the foot of the tel for a short way, then veered to the right, away from it. Taticus appreciated the order to get his men out of the city, to remove them from any temptation of deserting into the myriad alleys and streets.

After a mile and a half, the city gave way to larger estates and they reached a small river. Taticus called a halt to bivouac for the night. By the time they resupplied, it would be too close to sundown to begin a march. He ordered his Decharchs to meet with him with their supply wagons. He led these forty men back into the city to the quartermaster's warehouse.

After a wait, they were met by the Stratopedarches, the master of supply. "Orders?"

Taticus handed him his orders. "Komes Taticus. I need road provisions for four hundred."

The supply master examined his paperwork. "These orders are signed by Strategos Psellus."

Taticus remained silent, thinking, *Thank you for stating the obvious!*

The master handed him back the orders. "I can't help you. These supplies are allocated to Strategos Andrew."

Taticus was stunned. "What are you talking about? These orders assign me to Andrew." He pushed them back.

"Then you'll need a supply authorization from Andrew."

"These orders are from Psellus, who's superior to Andrew."

"Then you can draw supplies from Psellus. Until you have a requisition through Andrew's command, I can't release any supplies to you. The only way I can release supplies to you under Psellus' orders is through a funds transfer."

Taticus knew it would come to that as soon as he encountered resistance. "How much?"

"Four hundred men? Four days? I think three gold denarii would cover it."

Taticus looked him in the eye and stated flatly, "That's robbery."

The supply master shrugged. "Not my problem."

Taticus' lips were white. He could stand against a blood-crazed enemy with equanimity, but he'd never be able to deal with a bureaucrat with an even temper. He dug in his coin-purse and produced three gold coins. "I want a receipt."

"But of course. This way please."

23. Bosra
July 6, 634

The siege of Bosra was in its third day without event. It looked like the Roman garrison had elected to sit out the siege, hoping to starve off the attacking Muslims. The archers from the wall regarded the encamped Muslims just out of arrow shot. The Muslims, for their part, took advantage of the inactivity to recover from long weeks of forced marching, repairing their gear, replacing shoes and washing filthy clothes. Tamara worked during the day boiling bandages for the wounded and ministering their wounds. She hated these people, hated everything they had done to her, but she couldn't stand to see someone injured and in pain and not do anything about it. She justified it to herself that hoping that such acts of charity might serve as an example of how civilized people treated one another. The activity helped her keep her mind off the prospect of what awaited her after dark at the hands of Nu'man.

Tamara was just finishing hanging freshly boiled strips of linen to dry on a makeshift line when a sound caught her ear. Distant at first, carried on the slight breeze from the east, the sound of a church bell calling the faithful to holy mass could be heard from within the walls of the city. She thought for a moment and realized it must be Sunday.

The sound of the bell called to her, and facing the sound she dropped to her knees. Everything that had happened to her in the last three weeks came crashing in and tears began to flow.

Oh my God! God, why have you done this to me? Please, Lord, deliver me. . . rescue me from this torment! Oh, God, don't let me live like this for the rest of my life. Please, God, grant me a quick death, that I may be delivered from this evil into your arms!

Her silent prayer faded into incoherence, a wordless repetition of pain and horror and supplication as she cried. Several minutes passed as she gathered her thoughts.

Oh, my God, please accept the souls of Jamila, of my father, of all those taken by these heathens. Please forgive their sins and welcome them into your arms. Oh, God, why, why, why? What have we done to warrant this punishment? Jamila. . .

.Lord, she was my best friend! How can you look down on such evil and stay your hand? Take these heathen, Lord, smite them from the earth! Send these demons to Hell!

Again, her thoughts lost their words and her prayer became a parade of grief, rising and falling, threatening to overwhelm her like it had so many times before. In the silence of her mind, as the memory of the church bells of Bosra echoed in her head, she became calm and bits of scripture came to her, unbeckoned. *Fix your eyes on Jesus. . .who for the joy set before Him endured the cross, despised the shame and sat down at the right hand of God.*

Lord, I cannot carry this cross. For what purpose, Lord? How am I imperfect, that this will perfect me?

Consider the lilies: they neither toil nor spin; but I tell you, not even Solomon in all his glory clothed himself like one of these. . . .your Father knows what you need.

She found it so hard to believe this. Was there a purpose, a reason she was enduring this? Was she meant to do something that hadn't been made clear?

Lord, I am nothing. I have nothing. All that I am is yours. I place my soul in your hands. Use me as your tool. Or take me, Lord, deliver me from this horror, if you have no use for me.

Grant me the strength, oh Lord. Give me the strength to do your will. I know you would not ask that which I was unable to do. Give me the strength and courage, Lord, to do your will, to fulfill whatever purpose you have for me here. Protect me, Lord. Show me what you would have me do.

The act of surrender calmed her and she felt a wave of serenity slowly flow over her. Her life was in God's hands now. She'd be all right. She could survive this.

Wahid had heard that Nu'man's woman could provide him with bandages to dress Qutayba's wound. After several queries, he found the man brushing down a horse. "As-Salāmu `Alaykum! You're Nu'man?"

"As-Salāmu `Alaykum, I am."

"I've been told that you can provide bandage dressings for the wounded."

"Of course." He raised his voice. "Tamara!"

She didn't answer. Nu'man led them around the horse and tent. "Tamara!" Wahid saw a young woman on her knees, partially prostrated. Nu'man growled and stepped forward. "By

Allâh! I'll teach you not to respond to me!" His hands began undoing the rope wrapped around his cloak.

Wahid's huge hand fell on his shoulder and restrained him. "Hold, friend."

Nu'man's head snapped around and he glared up at Wahid. "What are you doing? Who do you think you are?"

Wahid shushed him with a motion and said softly, "Don't you see that the girl is in prayer? You cannot interrupt her!"

Nu'man looked more closely and, indeed, the girl was gently rocking, evidently in supplication to some unseen power. The scene riveted the two Arabs, tugging at deep-seated superstitions that transcended the prophet's teachings. "Thank you, friend," Nu'man finally said. "You have saved me from a curse. Come, sit with me and tell me a story until she's finished." The two men retreated respectfully.

Bashour and his companions were washing their clothes in the river north of the city. Someone had built a catch basin for washing and bathing. Bashour was thankful for the chance to rinse the accumulated dust and sweat out of his garments.

"I never thought I'd see Khalid placed over Ubaidah." declared Sameer.

"Khalid is Abu Bakr's darling," said Jabir. "Everyone knows that if you want results, you send Khalid." Bashour had learned from his time with the Muslims that Khalid's nickname was "The Sword of Allâh." He was undeniably some sort of god of war.

Wahid was washing his hair and beard. "If the results you seek are victory and destruction of the enemy. This tells me that Abu Bakr has no intention of negotiating with the Romans."

The others nodded in agreement, but Bashour was lost. "Why is that?"

Sameer answered, "If you wish to conquer, you send a warrior. If you wish to negotiate, you send a trustworthy man. If Abu Bakr was going to negotiate, Khalid would be under Ubaidah."

"They say Ubaidah is trustworthy, then?"

Jabir spoke up, "The Prophet, peace be upon him, said to the Christians of Nijran, 'I will send you the most trustworthy man.' All of us were looking forward to be the one selected. I was hopeful, but I knew there were others that the Messenger of

Allâh, May Allâh be pleased with him, regarded more highly. He then sent Abu Ubaidah."

Bashour had been wondering abut something for weeks and he finally felt comfortable enough with his companions to ask, "Why do you do that?"

"Do what?" asked Rashad.

"Why do you say 'Peace be upon him,' every time you mention the Prophet?"

The others just looked at each other in silence and Bashour had a sinking feeling that he'd just made a serious gaffe. "Well, it's how we show respect," Rashad said. "After all, he was Allâh's messenger."

Jabir said, "the Holy Qur'án instructs us: Allâh and his angels send blessings on the Prophet: O you that believe! Send your blessings on him and salute him with all respect."

"I heard," said Qutayba, "that he once said that an angel came to him from Allâh and said, 'Whoever among your followers sends Salah upon you, Allâh will record for him ten good deeds and will erase for him ten evil deeds and will raise his status by ten degrees and will return his greeting with something similar to it.'"

Bashour wondered what it meant to be raised by ten degrees. Was that a lot? But he didn't want to look too foolish asking too many questions like that. He took a different approach, hoping that some of his questions would be answered in passing. "What was the prophet, peace be upon him, like?"

Jabir started, "I have never seen such a man as Allâh's Apostle, peace be upon him. He was the most honest of men. Even his enemies knew of his honesty."

"He was very brave," added Qutayba. "He was the most generous person, gentle and compassionate and forgiving. He was brilliant, no man could match his powers of reasoning."

Wahid snorted quietly, but kept silent. Sameer began describing him, as if talking about a lover. "He had a broad, round face and pinched nose. His eyes were black and he had long eyelashes, like those of a camel. He had a gap between his two front teeth that you could see through when he talked. His hair was reddish and fell to his shoulders. He had a full beard and hardly any gray hairs, even until he died. His skin was white as milk and his palms were soft as silk." At this Wahid rolled his eyes and took to scrubbing his clothes even harder, but nobody but Bashour noticed.

Sameer continued, "There was no hair on his chest or belly, just some on his arms and shoulders and he had the seal of the Prophet on his back the size of a pigeon's egg. He was fastidiously clean and was always brushing his teeth and cleaning his mouth. His sweat smelled finer than the sweetest perfume."

Bashour began to feel slightly embarrassed. They were waxing like lovers over the man, to the point that it was becoming sexual.

"I never saw anybody," said Jabir, "who could see as far as he could, or could hear as well as he. And when he walked, he leaned forward, as if he was about to fall down. But no one could walk as fast as he could. Many became exhausted trying to walk with him, and he was tireless."

Bashour was more interested in the man, not what he looked like. "Did he ever laugh or get angry?"

"He never laughed so you could look in his mouth" said Qutayba. "He'd smile wisely when he was pleased. But oh, when he became angry! His face would get so red you thought he had a birthmark that covered his head."

Jabir added, "He had the sexual strength of a stallion camel. He used to visit all his wives in a round, both during the day and at night, and there were nine of them. We used to say that the Prophet was given the strength of thirty men."

The men contemplated the implications of this activity for a moment in respectful silence. Rashad spoke up quietly. "He never asked for any reward from the people for all his efforts towards their welfare, and tolerated their abuses and taunts with great patience. No one in Mecca paid any heed to his sincere and honest message. Some of them, including his uncle Abu Lahab, abused him, but he tolerated everything and continued his sincere efforts for the good of the people. He was the perfect man and we all strive to be like him in every way."

This made some things clear to Bashour. Often when they corrected him and he asked why, the answer was, "the Prophet did such-and-so." Now he understood that all Muslims had been called to be like Muhammad. He resolved to learn more about this man and follow him in every way.

24. Bosra, Syria
July 7, 634

Romanus ascended the steps to the parapet of the city walls at the summons of the sentry detail. After four days of siege, the routine had settled into a dull monotony. The Arabs surrounding the city seemed content to keep their distance, not challenging the marksmanship of the archers on the walls. The captain of the guard met him at the top of the steps and directed his attention westward.

"There, sir. It's been growing for the last half-hour." A cloud of dust hung low to the ground on the road to the west.

Romanus regarded the dust cloud for a moment, then his eyes swept the besieging Arabs. He could see no activity. "Any reaction from the Arabs?"

"No, sir. Either they're not aware of it, or they don't care."

Romanus turned to his aide. "Thoughts, Domnus?"

"I would have expected a relief column to come from the north. My guess is that these are Arab reinforcements."

Romanus chewed his lip. "I agree, but there's supposed to be an army forming near Jerusalem. Perhaps they've taken to the field." His guards and aides held their silence for long minutes while he turned over the situation in his mind. Then he spoke decisively. "Muster the troops and prepare to sortie through the main gate. If this is a relief column, we need to be ready to crush the Arabs from two directions."

Over the next hour, the soldiers of the garrison formed up and stood waiting in a vast column behind the gate, sweating in the afternoon sun. Romanus was concerned. A battle this late in the afternoon was inadvisable. But he had no control of the initiative. He considered a sortie to draw attention from the advancing column and decided against it. He simply didn't know enough and was still smarting from the two defeats he'd already suffered in the field.

The dust cloud finally resolved itself. It was neither a relief column nor enemy reinforcements, it was sheep – thousands and thousands of sheep. They were herded by a couple dozen Arabs on foot and camelback. Like a black-and-white tidal wave, they swept into the Arab lines and flowed around the city, dispersing into the fields beyond. It seemed as if they'd never stop coming.

Khalid had surrounded himself with his lieutenants. "We can sit out these Romans until they starve in the city, but I feel like I'm wasting my time doing this. Caesar is marshalling his forces while we sit here and wait. I want to keep these Romans off-balance."

"I could send for an army to replace yours," said Ubaidah. "We could maintain the siege here while you proceed up the Levant."

"No. I'll concentrate all my forces together. If we split them, we invite the Romans to defeat us piecemeal. I will strike them like a gloved fist."

"Why do we need this city anyway?" said Shurahbil. "Let us lift the siege and move on to conquest."

Khalid frowned. "No. No, we've started this attack and we must finish it. The Roman must know that we will strike terror wherever we go. We must not back away once the battle is joined. If he knows we will leave if something looks too difficult, he will be more inclined to resist. We must convince him that there's no hope when our armies arrive." He placed his hand on Shurahbil's shoulder, "I agree with you in principle, old friend. There's nothing we need in this city and given the choice, I'd bypass it and find the main body of the Romans. But we cannot quit the field now."

Dhiraar spoke up. "These Romans are farmers. They don't think like us. If we strike where their heart is, we can get their attention."

Khalid raised an eyebrow. "Go on."

Dhiraar made a small gesture with his hand and cast his eyes about. "The fields. They're cultivated and irrigated from the river. The Roman will react if we attack those, as if he had a knife at his throat."

Khalid stepped back from the group and did a slow circle, his eyes studying the plain. The desert was indeed under cultivation. Much like the fields of Medina when the Jews controlled the town. As an Arab, with the nomad Bedouin blood in his veins, he hadn't noticed this. He returned to the group. "Dhiraar, you have a keen eye. I will speak to the Roman commander of the city. I need a translator."

"I speak their language," Shurahbil said. "I will go with you."

Khalid paused thoughtfully to consider. "I will need to talk to these people more. Shurahbil, I need you at the head of my armies. You cannot always be at my side." Turning towards Dhiraar, he asked, "Didn't we pick up some converts in the high desert? Youngsters? Do they speak Greek?"

"I know the ones you speak of," said Dhiraar. "I'll check." He made as if to leave, but Khalid held him.

"Wait, my friend. Shurahbil, you'll accompany me, but say nothing. If one of these boys does speak Greek, I'll need to know if his translation is accurate. Dhiraar, take a hundred men with torches and spread them among the fields to the west, every ten paces or so. When you see banners, light the fields on fire."

Bashour had followed Dhiraar's summons to Khalid and stood in mute awe. The big man was donning his battle armor and issuing instructions. He finally turned and acknowledged Bashour and Dhiraar. "This is the one? Do you speak Greek, boy?"

Bashour nodded. "Yes, Sahib and Latin, too." Bashour's accent sounded sharp and clipped compared to the southern Arabs.

"Good. You'll be my mouthpiece when I talk to these Romans. You'll translate what I say to them. I'm not so foolish to think you'll translate directly, word for word. I want you to convey meaning. You may ask questions, if necessary, to be sure you understand the meaning I intend to convey. When the Roman talks, I want you to tell me not only his words, but what he's thinking, feeling. If he's scared, or unsure, or confident, I want to know your opinion. Can you do that?"

Bashour gulped. He managed not to stammer when he replied, "Yes, Sahib."

They strode out, three of them, Bashour, Khalid and another man that Bashour didn't know, towards the gate of the city. The nameless man carried a white banner held aloft. After ten paces, Bashour could see that the archers on the walls were already paying attention to them. Arrows were turned their way. Khalid held his hands clear of his body and instructed Bashour to do the same. When they had crossed halfway between the Muslim lines and the city gate they stopped and waited, motionless.

Minutes passed. Bashour could feel thousands of eyes of the Muslim army on them, waiting. After a few minutes, Khalid asked, "What is your name, boy?"

"Bashour bin Ghalib, Sahib. Of Tadmur."

"Where did you learn tongues, Bashour of Tadmur?"

"I studied at the feet of my teacher, Imad bin Najib. I learned mathematics, literature, history, philosophy."

Khalid snorted. "You wasted your time, except for the mathematics. You should have been learning to ride and to use a sword."

Bashour flushed. "Yes, Sahib."

They were silent for a time, standing motionless before the gate. Khalid spoke again, "What is a philosopher doing, joining Allâh's Jihad?"

"I've found answers in the book of Allâh's Apostle, peace be upon him. Answers that the priests couldn't provide. I'm following the path of truth."

Khalid smiled. "And I don't suppose that the idea of Allâh's reward in gold and women along this path has any attraction to a philosopher?"

Bashour flushed crimson and the big man laughed. Then, "Ah, they're coming to see what we want. Remember what I told you, philosopher."

The gate of the city had opened a crack and three men stepped out and strode towards them. As they approached, the man carrying the banner murmured to Khalid, "The one in front is Romanus. He's the leader of the city garrison. He's the one I spoke to before. Arrogant dog."

The Romans stopped several paces away from them and the two leaders glared at each other. Khalid broke the silence and Bashour translated his words. "Your city is surrounded and will remain so. As you saw, twenty thousand sheep have arrived to feed my army. There will be many more. We will feast here, even until midwinter if necessary, while you starve."

Romanus responded, "What choices do you offer me?"

"He's angry," added Bashour.

"He has every right to be," said Khalid. He produced a coin and handed it to Bashour. "One of these from every person in the city and his army to surrender all weapons." Bashour examined the coin. It was a gold denarius.

Romanus showed no reaction to the demand. "And if we haven't the gold to pay?"

“We will take the value in goods, supplies, slaves. But if you don’t decide, if you force us to wait, then when you crawl out of your city on empty bellies begging for food, we’ll take you as slaves and loot the city.”

“Assuming our army doesn’t show up and drive you back to the desert.”

Khalid smiled. “Yes, you can always hope for that, can’t you? But even then, how will you eat during the winter?” He nodded at Shurahbil, who lowered the banner slowly. As it nearly touched the ground, dozens of banners in the Muslim lines leapt into the air. Romanus looked around, alert for a trap, or for motion, but could see no danger.

Then smoke began rising behind the Muslim lines. Khalid looked over his shoulder and waited a few moments for it to become thick, then turned back to Romanus. “We will burn your crops for miles around. If you don’t surrender soon, you’ll starve either way. As for me, I have a leg of lamb waiting for me. If you have nothing further to say to me?”

He motioned to Bashour and whirled and strode away negligently, leaving Romanus white-lipped with fury.

25. Bosra, Syria July 8, 634

"Turmarch, what you propose is preposterous." The Bosra council was shocked that Romanus would advocate surrendering his command to the invaders.

"Then, your eminence, please tell us, what choice do we have?" Romanus had spent the night doing the calculations over and over, and couldn't find a solution to his dilemma.

"We stand and hold, until Heraclius sends a relief column." said the Mayor

"A relief column that may never come, Mayor. That second attack came from the north, from Soweida. There's no way they could have hooked to the north like that through the basalt fields of Al Laja. That column came from Damascus. For all we know, the rest of Syria lays in Arab hands."

The eldest member of the council and old veteran in his own right spoke up. "With all due respect, Turmarch, that's just crazy talk. That column did nothing more than skirt Al Laja to the south and capture Soweida before coming here."

Romanus was exasperated. He couldn't abide armchair generals second-guessing his military evaluations. "Even if that's true, where would a relief column come from? Every spare soldier in Syria was ordered to Palestine almost a month ago."

"Heraclius is building his army there and will strike east and relieve us."

"And that's just what these Arabs are waiting for. They'll wait until our army is strung out on the march and they'll strike the flanks and fade back to the desert. These are Bedouins, that's how they fight. Heraclius will try to lure them into a set-piece battle on the ground of his choosing, not let them nibble away at his flanks."

The mayor asked, "Turmarch, we should hold out as long as we can in the hope that we'll be relieved. Do we really lose anything whether we surrender now or later?"

Romanus' frustration sought release and he slammed his fist into the table. "Yes! These are barbarians, councilmen! If we surrender now and pay their tribute, we simply live under their control. If we delay, that dark bastard out there has promised to sell the entire city into slavery." Looks of skepticism greeted his outburst, and Romanus turned away, trying to control his rising anger.

One of the aides behind him stepped forward. "Sir, if I may?" Romanus waved him forward. He stepped up and laid out a sheave of papers. "We have enough supplies in the city to last for two months. Then we starve. We're two weeks past midsummer. In a month and a half will be harvest. How can we harvest under siege? And you saw the smoke yesterday. These Arabs have made clear that they're willing to burn all our fields if we don't surrender. So even if we are relieved in a month, there will be nothing to harvest. The city will starve, come winter, if we don't surrender now."

Romanus turned back, his temper again under control. "They've shown that they can keep their siege in indefinite supply, while we slowly run out of food here.

"For what?" He waved his hand expansively. "Those eight thousand Arabs have twenty thousand friends west of here. This city won't even slow them down. The sacrifice will be for nothing. Think! Do you really think that Heraclius cares about this place?"

The mayor said, "Thank you, Turmarch. We must discuss this. Please, you and your men return to your duties."

The messenger found Romanus in his headquarters three hours later with the message from the council: Surrender the city. He angrily crushed the paper and dismissed the messenger.

Tamara had avoided even thinking about the possibility for weeks. It was simply unthinkable, beyond comprehension. Fear gnawed at her, the not knowing, the dread of the prospect, what she'd do if it happened. She was sure it had been too long, and every day had caused the dread in her stomach to get worse.

The camp was in a general festive mood. The city of Bosra had surrendered and Khalid had ordered the army to stand down indefinitely. She and several other women had been ordered to begin preparing a feast to celebrate. Several men were butchering sheep and she was preparing a broth of lentils when a familiar cramp seized her abdomen. She gasped and gently massaged her side as it slowly went away. Later, when she went to relieve herself and found blood, the dread in her stomach drained away with relief. She wasn't carrying a child.

The relief was magnified that night. Nu'man, when he realized her condition, wouldn't even get close to her. She wondered what she could do to prolong this blessing as long as possible.

Bashour and Marid, along with dozens of other Muslims, were speechless. The myriad winding streets and alleys in the town hadn't impress them much, and the long thoroughfares lined with columns weren't even as grand as those in their home of Tadmur. The columns here were slender, more delicate than those of Tadmur. Bashour thought they looked more Greek than Roman. In his mind he associated Greece with grace and beauty; and Rome with raw, brute strength. The main roads here were paved with huge flagstones that had been absent in Tadmur.

But the group was awed as they approached the outside of the amphitheater. The entrance alone was three levels above the ground, rising higher than ten men. The huge square basalt blocks that formed the building gave it a sense of solidity, as if the entire building had been carved out of a mountain. As they entered, they realized that the floor of the theater was deep below ground level. The whole theater was built into a deep hole, much larger than the impressive outside suggested.

Entering onto the stage, Bashour could easily appreciate the way a drama could be portrayed here. The stage had no fixed backdrop, it was broken up by columns that ascended to the second level, providing crannies and hiding places from which a retinue of actors could come and go as the action required, without obvious artifice. Above the stage were numerous windows and portals from which a chorus could sing commentary to the action below. In front of the stage was a large, paved, circular court, ringed by steeply rising seats, two dozen high in two tiers. Bashour could easily imagine battles fought in miniature in the courtyard, and someone even suggested that the court could be flooded to simulate a naval engagement. Bashour didn't doubt it.

They explored the entire theater. At one point Marid found Bashour and said, "You're not going to believe this. Go up to the farthest seat." He pointed to the top of the seats. Bashour, puzzled, climbed the steep stairs while Marid stayed near the stage. When he got there he turned and waved at Marid below.

To his surprise he clearly heard Marid say, “Can you hear me?” Amazed, he waved again and came running down.

“It was like you were standing right beside me!”

“I know, isn’t it incredible?”

The recreation was short-lived. Soon enough they were put to work in front of the city hall, collecting, counting and recording the tribute being brought in by the citizens and other Muslims. The townspeople were paraded through and each marked with a purple dye on their left hand to show that they’d been counted. Marid was placed in service conducting a census of the Muslims and their mounts, so the spoils could be allocated correctly among those who’d fought in the battle. Bashour was inventorying weapons captured on the field and turned in by the garrison when the city had surrendered. Rashad was helping him, calling out items that Bashour recorded. Bashour was relieved that he didn’t need to deal directly with the townsfolk. Tensions were still quite high. Khalid had placed guards at all the city intersections and foot patrols combed the city, stopping trouble with a show of force before it started.

He was still at it two days later. They’d set up shop in a warehouse that had started empty and was filling rapidly. Bashour and Rashad had divided it in two. One-half was items that had been counted and sorted, the other were things remaining to be inventoried. The counting and inventorying seemed endless. Some Muslims had been put to work policing the battlefield and they periodically came to the warehouse laden with weapons, which they piled in the front to be counted. Jabir had joined them. Bashour wrote as fast as they could count and call out their inventory.

“Seventeen more Roman arrows,” called Rashad.

Bashour had developed a system of columns and made an annotation in the appropriate place. “Is it really that important that we even count the arrows?”

Rashad dropped the arrows in a pile in the back of the warehouse, then slumped on the edge of a table strewn with Bashour’s inventory. He upended a water skin and wiped his brow. The day was growing hot. Though the building’s windows were open to let light in, no breeze stirred the heat. Jabir joined them, grateful for a break in the counting. Inventories were boring, especially for young men, and any excuse to break the tedium was welcome.

"Oh, yes." said Rashad. "Why, after the battle of Khaibar, some of the faithful were hungry after the long siege. They butchered some captured donkeys and boiled them. Allâh's Prophet, peace be upon him, was furious! He ordered them to upend the pots and waste the meat, because they hadn't been counted or valued for the booty inventory."

"That's not why he did that, Rashad," said Jabir. "He forbade the eating of donkey's flesh."

"Why would he do that and still allow people to eat horseflesh? What's the difference?"

"Because Donkeys eat unclean things, so their flesh is unclean."

"Well, how about the time in Dhul-Hulaifa, when we butchered some camels and sheep from the war booty and the Prophet, peace be upon him, ordered us to upend the cook pots, again because they hadn't been counted? We can still eat camels and sheep, or did he make those haram, as well?

Jabir drank deeply and wiped his mouth. "It doesn't matter. Everything has to be counted, down to the last arrow. That's what Allâh's Apostle ordered and that's what we'll do. It used to be easy, but now the army is so large and the booty is so much. I'm glad you can write and do sums, Bashour."

The Muslims disdained sleeping in the city, preferring the more open air outside the walls. Bashour and Rashad had retired from the warehouse to their camp when it became too dark to see. Sameer was poking at the fire, waiting for the pot to boil when Marid appeared out of the darkness and plopped down beside Bashour. "Did you hear the news?"

"What?" Bashour crinkled his nose. Marid's breath smelled of wine.

"The city couldn't produce enough gold to pay the Jizyah, so Khalid ordered those who could not be paid for taken captive."

Bashour looked at Rashad. "What will they do with captives? If they can't pay, they can't be ransomed."

Rashad shrugged. "Sell them as slaves. That's what we've always done."

Marid took a drink from the goatskin he was carrying. "They say we can have a girl for the night from the captives. All you have to do is ask."

Qutayba snorted. “Back of the line, camel-holder. You have to have done something worth such a reward.”

Marid pulled himself to his feet angrily. “Camel holder?”

Qutayba rose to meet him and stepped close, then pulled back. Marid swayed for a second. Qutayba snatched the goatskin from him and put it to his nose. “Wine!” He emptied the skin on the ground and squeezed it dry.

Marid’s fists balled. “Hey!”

Qutayba threw the skin to the dust and shoved Marid in the chest with one hand. The boy stumbled, and the rest of group except Bashour, got to their feet. “Intoxicating drinks are forbidden by the Prophet, peace be upon him.” declared Qutayba.

Marid considered the group that had turned against him. Qutayba pointed. “Go!” Marid’s eyes regarded them all for a few seconds. Then he turned and left the circle of the fire. Bashour tried to look insignificant as the rest resumed their seats, not wanting any attention brought to himself because of his friend.

The idea of a map wasn’t new to Khalid, but never in this kind of detail. He’d diagrammed his plans in dust before, but part of the booty from Bosra included a finely drawn map of the area. It didn’t take long for Khalid to understand how to read it and see where the mountains, rivers and the cities were. This would save him valuable time. He could see what the terrain was, he didn’t have to send scouts to examine the lay of the land. He was fascinated and wanted to sit and examine it in detail, but his staff was assembled, waiting his instructions.

He could see the narrow gap between the basalt field and the mountains to the east that he’d led his forces down. Returning along that route had an advantage in that he was invulnerable from attack from his left flank, but it left little room to maneuver if he ran into a force coming from the north. No, the basalt fields didn’t extend as far as he’d feared to the west. He could return north with them on his right. He’d have to keep pickets out, but he had room to react if he was attacked.

His hand swept an arc across the map. “Shurahbil and I will move towards Damascus along this line. Ubaidah, you’ll copy this maneuver with Yazeed and Amr’s armies to the left of my flank. We will take Damascus, then strike for the coast. This will isolate Palestine. Once we've surrounded them, we can afford to attack them from their rear."

Ubaidah whistled silently through the gap where his front teeth had been. No wonder the Prophet had called Khalid the Sword of Allâh. Only a man as bold as Khalid could translate Bedouin tactics to a scale such as this! But Khalid was missing something.

"What do you expect their army to be doing while we're doing this?"

Khalid looked at him. "Eh?"

Ubaidah tapped the map southwest of Jerusalem. "My scouts have reported a huge buildup of soldiers, perhaps three times our number, in this region. While we're banging our heads against city walls such as Damascus, they could be marching on Medina. Also," he added, "you're not cutting off their supply. This area draws as much food from Egypt as it does from Anatolia, and they have seaports."

Khalid was unused to considering naval matters. How much food could you really ship in boats? He had no idea. But Ubaidah had a good point. Much of his strategy involved seeking the bulk of the Roman army and staying ready to react if and when they found them. But if he knew where they already were. . .

"Shurahbil, when will you be finished with the inventory?"

"Two more days should do it. We've finished the census and have extracted all the tribute we're going to get."

"Dhiraar, how are the troops? When can we march?"

"Sahib, they'll march tomorrow if you wish, but they won't be in top shape until the full moon. They need rest, food, and medical care."

Khalid knew this. Part of his genius as a general was knowing when to push his men hard and when to let them rest. An exhausted army was no army at all. Let the enemy fight exhausted, if he chose. "Supplies?"

"We lack nothing. We're fortunate that the city surrendered instead of being starved out."

He turned to Ubaidah. "How soon can you collect Amr and Yazeed and have them rendezvous at Jerusalem?"

Ubaidah was conservative in his estimate. Nothing would be more disastrous than to make promises to this man that he couldn't deliver. "Fifteen days."

Khalid pondered the map. What was he missing? What could the Roman do to unravel his plan? He could think of nothing. If the Roman came straight at them, all the better. If he moved south, Khalid's plan of encirclement would be realized. If he moved north, well, the Arabs could fade back east into the desert and strike north. If he stayed where he was, Khalid would have his battle.

"We march at the full moon to Jerusalem. Ubaidah, have the other armies meet us."

Ubaidah said quietly, "If you mean to take Jerusalem, I doubt they will roll over as quietly as this place did."

Khalid smiled. "I have no intention of investing Jerusalem. That fruit will be plucked when it's ripe. But if the Roman army is where you say, I mean to shatter it." He looked around, "Questions? Comments?" They answered with silence. "Very well then. Go with Allâh's blessing."

Khalid was glad that the men he sought as advisors had learned not to fill the air with trivialities and nonsense discussion. Now that they'd taken a break from the march, he had a newly acquired slave girl that he meant to have some fun with before they sent her south for auction. He hadn't indulged in such pleasure for far too long.

26. Southwest of Jerusalem July 9, 634

Taticus was at the head of his numeri when they reached the encampment at Elah. The signs of a military camp had been obvious for miles. Once sleepy hamlets were bustling with commerce and a tent city had sprouted along the road, all designed to service the army nearby and separate the soldiers from their coins as painlessly as possible. At the edge of the camp, the functional chaos ended, replaced by military order and cleanliness. He halted his men and was met by a decharch manning a sentry post. The decharch saluted him. "Orders?"

Taticus rummaged in his pack and produced the orders from Psellus. "Thank you, Komes. Please wait while I find your assignment." He turned and disappeared into his tent and was gone for several minutes. Taticus wiped his brow in the sunlit humidity.

The decharch finally returned and handed Taticus a simple map of the encampment. "You've been assigned to the Antioch turma, at the other end of the valley." He gestured eastwards. "Go two millarium, to where the valley turns to the south. Follow the valley another half millarium and you'll find your turma. You've got a good position, upstream from most of the army." He gestured to the location on the map.

The decharch stepped back and saluted. Taticus returned the salute. "Thank you, Decharch." Then over his shoulder ordered, "Ready up!"

Taticus regarded the valley ahead. The valley was level, about a half-mile wide. The hills rose gradually up from the floor on the north, more sharply and abruptly on his right to the south. The road they were to pass was lined with tents from the bulk of the army that had preceded them. He turned to the sergeant beside him. "Kentarch, dress the column. Parade march. Pass the word to look sharp." He'd mostly allowed an at ease march for the last three days since Jaffa. Now that they were on the final leg of their journey they'd be under scrutiny by their fellows and, more significantly, by senior staff on the hillside to the south. He meant to demonstrate that his men were disciplined, ready to fight.

"Group! Ten-hut! For-ard, harch!" roared his Centurion. The tramp of men in step was a comfortably familiar sound to him.

The road was militarily straight through the camp, wide enough for ten abreast to walk comfortably. Taticus studied the camp during the march. The valley was packed with thousands of men. Smoke rose from the field kitchens and men lounged in front of their tents, trying to stay cool in the humid air. Taticus could see no open ground to be used for training. This suggested an army on the move, but many of the tents had a definite air of semi-permanence. Some of these men had been here for weeks. He tried to keep an open mind, but he was getting the feeling that training wasn't a major emphasis for this army. Was he just being ultra-sensitive, having just come from a training command? Had he forgotten what it was to be in the field? He shook his head. No, when he'd campaigned under Heraclius, when they weren't marching or recovering from action, they trained. This army hadn't seen any action and they certainly weren't marching. Taticus felt a sense of unease, mixed with anger, rise in his chest. The lounging soldiers along the road took no notice of his column, a scene that no doubt had been replayed daily for weeks as the valley filled with Byzantine soldiers.

It took an hour to reach the position that had been described to him. He halted the column and had them take up rest positions on the sides of the road, so as not to block it, and went in search of the headquarters. He spotted a red and blue banner and headed for it. Finding the commander, he saluted. "Komes Taticus reporting, with the twenty seventh training numeri, four centuries!"

The commander had been sitting at a table in an open sided tent, fanning himself to stay cool and poring over sheaves of paperwork. He sat back, returned the salute casually and ordered Taticus to stand easy. "Welcome, Komes! I'm Turmarch Curcuas. Taticus. . . Taticus. . . Did we serve together? Nineveh?"

"I was there, sir, with Strategos Psellus."

The commander visibly relaxed. "Goddamned good to have you! There's not enough veterans in this army to go around. Sit, please. What's the status of your men?"

"My men have a day's remaining supply. We're a skoutatoi unit, lacking in a quartermaster section. We landed at Jaffa four days ago and have been marching since. But they're ready to keep marching when necessary. They're young and disciplined, but they lack advanced training."

"That's good time from Jaffa, for skoutatoi."

Taticus squirmed slightly in his seat. "We're skoutatoi on paper, sir. Last month these men were in training. Our equipment is old and truthfully we're equipped more like a menavlatoi with swords instead of pikes."

"Should I change the classification, issue you pikes instead?"

"Oh, no, sir. I don't think that would be a good idea. You need iron nerves to place a pike and hold fast against cavalry. These men are green and if I may be frank, I wouldn't be comfortable trusting them to hold against a charge." Taticus was embarrassed to admit any weakness of his command. "These men have been trained to the sword. They'll stand in battle if they can swing at the enemy."

Curcuas sat back and smiled. "I like you, Taticus. Most men wouldn't have admitted a weakness about their command. I need men I can trust. Now that you've shown that you won't bullshit me, see that you don't start."

"Yes sir!" Taticus smiled back. He had no idea of this man's competence, but it gratified him that he was evidently no martinet.

Curcuas poured wine from a flagon into two wooden cups and offered one to Taticus. Taticus took it, masking his reluctance. His men were baking in the sun, awaiting a billet assignment and he was sipping wine like an aristocrat. "Is there a Mrs. Taticus? Children?" asked Curcuas.

"She was taken in childbirth, sir. I have two children, a son and a daughter. My sister cares for them near Smyrna. The army is my life."

Curcuas bowed his head. "My regrets." He sipped the wine and wiped a bead of sweat from his forehead. The humidity was oppressive. "Taticus. Your family name is. . . ?"

"Yavos, sir."

"A fine name for a commander. I'm not familiar with the family, though. . . from Smyrna you say?"

"I came up through the ranks, sir. My family isn't notable."

"Excellent. Your merit is beyond question, then."

Taticus was uncomfortable discussing his private life with his new commander. “Sir, do you have any idea when we might be ordered to march? I’d like to continue to drill my men.”

Curcuas snorted. “March? Komes, the goat rope that passes for a command structure for this army likely isn’t going anywhere. Have you heard that the Emperor’s brother Theodorus has arrived? Oh, Andrew is still in charge, but will Theodorus interfere? Will Andrew let him? Who’s really in command? A combined command can be a wonderful thing, if the commanders work together, but it can be a terrible curse, a worse enemy than the one who fights you, if they disagree. Theodorus’ record is spotty, he’s known more for his brother and his negotiating skills than his generalship. Andrew’s is unimpeachable. The only battle Theodorus won was against Shahin in Anatolia, and the rumor was that he was already on a boat to Constantinople when the victory was secured.”

Curcuas leaned forward. “Go ahead and drill your troops, Taticus, if you can find room to do so. And pray that these Bedouins return to their desert satisfied, before we have to chase them, because I fear we won’t be able to get out of our own way.” He stood and shook Taticus’ hand as Taticus rose. “Report to the stratopedarches for your billet assignments and rations. I hold a staff briefing every Monday and Thursday morning. I'll expect you there. It’s good to have you, Taticus.”

“I’ve got a prime piece of real estate for your men, Komes,” said the stratopedarches. “Right near the bluff on the left bank, level ground, no one uphill from you. At least until they start loading the hillside with people. Now, there are a few local regulations you need to be aware of. The water isn’t safe to drink. Be sure to boil it first. You may only dig latrines on the uphill side of your camp and they must be dug at least six feet deep. Urinating outside the latrine areas is forbidden. All trash should be policed up and either burned or disposed of in the latrines if it will not burn. Some camp followers from the other end of the valley have figured out we’re back here and they’ve started to set up shop just beyond the end of the valley. You know you can’t stop them,” he winked, “but tell your men that some of those women have the pox, so be careful. “You didn’t bring your own kitchen, so you’ll chow with the chiliarchy. I’ll send a runner with your chow schedule when I’ve figured out how to fit you in.

"You submit any equipment requests through me. I probably won't be able to fill any though. We're having enough problems just getting enough food shipped here. Any questions?"

"Is there a parade ground? Any place I can drill my men?"

The quartermaster snorted. "Good luck! There's some level ground to the south, but we'll have that full of tents soon enough. Everything around here is limestone hills, lots of up and down."

Taticus put his men to work pitching a decent camp and digging latrines in the afternoon heat. He was troubled at the lackadaisical attitude he felt in the camp. These men were bored, with no sense of urgency. The commanders were preoccupied with sorting units, hoarding supplies and arguing about who was in charge of whom. Soon there would be fights, Taticus knew, because young men would find a reason. They always did. The only way to prevent it was to keep them too tired to fight, until the time came to fight the enemy.

And what if the enemy didn't want to fight? This army was too unwieldy to chase down the fleet Bedouins flooding into southern Syria. Taticus was sure that they'd soon be striking south, a spear into the center of the Arab power. Heraclius had defeated the Sassanids that way. Taticus had no doubt that the same strategy would be applied here.

27. Northeast of the Dead Sea, Jordan July 20, 634

Khalid's army had been marching for four days since they left Bosra. The desert vegetation had slowly become more plentiful. The sparse, light-green thorny scrub around Bosra had become so dense that it became difficult to walk for any distance off the beaten trail. This scrub was different from the desert that Bashour was familiar with near Tadmur, where only hardy grass grew beyond the oasis, and even then only for short periods during the rainy months.

Bashour had been aware for some time that to their right the flat desert had given way to a vast chasm, but it was too far away to see any details. The road they were on slowly approached it, until they were standing at the top of a long descent into a huge valley running north and south, as far as the eye could see. The far side of the valley was nearly obscured in the distant haze. Bashour was fascinated by how the flatness of the desert abruptly gave way to the descent into the depth of the valley, as if God had dragged a knife through the earth. Running through the center of the valley was a wide, dark strip. Bashour sucked in his breath. “Have you ever seen such green?”

Qutayba snorted, “That’s nothing. You should see the Euphrates river area. Green as far as you can see.” He squinted at the green strip below them and miles away. “The Euphrates is so wide, you would be able to see it from this distance. I can’t see any actual water down there.”

Bashour’s mouth grew tight and he stayed silent. Every time he made an observation or expressed a thought, one of the others, most often Qutayba, would denigrate his comment or correct him. He was getting tired of it, and resolved to keep quiet.

The column ahead had reached a split in the road. Dhiraar was there, seated on a camel beside a dead tree, directing traffic. “Wagons to the left, all others to the right!” The foot soldiers and cavalry began descending to the valley, the wagons loaded with the loot from Bosra continued on the southward road. Bashour forgot his resolution and asked, “Where are they sending the wagons?”

"They're going south to Medina," said Rashad.

Bashour thought about this for a moment. "What about our shares of the booty?"

"We won't need it where we're going. They'll be waiting for us in Medina."

Bashour felt uneasy about this. He hadn't considered that he'd be going as far south as Medina. He wasn't even sure how far away Medina was. He was certain it wasn't close. The more he thought about it, the more problems he could see with the idea of sending the loot south. Who would watch out for his interest in Medina? The others at least had family to represent them there, but he had nobody. He had a sinking feeling that if he ever made it to Medina, there'd be nothing there for him.

The column had slowed as those in front began their descent into the valley. The path was steep in spots and even those riding the sure-footed camels dismounted to lead their animals. As they approached the split in the road, Bashour could see that the dead tree beside Dhiraar was actually a stone column with writing on it. Qutayba turned to Bashour. "Well, what does it say, Christian?"

Bashour bridled. Qutayba had been trying to pick a fight with him today. "I'm a Muslim, like you, Qutayba Bin Faruq!" He looked at the stone and gestured into the valley. "It says that Jericho is that way."

He thought for a second and then it struck him – Jericho? Then the green belt below him must be the Jordan River. Trees and foliage crowding its banks obscured the river itself. Strange, it wasn't at all how he imagined it would look. He realized he must be standing near where Moses first looked upon the Promised Land. He examined the horizon to the southeast and found the peak of a low hill several miles south of them. That must be Mt. Nebo, where Joshua had led the Israelites across the Jordan, after which they attacked the town of Jericho. He felt excitement rise in his chest at the history that had passed under his feet. He almost said something, but didn't want the scorn of Qutayba to ruin the import of the moment for him.

The descent into the valley was slow. The way was too wide to be called a path, but had no business being called a road. It was impossibly steep in spots; in others it gently dropped along the sides of deep chasms that had cut their way into the valley wall. The sun had disappeared behind the mountains in the far west when the last of the column threaded its way onto the floor of the wide valley. Bashour saw signs of cultivation here, wheat fields and the occasional small orchard, but the people who farmed this land were mysteriously absent. The herds of cattle and sheep that the Arabs drove along with them feasted on the nearly mature wheat crop. The moon, a few days past full, bathed the landscape with enough light to see clearly.

Tamara went about setting up the tent and starting the fire over which she would cook the evening meal as unobtrusively as possible. Her monthly course had ended nearly a week before, but every time Nu'man approached her, she told him that the time wasn't yet finished, that she was still unclean. He took it at face value and did not pursue the matter, seeming ashamed about the whole thing. Was he really that stupid or naïve that he didn't know about such things? How long could she maintain this lie before he found out? Was she making it worse for herself by perpetuating this charade? Deep down it gnawed at her, but at the instant of decision when he approached her, she chose to delay the tribulation rather than face an immediate violent rape. She was afraid of her weakness and dreaded what the consequence might be if he figured out she was playing him as a fool.

The tactic had advantages. For nearly a week, she had been free of pain for the first time since she'd been taken from Qaryateyn. She had only the normal soreness from the march, which caused her to collapse in exhaustion every night.

Her encounters with the other women in the camp were grim. Each woman was locked in her own prison of shame and embarrassment. She'd been granted an occasional weak smile of recognition, a nodded head. But no one dared talk. Tamara was afraid that if she opened up to any of the women, she'd start crying and wouldn't be able to stop. Each of them dealt with their torment privately.

Tamara kept her eyes cast at the ground as she served Nu'man his food, then backed out of sight. He didn't acknowledge her. One doesn't acknowledge a slave, she realized, unless he wanted something. She stayed unobtrusive and made sure he lacked nothing, so he wasn't inclined to take notice of her. She could do without attention of the sort he had to offer.

They crossed the Jordan River the following day at midday. The road dropped steeply into the riverbed, which was much wider than the river itself. Bashour was amazed at the trees. He'd never seen such dense vegetation in such quantity. The oases at Tadmur and Qaryateyn were veritable gardens, where date palms dominated the desert water sources, not the sycamores and other leafy trees that Bashour found here.

He was disappointed at the river itself. He had a mental picture of a formidable body of water capable of sweeping away the unwary, like the flash floods he'd witnessed in the desert wadis. Instead, the river was a sluggish and greenish brown, no deeper than his waist – narrow enough to toss a rock across without effort. His companions snorted and proclaimed that they'd seen irrigation ditches along the Euphrates bigger than this. The real challenge was approaching the crossing. The vegetation was more than head high except on the established path. The trees were so dense in places that only a single file could pass. A bottleneck at the river held up the column as they crossed. Bashour spent the time waiting in fascinated examination of the limestone sculptures that the river had carved in its narrow banks over the years.

The road gradually climbed away from the river behind them. Bashour was again overcome with history, realizing that he'd just crossed into the Promised Land, entered the land that had been forbidden to Moses. Had Joshua led his armies along this very road? He eagerly kept his eyes out to spot some monument to their passage, but of course found nothing. Unable to contain himself, he finally exclaimed aloud, "I think this is where Joshua led the Israelites across the Jordan to attack Jericho."

Qutayba rolled his eyes. Jabir asked, "Who's Joshua?"

"Joshua? He was the general under Moses, who led the Israelite army to conquer Canaan, after they wandered in the desert for forty years."

Jabir looked interested. "Why didn't Moses lead them? Were they lost for forty years? How can that be?" Jabir had crossed huge tracts of Arabia and Mesopotamia in the previous year. Even as big as the desert was, could you be lost for so long? He didn't think so.

Bashour told the tale. "They weren't lost, but they were all prohibited from entering Canaan by God. After they'd left Egypt, Moses sent Joshua and eleven others to scout Canaan and report back. All the scouts but Caleb and Joshua reported that the land was impossible to conquer, that the people were too mighty, the cities too strong. Joshua and Caleb said that with God at their side they could defeat Canaan. The people wept at the reports and God grew angry and told them that even after the wonders they'd seen when they left Egypt, they still had no faith in him. He decreed that no adult who left Egypt would live to enter Canaan, except Joshua and Caleb, because they believed. So they lived in the desert for forty years and after Moses died Joshua was free to attack Canaan."

"That was harsh," said Sameer. "Moses saved the people, just to let them all die in the desert?"

"In a way, yes, but it was God's way of purifying the Israelites. Those who'd lived in Egypt all thought like slaves. You can't make an army from slaves, so a new generation had to be raised and taught to fight. God let the slave mentality die in the desert. It wasn't just individuals he saved, but the whole tribe."

Qutayba said, "These Israelites, they are Jews, right?"

"Yes, the Jews are Israelites."

Qutayba spat. "Pah! Jews are descended from apes and swine, for the transgression they committed at Sinai. Allâh has cursed them for transgressing his law and altering his words. Jews are meant to be nothing but slaves of the righteous followers of Allâh!"

"The Jews are the chosen people of God. They inherited the covenant of Abraham."

Qutayba glared at him. "The Covenant of Abraham, peace be upon him, wasn't just for the children of Israel, boy. The children of Ishmael were Abraham's children, too!"

"If the Jews are the chosen ones of Allâh," asked Jabir, "then why did he command Muslims to kill them in Medina?"

Bashour felt off balance. "What?" he asked with astonishment.

Jabir recounted, "On the day of Al-Khandaq after the battle of the Trench, Allâh's Apostle, peace be upon him, was taking a bath when the angel Gabriel came to him and said, 'You have laid down the arms? By Allâh, I have not laid them down. Go out and attack them.' The Prophet asked, 'Who?' Gabriel pointed towards the Banu Qurayza. So Allâh's Apostle besieged them. They then surrendered to the Prophet's judgment. The Prophet was upset because Sa'ad had been wounded by the Quraysh and allowed Sa'ad to pass judgment. Sa'ad said, 'I give my judgment that their warriors should be killed, their women and children should be taken as captives and their properties distributed.'"

Bashour was confused. "But these Banu Qurayza. . . they were Jews?"

"Oh, yes. They were the last of the Jews in Medina. The Banu Qaynuqa and Banu al-Nadir had provoked the Prophet and we drove them out of Medina. The Banu Qurayza sided with the Quraysh in the battle of the trench and we killed all their men that afternoon in the town square."

Wahid, normally silent, spoke up. "I was there. I never fought any Banu Qurayza, nor do I know anyone who did."

Qutayba looked impatient. "Wahid, they lived in Medina just as we did, when the Quraysh attacked, they did nothing to defend the city. They were hoping for a Quraysh victory."

Wahid shrugged noncommittally and Bashour retreated into silence. He wanted to ask Qutayba how it was that David conquered his enemies and forged a great nation of Israel if the Jews were cursed as Qutayba stated. But he felt that the general opinion would support Qutayba.

What difference did it make? He had no special love for the Jews anyway.

But the lineage of Ishmael posed an interesting line of thought. "Were there any other Prophets born of the line of Ishmael besides Muhammad, peace be upon him?"

Qutayba looked suspiciously at him. "Eh? What are you talking about?"

"Well, the children of Isaac grew into a great nation and many times God selected a prophet to lead the people, or to warn them to mend their ways. Surely Ishmael's offspring had similar experiences."

Rashad smiled. "No, Bashour. Until Muhammad, may he be blessed, Allâh gave no guidance. The Arabs were polytheists and the Ka'aba had been turned into a temple of many false idols. Every family had a special idol that they worshipped. When the Prophet of Allâh returned to Mecca, the first thing he did was to go to the Ka'aba and smash and remove the false idols."

Bashour looked puzzled at this, unsure what to make of this information. "Something bothers you?" asked Jabir.

"I just don't understand how Allâh took such an interest in the Jews of Israel and ignored the children of Ishmael, then out of the blue his last prophet comes from the house of Ishmael."

Qutayba laughed. “That’s easy. Allâh realized that the Jewish prophets were worthless, that no one would listen to them and that their word would be twisted and corrupted and forgotten. So he gave his Qur’án to a real man, who would ensure that not a single word was altered.”

Bashour decided that was logical. It explained the endless debates over the nature of Jesus, based on the misunderstanding that he was like Allâh and not just a prophet. He spent the rest of the afternoon pondering this insight, realigning everything he thought he’d known before in light of this new understanding.

Khalid relaxed as they left the river behind. He never liked moving through overgrowth. He preferred being able to see his enemies from a great distance. Ubaidah approached and rode beside him and reported what he’d heard from returning scouts. “They say there is no garrison at the town ahead. It might have two thousand inhabitants, nothing more. Not even a proper city wall.”

Khalid grunted and was silent for a time. Ubaidah rode patiently alongside him, content that the man would talk when he was ready. Finally, he said, “Order the scouts to avoid contact. We’ll pass to the south of the town and encamp for the night at the base of the mountains.”

The west side of the valley was a series of steep bluffs, occasionally cut by deep canyons where creeks had weathered away the limestone. Ubaidah disagreed with the directive. “We will not invest the town then?” he said placidly. “I’m afraid I don’t understand. Are we going to conquer this country, or just pass through it?”

Khalid waved his hand ahead. “Two day’s march from here is a force three times our size, assuming our friend Amr bothers to show up at the appointed place. I don’t want to give that army time to get organized, much less time to march on us, while we count our treasure from every little wide spot in the path on our way. No, Abu Ubaidah, we will bypass this town, and Jerusalem as well, to get at the Emperor’s army. Insha’Allâh, when we have defeated that army, we can invest towns like this at our leisure.”

Ubaidah admired Khalid. The man was made for war, and war was made for Khalid. What other Arab would pass up a treasure at hand to get at the throat of a far-off enemy? He regarded his dark companion, who rode ahead stoically. Ubaidah could see why Muhammad had hailed him the Sword of Allâh. Never had he seen such a general!

28. Damascus
July 21, 634

Jonas Tournikes stepped out of the warehouse and squinted at the afternoon sun. He held a hand up to shield his eyes from the glare and took a deep breath. Nicetas had kept him in the warehouse all day, inventorying goods. He put up with the boring task impatiently. He hated this work and would have had none of it, if it hadn't been for Eudocia. God, he couldn't wait to marry her. Not only would he be able to hold the body that she'd been denying him for so long, but the wealth of Nicetas would finally solve some of his debts.

As his eyes adjusted, he tugged on his tunic to smooth out the folds and began casually striding towards the market quarter; his mind on the games he was planning to host that night. He turned the corner and merged with the bustle of the market. He paid the vendors no mind. Haggling for bargains was beneath him.

He failed to notice a large shape that came up behind him, or the man approaching him from in front with his eyes cast to the ground. He was passing an alley when the man approaching him unexpectedly veered and slammed into his shoulder, knocking him off balance. Before he could exclaim, he was hit hard between the shoulder blades and the two men enveloped him and spirited him into the alley.

Jonas was off-balance and ineffectually flailed at his attackers. His arms were grabbed and pulled roughly behind him and his face shoved against the rough mortar of the wall. He smelled garlic on the breath of the man who leaned over his shoulder.

"Kostas wants his money!"

He could barely talk with his face being smashed against the wall. "Tell. . . tell Kostas to be patient. He'll have his money, plus interest, when I'm married!"

Someone sank a fist into his kidney, causing him to gasp in pain and his legs buckled, "Kostas is tired of waiting!" They pulled him away from the wall and as he turned his head to see his attackers, he was hit, hard, in the jaw. "If you want to live to see your wedding, a down payment would be advisable."

They dropped him and he curled into a ball as they kicked him several times, then disappeared. He felt a tug at his belt, then they were gone, his coin purse with them.

Jonas rolled over painfully in his bed at the sound of the door opening. He heard his mother saying, "He's been sleeping. He's in a lot of pain, but I don't think it's serious. The doctors said there's no bleeding inside, there's no blood in his urine and nothing's broken."

Then Eudocia timidly entered the room and gasped when she saw his face. She didn't try to be quiet when she saw his eyes on her and he smiled weakly. "Oh, Jonas!" She sat by his bed and ran her hand over his brow. "Do you know who did this to you?"

"Just thieves. I didn't see faces," he said thickly.

His mother spoke from the doorway, "Common thugs! Attacking a man in broad daylight! Honestly, the crime in this city is getting worse. I wouldn't be surprised if they were soldiers. Heaven knows they're paid little enough as it is."

Jonas snatched that thread and amplified it, hoping to deflect more questions that might lead to his gambling problem. "Yes, soldiers, I think. . . ." That accusation would be easy to make. The soldiers that had been arriving from Antioch had a natural antipathy to people like Jonas. He was their age and not under arms.

His mother declared, "Well, somebody should do something. Don't tire him, dear." She disappeared, muttering.

Jonas grabbed Eudocia's hand. "I love you."

"I love you too, honey." Worry lined her face and she gazed into his eyes.

"Let's. . . .let's get married as soon as possible. I don't want to wait anymore." He squeezed her hand.

She patted his hand with her free hand. "Oh, my love, I want to, but there's so much to be done! And Father. . . Father's so concerned about the Arab invasion. They keep saying that the Arabs might attack Damascus. He hasn't had any time and he says you've got to learn more about the company."

Jonas' heart dropped. He needed to get access to money and soon. "I thought you loved me."

Eudocia's face fell and she leaned over and kissed him gently, saying between kisses, "Oh, honey, I do, I do! But there will be time. If you love me, you'll be patient, because I want our wedding to be perfect. And I want you to be a partner in Father's business. Please, be patient, my Love."

Jonas repressed the urge to snort. Partner? As a common merchant? Jonas' view of his future involved a box seat at the races, dressed in finery with good wine and with sycophants hanging on his every gesture. It didn't include sums and figures and accounting and haggling like sellers at the marketplace. Such things held no interest for him, though he hid that in public, pretending to be the obedient son-in-law. Once he had Eudocia's ring on his finger, he could hire people to perform such menial labor.

"Oh, Jonas, what if the Arabs do attack here? How could we get married if there's going to be a battle? Would you go off to war? How could I live if you were gone for years at war?"

"I'm not going to war, Eudocia." Certainly not! The only thing worse than being a merchant in Jonas' mind was being a soldier, or perhaps a priest.

They continued talking for some time. He begged, he wheedled, he plead, but Eudocia held firm and rebuffed his desire to wed. He began to grow angry. Before she could respond in kind, his mother arrived and indicated that he should rest and led Eudocia away.

"Why do you think they'll attack here?" asked Azrail. They were in Thomas' office. Azrail had made a habit of conferring with Thomas every few days, to observe the preparations for the siege. This time he and Harbis had found Thomas and Nicetas poring over a map of Syria. "Why not Jerusalem? Or one of the coast cities?"

"Jerusalem is virtually impossible to capture without a long siege and once captured, would take too many of his men to hold. No, look here." He pointed to the map. "If he takes Damascus, he can use it as a springboard for action throughout the region. His rear to the south and east is already secure and there are only two mountain pass approaches from the north and west. This would make an excellent base of operations for him. He'd have complete freedom of action and it wouldn't take much at all to hold the city. He's headed this way, but he needs to deal with the army in Palestine first."

Harbis spoke up, "We think he's got no more than thirty thousand men at his disposal, do you really think he'd attack an army three times his size?"

"Normally, I would say no. But I've heard some of the tales from Persia. This Khalid, I think he would. And he'd do so with a ferocity that might just earn him a victory."

"At three to one? I'll take that wager." exclaimed Azrail.

"I wouldn't give it," said Thomas. "But I also don't have as much faith in our army. There aren't enough veterans, and Heraclius hasn't moved into the field yet."

Nicetas spoke up. "I'm no military man, but suppose the Arabs beat our army in Palestine. What would we do then?"

"Riding against the Arab is a fool's game," said Azrail. "They would avoid a fight all day, until they found a place suited to them."

"Exactly!" said Thomas. "Their strength is their mobility. We can stand a siege, but we can't rely on relief. Their superior mobility would cut anyone trying to relieve the siege to ribbons. Unless. . ."

The all looked at him expectantly. "What if he couldn't afford to move away from the siege?" asked Thomas. He looked at Azrail. "If we had a large enough force here to threaten a breakout, he wouldn't be able to afford to strip the siege to engage a relief force."

Azrail pursed his lips. "We'd need twenty thousand more soldiers. I don't know if Heraclius would be able to provide that."

"I don't think he would. Not for a garrison. Heraclius is always thinking about attack. Try to sell him on the idea of making Damascus the rally point for a southward offensive. He's got to be thinking along those lines anyway. Get the troops here, assemble them for an attack, and if it turns out they defend. . .?" He shrugged.

"Yes. . . Yes, I can do that. I'll draft the letter this afternoon. Now, how goes the preparation?"

Nicetas had grabbed a quill and was furiously scribbling figures. "Ask me tomorrow. All my figures are based on the current population and garrison. Now you want me to add thousands more."

Harbis pointed out, "Nicetas, don't neglect that the new garrison will likely be Armenians, and they're all vegetarian."

Nicetas stopped writing and glared at him sharply. "Tell me you're kidding."

Harbis shrugged. "Yeah, I'm kidding." This earned him another glare.

"Well, Nicetas," said Azrail, "Hopefully if we get the extra soldiers, a siege won't be necessary. Oh, I heard news that your daughter's fiancé had a spot of trouble the other day?"

"Yes, someone beat him up in the market and stole his money. No one saw anything, even though it was late afternoon."

"I'm deeply sorry. I'll press the captain of the guard to see to it."

"He thinks it may have been soldiers, if that's any help."

Azrail and Harbis exchanged looks. "I'll do what I can. Good day, gentlemen." He nodded and they left.

29. Emessa, Syria
July 21, 634

As the servants cleared the dishes from the meal, Heraclius reclined awkwardly and shifted his weight to the arm of his chair, twisting slightly to try to relieve the stabbing pain in his back. A serving girl was placing mugs of wheat beer before the assembled generals and clergy. He motioned for warm milk instead, hoping to quench the growing fire in his belly from the meal. He normally ate less to try to avoid the burning, but at a meal of state such as this it was difficult to do.

"Gabras, what news do you hear from the Danube?" he asked.

Down the table one of his generals spoke. "Our outposts have been quiet. The Avars seem to have their hands full with an internal uprising. We've been smuggling weapons to the Khan Kubrat and he's giving the Avars a fight over the control of Pannonia. Fortunately, the barbarians have more loyalty to their clans and their Khans than they do to the nation."

Heraclius snorted, "Nation! Nations build and create. What have these barbarians done but loot and steal? I applaud the initiative of whoever thought of arming the enemies within their ranks. It's always good to fight your enemy by proxy, is it not?"

Gabras smiled and nodded, then continued, "There's an issue with refugees, however. Some Fifty thousand Bulgars are seeking to cross the frontier to escape the fighting. General Nicerite has denied them entry, pending a decision from you."

Heraclius pounded the table with his open palm, startling everyone around. "No!" he thundered. "I will not allow more damned barbarians into this empire! You look at what happened to Rome. The Ostrogoths canvassed for asylum when the Huns invaded the Danube valley and Marcian foolishly allowed them in. Then, when he required they pay taxes and provide legions for the empire, they revolted and ended up sacking Rome. No, I will not allow barbarians into this empire who aren't culturally equipped to accept the responsibilities of being a citizen!"

Gabras bowed his head in assent and Heraclius inquired, "These refugees, does it look like it could get ugly? Does

Nicerite have the forces necessary to repel them if they attempt to invade by force?"

"My understanding is that they're mostly non-combatants, families and herds. I think Nicerite is more concerned with the measures he should take if they choose to just ignore the border and enter without permission."

Heraclius' face grew hard. "You tell Nicerite that I'll support him in whatever measures he finds necessary, but those people are not to enter the Empire!"

An older priest glanced at the bishop inquiringly. The bishop nodded slightly and he spoke up. "Basileus, as Christians. . ."

Heraclius cut him off. "Father, Christianity is not a suicide pact. When thieves fight, the wise Christian bars his door. He doesn't invite the lesser of the thieves into his home and succor him until the thief is strong enough to murder him in his sleep. If this bothers your conscience, you're welcome to travel to Pannonia and minister to the Bulgarian tribes. I'm running an Empire here, not a monastic sanctuary!"

He turned his attention back to his generals. "Psellus, what news of the Arab problem?"

Psellus quickly cleared his throat and spoke so everyone at the table could clearly hear him. "We've lost communication with Bosra. None of our messengers sent there have returned. We fear that the city is either under siege or has been captured. There's been a sharp drop-off in raids staged out of Paran. They may have withdrawn back into the desert, but I doubt it. We're not sure where the main force of Arabs is. I suspect they're moving north towards Damascus from around Amman.

"Our army is assembled near Jerusalem. On your order, we can march northeast from Jerusalem and find out what's happening at Bosra. If the Arab is moving north, this will cut off his line of communication and retreat."

"How large a force of Arabs do we expect in this army?" asked Heraclius.

"If they've consolidated the raiders in the south to their army, I think some twenty-five to thirty-five thousand. That might be low. They estimate five thousand appeared out of nowhere east of Damascus, then turned south. They may have joined the main force. It gave Damascus quite a scare."

"Why don't you know where their army is, Psellus?"

"Basileus, our scouts have reported nothing. These Arabs move like the wind when they travel. There's no telling where they might appear . But we expect them to strike at Damascus. That would be a perfect base for them to consolidate their occupation of Palestine, and it would be virtually unassailable from the north and west."

"Is Damascus aware of this?"

"Oh, yes. They got quite a wake-up call when five thousand Arabs marched past not twenty millarium from the city. Azrail has been laying up supplies and has requested twenty thousand more soldiers for his garrison."

"Can we support that?"

"I can't, no, sir. All my forces are with Andrew and your brother in Palestine." He glanced at Caloiis.

"I can provide a meros of cavalry from Anatolia," Said Caloiis. "We can assemble and be in Damascus in a month's time. This would fit with the hammer and anvil plan, if Andrew's army can cut them off in the south."

"Make it two weeks," growled Heraclius. "Libanius should be back in a month. I'll send him on to you as soon as he arrives. Psellus, draw up orders for Andrew to divide his force into three Themata. Two of them will march to Bosra, the third, under Theodorus, will prepare to strike south at the seat of these barbarians. I want an end to this nonsense. I want their leader brought before me in chains."

Bishop Macedonius looked as if he'd bitten a lemon. "Do you think that wise, Basileus?"

Heraclius declined to answer for a long moment as he shifted his weight again. His back was killing him, a pinched nerve that refused to accept a comfortable position. "Speak your mind, Your Excellency," he said irritably.

"Well, they call this man a prophet. Seems that the last time a prophet was brought before a court of Rome, that governor became the most reviled man in history."

"Are you saying you think this man is a real prophet?"

The Bishop shrugged. "I'm saying you don't need to create a martyr."

"It's no matter. I understand their prophet died some two years ago. That's what started the civil war they had."

"As may be. I'd be careful with how I treated any of their leaders. For all we know they may have started a dynasty of prophets, eh? Better that their leader die a quiet and ignominious death and we poison their wells, dismantle their city, salt their fields and scatter their seed to the winds."

"Your point is taken, Bishop, but there's other reasons I need to make a public display of this 'Islam'. Some years ago one of their sycophants appeared before me in court. I questioned him and he gave me serious answers. The man was a fool and may have been speaking out of fear of his companions. I mocked him and proclaimed in jest that this prophet must truly be a holy man of God. Unfortunately, tongues wag and that proclamation has been taken out of context and rumor has spread that I follow an Arab barbarian instead of our Savior. I need to make a public display to dispel this."

The bishop bowed in acquiescence. "As you wish, Basileus. But be careful that in fixing a minor short-term problem you don't create a major long-term one."

Heraclius sniffed at this. His greatest desire was to clean up the corruption and turmoil caused by Phocas, the predecessor that he and his father had overthrown, and restore order to the life of the empire. The judicial system needed to be reformed and he was trying to find funding for a plan for public education for everybody. He was also working on a plan to reorganize the empire into a hierarchy of small, local governmental bodies which would be more responsive to the citizens. All of this was a pipe dream, though, unless he could find a way to end the constant diversions the empire faced in the form of wars, invasions and unrest on its borders.

30. Jericho
July 22, 634

Looking west from Jericho, the mountains looked like an impenetrable wall, rising sharp and brown off the green valley floor. Bashour had been disappointed that Khalid had forbade anyone from entering Jericho. He'd heard rumors that the tree that Zacchaeus had climbed still stood and it would have been wonderful to have been under it, knowing he stood right where Jesus had once stood.

They took the westward road that ran south of the town, and began ascending through a deep canyon. The walls closed in on them and Bashour marveled at the sight of vertical sandstone cliffs on both sides of the road. He studied the layers of rock, wondering at how each layer had a slightly different hue. Some layers were softer than others; the rock rose more steeply on the harder layers. The road grew narrow, hemmed in by the wall on the right and a drop to a small stream on the left.

Rounding a turn, Bashour was amazed to see a building clinging to the side of the wall, nearly directly above where they would pass. Someone had built a foundation that rose to dizzying heights so that it looked like a natural part of the cliff. Perched atop it was a dwelling of some sort. He could see someone at the top of the parapet looking down at the approaching column, having just pulled up the only ladder that provided access. A shout from the front of the column was met by the figure raising a cross. The Arab column passed without challenge.

The canyon widened and gave way to rugged rolling hills after that. The mountains Bashour had grown up with were long, featureless hills. He'd never seen anything like this. The land was like a rumpled blanket, the road winding through sculptured hills, softened by weather into fantastic shapes. Every turn brought surprises, new vistas that he could never have imagined. The canyon made him uncomfortable. He was used to being able to see for miles, all the way to the horizon, but here the mountains broke up his view and the world seemed to close

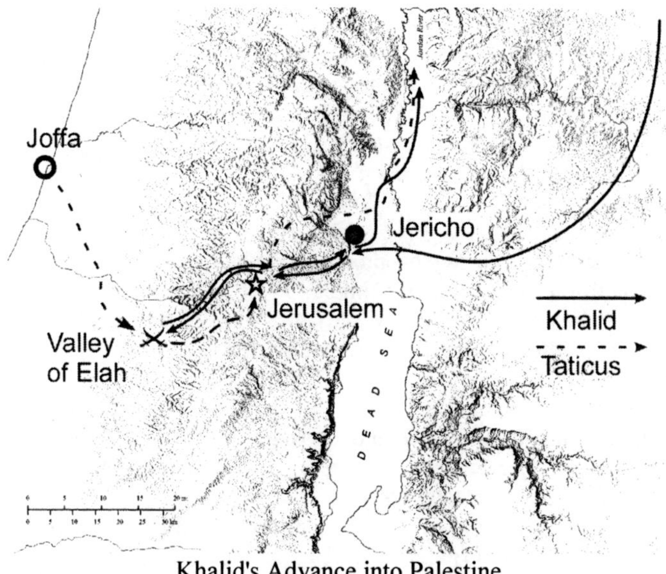

Khalid's Advance into Palestine

in on him. Had he been alone, he would have yielded to the urge to climb the highest hill he could see, just so he could look around.

By midday they were tired, having been climbing virtually all morning. Then, reaching the top of another of the seemingly endless climbs, the road leveled out. The landscape changed abruptly at the summit and the tan hills started to show signs of green. Soon they were passing small settlements. Farmers paused from their work in the fields and orchards to watch the column pass.

The tan grasses gave way to yellow rock, from which stubby evergreen trees and small figs and sycamores made a valiant but incomplete attempt to keep the desert at bay. They began descending in late afternoon and were winding their way among a tangle of hills. The column had spread out in an olive orchard. Bashour and his companions were working their way through the orchard when the ground dropped off abruptly in front of them and there, spread before them was the greatest city Bashour had ever seen.

They were looking across a wide, deep valley. The west side of that valley rose steeply to the base of an enormous wall that seemed to stretch for an impossible distance. South of them the valley and wall turned westward. They were above the top of the wall and could see that the area right behind it was wide and flat and empty, like a parade ground. Beyond this, the land rose, covered with buildings, mostly in shadow since they were looking into the late afternoon sun. Bashour couldn't see the far side of the city.

"Is that. . . ?"

Wahid laid a heavy hand on his shoulder. "That is Ilya, what you call Jerusalem," he said simply.

Jerusalem! The City of Peace! Zion, Ariel, the City of David! Excitement gripped Bashour's chest.

Khalid regarded the walls of the city analytically. The defenses hinted at the tremendous wealth of the city. Shurahbil approached. "As-Salāmu `Alaykum, Sahib! A messenger from the city wishes to speak with you."

Khalid glowered at him. "I sent you to gather intelligence about the city, not bring me messengers."

Shurahbil smiled. "Yes, Sahib. I've done both. We questioned several farmers and travelers. The city's fortified with 25,000 men and enough food to last for more than a year. There's a well, water in deep caverns, so they will not thirst."

"Very well. Send the messenger away."

Ubaidah, riding beside him, asked, "You don't want to at least hear him? He may be here to surrender the city."

"He's not. We haven't enough men to force those walls and they can wait in there while we starve. Even if he were, you have to think ahead. If we take this city, we must hold it. Somewhere nearby is an army three times our size, and I have no wish to be besieged by it in this city. Our only advantage is maneuver and surprise. I don't want to talk to anyone from that city and be forced to make threats I'm not prepared to act on.

"We camp tonight north of the walls. Put listening posts as close to those walls as you dare and watch the gates. I don't think they have the nerve to come out and try us, but I don't want to be surprised."

As they finished evening prayers and began collecting the small rugs they used to kneel on, Rashad spoke, "Once we prayed towards Jerusalem. Then Allâh's apostle, peace be upon him, instructed us to pray towards the Ka'aba in Mecca. Tonight I have faced both."

Bashour regarded him quizzically. "Really? You used to pray towards Jerusalem?"

"For about a year and a half," said Jabir, "after the Muhajirun migrated to Medina, we prayed towards Jerusalem. We did so in respect to the Jews of Medina who invited the prophet, peace be upon him, to teach there and helped him financially. But then the Jews were revealed as traitors and turned their backs on Islam; and Allâh's apostle, may he enjoy Allâh's blessing, wished that his Qibla would be the Ka'aba. Allâh then revealed to him that he may change the direction of his prayer."

They were camped on a hill north of the great city and could see the lights of fires in the city. After the meal, Rashad was instructing him on passages from the Qur'án. "I think we were reciting The Heifer." He began to recite, with Bashour repeating each ayat.

"O Children of Israel! call to mind the special favor which I bestowed upon you and that I preferred you to all others for my message.

"Then guard yourselves against a day when one soul shall not avail another, nor shall compensation be accepted from her, nor shall intercession profit her, nor shall anyone be helped from outside.

"And remember that Abraham was tried by his Lord, with certain commands, which he fulfilled; He said: 'I will make thee an Imam to the nations.' He pleaded: 'And also Imams from my offspring!' He answered: 'But my promise is not within the reach of evildoers.'

"Bashour! Are you listening?" Bashour had failed to repeat the last ayat and was staring at the city, deep in thought.

"I'm sorry, Rashad. I was just thinking that Christ was crucified here, in this city. I wish we could go inside the walls and see. My teacher back home, Imad, told me that they'd built a chapel on the site of his tomb, where he rose from the dead."

Qutayba snorted loudly. "That's a lie that Christianity teaches! I thought we taught you that? Jesus was never crucified. Allâh confused the crowd and made them see Jesus, but they really crucified Judas the traitor."

Bashour knitted his eyebrows. Yes they had said that, but now, here looking at the city, he wasn't sure if he believed it. "Where did you hear that?"

Qutayba's eyes flared and he made as if he would rise from his seat by the fire, but Jabir placed a hand on his shoulder and said quietly to Bashour, "Such was revealed to the Prophet, peace be upon him. In the sura of Women, it says, 'And for their saying, "Verily we have killed the Messiah, Jesus the son of Mary, an Apostle of Allâh." Yet they killed him not and they crucified him not, but they had only his likeness. And they who differed about him were in doubt concerning him: No sure knowledge had they about him, but followed only an opinion and they did not really kill him, but Allâh took him up to Himself. And Allâh is Mighty, Wise!'"

Bashour digested this information for some moments. Then he said, "So you say that when they came for Jesus, Allâh placed a confusion on them, and they seized Judas, thinking he was Jesus, and they crucified him in Jesus' place?"

His companions all smiled and nodded.

Bashour continued to regard the city as the stars turned above them. What the Muslims taught him made sense, more sense than believing that someone rose from the dead. Would it be less effort for God – Allâh – to place a geas of confusion on the Jews, than it would be for a man to die and then rise again? It had happened before, in the wilderness of Tekoa, when the Lord had confused the enemies of Jehoshaphat and they turned and killed each other in their confusion.

That would explain the apparent resurrection. Even Jesus' disciples had been confused and they believed he'd risen from the dead and all of Christianity was based on something that had never happened.

Bashour felt a sense of clarity. Islam had removed the confusing questions of Christianity and replaced it with something that actually made sense. He gave silent thanks to Allâh for guiding him on this journey of discovery and showing him the truth.

31. Damascus
July 22, 634

Thomas enjoyed getting out of the bustle of the city during the short walk from the Damascus east gate to the monastery. In less busy times, he and Epiphina took horses into the orchards beyond the city to picnic and enjoy the quiet of nature, free of the commotion and smell of the crowded streets. He'd hoped that at Damascus life would be more sedate and give him more time for the leisure he longed for. The Arab invasion had rudely interrupted those plans.

A young friar answered his summons at the Monastery and called for Abbot Lecanepus. "Thomas! A surprise! Come, I must show you my melon crop. They're nearly ready to harvest." As they walked through the monastery towards the gardens, he went on, "We have an excellent crop of turnips as well, more than we can possibly eat. You're welcome to take the excess and add them to your stores."

Thomas demurred, thanking the Abbot for his generosity and hinted that he'd send someone around to pick up the bounty. "But Father, don't you think you should transfer the monastery inside the city walls until the emergency is over?"

The Abbot stopped and regarded Thomas intently. "Do you really think that the Arabs would mount a siege against Damascus?"

Thomas considered for a moment. "I do, Father," he said firmly,

The abbot resumed walking. "I understand you haven't sent your wife to be with her father."

Thomas understood what the Abbot was driving at. "No, we discussed it and decided that doing so might cause a panic."

"And so might moving the Monastery into the city. No, Thomas, even should the worst happen, I think we'll be quite safe here. From what I understand, these Arabs seem to have a great respect for religious devotion. Besides, if they do put the city to siege, how could we witness to them from inside the walls?"

Thomas regarded the Abbot. "Are you very brave? Or a fool?"

The Abbot laughed with him. "A brave man does what he must, despite his fear. A fool doesn't know enough to be afraid. I'm afraid by that definition, I'm a fool. Here, look at these melons. Have you ever seen such a succulent crop?"

Thomas made appropriate noises of praise, though he knew nothing of melons or gardening. Then he asked, "Surely you wouldn't object to storing the monastery's valuables in the city for the duration? I think it could be time to have your gold works polished and mended, could it not?"

"Greed does have a way of interfering with piety, does it not? Yes, your point is well taken. I think we should lead our adversary not into temptation. I approve of your suggestion, Thomas."

"Very good. I'll have Azrail send a guard detail to escort your consignment. Is tomorrow too early?"

32. Southwest of Jerusalem
July 22, 634

Andrew excused himself from the command tent and walked into the midmorning sunshine. He stretched and looked at the sky, then paced slowly along the top of the ridge. His headquarters was set up among the ruins of an ancient fortress on the low hill south of the Valley of Elah. From here he could nearly see the entire valley below him, from the west entrance of the valley all the way to where it turned south to his right. He imagined the history that this valley held. Locals insisted that David slew Goliath here. If so, then he must be standing where the Philistine generals stood and the Israelite army must have been arrayed in the low hills to the north, across the valley from him, about a millarium away.

It must have been a simpler time then, when people rallied around a king to defend their land. Now. . . Now they had no king, just an Emperor – a Basileus, as he styled himself. His power derived from his ability to seize his throne and maintain it. Not a king, like the biblical kings, whose power derived from divine decree. How much loyalty did he owe to a man who'd seized power by defeating and executing the previous Emperor Phocas; however much Phocas had it coming?

He had to admit that Heraclius was a masterful strategist. But Heraclius was 300 millarium away. Andrew would have been more comfortable about his command, had not Heraclius' brother, Theodorus, not shown up. Andrew was still in nominal command, but unsure if Theodorus had the authority to overrule him at any time. Too many of his staff and commanders were political appointees, with no real battle experience. They treated this as a lark and were uninterested in drilling the troops or preparing for a long march. Now they were bickering over how the march would be divided. Orders had arrived last night to march two-thirds of his army towards Bosra and the rest to strike south into the heartland of Arabia. Theodorus was maneuvering to take command of all the elite units with combat experience, on an expedition that showed little chance of meeting an armed resistance. Andrew had spent the morning making the case that the few combat seasoned units belonged under his command, where they would likely meet the Arab army hiding somewhere in the Syrian desert.

Drawing up marching orders was hard enough without such a complication. He had to determine the order of march, individual units needed to be given their position instructions. Supply units needed to be prepared and instructed where they needed to be. Provisions for the march needed to be issued. If any other commander had caused this sort of problem, Andrew would have simply relieved him, but you can hardly relieve the brother of the Emperor, can you?

He closed his eyes and was taking deep, calming breaths, when Theodorus called out to him. "Andrew! Come quickly!"

He pursed his lips in irritation about the informal familiarity and returned to the headquarters. A messenger was there sweating and panting. As Andrew entered, Theodorus commanded, "Repeat what you just told me."

"Yes, sir. Uh, a large force of Arabs, some thirty or forty thousand, camped outside Jerusalem last night. They made no attacks and refused to meet the delegation that we sent. They came from the east, from Jericho."

Andrew and Theodorus looked at each other. "The reports of riders that people have seen from a distance. . ." started Theodorus.

"Scouts!" exclaimed Andrew. "You can bet they know we're here." He turned toward the messenger. "When were you sent?"

"Before dawn, sir. The sky was just turning light."

"Were you followed? Do you know where they went?"

"No, sir."

He realized he had no time to deliberate on this news. "Assume they're coming this way. Strike the camp. Deploy the army on the south slope, off the valley floor. I want that valley clear, with nothing for anyone to hide behind. I will not tolerate an obstructed range for the archers, do you understand? If it won't move, I want it leveled or better yet, buried. Once established on the south slope, instruct the men to dig in and prepare for an archery attack.

"Theodorus, you take the themata on the left, Exazenus, you'll command the right and I'll be in the center.Get scouts out. I need to know where that army is, where it's heading and exactly how big it is. How many of them are foot soldiers and how many cavalry?"

For once, Theodorus didn't add anything or argue. His commanders scrambled to get to their units. Soon horns could be heard throughout the valley and the camp burst into life.

The Muslim army rested at midday as Khalid took a small reconnaissance force forward. Scouts had reported contact with the main enemy force in a valley a day's ride from Jerusalem. They'd spent the morning clambering up and down hills that seemed to run crossways to the direction of their march, but now the nape of the hills ran in the direction they were marching. They were riding a tree-lined slope, staying off the ridge line to keep from exposing themselves to view. Dhiraar had nervously put outriders fanning in front of them to warn of a possible ambush. Soon the small valley along which they were moving merged with another and grew wider. Khalid led them across the valley and west over a small rise. They found themselves looking over a wide, long valley with a small stream, but no crops. The valley floor was brown and beaten. Across, at the base of the far slope, Khalid could see the remnants of a large group of men clambering up the hill. His eye cued to the scale; soon he could pick out positions on the steep hillside, and realized that the far side of the valley was crawling with soldiers.

Khalid gestured. "Abd ar-Rahman, your force will bivouac on the right along this slope. Sa'id ibn Amir, you'll move to the left and set up on that west-facing rise, from that outcrop south. Mu'adh ibn Jabal, you'll take the center position, from right here to Sa'id's flank. Yazeed will be in the small wadi behind us with the reserve. Shurahbil, you'll transfer your foot infantry to Sa'id and protect the left flank with cavalry. Ubaidah will do the same on the right, with his foot soldiers going to the son of the Caliph. We will establish our positions and wait. The men need rest. If we can avoid fighting for a day or two, so much the better. Any questions?"

No one answered, and the commanders separated to examine their assigned terrain before returning to the army to issue deployment instructions.

33. Southwest of Jerusalem
July 25, 634

"How's the arm?" asked Bashour as he seated himself across from Qutayba.

Qutayba flexed his arm, making a fist and winced. "It hurts less every day. Praise be to Allâh, it escaped infection."

They were camped near the top of a reverse slope, well behind the lines the Muslims had formed on the north slope of the valley, across from the Byzantine army. Here were the non-combatants, mostly women and the herds that the Muslim army dragged with them and collected on the way. Bashour and Marid had been detailed to help guard the camp, along with the walking wounded such as Qutayba. The rest had been sent into the line.

Qutayba tipped a pot into the dust. A thin trickle of water moistened the soil. "We need water."

Bashour took the empty buckets and started working his way through the camp to the stream. The camp was mostly women and they chattered a lot. He was greeted as he went, the ubiquitous, "As-Salāmu `Alaykum!" which he returned in kind. These were Arab women who'd followed their men into war, and they treated it like an outing at the summer fair. Among these women were silent wraiths, slave girls and those captured by the Muslims on their march. They avoided his eyes and slipped by unobtrusively, nervously.

The bank to the streambed was steep and slippery with spilled water on the limestone dust. A woman was struggling to climb it as he picked his way down. Just before he reached her, she slipped, spilling her water. She dropped the jug she'd been carrying and let herself slide to the bottom and sat there, her face buried in her hands, shoulders heaving.

Bashour was concerned and reached the bottom through a controlled slide. He put down his buckets and picked up her jug and refilled it and carried it back to her. He squatted beside her and laid a hand on her shoulder. "Don't cry, Sister. I'll help you up the hill."

She flinched away violently at his touch and glared at him. The movement caused her headpiece to come loose and fall on her shoulders. His heart caught as he recognized the girl he'd stopped in the desert weeks before. He suddenly didn't know what to say.

"I. . .I'm sorry. Look, I'll help you." He took her jug and scrambled up the slippery path and set it at the top. She followed and had some trouble. He offered his hand. After a moment's hesitation, she took it and he hauled her to relatively level ground. "I'm Bashour," he said. "You're Tamara, right?" He had been repeating the name to himself since the night he saw her in the high desert.

She averted her eyes and said in a small voice, "Yes." He struggled for something to say in the awkward silence. Her eyes filled with fear. "I have to go," she said, and picked up her jug and hurried off.

Bashour filled his water buckets, kicking himself for acting like a fool, standing there without knowing what to say. Did she remember him, did she recognize him from the night he'd stopped her escaping? No, it wouldn't do to remind her of that. God, I'm an idiot!

Theodorus grimly surveyed the valley and the Muslim encampment on the north slope. Yes, Andrew was correct, the fight would be here, in the valley. Flankers on either side were eyeing one another warily, each unable to get around the other for an advantage. As he watched, a lone Arab horseman rode onto the valley floor and pranced in front of their lines. The faint shouts of Arabs reached his ear, as the other army cheered their champion. With a flourish, he removed his cloak and flung it, leaving himself bare to the waist. Then he turned his horse and leisurely started riding across the valley. Theodorus motioned one of his aids closer. "Mount three squads of cavalry and capture that maniac. I want him questioned."

The bare-chested horseman was within easy arrow shot of the Byzantine lines and had turned to ride down the lines when a dozen cavalry reached the valley floor and converged on him. Unalarmed, he casually turned his horse and leisurely cantered back towards the Arab lines. As his pursuers drew near him, he increased his pace to a canter, not too fast to outrun them, but to make the chase longer. Theodorus suspected a trap and hoped the cavalry commander had the sense to stay out of arrow range.

The lone horseman suddenly whirled his mount around and produced a lance. He charged, surprising the pursuing cavalry.

He'd run through the first and had dismounted a second before anyone could react. The others reacted with surprise and got in each other's way in the turmoil. Riderless horses dashed about, adding to the confusion, and the lone Arab calmly dispatched two more cavalrymen. He moved as if the horse and he were one, sidestepping and turning so he was only facing one attacker at a time. The cavalry swords were no match for the reach of his lance and the man was a master at his weapon, keeping it moving, not allowing it to be trapped or broken. More than half a dozen men were dismounted; of those only two were moving, scrambling back across the field. The lone Arab charged two more, sending them scattering.

Theodorus ordered, "Two more squads! Quickly!"

The remaining cavalry on the field lost their nerve and fled, meeting their reinforcements at the base of the hill. The lone Arab held his lance over his head in triumph and galloped back to his lines.

Khalid strode through the cheering Muslim soldiers as Dhiraar pulled his horse to a stop and began picking its way up the hill. The horse was blowing hard and Dhiraar was grinning broadly. He dismounted in front of Khalid, who scolded him. "What do you think you're doing? I sent you to reconnoiter their lines, not to instigate an attack and start a duel!"

Dhiraar's smile didn't falter. "By Allâh!" he said loudly, "If I hadn't known of your disapproval, I would have pursued the Christians and killed every one of them!" The soldiers cheered at his proclamation.

Khalid took him roughly by the arm and marched with him. "By Allâh, you'll damn well start following orders!" he said quietly and roughly through gritted teeth. "I'll be the one who decides when to start this battle, not you!"

Dhiraar showed no remorse. He just smiled and waved at the soldiers who clapped and cheered their hero.

34. Southwest of Jerusalem
July 25, 634

Andrew and Theodorus were in the command tent after sunset, reviewing their dispositions with the command staff. A messenger appeared and whispered to Exazenus, who nodded. "Sir," he said to Andrew, "There's someone here with information about the Arabs."

"Well, let's hear him."

The messenger ushered in a man dressed in plain woolen weave. He introduced himself. "I am Diya Al Din ibn Hadaad, a farmer with a small piece of land just to the north. My family is from Arabia and we are Christians. I've spent the last two days with the army you face, selling them vegetables. I have seen many things." He looked from person to person, their faces impassive. He swallowed and wondered if he should wait for a coin before continuing, then decided that he stood to be rewarded more, if he didn't force the issue.

"Yes, go on," commanded Andrew.

"These men, they are strange, not like the Arabs my father told me about before he moved here. These men, they live like monks during the night, by day they're like warriors. If the son of even their ruler were to commit theft, they'd cut off his hand. If he were to commit adultery, they'd stone him to death. They are severe and enforce righteousness upon themselves. Never have I heard of such discipline."

Exazenus crossed himself. "If this is so, I'd rather be laid in the ground rather than meet such an army on its surface. I fear that such adherence to God's laws are pleasing to the Lord and I would not receive his blessing if I battled such a people."

"Silence!" roared Andrew. "Cubicularius, have you lost your nerve? What kind of talk is that? Has your piety gotten in the way of your command ability?"

Theodorus tried to calm the meeting. Exazenus was obviously near panic. "Andrew, these are not decadent Persians, nor are they the desert barbarians we thought them to be. Perhaps they could teach Christians a thing or two about piety?"

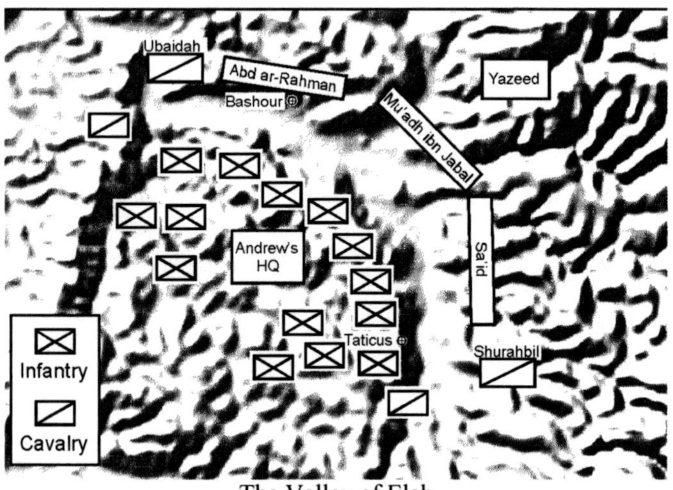

The Valley of Elah

Andrew bunched his fists in anger and suppressed an urge to respond angrily. "Clear the tent," he demanded. Aides and lower ranks scrambled out, leaving only the three commanders.

Andrew placed both fists on the table, leaned forward and said quietly, "We're on the eve of battle. We face an enemy who not only intends to kill us, but went out of his way to seek us out and challenge us. Under our command is a half-trained army of highly superstitious men, and if they hear talk like this from their commanders, they'll desert the moment the first arrow flies! I don't give a goddamn if you think that Christ and his twelve apostles are at the head of that army; if you breathe one more word of this, I'll relieve you of command, clap you in irons and ship you to the Bulgarian frontier! If necessary, I'll cut your tongue out in the process to keep you from infecting my army with your wild notions!" He glared at Theodorus, "If you have a problem with that, take it up with your brother, or take over this command here and now and answer to Heraclius yourself."

Andrew knew he'd overstepped propriety, but was too furious to care. Talk like this cost lives. The die was cast, the next moments could be the end of his military career.

Theodorus blinked first and lowered his eyes. Andrew drew himself up. "If either of you harbor any doubts about your ability to command, say so now, and I'll reassign you to the rear with a full recommendation."

After a quiet moment, Exazenus muttered, "Not necessary, sir." Theodorus just shook his head.

Khalid moved like a cat through the Muslim lines, stopping occasionally to speak to the soldiers. Across the valley they could see the many fires of the opposing army. They had many more fires than the Muslim camp. Khalid was worried. He'd never fought a pitched battle such as this before, on an open field with no room to maneuver. He considered the possibility of withdrawing under cover of darkness and seeking a more hospitable battlefield. Had this been the open desert, that's just what he would do, but this country, it was broken and hilly, with draws and wadis and scrub forests that one could lose an army in. He knew that in such terrain he couldn't maintain command control, nor could he use his superior mobility to its best. No, the flat open land of that valley was the best place to meet these infidels, even if they outnumbered him three to one.

He entered the circle of one fire and was greeted warmly. He inquired about the rations and was satisfied that spirits were high. Then he encouraged the men. "Know that you have never seen an army of Rome as you see now. If Allâh defeats them by your hand, they shall never again stand against you. So be steadfast in battle and defend your faith. Beware of turning your backs on the enemy, for then your punishment will be the fire. Be watchful and steady in your ranks and above all, don't attack until I give the order." He left them nodding enthusiastic agreement.

He encountered a band of archers further down the line. Again he stopped and inquired of their welfare and again he was impressed by their morale. "You saw how the Romans at Bosra employed their archers? How the arrows rained from the sky and if you stepped away from one, you stepped into another?" They nodded solemnly. " I want you to shoot like that in this battle. No more shooting arrows individually. There will be too many enemies to pick out targets, and our forces will be engaged across your line of aim. I want your barrage to fall like hail among their second ranks, in clouds of arrows like blackflies. All of you draw and loose at the same time, so the Romans cannot get out of the way. I know you haven't fought like this before and no one will be able to count your glory, but the glory is Allâh's and all praise goes to him!"

He continued through the night, touching as many men as he could individually with his words, and every man felt singled out by their commander and worthy of his faith.

Taticus wasn't on guard detail, but was outside his line when he heard a noise in the darkness. "Halt! Who goes there?"

"Andrew, Strategos of the Army!"

"Come forward and be identified."

The man stepped forward and Taticus studied him in the weak light of the distant campfires around them. Satisfied, and a bit embarrassed for challenging his senior general, he saluted stiffly. "Welcome, Commander."

"At ease, Komes. Your name?"

"Taticus, of the twenty-seventh skoutatoi of Antioch, sir."

"I said at ease, Taticus. You did perfectly right in challenging me in this darkness. No sane person moves around at night in an armed camp."

"Yes, sir."

"How are your men, Taticus?"

"Rested and ready, sir."

The two men regarded the Arab fires across the valley. "As far as I'm concerned, Taticus, your men can get all the rest they need. I'm content to wait here in this stalemate for the rest of the summer."

"Sir?"

"How long have you served, Taticus?"

"Going on seventeen years, sir."

"You fought the Sassanids?"

"I was with Heraclius at Nineveh, sir."

Andrew nodded. "What's your analysis of the situation, then?"

Taticus swallowed. "Permission to be frank, sir?"

"I insist."

"The enemy has our lines bent on an inside curve. This valley is a poor place to pick a fight; it's narrow and long and has no room to maneuver."

"Yes, quite correct. But we have an overwhelming numerical superiority. We have no need to maneuver."

"Yes, sir," Taticus reluctantly agreed. "But our army is mostly poorly trained recruits and has no experience in coordinating operationally. They're untested and the enemy is battle-hardened. The numerical advantage might not be as significant as it sounds."

Andrew regarded Taticus' profile in the dark, as the other man continued to study the enemy's positions. How many of his officers would have the courage to say what they thought, even if it wasn't what he wanted to hear? "Exactly, so, Komes. Which is why I'm not eager to fight. Every day we wait here is a day more that the cities to the north can prepare in the event we somehow fail."

"Yes, sir."

"I've got to check the rest of the line. Good work, here, Komes." He started to go, then turned back, "Taticus?"

"Yes, sir?"

"You're in a position below your ability. Be sure you come see me when this is over. I have a posting for you more in line with your abilities."

"Yes, sir!"

35. Southwest of Jerusalem
July 30, 634

Andrew was awake as dawn broke over the valley. The strange chanted calls to prayer came drifting across the valley from the enemy camp. Beside him was Sergius, the bishop of Joppa, who'd marched with the army. "What is that sound?" asked Andrew.

"I'm told that it's their call to prayer, which they do as the first thing every morning," said Sergius.

Andrew accepted a cup of hot wine from an aide and sipped it, muttering, "I wish that all they did was pray. Why couldn't they stay in their desert if all they wanted to do was pray?"

The other side of the valley was still for some time, then a trickle of soldiers descended from the opposite hill and took up a position on the edge of the valley. Andrew had withdrawn to his headquarters and was finishing breakfast when he was notified of the movement. Hurrying to the top of ridge, he saw the Arabs forming in battle lines. He quickly issued orders to deploy for battle, causing a mad scramble as trumpets blew to alert the army along the line.

Andrew went to Archbishop Sergius. "Old friend, may I ask a favor of you?"

Some time later, Sergius walked past the front line near the center of the valley, wearing his robes and carrying his crozier and wearing his miter. With him was an unarmed soldier, who claimed to be fluent in Arabic. They strode confidently across the field until they'd reached a point halfway across the valley, at which point they stopped and stood.

Minutes passed and Sergius could feel thousands of eyes on him. Then a man rode forward on a fine horse and approached him. Sergius studied the big man with the black chain mail and a bright-red turban over his iron helmet. The man pulled up and regarded him from atop his horse, looking down on them.

"Are you the commander of this army?" he asked through the translator.

The big man replied with a sweep of his arm towards the Muslim lines. "So they regard me, as long as I obey Allâh and follow the example of His Prophet, peace be upon him. If I fail in this, I have no command over them and no right to be obeyed."

The Bishop pondered this for a moment and muttered, "It is thus that you conquer us."

"Your Excellency?" asked the translator.

"Never mind that. Tell him, know that you have invaded a land that no king dares to enter. The Persians entered it and returned dismayed. Others also came and many paid with their lives, but could not attain what they sought. You've won so far, but victory doesn't permanently belong to you.

"My master, Andrew, is inclined to be generous with you. He has sent me to tell you that if you take your army away from this land, he will give each of your men a dinar, a robe and a turban. For you, there will be a hundred dinars and a hundred robes and a hundred turbans. We have an army numerous as the stars and it is unlike the armies that you have met before. Heraclius has sent his mightiest generals and his most illustrious bishops with this army."

The Arab threw back his head and laughed. "You think you can buy peace with such a trivial tithe from the vast riches of your cities? Why would I settle for such a thing when I can have all that and much, much more after I've defeated you?" He leaned forward in his saddle, looking the Bishop in the eye. "Go back to your master and tell him to pay the Jizyah for every man woman and child in this land in perpetuity, accept Islam, or die!"

He wheeled his horse and kicked it into a canter and returned to his lines.

"He what?" roared Andrew.

"He said. . ." started Sergius, but Andrew cut him off.

"The nerve of that son of a bitch, to dictate terms! Exazenus! Theodorus! Order the archers and slingers forward. Start a barrage on their line. Screen them with skoutatoi. If the Arabs advance, have them pull back as necessary."

The ranks of archers and slingers marched out in formation. Taticus eyed their deployment critically, noting how the units tended to waver and grow ragged near the edges; a sign that they hadn't been drilled enough. When they were within range of the Muslim lines, some ways beyond the center of the valley, the formations stopped, the slingers in front of the archers. On command, they unleashed a barrage into the Muslin line. It wasn't as crisp as Taticus would have liked, but the ragged flow of arrows was still powerful enough to be effective.

The Muslims scrambled for cover. Some ducked behind rocks and what short trees they could find, most tried to make themselves small under their shields. Some few stood and bellowed their contempt. Those didn't last long. The plunging fire was thick, and accuracy wasn't an issue when there was no way to move to escape the falling arrows. Men cried out as stray limbs were pierced.

In Yazeed's command, Muadh ibn Jabal, one of the companions of the prophet, began rallying his men between barrages, exhorting them to rise and advance on the archers to disperse them. As he moved from position to position, Khalid found him and called to him across the battlefield. "Muadh! What are you doing?"

"Sahib, these Romans have superior bows to ours! We can't reach them and counterattack! We must assault their lines and stop this barrage!"

Khalid quickly closed the gap between them and together they hunkered down, seeking what cover they could. "Muadh, stand down! It's far too early to start this battle. We can't fight until late in the day, or else the weight of the Roman numbers will overwhelm us."

"But Sahib, are we to just sit here and die? How can we win if we don't attack these dogs?"

"By Allâh, I will not give these infidels a whole day to practice slaughtering the faithful! Allâh will grant us victory, but just in case, I want darkness close at hand should we have to retreat. You'll get your chance, Muadh, but on my schedule, not yours."

Khalid continued to move among his men, exhorting his commanders to stay put and absorb the barrage. After half an hour, the downpour of arrows fell off to a gentle rain, as the archery units were firing their arrows faster than they could be supplied from the enemy lines. This gave little respite, because the slingers seemed to have an inexhaustible supply of stones from the creek bed. The Muslims learned quickly and the casualty rate dropped off as those who hadn't been wounded in the first attacks learned to keep their limbs under cover. Some scraped shallow holes in the hillside and piled up thin walls of rock to reduce their exposure.

Dhiraar encountered Khalid. “Sahib, why do we wait if Allâh is on our side?”

“Patience, Dhiraar, you’ll have your chance.”

Dhiraar took to following him, ostensibly as a shield bearer and bodyguard, but Khalid could feel his disapproving gaze at his back. No one else said anything to him directly, but the volume of the grumbling gradually increased throughout the long, hot morning. The withering fire finally began to taper off as the archers ran low on their reserve of arrows. Khalid reluctantly turned to Dhiraar. “Select your champions and you may challenge the enemy. Be careful not to start a general assault, Dhiraar. Your job now is to delay their attack until well past midday.” As Dhiraar turned to go, he added, “And wear some armor!”

Marid found Bashour in the rear guard encampment. “Come on!” He urged, “Dhiraar is going to challenge their champions!”

“We were told to stay here with the reserve and guard against infiltrators to the rear,” said Bashour.

Marid just looked at him with an impatient expression. “Who’ll blame us for wanting to fight?”

Bashour hesitated for a moment, then followed Marid through the scrub towards the front line. He found his companions, Rashad, Wahid and the others at the base of the hill. Jabir said, “Aren’t you supposed to be guarding the women?”

“What and let you guys have all the fun?”

“You stay on my left and do exactly as I say,” said Wahid. “Unless you’re eager for paradise today.”

As Taticus watched, a lone horseman broke free of the ranks across the valley and galloped towards the lines of slingers, who melted away at his approach. Horns sounded and the lines of slingers and archers began a somewhat orderly reverse march towards friendly lines. The lone horseman began cantering back and forth, growing ever closer to the Byzantine line. “What is he doing?” asked a soldier at Taticus’ elbow.

“He’s challenging us to a duel,” said Taticus grimly.

Andrew also watched Dhiraar ride back and forth, taunting his soldiers. He ignored the occasional arrow fired his way. One or two even hit his armor and ricocheted off. Theodorus approached him, his eyes on the rider. "Should we engage their champion?"

Andrew shook his head. "No. There's no need. We have an overwhelming numerical advantage. We have nothing to gain by defeating their champion; but should we lose, it would demoralize our soldiers."

Theodorus's eyes were still on the man. "Andrew, I'm afraid I don't understand this. Is this some kind of ritual? Why don't they just attack?"

"The duel before battle has a long history, Theodorus. The idea is that if your champion can defeat theirs in one-on-one combat, the enemy will grow fearful. You might convince him that he's the inferior force and make him afraid enough to quit the field." He thought for a moment. "As a matter of fact, one of the most famous duels in history occurred right here."

"I'm sorry, I don't follow you."

"Remember the Old Testament? This is the valley of Elah, where King Saul's army met the Philistines. The armies were arrayed just as we are today, but they were evenly matched and neither side dared to start the general attack. For several days the Philistine champion taunted Saul's soldiers, until finally a boy stepped forward and killed him with his sling."

"David and Goliath? That was here?"

"The very place. The Philistines were so dismayed that their best man had been killed by a boy that they fled all the way back to Gaza. Thus is the power of a demoralizing duel. I refuse to give my opponent such an advantage." He motioned to one of the junior officers nearby. "Pass the word that no one is to accept the challenge of that maniac."

Dhiraar trotted in front of the enemy lines, bellowing his challenge. "Come out, infidels! Come and earn your glory!" After some time without a response, he began to be more abusive. "Is Caesar served by women? Why will no one fight me?"

He rode closer to the line, close enough that he could pick out a face and he pointed. "You! Are you a lover of boys? Why are you on this battlefield, little girl?" He dodged a desultory arrow shot his way.

"When you speak of this day to your women, your balls will crawl into your belly and you will hide your face with shame."

In frustration, he tore off his armor and his tunic and threw his hands wide. “Come and get me! I’m unclothed! Are you cowards too frightened to even fight a half-naked man?”

A runner approached Andrew and drew himself up, “Sir! The men who speak Arabic are beginning to grumble at the accusations of this man. They’re wondering why you won’t let them respond.”

“What is he saying?” asked Andrew.

“He’s accusing the men of being cowards, women and lovers of boys, sir.”

Theodorus exchanged looks with Andrew. “We won’t be able to keep discipline long with that sort of talk.”

Andrew made a curt motion. “Send a decade of horsemen to intercept this fool and bring him down. No one is to engage him one-on-one, understood? I don’t want a repeat of yesterday.”

Dhiraar spotted the horsemen as they broke the front ranks and trotted to intercept him. He kicked his horse into a canter and bellowed, “Is this how you meet your challenger? With a ten to one force? Are the soldiers of Caesar without honor?” He cut diagonally from the Byzantine front line, keeping out of range of the approaching cavalry.

Andrew was intently watching the cat-and-mouse contest between Dhiraar and the horsemen he’d sent. He missed the activity across the valley until one of his aides drew his attention. A dozen Arab horsemen had left the enemy line and were approaching the squad chasing Dhiraar. The lone Arab danced this way and that, avoiding capture or encirclement. From a distance, it looked as if he was laughing; he seemed to be enjoying the game. Andrew muttered under his breath, “Come on, damn you, capture him!” The last thing he wanted was a general melee between the enemy’s horsemen and his, for the same reasons he refused the champion’s challenge.

A half-dozen Byzantine horsemen left the friendly lines and added their support to the developing brawl in the valley. Andrew whirled on one of his officers, “Domestikos! Find out who ordered those men to break ranks and relieve him at once.”

He watched helplessly as the Arab cavalry finally converged on his men. The Byzantines were no match for the Arab veterans. Soon confused, riderless horses returned to the friendly lines, leaving their motionless riders on the valley floor. More Arabs left their lines to meet the horsemen who’d broken ranks and in return several more of his horsemen left to intercept them. Andrew felt the situation was quickly spiraling out of control. His men were being destroyed piecemeal by the superior Arab riders. The men at the base of the hill on which he stood surged like a living thing, eager to join the battle with their mounted comrades.

Theodorus commented, "The men are eager to join the battle, sir. Is there a reason not to attack?"

Andrew was in a quandary. He didn't want to expose his men to an uphill attack against an entrenched enemy, though the slope on the north side of the valley wasn't as steep as the one he stood on. What if the Arabs refused the field and stayed in their positions? How far would his men have to advance under attack from Arab archers? He understood his mission was to delay the Arabs as long as possible, but with his numerical superiority he should be able to carry the day, if they'd stand and fight.

"Pass the word to advance, but be ready to halt on my order. I don't want to advance into their archer's range."

"Sir, once you commit, you won't be able to withdraw the front ranks. The men behind them will be in the way. . ."

"I know, damn you! Execute my orders, sir!"

Taticus heard the trumpets sounding the advance and saw century banners being raised along the line. "Up and at them, boys!" he shouted. "Form ranks abreast!"

They would be three or four ranks back, not on the front lines. They watched as the front ranks departed the hillside and started across the valley. As each rank left they shifted down the hill. Taticus moved along the line of his men, calming them. He'd watched the horsemen duel farther down the valley and knew that the commanders were on the verge of losing control of the army. He did his best to assure the men otherwise, convincing them that everything was going according to a carefully conceived plan.

Khalid met Dhiraar as he reentered the lines on the north slope of the valley. The men cheered the half-naked horseman and his grin reflected their adoration. Khalid smiled gamely at him as he dismounted and proclaimed "By Allâh! These Romans will be easier than I thought!"

Khalid took him by the arm, still smiling and pulled him aside. He was still smiling to outward appearances as he hissed. "What in Allâh's name do you think you were doing? Your task was to delay the attack, not precipitate it. Look what you've done." Dhiraar's eyes followed Khalid to where the Byzantines were forming up and marching across the valley floor.

Dhiraar was still basking in the acclaim of the rest of the army. "If it's Allâh's will that the Byzantines die today, then who am I to say otherwise?"

"Fool. If you weren't the bravest fighter in the army, I would return you to Medina!" At that he took Dhiraar's hand and turned towards the men and raised both of his arms above his head. A great shout went up among the soldiers. As furious as he was at Dhiraar, he recognized the need for the men to have a hero, a champion.

As the blazing sun passed the meridian, the Byzantine army pulled up to a stop, midway across the field. Khalid paced around his hillside, regarding the enemy army, trying to figure what the enemy commander was doing. He clambered down the hill to his front pickets, snatched a bow from the hand of one of his archers, pulled it as hard as he could and loosed an arrow in a high arc across the valley. It fell short of the enemy line. The short cavalry bows of his men were no match for range against the more powerful bows of the Romans.

He encountered Mu'adh as the two moved along the lines, steadying the soldiers. "What are they about, Sahib?" asked Mu'adh.

"Only Allâh knows," replied Khalid. "The only thing I can think of is that their commander is shy about attacking up a hill. I can't believe they've got some sort of trap they want us to step into."

Mu'adh kept his silence, watching Khalid think. Finally, Khalid eyed the sun, then swept his eyes from one end of the valley to the other. "Here's what I want you to do. Contact Sa'id and tell him to anchor his left flank at their current positions. You will then return to your command post and order your army forward. Sa'id and Abd ar-Rahman's forces will maintain contact with yours during the advance. Engage the enemy and slaughter him. Pass the word that the line must maintain its integrity. If the enemy provides a breach, ignore it. Do not exploit it. If we try to maneuver on foot, he'll use his superior strength to crush us. Today we stand and harvest Allâh's glory!

"We will begin after the afternoon prayer. Wait for my signal to begin your advance."

The line had remained quiet for some time. The men who'd drawn up short in the valley were sweating under the hot sun and runners were passing water through the ranks. Andrew and Theodorus moved cautiously forward to inspect the situation. As they slid through the ranks to get to the front, they heard the weird ululating call that they'd learned to recognize as a call to prayer. A short time later, the army on the slope in front of them rose en masse and began bowing and kneeling in prayer. They were facing Andrew's army and it looked like they were worshipping the Byzantines.

"If we could predict when they're going to do this, what a wonderful time for an attack," said Theodorus.

"Wouldn't it be? Unfortunately, they'll be done before we can get the army moving this time," replied Andrew. Even as he spoke, the enemy was finishing and straightening up. Then a yell came from their center and banners snapped upright. The Arab army started moving forward.

Theodorus tugged at Andrew. "Come, sir, this is no place to be."

The Muslims moved purposefully forward at a quick but steady pace. As the lines closed, Arab archers let loose a coordinated volley that decimated the front rank of the Byzantine army. The two lines clashed with a roar before they could loose a second volley. Bashour felt swept along as if by a tide, concentrating on keeping his right shoulder in contact with the huge bulk of Wahid by his side. The long, curved sword with which he'd been practicing felt heavy and unfamiliar in his hand. He watched as several enemy soldiers in front of him collapsed just before the lines closed, arrows seeming to spring magically from their bodies. As the crush of men around him slammed into the enemy line, Bashour tripped over a body and fell headlong. He'd scarcely touched the ground before he was hauled to his feet by the scruff of his shirt. "Calm down and watch your step!" growled Wahid. The big man then started laying about him with his sword, his reach extending past Bashour's and keeping the short swords of the Romans away from both of them.

Andrew was almost jumping up and down, trying to see over the tumult to get an idea of what was going on. "I can't see, damn it! I need high ground!" He looked around for runners and saw none. He was away from his headquarters, cut off from his means of communicating and directing his army. Even if he could see, he had no way of issuing meaningful orders. He hated to move away from the fight, but he needed to be on the southern wall of the valley where his headquarters was. He started trotting, Theodorus struggling to keep up.

When he reached his command center he could see most of the valley and assess what was happening. Along a swath that ran diagonally across the bend in the valley, cutting the corner, the two lines were locked in combat with no room to maneuver.. The ends were anchored on the far edges, where the Arabs still held fast on the opposite valley slope. "Runner! Order the flanks to advance and try to seize the hillside positions on both flanks."

As the runner left, he turned to Theodorus. "If we can make the slope on either side of the fight, we could turn their flank."

They watched as the flanking units entered the fight, but it was too far away to see if there was any success once they reached the other side of the valley. Casualties started arriving in the headquarters, men bloodied in a variety of ways. Some walking wounded were injured severely enough to take them out of the fight, but remained coherent. Andrew stopped some as they passed and queried them.

"Sir, they fight like maniacs. Approaching their line is like walking into a scythe. You get the turn on one and his partner will likely cut your arm off. You can't stop those curved swords, they just slide past a parry and cut you open."

Taticus had no awareness of the larger fight, he was concentrating on the bit directly in front of him. Three ranks back, he left a space between his men and the ones in front to allow motion, if need be. He paced back and forth, trying to keep his men together. "Do not break ranks! Hold your position in formation! Don't let the wounded pass through your ranks! Make them go around!" Opening ranks to allow the wounded to pass back would do more to disorganize his unit cohesion than any enemy action. It was a cold way to handle the wounded, but upsetting his formation could get even more men killed and could cause a disruption that could easily turn to panic. Soon enough they'd get their turn at the bleeding edge of the battle.

A runner caught Khalid, "Sir! The enemy has closed to contact all the way into our line of departure position on the left, but we're holding and denying him an advance into the high ground."

Khalid grunted, "Very well, send Sa'id Allâh's blessings and tell him to keep those infidels off that slope." He was pleased with how the battle was going. His veteran troops were holding their own with minimal casualties, neither advancing nor retreating, but holding their position and slaughtering the enemy. They were so effective that they could take short breaks while the enemy soldiers moved the dead and wounded in front of them so they could get at the Arabs.

Bashour had found his niche at Wahid's side. The big man did enough fighting for both of them, but Bashour saw a pattern to his swings and used his sword to cover the left when Wahid was occupied on his own right. He didn't have the skill or the desire to press a real attack, but satisfied himself keeping the blur of swords away from Wahid when he was looking elsewhere. The first few moments of battle were terrifying and several times he'd received a knock by Wahid to motivate him to keep his sword up and swing it. He'd taken to using two hands, when his right arm became tired.

Wahid was engaged on the right when a pike was forced through the rank at Bashour's face. He pulled back and batted it aside, but left himself open for a blade to strike his torso. His leather armor turned the edge, but the force of the blow knocked the wind out of him. He crumpled, trying to keep his feet, his eyes growing wide as his body demanded air that wouldn't come. Another sword hit his helmet, causing him to see a flash of light behind his eyes, as if a bolt of lightning had hit his head.

Then he fell backward, realizing as he hit the ground that he'd been pulled back by Wahid, who stepped in and filled the void he'd occupied. Hands snatched at him and dragged him back. He fumbled for his sword, but it slipped out of his fingers and he thrashed his legs to try to regain his feet. "Quiet down," said a voice beyond the hands that pulled him. "You're out of the fight for awhile."

He spent several minutes sitting on the ground behind the battle line, holding his head and squeezing his eyes closed. A strange man came up to him and looked him over quickly. "Is any of that blood yours?" Bashour gave him a blank look, so the man quickly ran his hands over Bashour, then removed his helmet and examined his head. "You're going to live, but you're done fighting for today. Can you stand?" Bashour attempted to get to his feet and succeeded, but the world began to swim around him and he felt like vomiting. He collapsed against the stranger, who beckoned to others. “You there! Carry this one back to the camp!” Arms went under Bashour’s and supported him as he stumbled out of the valley.

The light was failing as the sun began to set. Andrew was having trouble seeing the front line from atop of the south slope of the valley. The east side of the valley, where it turned south, was already in gloom. Soon it would be too dark to see. “Command the army to disengage and return to the slope. If the Arabs follow, make it a fighting withdrawal. Don’t turn your back on them!”

Taticus heard the trumpets sound the withdrawal. His men hadn’t tasted blood that day, had never been given room in the line facing the Arabs to advance. He heard grumbles, but as a veteran he was grateful. The rank behind him began pulling back and he issued orders to follow them. He had torches lit, since it would be too easy for his men to scatter in the gathering darkness. The sounds of battle grew quiet, unnaturally so, as if a door had been closed, and all he could hear was the muted shuffle of a voiceless army shifting through the trampled fields.

Torches and fires were lit on the slope occupied by the Arabs, and Khalid greeted his men as they returned off the line. He found Dhiraar, still stripped to the waist, covered in gore and blood. The weary grin on the man’s face reassured him that none of the blood was his – at least not enough to matter, anyway. He came up to Khalid. “By Allâh! I thought you’d gone soft when you delayed the attack as long as you did. But if we’d attacked any earlier, I would have fallen in exhaustion! I killed infidels all afternoon and there was still an endless supply of them.”

Khalid was worried. They’d made a great slaughter this day and their losses were light. Even so, the Byzantine army could still overpower them on the morrow just with their weight of numbers.

“Dhiraar, when you have cleaned yourself and made your prayers, come to my tent.” He turned to the waiting runners that trailed him. “Notify the commanders to meet me in my tent as soon as possible.”

36. Southwest of Jerusalem
July 30, 634

Ubaidah had campaigned on Jihad with Muhammad many times. He was used to the messenger of Allâh embarking on long diatribes proclaiming his greatness, calling on the power of Allâh and denigrating the enemies as infidels. Allâh's messenger would often become so angry when condemning his enemies that his face would become as red as a pomegranate. Coming from anyone else, Ubaidah would have thought it was all a massive show to work up courage; but Allâh had blessed his messenger and apparently heard every word.

Khalid was a different sort altogether. They sat in a circle in front of his tent on cushions and quietly drank tea. Braziers were lit above them, so no glare was cast in anyone eyes. Khalid's eyes were distant as he softly voiced his thoughts. "The enemy army is a monster. We've dealt it a tremendous wound today, but not a killing one. Like an injured monster, he'll come back and he'll want blood."

He fell silent for a time and no one spoke. In Khalid's presence, they were all students of the art of war and they knew it. Far off, a man screamed in pain.

"The timing today was perfect. We were able to end the battle before our mujahideen collapsed with exhaustion. He won't give us that choice tomorrow. Tomorrow he'll fight us from sun to sun, and he'll roll over us with his numbers after our men can no longer raise their swords."

Again, he lapsed into silence. He threw his head back and contemplated the stars above them. They shone fiercely, brightly, with no moon to dim their majesty. Then he continued his musing. "We need to cut the head off this monster. We need to get at their commander."

Dhiraar spoke up, "We're at a disadvantage. We could offer to meet with him for a negotiation, then kill him."

"Aye, and you can be sure that he'll consider doing the same back to me the moment such a proposal is put to him."

"So? Would he expect an assassination attempt? To offer to negotiate would only assure him of his advantage."

"Hm. Yes. Yes, I can see that it could be done. . ."

Khalid thought some more, then sat forward decisively. “Here’s what we’ll do. Do you know that knoll in the center of the valley, where it turns to the south? We’ll meet him there. Send a messenger to the enemy. Tell him I wish to meet their commander before sunrise under a flag of truce to negotiate our withdrawal. Tell him enough blood has been shed. I wish to speak to him alone. He may bring a translator and a personal bodyguard if necessary.

“Dhiraar, take ten men and get into position near the base of that knoll, facing their lines. When you hear my signal, you may spring the trap. Cut off his escape and kill him. Start selecting your men now.”

“Yes, Sahib!” Dhiraar rose and disappeared into the night.

“Shurahbil, find that translator of mine, the boy from Tadmur, Bashir, Bashar, something like that. I want him with me.”

Yazeed asked quietly, “If we cut off the head, the beast will still thrash around. How can we kill such a thing before it grows a new head?”

Khalid smiled. “I have a plan. We can use the shape of this valley to our advantage. Now here is what I want you to do. . .”

Andrew’s commanders stood at attention before him as his fury washed over them. “An army that cannot communicate is a mob!” He stopped and moved face to face with one of his cavalry commanders. He had no idea if this man was the culprit, but at the moment it didn’t matter. As far as he was concerned, they were all culpable. “Did I not give the order that no one was to engage those ‘champions’ of theirs in one-on-one combat?”

The man stared straight ahead. “Yes, sir!”

Andrew resumed his pacing. “An army is an animal. An animal that must coordinate the actions of its various limbs, or it cannot even move. This isn’t some Greek democracy where every man has a say in how affairs are handled and every man has the right to veto his orders and do what he wants! I cannot make this army fight effectively if I can’t count on my orders being followed. I cannot know what’s happening on the battlefield if my sub-commanders don’t communicate with me. And I will not allow the lack of discipline in the ranks of the men you’re responsible for to dictate the time and tempo of battle!

“Theodorus, what is the current casualty count?”

"Um, some twenty thousand combat ineffective, sir. Of those, we believe some seven thousand are dead."

"Twenty thousand men!" Andrew shouted, "A whole Themata! Pissed away in a few short hours! Had we done similar damage to their army, we'd be sitting in their camp right now!"

He sat down, not looking at anyone. They stood in uncomfortable silence for long minutes as his anger subsided.

He finally said, "Stand at ease. What's happened has happened. I need suggestions."

The men shuffled uneasily as they relaxed. One spoke up, "We can hold this side of the valley and make them come to us, make them fight uphill."

Andrew cut his hand in a negative gesture. "No. The battle has been joined. I will not withdraw to a defensive position. Not when we still outnumber him more than two to one."

"We can try to flank him, use our numbers to extend our lines and envelope him."

One of the cavalry commanders spoke up. "That's not an option. We probed their flanks today and were repulsed. He's placed his mobile light cavalry on the flanks and they can run circles around us. Given the difficulty of the ground, no. It's not a good place to attempt a flank. These hills have wadis and defiles throughout. We'd get split up and cut to pieces if we tried."

Theodorus said to Andrew, "That commander, he deliberately held off attack, even during our barrage of arrows, just so his men wouldn't get tired before sunset. He's a sorcerer, that one."

"Yes. Yes," said Andrew, "if we could rid ourselves of that warlord that's commanding them. . ."

A runner entered the command tent and handed a dispatch to Andrew. "A messenger from the Arabs, sir. Says he has a message for you from the enemy commander."

Andrew exchanged looks with Theodorus, then said, "Well, bring him in!"

The turbaned man entered the tent and bowed. "As-Salāmu `Alaykum. Our commander, Khalid bin Al Waleed, wishes to meet with you at a neutral place to discuss the terms of our army's withdrawal from your lands." He went on to explain the details of the proposed meeting.

When he finished, Andrew pursed his lips, considering the proposal. Theodorus stepped forward, saying, "Andrew, this could be a . . ."

Andrew cut him off with a motion of his hand. He turned to the messenger. "Tell your commander that I agree to his terms of the meeting. We will be there." He motioned for the man to be escorted out. When they were safely gone, he whirled on Theodorus. "Don't you have the common sense to keep your mouth shut in the presence of an enemy spy?"

"My apologies, but this is obviously a trap. How could you agree to such a meeting?"

"It matters not that I agreed to meet. If I decide there's no advantage to the meeting, I simply ignore it. My options are still open, more than if I'd outright declined the meeting."

He turned to one of his more trusted commanders. "Bekkos, this spot he mentioned. You know of it?"

"Yes, sir. We used it as a survey point when laying out the original camp in the valley."

"Can a decade of your scouts make their way there quietly, without being observed?"

"Yes, sir. There's no moon tonight, we could march there holding banners and no one would see us."

He turned to Theodorus. "The Lord has delivered the enemy into our hands, Theodorus. Just as you suggested ridding us of that sorcerer."

"Likely he's planning the same for you," said Theodorus.

Andrew dismissed his concern with a wave. "He's frightened. He knows how angry I am and that I'll strike at him as soon as it's light enough to see. This time his men will fight all day and eventually collapse. He's trying to find a way out."

"Then ignore him and crush him just as you propose. You have nothing to gain by meeting with him."

"And how many more of our men do you condemn to death with that plan? No, I'll seek any advantage I can get. This Arab has realized he's bitten off more than he can chew and is trying to find a way to escape with his tail between his legs."

He turned towards Bekkos, "Send your men ahead of me. Raise the alarm if they encounter anything. Tell them to listen. If he doesn't surrender, or refuses my terms, come out of hiding and seize him."

Every loose object had been secured with leather straps. Their armor was sheathed in cloth to prevent noise and their forms were softened by capes to break up their outline. They left the Byzantine lines and slipped silently across the valley floor like wraiths in the nearly complete darkness. To the men every step sounded like a cacophony, but from ten feet away, no one would have noticed their passing.

The trip across the valley was swift and silent, with a delay as they clambered across the dry creek bed near their destination. They reached the designated spot and began a careful search for a place to secrete themselves. The leader stopped and touched the shoulder of the man behind him and pointed up the hill, then began ascending the slope. Each man in turn did the same.

None noticed that the last man did not start the ascent. He died silently as Dhiraar's dagger cut his windpipe. Dhiraar took his place and began stalking the next man in line.

The slope leveled out in a small shelf some yards up. The group bunched up as they reached the flat area and waited for their tenth man. Confusion grew as the seconds ticked by and he failed to show.

"I heard him right behind me," whispered one man to the leader.

An arrow sprouted from the leader's throat, cutting off his answer. More arrows whistled in the darkness, followed by a brief melee as what they had mistaken as boulders instantly transformed themselves into demons, hell-bent on slaughter. In a moment, it was over.

Dhiraar was breathing heavily. "It seems Khalid wasn't the only one with this plan." He chuckled softly.

"Shall we hide the bodies, Sahib?"

"Yes. No, wait." An evil smile spread over Dhiraar's face and his men could see his teeth in the darkness. "Take their clothes and disguise yourselves."

Bashour had been awakened by an urgent summons from Khalid. His head throbbed, but he felt steady on his feet. Now he was walking beside the big man's horse, holding a stirrup to guide him through the darkness. In the east, the sky was turning purple with the coming dawn.

They reached the foot of a knoll that thrust out into the valley where it turned southward and waited, looking towards the Byzantine lines. They could see fires along the far slope, as the opposing army began to warm their breakfast.

In the predawn gloom they could see three horses picking their way across the valley. They were a respectable distance away when they stopped and dismounted. At this gesture, Khalid did the same. He tied the horse to a bush and stood waiting.

One man motioned the other two to stay where they were and approached Khalid and Bashour. Bashour felt like a puppy that found itself between two mastiffs squaring off to fight. He swallowed and tried to keep his voice steady as he translated the words of the enemy commander.

"Are you prepared to lead your army back to the wretched desert from whence you came?"

Khalid smiled wickedly and bowed. "This is your last chance, General, to accept Islam, or pay the Jizyah and accept the dominion of Allâh over your land." Bashour had difficulty translating the word "general," and instead substituted the generic "commander."

Andrew's face became furious and he shouted, "Seize this man!"

Khalid felt a stab of fear race through his bowels as Roman soldiers rose out of the rocks above and to either side of them and descended, converging on their position. His hand went to his sword and he thought of paradise. He kept his eyes moving, looking for an advantage, prepared to start the fight and thin the attackers at the slightest opening. Then, in the gathering light, he recognized Dhiraar's smile and his shoulders visibly relaxed.

Andrew stood, almost laughing at Khalid, a look of supreme triumph on his face as the men converged on the small group. Then he saw Khalid smile and a look of confusion swept across his face. He looked in Dhiraar's direction and saw for the first time that this soldier wore nothing under his cape. Realizing what had happened, he snatched a knife from his belt and leapt towards Khalid.

Bashour was uncertain of what was happening and was sure that he was about to be captured, or worse, killed. He was frozen to the ground, rooted with fear, when the other commander did the inexplicable and attacked Khalid. Without thinking, Bashour lunged as Khalid stepped back to avoid the strike. He tried for the hand with the knife and missed, but his body slammed into Andrew, causing both of them to stumble. Before Andrew could regain his balance, Dhiraar's sword flashed and the man's head tumbled to the ground. The body stiffened, then fell thrashing into the dirt.

Dhiraar yelled something unintelligible and pointed at the two men waiting for Andrew, who turned their horses and bolted back across the valley before anyone could do anything about them.

Khalid grasped Bashour's wrist and hauled him to his feet. "Well done! That was courageous, even if unnecessary. I shall see that you're properly rewarded."

Bashour looked around at the gathered soldiers. Seeing their grins, he muttered something inaudible, then bowed and touched his forehead.

37. Southwest of Jerusalem
July 31, 634

Theodorus waited uneasily at the hilltop command post for Andrew to return. It didn't surprise him when, just after the sun cleared the eastern horizon, the bodyguard who'd been sent with Andrew galloped up and dismounted his horse, breathlessly.

"Andrew. . . they've killed him. . .it was an ambush!"

Theodorus looked disgusted. He'd expected something like this. "The question begs, why are you still breathing?"

The bodyguard drew himself up, breathing more evenly, "The enemy commander only had an unarmed interpreter, naught but a boy. Andrew ordered us to lay back, so as not to frighten the man, in preparation for our surprise. But we were the one surprised. Their men, they were dressed like ours, but they killed Andrew and we ran."

Theodorus was furious, but with nothing at which to direct his anger. He waved the guard away. This had been totally unnecessary!

"Strategos, they're moving!" called one of his aides. He strode to where he could look over the valley. From the center of the enemy line, men carrying banners began marching in separate directions. As they passed the enemy surged forward, creating an ever widening "V" crossing the valley.

"Order the themata forward. Frontal attack!" Today he would drive these barbarians from Palestine, or crush them beneath his boot!

Khalid had set a crushing pace as they raced back from the base of the small hill in the gathering dawn. As the adrenaline from the predawn action faded, Bashour felt exhausted and numb, stumbling through the half-darkness, oblivious of everything but Khalid's heels before him.

Dhiraar touched his shoulder when they reached the friendly lines. "Rejoin your comrades. Today, Insha'Allâh, we will have a great victory!" Bashour said nothing in return, just nodded and moved off.

Bashour's head was throbbing where he'd been hit the day before as he staggered back to his group. They were just waking, preparing for morning prayers, and rose at his approach, questions half-formed. But their questions were unspoken when he pitched forward onto his face just short of their circle. Sameer and Rashad knelt to check him. Wahid reached down and peeled back an eyelid and saw the eyes rolled back in his head. “Carry him to the infirmary area. He’s in no shape to fight today,” the big man rumbled.

Khalid had placed himself at the front and was one of the first to step off across the valley. He led his men at a walk, keeping the same speed as the banner bearers who walked sideways along the departure line, releasing the men in their wake. The result was a wedge approaching the enemy line, Khalid at the apex.

He saw the enemy leave their positions at the base of the hill and come to meet his army. They marched in a straight line, as opposed to the arrow shape formation his tactic had developed. He smiled. The Roman commander, whoever he was now, was playing his part perfectly.

As the lines approached one another, Khalid kept his eye on the sky, looking for the arrows that he was sure were coming. When he caught sight of the dark cloud ascending from behind the Roman’s front line, he yelled, “Let’s go!” and broke into a run. They had to cover the ground between them and the Romans as quickly as possible to minimize the time they’d spend in the murderous storm of arrows.

The first arrows fell well behind him, but he didn’t have time to contemplate it as they crashed into the Roman line, which barely had time to brace itself for the impact. Their momentum carried them through the first ranks and the front wavered. Would he actually be able to break through like this? The thought had occurred to Khalid when he proposed this plan, but he’d dismissed it. There were too many enemy soldiers to allow that. No, he wouldn’t create a trap for his own men to fall into. “Close ranks!” he yelled. As his men recovered their organization from the initial contact with the enemy and began the earnest task of killing, he stepped back off the line and out of the fight. He had to move to where he could see what was happening. His plan required coordination.

He moved along the line, prodding, poking and dressing the line to be sure it would hold for the moment.

Behind him, in his departure line positions, he saw banners rise all along the line. Excellent. The entire army had left their positions. Now, all he had to do was hold until they were engaged all across the valley. After ten minutes, the banners were dropped in succession from the edges inward. His whole line was engaging the enemy now. The time had come to set the trap and see if the enemy would stick his head in it.

Moving to the apex of his line, where he'd led the men forward, he touched his men and ordered them to fall back. Passing the word in both directions, his line fell back in an orderly inverted V, extending the enemy's lines as they took advantage of the sudden retreat.

Theodorus watched the battle unfolding. His archers did less damage than he'd hoped they would before the battle had closed, but it was no matter. He had the numbers to crush the enemy.

"Strategos! Their line is collapsing!" One of his aides was gesturing at the center of the valley, just west of where it turned south. Yes, no doubt about it, a breach had been opened and was widening. It had happened much sooner than he'd expected and it couldn't have happened in a better spot. They would split the enemy in two and crush them piecemeal.

Events were developing rapidly; he must move immediately to maximize the shock value of his sudden advantage. "Order up the reserve! Commit them to that breach! All of them!" Perhaps the enemy commander had become overconfident that his assassination of Andrew would be a decisive military advantage. He smiled fiercely as thousands of troops, a full turma at least, descended and joined their comrades in the newly opened breach.

Khalid guided his men in an orderly advance to the rear, fighting steadily, giving way but making the enemy pay if they pushed too hard. The integrity of his line was maintained. Excellent! They slowly and methodically gave way until he placed his foot on the slope that formed the northeastern part of the valley. Signal men were waiting for him, here where his army had started the morning. He signaled to them, and they raised their banners high. Now, hopefully, Mu'adh and Sa'id would do their part and stop the line from collapsing further. He scrambled up the hill and stopped for a moment and surveyed the line. A huge V had formed, pointing at his camp. And, as he'd hoped, the far side of the valley was black with the Roman reserve rushing into the breach to exploit the weakness. The Romans had taken the bait. Now to spring the trap.

He waited until the entire enemy's reserve had entered the area of his retreat, then ascended the rest of the way to the top of the hill and found the signalmen waiting there. They waved their banners and lit the signal fires. Up the wadi that led out of the valley to the northeast, he heard Yazeed's men shout to Allâh and the ground trembled under their hooves. The reserve burst onto the valley floor and separated, going to either side of the apex of the vee formed by his retreat. Six thousand horsemen added their din to the battle below.

Yazeed's cavalry disdained adding their weight to the fight at the apex of the vee. They galloped along behind the lines to where Mu'adh and Sa'id held the line from spreading the retreat further. There, they plunged into the Romans, forming a pincer at the base of his penetration. At the same time the men who'd been content to fall back when ordered and stand fast when ordered to stop, suddenly began fighting forward, pressing the Roman defenders.

The result was chaos inside the Roman lines. Pressed from both sides and their line of retreat threatened, the Romans were quickly losing room to even turn around. The problem was exacerbated by the addition of some fifteen thousand reserves into the perceived breach.

The envelopment narrowed and closed in. The horsemen to the left and right broke through the concavities in the Roman line and met behind the embattled Romans, turning their rear into a cauldron of killing. Men on the flanks perceived what was happening and tried to flee, causing the Roman line to begin to collapse from both directions. The pressure to get away from the battle squeezed the men even tighter. In some places, men were hemmed so tightly that they couldn't even raise their weapons or do more than turn their heads. The Muslims shouted and doubled their effort. The rocky ground soaked up the Roman blood and Muslims fought to keep their balance as they advanced over piles of bodies to keep the pressure on the encircled enemy. When it seemed like it couldn't get any worse for the Romans, the Arab archers began shooting into the cauldron, adding to the death and confusion. The bodies were packed too tightly to escape the deadly rain, and every arrow launched found a mark.

Theodorus watched in horror as the center of his attack was squeezed and ruptured. His breach had been broken and at least a third of his men were encircled. The breakthrough of the Arab cavalry had split his forces and flanked those who weren't encircled. About half the horsemen that had broken through at the base of his penetration were turning on the lines with which he still had communication and were rolling them apart.

"Strategos! What shall we do?" asked one of his aides. Theodorus looked at Exazenus, who'd lost interest in the battle and was on his knees, trembling and praying fervently.

"First, throw a blanket over him, so he doesn't demoralize the men." He turned and surveyed the disaster below him. "Order the line back to the hill. Try to form a defense line they can defend with a height advantage."

How was he going to explain this to his brother?

Taticus was having some local success on his section of the battle line. He was on the right wing of the army, where the lines ran almost north and south. He'd ordered pike men into the second rank with their pikes, or kontaria, over the shoulders of the men in front of them. The kontaria formed a hedgehog advancing into the enemy, restricting their employment of their long, curved swords. As they beat at the kontaria being thrust in their faces, the fighting front rank threatened to spill their guts with their spatha double-edged swords. This combination allowed him to make slow headway into the enemy line, but he couldn't press too far without losing contact with the units on either side of him.

He saw signs of confusion on his left. At first he ignored it, but the pace of the battle seemed to change and he sensed that the front was beginning to waver. He backed up away from the line to get a better view and saw that the line was collapsing on either side of him. Men were breaking and running for the shelter of the hills that they'd been camping on. Just then a rider came by yelling, "Retreat! Pull back to the hill! Retreat!"

The green soldiers on either side of him, terrified as they were from their first taste of real battle, took the order literally and many of them dropped their weapons as they turned and ran for the hill. Taticus roared to his men, "Hold your line! Fighting withdrawal! Fall back by the pace! Hold position on your line! To the rear!"

Maintaining discipline and keeping an organized retreat was a monumental effort, especially when his men became aware of the line disintegrating around them. The Arabs in front attacked ferociously and others were flowing behind them. Taticus wheeled his formation to the right to meet a flanking attack. Many Arabs chose to ignore the tough knot of fighters and swept by them in pursuit of those who'd fled.

Amazingly, Taticus soon realized that the way was more open to his front than it was behind him. Looking back, the scene was chaotic. Arab soldiers didn't allow the Byzantines time to regroup, but pursued them right up the hill, which crawled with soldiers from both sides. Arab bands hunted down pockets of resistance. Taticus realized that the army had been shattered and made a decision.

"This way!" he ordered and gestured with his sword towards the hills to the east, where the Arabs had come from. They met little resistance; no one expected an attack in that direction after the catastrophe that had befallen the Christian army. No one challenged them with any serious opposition as they made the slope of the hills. They swatted aside the odd Arab soldier that got in their way. They ran right through the Arab encampment, passing women and wounded without giving them any heed. The terrain then turned into a maze of steep, dry wadis and small limestone hills. Brush and small caves littered the landscape and they took care to stay out of sight once they'd broken contact with the enemy. They worked their way further east, avoiding ridges so they didn't skyline themselves. Several times they heard horsemen nearby and took cover, but they managed to spend the rest of the day without being seen. Taticus took stock of his small command. Of the original four hundred he'd led from Antioch, some hundred and fifty were left.

38. Southwest of Jerusalem
July 31, 634

Bashour watched the cloud high above him. It looked like a dog, then slowly changed to the face of a cow, then transformed into something unrecognizable. The change from the familiar to the unfamiliar made Bashour sad. He turned his attention to the blueness of the sky surrounding the cloud. He could hear soft conversation around him, mixed with the cries and moans of the wounded, but he was oblivious to all of this, content to study the peacefulness of the sky. The sky had always been there and always would be long after his time had passed. How eternal was the sky, how pure and untouched by the affairs of men. He imagined what it would be like to be in the sky, looking down on men as if they were ants. He concluded that the affairs of men were of as little consequence as those of ants in the larger scheme of things.

The background noise changed abruptly. Ululating yells and cheers of celebration swept across the hill he was on and the camp seemed electrified. He turned his head on the pallet he was laying on and realized that as inconsequential as the affairs of man might be, it didn't hurt any less.

An involuntary groan escaped his lips and one of the women nearby heard him and came to his side. He grimaced as she raised his head and held a cup of warm tea with honey to his lips. He drank thankfully. As she laid his head back, he got a good look at her and thought he must be dreaming. This was the beautiful girl that had been occupying his thoughts at night. Tamara. That name had danced on his tongue for days since he first heard her say it. She turned away and left him looking again at the sky. He faded back to sleep.

When he woke again, he heard women crying. He tentatively raised himself, steeling himself against the shock of pain in his head that never came. He carefully moved his head back and forth. The pain was there, but a mere shadow of what it had been. He sat up and looked around. A woman was on her knees and other girls around her. He studied the scene for a second and realized it was Tamara they were paying attention to.

He caught the eye of one of the women and motioned to her. "What's wrong?" he asked.

"News has come that her husband has been wounded and will probably die."

At first Tamara felt a wave of relief as the impact of the news sank in. She'd hated Nu'man with every fiber of her being for the apparent enjoyment he took in inflicting pain on her. She hoped that his wound was both painful and fatal.

Then she realized that his death would change nothing for her. She'd be placed for sale again, sold like an animal to the highest bidder. Her mind refused to dwell on what horrors that might bring, but her fear insisted that the result would be a new set of humiliations, pain and torment that she couldn't begin to imagine. She suddenly found it hard to breathe. The fear swelled inside her and threatened to overwhelm her. She sank to her knees. Her mind began racing, trying to find a way to escape, to flee the fate she was sure was in store for her with Nu'man's death. But no escape was possible. She entered into an ever-tightening spiral of thought that threatened to plunge her into madness. Her vision began to close in and darkness engulfed her.

She flinched away as other women touched her. They made soothing, consoling noises and she realized that they thought she was grieving for Nu'man. She clamped down hard on her self-control. She was afraid she'd start screaming hysterically. Oh, my God! How could they think anyone would grieve for an animal such as that?

"What will happen to her?" Bashour asked.

The girl swallowed and her lips quivered. Bashour couldn't understand why. "Likely she'll be sold or give to another mujahideen who's distinguished himself today. Plenty of heroes after a victory like this," she said bitterly.

The following morning Qutayba and Sameer showed up at the infirmary area in search of Bashour. Their spirits were high, still flush after the victory of the previous day. "Come on, lazy, you've had enough rest. We require your prodigious mathematical skills. There's so much loot on the battlefield, we don't have enough fingers and toes to keep track of it all."

Bashour went with them, listening to their endless tales of bravery as they relived the previous day's action blow by blow for him. He caught his breath in shock as they crested the hill and looked south across the valley. The once peaceful looking expanse was littered with bodies and equipment. The stench of death assailed his nostrils as they descended to the valley floor. He followed his companion's example and loosened his keffiyeh so he could pull it across his nose.

Teams combed the battlefield, searching bodies. When they found a Muslim body, they respectfully rolled it in tent cloth and carried it from the battlefield. The rest they left where they lay, after stripping them of armor or anything of value. Jabir saw them and came over, proudly opening a bag filled with gold bracelets and rings for their inspection.

"Quite a haul, eh? A lot of infidel widows will be crying when they hear about this."

Sameer tried a ring on experimentally. "We'll have to reunite the widows with their wealth, won't we? They just have to come to my tent and be my wives!"

Qutayba snatched the ring from him and threw it back in the bag. "Not until it's been counted and your share is determined. Besides, you've got all the wife you can handle right now, so don't torment yourself dreaming of another."

Jabir winked. "What would Dimah say if she heard you talking like that?"

The happiness disappeared from Sameer's face, replaced by distress. He looked at each of the others. "You're evil men, for whom nothing good will come. You won't let a starving dog even think of bones." Then he looked worried and studied the other two. "You. . . .you wouldn't tell her? Would you?"

Bashour quit listening to the exchange. His attention was drawn to a line of prisoners being marched close by. They were lined up and their guards stood, waiting.

Rashad dug his elbow into Bashour's ribs. "I heard there's a reward in store for you. Are you going to tell us what happened when you were with Khalid?"

"Reward? Oh. . . yeah, I . . .I hadn't thought about it that much. It was nothing, really." Jabir looked skeptical. "Khalid is a master campaigner and has seen endless battles. He doesn't reward people lightly. Tell us what happened."

Bashour related the tale without embellishment, then asked, "What would such a reward be?"

Wahid broke his usual silence. "Likely a cavalry share." Riders got a normal share of the loot and two shares were given for the horse.

Bashour's face fell slightly in disappointment. Rashad caught his expression. "What? What were you hoping for?"

Bashour had a half-formed thought about pressing Khalid to reward him with Tamara, the slave girl he saw in the hospital area. But that was too much to ask, he felt. "Nothing. Never mind." Rashad and Sameer looked at each other and grinned. "Come on, farmer boy, you've got something in mind."

Bashour shook his head. Jabir looked at the sky thoughtfully., "This shouldn't be too difficult to figure out. While we were killing infidels, our young friend spent the day surrounded by attractive slave girls, catering to his every want and need." Bashour snorted at this and Jabir continued. "It stands to reason that he finds himself smitten and was hoping Khalid would reward him with a nighttime companion."

Qutayba joined in. "The faithless rogue. Isn't Shai-tan a warm enough bed companion?" They laughed at the idea of anyone sleeping close to their homicidal camel.

Rashad asked Bashour directly, "Is that it? Were you hoping for a woman?" Noticing Bashour's wistful look, he continued, "That's it! By Allâh, you're right, Jabir!"

Jabir bowed for all. "Simple deduction."

"Oh, come on, guys!" said Bashour.

Wahid said, "Why not?"

Everyone stopped and looked at the big man. "What do you mean?" asked Sameer.

Wahid shrugged. "Why not? Allâh's apostle, peace be upon him, frequently gave girls from the booty we collected on raids. If anyone had his eye on a particular girl, all they had to do was ask the Prophet. The only danger was if the Prophet, may Allâh be pleased with him, decided he liked the girl too and took her for himself."

Bashour looked confused. "Why would he do that?"

Qutayba rolled his eyes, "Why do you think, stupid? Allâh's messenger, peace be upon him, liked a beautiful woman as much as anyone."

"But. . . but he was married, wasn't he?"

"Yes, many times. So?"

Bashour opened his mouth, not sure how to respond. Rashad saw his confusion and explained to him, "Allâh permitted this, for he spoke in 'The Allies':

"O prophet! We have made lawful to you your wives to whom you have paid their dowers; and those whom your right hand possesses out of the prisoners of war whom Allâh has assigned to you; and daughters of your paternal uncles and aunts, and daughters of your maternal uncles and aunts, who migrated with thee; and any believing woman who dedicates her soul to the Prophet if the Prophet wishes to wed her -- this only for you and not for the Believers; We know what We have appointed for them as to their wives and the captives whom their right hands possess -- in order that there should be no difficulty for You. And Allâh is Oft-Forgiving, Most Merciful."

Bashour digested this. "Were there any women forbidden to the Prophet?"

Wahid glared at him and Qutayba stepped forward and shoved him. "You keep a civil tongue, Farmer Boy!"

Rashad stepped between the two. "Easy, Qutayba. He's still learning. He didn't mean anything."

Qutayba relaxed some, the fire in his eyes fading, but pointed at Bashour. "You keep your filthy mouth off Allâh's apostle, Boy!"

Wahid moved forward, saying, "Not now." He motioned at the line of prisoners who'd been waiting a short distance away. Their guards were forcing them to kneel as Khalid strode up. The big man removed his helmeted turban and ran his fingers through his sweaty hair. He looked around, then turned and said something to the guard, who shook his head. Khalid looked around in frustration and spied Bashour standing nearby with his friends and brightened. He pointed at Bashour. "You! Translator! Come here!"

Bashour tried not to look at his friends as he complied. "Yes, Sahib?"

Khalid motioned brusquely at the first prisoner. "Tell him I will spare his life if he accepts Islam."

Bashour asked the man, "Do you speak Greek?"

The soldier was bound with his hands behind his back. He glared at Bashour defiantly and said simply, "I do."

"This is Khalid, the commander of the army that defeated you yesterday. He says he will spare your life if you accept Islam."

The man looked suspiciously at him. His bound companions were paying careful attention. "What do I have to do?"

"It's quite simple, really. All you have to do is declare that there is no God but Allâh and Muhammad is his prophet."

"I will not bow to a foreign God. I choose death."

"Allâh is not a foreign God. . ."

"Enough!" commanded Khalid. "What's he saying?"

"Sahib, he has questions. Please, give me a chance to persuade him."

Khalid looked sour and motioned for him to continue.

"Allâh isn't a foreign god. Allâh is the God of Abraham, the same one you worship as a Christian."

"I see no reason to take an oath of faith to the God I've worshiped all my life. I have no idea who this Muhammad is. I know of no Prophets."

"Muhammad was the Messenger of Allâh, who gave us Allâh's words in the Holy Qur'án. . ."

"Quiet, boy," the man said wearily. "If I'm going to die today, I'd prefer to do it without having to listen to you prattle on about some ridiculous cult belief you have. Now leave me be to say my final prayer."

Bashour was surprised at the man's attitude. He stood speechless, trying to think of something to say.

"Well?" Khalid prompted. "What did he say?"

"He . . . he said no."

"Step back," said Khalid, and when Bashour did so, he motioned at one of the guards. A scimitar flashed and the prisoner's head was cut cleanly from his neck. The body spasmed and flopped forward, twitching violently. Down the line of prisoners a man moaned in despair.

Khalid studied Bashour's shocked reaction. "Don't start so. Allâh commanded this man's death before the earth was made, in the Women sura:

"You will find others who desire that they should have security from you and security from their own folk. So often as they are returned to hostility they are plunged therein. If they keep not aloof from you nor offer you peace nor hold their hands, then take them and kill them wherever you find them. Against such We have given you clear warrant.

"This man made war against the servants of Allâh. We offered him mercy and a chance to repent and he refused. His death was quick and painless." Khalid looked at the line of prisoners and sighed. "I'm not going to spend all day at this. Tell them that any man who accepts Islam and joins us will live and be welcomed, right now. Tell them my patience is wearing thin."

Bashour did so and pleaded with them to take the simple step to save their lives. No man spoke. They uniformly stared at the ground before them.

"So be it," said Khalid. He took Bashour's arm and started leading him away, making a small motion to the guards. "Make it quick and clean."

The shirtless Dhiraar fell in behind them as they moved across the valley towards the enemy's former positions. Bashour tried not to think about the carnage occurring behind them. After a time Khalid spoke. "You acted bravely yesterday morning. I wish to reward such an action. Dhiraar here suggested a cavalryman's share of the booty. That would be three times the share you would receive. Do you find that acceptable?"

Bashour swallowed and remembered what Wahid had said. Would it hurt to ask?

"There. . .there's a girl in the infirmary area. Her name is Tamara. . ." He was cut off by the laughter of the two men.

Khalid clapped a heavy hand on his shoulder. "By Allâh, a young man will always jump over piles of booty to get at a woman. Dhiraar, see if you can make that happen.

"Return to your friends, translator. Don't wear yourself out with your new prize."

39. Near Bethlehem
August 1, 634

Taticus was thirsty, but it wasn't the parched killing thirst that one experiences in a desert. The humid air made him sweat and long for water, but at least he could still spit. He and his men were hidden behind scrub bushes at the bottom of a wadi. The light from the rising sun chased the shadows from the hillside above them, but hadn't yet penetrated to the bottom of the steep slopes.

After breaking contact the previous day, he'd led the men due east cross-country, careful to stay off the roads and away from the crests of the hills. He'd pushed them until it was too dark to see. Had there been any kind of moon at all, he would have driven on through the night. They didn't dare light a fire for fear of being discovered.

He estimated that they must be almost due south of Jerusalem by now. He moved among the men, rousing them from sleep. When he reached the end of the line, he stopped and thought about his next move. They were at the base of a steep slope some 600 feet high to their north and east. He grabbed the nearest soldier. "Leave your gear and scout the top of this ridge."

The man returned a half-hour later. "I met a farmer near the top. Bethlehem is two millaria southeast and Jerusalem is four millaria northeast. Beyond this ridge is another deep valley like this one. He says if we follow that north and turn right, it will widen out and take us to Jerusalem."

Taticus whistled sharply to get his men's attention and motioned for them to get up and start climbing the hill.

As they approached the city, they joined other small groups of soldiers who'd escaped the carnage of the previous day's battle. They were all hungry and tired; some had fled more than twenty miles in efforts to avoid roaming Muslim search parties. They all told a similar story about the battle. Their portion had held, but when they realized they were surrounded and that the Arab army had broken through and were investing the headquarters, the line had collapsed.

Elements of the Jerusalem garrison had deployed on the road that led along the wall of the city leading to the Joppa gate. All the other entrances to the city had been sealed. Garrison soldiers shared water skins with the refugees from the Valley of Elah, but no questions were asked. Everyone seemed to know what had happened and centurions along the way herded the men along and prevented them from stopping or bunching up. Taticus examined the high walls on his right, set atop a short but steep bluff. His military eye saw it as a difficult approach to an almost impossible obstacle.

They were herded through the gate and along the main east-west road through the city toward the old temple area. Taticus learned that they'd be using it as an open-air bivouac for the survivors of yesterday's battle. He decided it made sense. Thousands of men would be straggling in over the next few days. The city was surely not equipped to host so large a force on such short notice. Judging by the order being enforced by the centurions along their route, the garrison commander had organized things well in a short time.

The temple mount area was relatively flat and no one had built on it. Not quite a parade ground, but close. Upon reaching their assigned area, Taticus ordered the men to stack their arms in the center of their area, then established a security perimeter to prevent theft of their meager resources. He detailed several men to collect water skins and go to fill them at the city well. The remaining men rested. None of them had slept the night before. Taticus moved among the men, inspecting their feet after the long march of the previous day. Many men had minor wounds that they mutually treated, bandaging them to keep the persistent flies away.

Taticus was aware of the other units bivouacked around them. Some were organized as efficiently as his group, but others – far too many by his reckoning – seemed to have no organization at all. Men left alone without direction could cause all sorts of mischief. This truth was already becoming apparent as Taticus heard angry voices and bickering. Soon there would be fights. He suppressed his natural inclination to find the source of the problems and squash them while they were still small. He had enough to worry about with his own men.

The midsummer sun beat mercilessly on the open ground and the men were soon uncomfortable, seeking what little shade they could find. Near noon a garrison soldier came through the camp with large baskets of bread. Shortly after that, a non-commissioned officer came looking for Taticus. "Komes, the city Turmarch wants all unit commanders to report to him as soon as possible. Follow David Street back to the gate you came in, the headquarters is on the left."

Taticus didn't recognize any of the other commanders assembled. After more than an hour, the commander of the garrison showed up. Taticus didn't join in the obligatory grumbling about the delay. He'd been in the army too long to expect things to happen promptly. He carefully positioned himself close to the dais at one end of the hall, so he'd be up front when the commander spoke.

The Turmarch looked grim when he finally showed up. He ascended the speaker's platform and silence fell over the hall. He paused to gather his thoughts. "I guess there's no point in discussing the events of yesterday. You all know what happened better than I. Let me bring you up to date on the current situation.

"I've dispatched horse scouts around the area to gather intelligence. The bulk of the survivors from the battle are fleeing towards Gaza or Joppa. We've received four or five thousand here and we expect several thousand more will straggle in over the next few days. The Arabs have given up pursuit for the most part and are apparently consolidating at Elah. After a battle that big, I'm sure they have a lot of casualties. I expect them to hold there for several days while they lick their wounds. I don't suppose anybody here knows if the army's baggage train was put to the torch during the overrun?"

Men shuffled their feet and looked from one to the other. No one spoke up. "Very well, we'll have to assume they captured the baggage train and have no supply issues to worry about. We watched them pass by the city several days ago and judging by the herds they were driving and picking up as they went along, I don't think supply was a big problem for them anyway.

"Which brings us to the next problem. This city is well fortified. We have an internal water supply that can't be interfered with and we have enough supplies to hold the garrison for nearly a year if necessary. But we can't accommodate another five to ten thousand soldiers. Having your forces here is an embarrassment of riches. We don't need you to hold the city. Our assigned forces are plenty to hold these walls against a force twice the size of the army you faced yesterday. But if we're put under siege, the number of mouths we have to feed will have a direct effect on how long we can hold out.

"Therefore, I'm going to allow two days of rest to recover from yesterday's debacle. Then you're to march north towards Galilee, perhaps to Damascus. There you'll form the cadre of a reaction force to come and relieve the city once the Arabs put us to siege, which I'm sure they will within a week. Now, who's the senior officer here?"

With a few exceptions, no one really knew each other. Again they cast looks back and forth.

"Come on! Are there any Drungarios here?" An infantry drungus was about three thousand soldiers. Nobody spoke. "Any chiliarchs?" A chiliarchy was a thousand soldiers. Again, silence.

"Did you all murder your commanders?" This drew nervous laughter from the crowd. "Komes? Surely there is a Komes among you."

To this more than a dozen raised their hands, including Taticus. "Ah, Komes, to the front here, all of you." Taticus eyed the others as they shouldered through the crowd, surprised at the relative youthfulness of the others. Did he ever look so young? One old veteran like him was also sizing up the crowd.

The commander looked them over and motioned at Taticus and the other veteran. "Which of you is senior?"

Taticus squared his shoulders and announced, "I am Taticus of Antioch. I have served the Emperor for almost seventeen years."

The other veteran did the same. "Silvanus of Sastos. Eighteen years."

The commander looked around the room. "Does anyone challenge the seniority of Silvanus of Sestos?" Silence answered. "Very well. Silvanus, the remnant of the forces from yesterday's battle are yours. You will march in two days for points north. You'll refit as opportunity presents itself and await instructions from the Emperor."

Silvanus protested, "Turmarch, you can't possibly expect these men to continue marching. They're exhausted. We need more time to recover from the battle."

Taticus spoke up, "When I campaigned under Heraclius at Nineveh, we marched and fought and continued to march in the same day. What does fighting have to do with walking? Are these soldiers all untrained recruits?"

Silvanus glared at him. "Yes, I'm sure you were all made of iron at Nineveh, but these are real men, not the iron golems of your bygone days."

Taticus turned to face the other man fully. "Where did you serve, Komes?" He challenged, his voice was filled with disdain.

"Enough, you two!" interrupted the Commander. He asked Taticus, "You served at Nineveh?"

"Yes, sir."

The commander massaged his temples with one hand, contemplating the situation. "Silvanus," he finally said, "You'll remain here and organize what stragglers arrive after the main body has left. Taticus, you're promoted to Drungus. Lead these men north in two day's time."

"Begging your pardon, sir?" asked Taticus, raising a finger.

The commander didn't try to mask the look of irritation that crossed his face. "What is it?" He snapped.

"Sir, two days hence is Sunday. I request permission for my men to observe the Sabbath and we will march at dawn on Monday."

The Commander looked exasperated, then nodded. "Permission granted. But I want you and your men out of this city before Monday noon. Don't get trapped here when those Arabs lay their siege.

"Now get out of my sight. The sight of you lot reminds me of your defeat yesterday and makes me ill. See my Stratopedarches if you have any needs. And keep your men under control. I expect discipline among your lot."

40. Southwest of Jerusalem
August 2, 634

After the mid-afternoon prayer, Khalid called his commanders to a meeting. "Ubaidah? Do you have anything to report?"

"My men have returned from chasing the infidels to the northwest. Some riders came in sight of the ocean. There's no organized resistance. The enemy is scattered through the countryside. We killed those we found. I suspect that some of them are masquerading as farmers."

"Shurahbil?"

"Same story to the southwest. The bulk of the enemy forces are retreating along a road towards Gaza. They're organized and have repelled assaults on their column, but they're withdrawing rapidly. They're leaving a trail of abandoned weapons and wounded who can't keep up. I don't think we have to fear a counterattack from that direction."

"Yes, soldiers don't throw their weapons away if there's any leadership or discipline. Yazeed?"

"We invested their headquarters and supply dump. Their command staff was wiped out, except for one of their generals we found cowering under a blanket." Everyone laughed at this. "We're still counting the weapons we captured. I need instructions regarding the supplies."

"The foodstuffs are not booty and should be exempt from the count. I'm commandeering it all in the name of the Caliph to distribute to the army." This drew nods of assent "Dhiraar, how are the men?"

"Morale is high, Sahib. The wounded are being cared for. The serious cases have already been evacuated to Medina. The rest will be ready to march soon, but if we could have a week of recovery, it wouldn't hurt."

"You shall have your week, then. Were you able to take care of that matter with the translator?"

Dhiraar smiled evilly. "Yes, Sahib. Nobody objected. She's been through two husbands since she joined us; the men think she's unlucky. One man said it was one thing to go to Paradise for Allâh's cause, but he wasn't going to tilt the odds on account of a slave girl. I delivered her myself."

"Excellent. Sounds like everyone wins then. Comrades, let the men know how proud I am of them. We met and defeated a force three times our size, praise be to Allâh! Allâhu Akhbar!"

"Allâhu Akhbar!" chorused the men.

"You're joking!" said Marid, as they dried themselves from bathing in the stream. Bashour smiled and shrugged smugly. "You're serious!"

"Wait until you see her, Marid. She's so beautiful."

Marid adopted an air of indifference, not wanting to encourage his friend. "Good for you," he said.

Bashour had known Marid all his life and could sense the jealousy. He'd always been uncomfortable around the girls, while Marid was the ladies man. He'd often grown tired of Marid's subtle boasting of his successes. Tadmur had been a small community and Bashour knew that much of Marid's experience was all in his imagination.

They approached where Bashour and his companions were camped. They'd moved camp upwind from the valley, because the stench of the decomposing bodies was becoming obnoxious and flies were a growing problem. Bashour saw Tamara, a huddled figure poking at a small cook fire, her head down, trying to ignore the others. When they saw him and Marid, they rose to hail him.

"Here's the heroic lover boy now," said Sameer.

"And to think I was wondering if he was a lover of boys," said Qutayba.

As they entered the small circle, Rashad said, "Bashour, to celebrate your good fortune, we've procured a lamb for a feast. Since Jabir is basically useless as a cook, we've engaged your lovely lady to prepare it for us. Judging by the smell, I'd say you're lucky twice!"

Qutayba scowled. "We'll see how lucky he is. Word has it that this one has a curse. Both of her previous husbands have died shortly after they took her."

They looked expectantly at Bashour. "Are you going to marry her or just keep her as your slave?" asked Sameer.

"I. . . I hadn't thought about it." Things had happened so fast, Bashour was trying to catch up.

"Well, take your time," said Rashad. "You can keep her as a slave and if you decide you like her, you can manumit her and marry her."

"Just make sure you marry the right one and not her sister," said Jabir.

"Hey!" cried Sameer.

Bashour left the laughter of his friends and approached Tamara. He leaned over her and touched her back. He felt her stiffen. "Are you okay?"

She hesitated, then nodded. "Yes."

Bashour was dismayed. He wanted her to accept him, to feel about him the way he felt about her. "Are you sure?"

"Go to your friends. I'll have your food in a minute." She never lifted her eyes to meet his.

"Bashour! Here!" Jabir was offering him a bowl of sweet dates. He enjoyed the taste as the sweetness exploded in his mouth. He passed the bowl on, determined to be moderate. He'd made himself sick on dates more than once as a child.

Wahid broke his usual silence. "Well? Are you going to tell him?"

Rashad stood to make an announcement. "Bashour, even though your contribution in battle is to merely dull the edge of our enemy's sword with your helmet," Bashour smiled sheepishly as the rest of them laughed, "we appreciate that you have, at great risk to your physical person, taken the primary duty of caring for our beloved Shai-tan." Almost on cue, from outside the circle, the camel chose that moment to spit. It fell short, but her intent was clear. Again, the group erupted in laughter.

Recovering his composure, Rashad continued. "Nevertheless, you must have done something noteworthy for Khalid, and your honor reflects upon us all." The others mumbled assent around the circle. "So we, your friends, have determined that it simply wouldn't do for you to enjoy your first nights with your new slave girl under the open stars with the mosquitoes and the watchful eyes of the lechers of the army."

Qutayba chose this moment to slap the back of his neck with a loud curse, then examined his hand to see if he got anything. This caused more laughter.

Rashad continued, "So we collected our resources and present you with a tent of your own." At that he waved at a small tent, approximately eight feet to a side, standing a discrete distance away. Bashour had seen it but had thought it belonged to another group.

Bashour was speechless. "Thank you!" was all he could say at first. His friends exchanged knowing smiles, and he finally said, "I don't know what to say. You're the greatest friends a man could have!"

"No, Allâh is greatest! " said Qutayba. "Allâhu Akhbar!"

"Allâhu Akhbar!" they chorused.

Tamara cringed at the chant. She'd heard 'Allâhu Akhbar' too many times in the previous weeks and it never meant anything good. She'd first heard the cry when they'd cut Jamila's head off. Tears welled up as she thought of Jamila.

She removed the mutton from the heat, basting it one last time with drippings laced with spices, as her mother had taught her. Much as she hated these people, she couldn't find it in herself to ruin food by cooking poorly. She served the men with her eyes cast down, avoiding their stares, trying not to be there.

They ate quickly, for the sun was approaching the horizon. They'd just finished and thrust their plates and utensils at her to clean, as the ululating cry to prayer echoed across the camp and they began cleansing themselves using a pot of water she'd fetched from the stream.

As she washed, she kept her mind blank. She knew what was coming as the night fell, what would be expected of her. This new man, no more than a boy, really, seemed somehow different, but she knew that deep down, men were all the same. She was sure that under his awkward exterior lurked another rapist like the rest. The panic was hiding, threatening to erupt and consume her, snatch away her breathing and buckle her knees. She knew escape was impossible. Part of her wanted to fight, as Jamila had done, but another part wondered if it would be easier if she just submitted and let him do what he would. She never knew how she'd react. Every day she'd vowed to fight and if it came to it, die. But when night fell, she was too scared to fight, too terrified of the consequences and she was humiliated by her inability to control herself. Every time the spark of rebellion had risen, the memory of Jamila's headless body collapsing in the dust extinguished it.

The prayers were over and the men approached her. They were joking and laughing, giving her new master – she refused to think of him as a husband – a hard time.

"Bashour, you'd better take your woman and go. You have a long night ahead of you," laughed one. She went rigid as Bashour gently took her arm and led her towards the tent they'd set up. She fought to quell the panic, taking deep breaths. Her mind was blank, the expectation of what was to come was hammering for attention and she did everything she could to ignore it.

They paused as one of the others called, "Hey Bashour!" She kept her head down but saw out of the corner of her eye one of them making a rude gesture with his index finger and the other hand making a small circle. "It goes like this!"

Bashour grinned and made a rude gesture back, then ushered her into the tent.

Tamara stood trembling as he closed the tent flap behind them, to the cheers of his companions. Her head just brushed the top of the tent. Pillows had been thoughtfully arranged around their bedrolls. "I hope no mosquitoes got in," said Bashour. He turned and stepped around her and regarded her in the faint light. "Should I light a lamp?" he asked. She just stood there.

He removed his cloak and sat on a pillow. "Please sit down?" he said quietly.

She hesitated and sat primly, keeping her head down, avoiding his gaze. The panic was gone. Expectation was behind her; this was the reality. What happened now would happen. The uncomfortable silence stretched on.

"So . . . here we are," said Bashour awkwardly.

She refused to respond to him. He reached out to cradle her chin with his hand. She flinched away violently and he withdrew it hastily.

"Do you remember the night in the desert when you tried to run away?"

That bought him a surprised look. For the first time, she regarded him with something like interest. He smiled gently and nodded. "That was me."

Tamara was lost. This was a new experience. No man had talked to her like this since she'd been taken. They just took what they wanted and discarded her. She didn't know how to respond.

"I thought about you every night since then."

Oh, please. Did he really think he'd talk her into giving him what he obviously wanted? He actually wanted a girlfriend, not a slave girl! This was becoming maudlin. She halfway wished he'd shut up and just do his business. She could hate him so much more easily if he just didn't talk to her.

"You're very beautiful."

This led to an awkward silence. Panic started to grow in her belly again.

The fear coming off the girl was palpable and it broke Bashour's heart to think that she was so afraid of him. He wanted so badly to embrace her, to tell her everything was okay, but she'd erected a wall between them. He'd had experience with dogs that had been beaten and were cowed. He knew that if he forced the issue he'd only make things worse. He resolved to give her space and see if she would come to him eventually. She started as he moved to reach for some blankets. "Relax. I'm not going to hurt you." He took a blanket and laid it gently on her shoulders, then took another and retreated as far as he could in the tent and curled up with his back to her.

She sat in shocked silence for long minutes. This was totally unexpected. Was she safe tonight? Would he wait until her guard was down and come and force himself on her? Was he not interested in her? Was there something wrong with her? The air was warm and stifling in the tent. Eventually she lay down, arranging the pillows around her. She lay awake, tensing every time she heard him move, expecting him to touch her, wondering if she would scream when he did.

Bashour lay awake, acutely aware of the beautiful creature near him. He dreamed of her recognizing him as a savior and embracing him. Hours passed and he stayed still, listening to her breathing. It never settled into the long steady sound of someone asleep and a couple of times he wondered if he heard her softly crying. As the hours passed, he faded in and out, never quite asleep and never quite awake.

41. Jerusalem
August 2, 634

"I can give you four days rations per man, no more," the quartermaster informed Taticus.

"And how am I to reach Tiberias on that?" retorted Taticus. "I need a week's supply. Plus we need to replace the weapons that have been lost."

"Five days. I simply can't deliver more before you march. And forget about the weapons. We will need everything we have for the coming siege. You can re-equip in Galilee."

Taticus studied the man. He'd dealt with this sort before and he knew when he'd hit the wall in negotiations. The Jerusalem garrison commander had no sympathy for him; he'd made it clear that he'd just as soon turn Taticus' new command out without a crust of bread. Taticus turned towards his new logistics officer. "Handle the distribution. Five days road rations to every man. Make sure they march with plenty of water." With one last look at the smug quartermaster, he turned and left.

The mid morning heat and humidity of Jerusalem hit him like a wet rag when he stepped out of the building. He squinted his eyes against the glare, made worse by the white limestone that was the building material of choice in the city.

When he reached the temple area he made his way to his headquarters, where an ad hoc team of commanders were busy drafting orders and trying to organize the ragtag army that still trickled into the city three days after the defeat at Elah. He'd been considering what he was about to do all morning. "Form the men up by centuries. I want to address the army. Get me something to stand on so they can all see me. You have one hour." He waved off questions and returned to his command tent, a luxury that few men had in the heat. There he absently shuffled through manifests, orders of battle, equipment reports and a myriad other things that made the difference between an army and a disorganized rabble. He idly wondered if the Arab commander faced the same plethora of paperwork.

When the hour was up, he put on the cloak of a commander and emerged from the set. He set his jaw in a firm, angry war face and strode to the open area where his commanders had assembled the men in passable ranks. Someone had stacked a pair of column sections and made makeshift steps in a pile of rubble to ascend it. The men were called to attention at his approach.

He ascended to the flat top of the column, about six feet high and was pleased that everyone could easily see him. He glared angrily at the group.

"Kentarchs! Order the men to count off by ten!"

The order was relayed and each rank of one hundred eighty counted off.

"Ones, step forward!" A tenth of his army took a single pace forward.

Taticus bellowed his words so everyone could hear, speaking slowly so he could be understood at a distance. He made his points in short sentences, with long pauses to let them set in. "Three days ago, this army was humiliated on the battlefield! An unruly mob of camel herders a third your size drove you from the field!" He paused and let them squirm as he glared at them.

"In years past, I, as your commander, for cowardice in the face of the enemy, would order this army to be decimated!" He yelled the last word as loud as he could for the greatest effect.

"Look around you! I could order you to kill those men who have stepped forward! Their blood would absolve the stain of your shame! "Should I do this?"

The question hung in the hot air. Decimation was ancient history. No Christian would consider such barbarism. Were they being led by a madman? *Let them wonder*, thought Taticus.

"We march north at first light the day after tomorrow. We will march quickly. I will not tolerate any man falling out. I will not tolerate any man breaking ranks. I will not tolerate any man slowing this army. We will not stand around! I'll flog any man who slows this army and he will still have to keep up!

"Dismissed!"

As he descended from the dais, he ordered his centurions together. When they'd assembled, he gave them quite a different talk. "We're going to force march to Galilee. We will travel from first light until it's too dark to see. Five minute breaks every hour, no more. Look to the feet of your men, make sure they have good foot leather. "The level of training of these men is abysmal. This will change. For now, I'll be happy just to get them out of reach of that Arab army. You can expect we'll probably be back here in a month's time to relieve a siege of this city. Keep your men together, keep them in formation. Use the lash if necessary, but don't be too hard on them. It's your fault that they're untrained, not theirs.

"I'm not going to pull a wagon train on this march, it would slow us down. Each man carries his rations on his back, a cloak and his weapons, no more. Orders will be issued this afternoon with the marching order. Get your men organized so there are no surprises Monday morning. We'll start as soon as it's light enough to see. I want these men to look proud and professional as they leave the city gates. Training is canceled for tomorrow. Mass will be celebrated, and the men will be given the day free. You will be responsible for keeping order, and seeing that every man is back in the area by sundown. I don't want any men left behind in a brothel come Monday. Let them know that the garrison commander has given orders that any man who misses movement Monday will be severely punished. Hell, tell them he's threatened to have them executed for desertion." The garrison commander had said no such thing, but he needed something to hold over their heads, or half the army would evaporate into the streets and alleys of the city on Sunday, never to be heard from again.

"Any questions? Dismissed."

42. Emessa
August 2, 634

Heraclius reclined on the cushions, trying to relieve the pain that seemed to constantly plague him and cripple his movements. He recalled the soreness of a long horseback ride when he'd been too long out of the saddle. His body felt like that now all the time. He admired his young wife across the table and reflected on how lucky a man could be to have such a treasure.

He let his irritation show when he heard someone in the entry of his chambers seeking to speak with him. Couldn't they leave a man in peace for even a single meal, without bothering him with affairs of state? The young guard came in and announced, "A message from the Army of Palestine, sir."

He brightened at the prospect of good news. "Show him in," said Heraclius, as he struggled painfully to his feet. He would never accept an outsider while lying down. He was still a soldier, not a sybarite.

The messenger entered brusquely. Good man, he was still sweating and dusty from the ride. He must have come straight to the palace upon arrival. He bent to one knee and bowed his head. Heraclius felt a tinge of concern. This was unusual.

"Basileus," said the messenger, "The Army of Palestine has been defeated. Andrew is dead and your brother is missing."

"What?" The room suddenly swam around Heraclius and he felt faint. His mouth felt dry. Unable to steady himself, he fell to a knee and gripped the low table. As he knelt there trying to command breath into his lungs, Martina rose and said, "I'll get Psellus."

The scene was unchanged minutes later when Psellus and Caloiis entered the room. Psellus went to Heraclius and helped him recline into his pillows, then commanded the messenger, who was still bowed on one knee, "Rise and report!"

The young man stood and swallowed and studiously ignored the sight of his Emperor on the pillows. "Yes, sir. The Arabs . . ." He paused, collected his thoughts and started again with more authority in his voice. "The Arab army bypassed Jerusalem and met our army in the Valley of Elah. Andrew deployed the army on the south hillside of the valley, the Arabs on the north. They declined battle until late in the afternoon, even though we punished them with arrows. On that first day nothing decisive occurred.

"That night, Andrew received an offer for negotiation. He sent ahead a patrol to kill or capture the Arab leader, but we don't know what happened to them, because Andrew was killed in the negotiations."

"That fool!" exclaimed Caloiis. Heraclius waved him to silence.

"The next day the Arabs attacked at dawn. They met us all along the front, then collapsed their center. Theodorus ordered the reserves into the breach, but it was a trap. The Arabs squeezed the pocket, cut it off and isolated it. They broke through the center and routed the army."

"Just like Hannibal at Cannae," muttered Heraclius to himself.

"Is there anything left of the army?" asked Psellus.

"I can't say, sir. Several cohorts have fled to Joppa. That's where my unit went. I've heard tell that more went towards Gaza and some managed to get through to Jerusalem."

"We're defensive, Psellus," said Heraclius. "We have no army assembled that can meet these demons. They're free to strike anywhere in Syria."

"Basileus, we should garrison the mountain passes north and west of Damascus, to prevent them from coming further north."

"Psellus, they came out of nowhere in eastern Syria. They passed not fifty millaria from here. How many more Arab armies will materialize out of that desert? No. Emessa is too vulnerable now. We must move the court to Antioch. These barbarians care nothing for terrain; they will go over the mountains as if they weren't even there.

"Psellus, travel ahead to Antioch and begin assembling an army to meet these Arabs. Leave at once. Caloiis, how many horsemen are at your command?"

"Five thousand, Basileus."

"Take your themata and reinforce Damascus. Use Damascus as your base and patrol aggressively southwards. Try to disrupt any movement of the Arabs. If Damascus is attacked, stay mobile and do what you can to relieve the siege. I'll send Libanius on to you as soon as he arrives."

"I shall return with their leader's head on a lance!" proclaimed Caloiis.

"Just see that you don't end up on his lance," said Heraclius, darkly.

"What of the Jerusalem garrison, Basileus?"

"They can stand a long siege. They will remain in place. We can't afford for the Arab to take that stronghold. If they get in there, we'll never get rid of them. It stands right on our main line of assault if we attack into Arabia. If they're besieged, it'll tie down the bulk of the Arabs and we'll be able to raise a relief.

"Order what remnant you can find from Andrew's army to assemble at Tiberias. Maybe we can get enough together to form the cadre of a reaction force. And tell my brother to report to me if you find him."

43. Medina
August 2, 634

Abu Bakr winced as he prodded the mass in his abdomen. He thought it was getting larger every day. He was having trouble keeping solid food down and was relying more and more on camel and goat's milk to keep his belly full. Insha'Allâh, he would feel better soon.

Cries of "Allâhu Akbar!" filled the air outside the mosque. He smiled. Good news always entered Medina thus. He waited as the noise grew closer and finally burst into the room with a flood of people.

"As-Salāmu `Alaykum, Caliph! Good news! Khalid has met the Roman army and defeated it in a glorious battle, Praise be to Allâh!"

"As-Salāmu `Alaykum," replied Abu Bakr with a smile. "Khalid is indeed the Sword of Allâh."

A man pushed forward. "Caliph, I shall lead a thousand men to join Khalid and his army."

"Al Qasim, you are very brave to join the fight when the battle has already been won," commented Abu Bakr drily.

Abu Sufyan worked his way through the crowd, which was starting to settle down. "As-Salāmu `Alaykum, Caliph. With your permission, I'd like to join my son, Yazeed, in Syria."

Abu Bakr generously bowed his head. "Indeed, Abu Sufyan, you should leave at once if, Insha'Allâh, you're to catch them before they start moving again. The women of Khalid's army arrived from Persia several days ago. Take them with you. They should be with their men."

Someone else asked, "Caliph, many of the rebels from the Riddah wars who were returned to Islam wish to go fight with Khalid. Is this permitted?"

"No!" exploded Abu Bakr. "By Allâh, those dogs are lucky to have their heads! I will not allow them to get rich by riding Khalid's cloak. Don't bother me with this again!"

A wave of nausea swept over him and he did his best to hide it. "Thank you for the good news. Now leave me in peace."

The crowd bowed and backed out of the room. His daughter Aisha stayed and fretted about him, obviously worried. “Are you well, Father? You look so pale.”

He just shook his head. “My stomach still bothers me. I don’t know what this is, growing right here. Insha’Allâh, I pray that it will go away soon.”

44. Southwest of Jerusalem
August 5, 634

Tamara lay awake, facing the wall of the tent. The camp had been quiet for several hours. An evening breeze from the east had driven the stifling humidity of the day away. It had taken a long time, but finally she heard the deep regular breathing of Bashour that told her he was asleep. Over the last several nights, the scene was always the same. They would go to bed in the tent and there would be an awkward moment of intimacy due to their forced proximity, which Bashour would always break by wishing her a good night and lying down to feign sleep. Every night they'd lay in silence, acutely aware of each other, until he would go to sleep. When his breathing told her he was asleep, she'd shift into a more comfortable position on her back.

The mornings weren't so awkward. Long before the sun had peeked above the horizon, as soon as the dawn was bright enough to clearly see things, someone would start calling as loudly as he could, "Allâh is Greatest, I bear witness that there is no God except Allâh, Come to prayer! Come to success! Prayer is better than sleep! Allâh is Greatest! There is no god except Allâh!"

This provoked an intense frenzy in the camp and anyone still asleep was roused and hurriedly assembled for their morning prayers. She was glad of this, because it allowed her some privacy to make herself more presentable after sleep. She had no desire to make herself look attractive for any of these animals, but she stubbornly clung to a certain amount of pride which was the last thing she owned. She refused to let them take that away from her as they had everything else.

She lay there and thought about this strange young man, just an arm's reach away from her. Her fear of him was gone; the last few days taught her that she could trust him not to make any uninvited advances on her. She recognized that he was smitten by her, and found it almost charming. The charm was erased by the situation she found herself in. She was the de facto possession of a boy who had a crush on her. He could do with her whatever he pleased, and from everything she could see no one would say a thing. That idea terrified her, and if she dwelled on it she felt herself sliding towards a black abyss of panic from which she wasn't sure she'd be able to escape.

She felt so mixed up. This morning she'd actually smiled at him, before she caught herself. He'd returned with the men from a foot patrol. The battlefield had been plundered and now they were foraging across the countryside, pillaging any villages they come across. They'd been laughing and poking fun at each other in the usual way, comparing jewelry they'd looted from somewhere. She'd cooked a pudding made of wheat, milk and dates, and when he first tasted it Bashour's face had lit up and he complimented her profusely on how good it tasted. She felt good that he liked it, found herself smiling. What had she been she thinking?

A day or so before, she'd been serving a stew that she'd made, when one of Bashour's companions – she thought his name was Qutayba, the one with the wounded arm – had patted her backside and pinched her. Bashour had leapt to his feet and knocked Qutayba's bowl out of his hand. The two men had almost come to blows. Heated words were exchanged. Tamara thought it was about to get physical when the big man, the one called Wahid, had intervened and told Qutayba to back down. Tamara considered Bashour and Qutayba, and she thought that Bashour was fighting way out of his weight. Bashour was no small young man, but Qutayba was just mean and hard. She found herself thinking that Bashour was noble and sweet for the way he defended her, again catching herself with the reminder that she was his slave.

He was kind to her, though, and clearly infatuated with her. Compared to the rest, she realized that she'd much rather be with him, if she was to be a slave at all. She knew he wasn't from Arabia like the rest. His accent suggested he grew up close to where she did, Tadmur, maybe. His friend Marid had the same accent. She didn't like the way he leered at her when he was around and was glad he slept elsewhere. She felt less safe around him than even the close companions of Bashour.

As her mind drifted in the dark, she found herself missing her parents, the easy days of her youth, the house filled with the smell of baking bread. But even those memories darkened with the vision of her father being executed from a distance, and that brought the waking nightmare of Jamila, her head flying from her shoulders, the blood. . .Stop!

Tamara forced herself to think about something else. She knew that dwelling too much on what had happened would lead to madness. As she pushed her imagination back into its cage, she again listened to the rhythmic breathing of Bashour. She'd normally been more attracted to men a few years older. She and Jamila had often discussed who the most eligible bachelors were in Qaryateyn. It had been a small town, the options had been disappointing to contemplate. She noticed her tendency was towards men five or six years older than her. She and Jamila had fantasized about going to a big city like Damascus and having suitors by the score, young muscular men vying for their favor.

Perhaps she should give Bashour what he wanted? Would he get tired of always sleeping on the other side of the tent and get rid of her? He'd been nothing but proper to her, friendly but not pushy. He was younger than she liked, but he wasn't unattractive. He was tall and his muscles would fill out. And it wouldn't be like rape if she went to him, would it? Could she even touch a man like that and enjoy it, after the last few weeks?

No. Maybe in a different situation, but Bashour was a Muslim like all the rest of them. She'd been listening without saying anything to the lessons he'd been taking from Rashad in the evenings. This belief was so wrong, so evil. No good person could believe and profess such things. Her father had taught at the school sometimes, taught the boys scripture. She used to sit quietly when he'd let her come and listen to the stories he'd tell from the scriptures, sometimes reading them, sometimes ad-libbing and embellishing for the children. As a girl, she wasn't expected to know much of such things, but her father believed that girls shouldn't be excluded and saw that her curiosity was rewarded as much as any boy's. She knew enough about scripture to know that what the Muslims were teaching was wrong. They thought that dying in battle to convert people was some sort of holy calling!

Bashour wasn't an Arab Bedouin. He was a Ghassanid, like her. Why had he professed a belief in this Islam?

Tamara had a stubborn sense of righteousness. It had gotten her in trouble occasionally when she would argue with boys, made all the worse because she was usually right. Most of these warriors were obviously brainwashed into this cult of Islam, but maybe she could find out what was going on inside Bashour's head and convince him he'd made a mistake? If she could appeal to his Christian upbringing, there might be a chance to make him see his errors. She was sure he'd been raised a Christian; he'd said some things to Rashad that told her that much. Yes, it was time to start finding out what made him tick.

The truth was that she was becoming desperate for someone to talk to, some social connection. The other women in the camp were in two groups. The ones from Arabia, the camp followers who'd accompanied their men to war; they just treated her little better than an animal. She was just a slave and the only things spoken to her were brusque orders. Even when they talked to each other, they spoke as if she wasn't there. Then there were the girls in the same situation as hers. They lived in their own personal hells and were mortified with embarrassment at what happened to them every night. They wouldn't meet her eye, they'd look away when greeted. To talk to another slave girl risked shattering a fragile emotional barrier. You could never tell if someone was going to break down and start crying, or worse. That would draw attention and perhaps a beating.

Tamara had never felt so alone. A kind word, a smile, a touch that didn't promise pain and grief; she'd never realized how important these things were until they were gone. And lying right next to her was a young man who offered these things if she wanted them. How long could she steel herself to recoil against what he was? Would she turn into one of them?

45. Damascus
August 7, 634

Jonas Tournikes was taking the long way to Eudocia's house on his way to have dinner with her parents. He stayed on the well-traveled boulevards and marketplaces, well away from deserted alleys and streets. He sought out crowds on the theory that Kostas' men wouldn't get physical with him in public. Nicetas had been pleased with the way he'd thrown himself into his work in the warehouses after he was attacked. He had no idea that Jonas was doing his best to maintain a low profile in public until he could find a way to settle the gambling debts he'd incurred.

He made his way through the market, ignoring the stalls and their goods that spilled into the wide thoroughfares. He did his best not to make eye contact that might lead to a conversation and delay his journey. As he turned a corner into an open square where food vendors tended braziers with delicious smelling strips of meat, he saw three of Kostas' men. Before he could turn and fade back into the lanes of fabrics and clothes, they spotted him. They watched him intently but made no move towards him, so he decided to brazen it out and continued, with just the slightest hesitation.

A few steps farther and he saw Kostas himself sitting at a small table in a relaxed pose with a small group. The two men locked eyes; Kostas smiled broadly and waved him over.

Kostas didn't rise to meet him, but engulfed his hand in his fleshy grip. "Jonas, my young friend! We've missed you at the games lately!" He made no effort to introduce the other men at his table.

Jonas smiled gamely. "I have. . .other engagements."

"A young man of your stature? You're far too young, my friend, to be a slave to enterprise. You must enjoy your youth. Tell me, what is it that keeps you so busy?"

Jonas was thankful that he had a legitimate, important sounding excuse. "We've got a huge provisioning contract with the army quartermaster corps. I've had no time for anything but work."

Kostas leaned forward and fixed him with a hard stare. "You should pay such attention to all your obligations, boy."

Jonas raised his hands and took a half-step back defensively. "I told you I'd get your money as soon as I get married, Kostas. That's the truth."

Kostas leaned back and glared at him long enough to make him uncomfortable, then looked away, waving his hand dismissively. "Get about your business, boy. You have obligations." He proceeded to ignore Jonas' presence.

Jonas tried to avoid looking around as he left that area of the market to see if Kostas' men were following him. He hurried to the Nicetas home. On arriving he fixed a smile on his face and tried not to let the worry in the pit of his stomach show on his face.

Eudocia met him at the door and gave him a chaste kiss. "Oh, I was afraid you might be late! Dinner is almost ready and we're just waiting for Daddy."

She led him to the back patio where servants were laying out the evening meal. They encountered Nicetas coming in from his offices. "Eh, Jonas, good to see you, boy. Go ahead and start without me, I just need a quick wash."

He joined them shortly and Jonas fielded pleasantries with Eudocia's mother. Nicetas complimented Jonas, "I want to thank you for all the work you've been putting in at the warehouse lately. It's important for you to show that you're not above rolling up your sleeves and helping with the heavy lifting. The men who work for you won't respect you, if you ask them to do anything you're not willing and capable of doing yourself."

"I'm just doing what I see needs doing," said Jonas modestly. He didn't tell them that he loathed every moment of it.

"Daddy," said Eudocia, "we need to talk about a date for the wedding."

Nicetas face grew serious. He looked at his wife, who just raised an eyebrow and subtly shook her head. "Eudocia, your mother and I have been discussing this and we think that the current emergency isn't the best time to hold such an important event. Why, everyone is running around preparing for a siege or war. No one has time to consider things like wedding rehearsals and a celebration. And a siege is no place for a young bride, if the Arabs should come north."

Eudocia's face fell. "Daddy, if they come north, will we evacuate?"

Nicetas looked at his wife. “Dear, what do you think?”

“We lived under the Sassanid occupation,” she said. “I’ve no wish to have my gardens and house trampled just because the city answers to a different ruler. I’m staying.”

“Jonas, has your family discussed this?” asked Nicetas.

Jonas looked indifferent. “No we haven’t. Do you really think it’s a serious possibility? We thought it was all just idle speculation.”

“My boy, all that food we’ve been storing isn’t just for show. Haven’t you heard the news? Our army was defeated in Palestine. Thomas thinks that the Arab army will be headed this way.”

“Daddy, if they come here, how long would we be under attack?”

“That depends on many things. Will Heraclius relieve the siege? Do we have the food to hold out all winter? If Heraclius can’t relieve us, can we negotiate an acceptable surrender? It’s hard to say.”

“Daddy, suppose the worst happens and they take the city. Will that cancel our wedding plans?”

“No, Sweetheart,” Nicetas smiled. “Once the war has passed, your wedding will go ahead as planned. This city might change hands, but life will go on and people will still need trade. It won’t matter if you’re married under an Arab sheik or an Emperor.”

After the dinner, Eudocia’s parents left them on the patio and retired discreetly. Eudocia led Jonas to a fountain where they could talk without being overheard. “Jonas, if you want, we could elope. We could ask the priests at the monastery to marry us. We could go north to Antioch or even Constantinople.”

The thought appealed to Jonas for a moment. It would certainly solve his debt problems, but what sort of life would that give them? His family had money. Even though he didn’t have access to it at the moment – he was afraid to admit his debts to his father and beg for money – he still lived a fairly decent lifestyle. The addition of the money from Eudocia’s family held an even greater allure.

“No. No, we’ll do as your father says. There’ll be time enough. He’s right; everything will be fine when this little war blows over. Everyone’s getting excited over some Arab bandits. It’s a lot of fuss about nothing.”

She hugged him, but avoided a kiss, in case her parents might be spying on them. "I'm sorry Jonas."

"Relax," he said with bravado, "I don't think they're going to come this way. It's too far. All this is just a lot of people panicking for nothing."

Things were going to get difficult. The marriage was obviously on hold until the Arabs were satisfied and went back to the desert. Jonas started thinking of a plan to let him skim some profits off the warehouse operation to keep Kostas at bay while he waited for that to happen.

46. Southwest of Jerusalem
August 7, 634

The word had been passed that they'd be breaking camp and marching the next day. Bashour and his companions had been busy making preparations. For his companions, that had consisted of packing consignments of their share of the booty from the battle to be returned to Medina for safekeeping with their families. Bashour had no connection to Medina and was at a loss for what to do with his share. Rashad had helped him out. They held a small sale and he'd traded away the weapons and goods that he couldn't carry to other Muslims for gold. He was relatively wealthy now by the standards of his youth, but here in a mobile military camp, prices were inflated. He stashed the gold in a pouch in his small pack of possessions and tried to forget it. His most prized treasure was Tamara. He was sad that she still seemed so reluctant to associate with him, but now and then her shield slipped and she'd break her stoic reserve with a smile. He longed to hear her laugh.

After the evening prayer, they retired to Bashour's tent as usual. He wrapped himself in his cloak. "Good night, Tamara." Then he lay down. Instead of lying down and feigning sleep as she usually did, she sat cross legged and regarded him.

He felt her eyes on him, aware that she hadn't laid down with her back to him, as usual. He rolled over to glance at her and in the meager light he found her eyes locked on his. She'd never met his gaze so directly before. He rolled over and braced himself on an elbow and regarded her back, quietly. He almost asked her what was on her mind, but decided to let her be the one to break the silence.

"Where are you from?" she finally asked. "You're not like the rest of them. You're a Ghassanid, like me." She nearly spat the word "them," filling the word with as much loathing as she could muster.

"I'm from Tadmur."

"That's what I thought." She was silent for a few moments. "And your friend, Marid? Him too?"

Bashour nodded. "We've been friends as long as I can remember."

She pursed her lips with disapproval at this, but didn't say anything. She decided that telling him how she felt about Marid wouldn't help her in any way.

He waited patiently until she asked, "Why are you with these people?" She struggled to elaborate, but words failed her. The idea that anyone, especially someone of her tribe, would willingly join these barbarians was so wrong. She couldn't find words powerful enough to express the outrage.

He found himself taken aback. He'd spent the six weeks since he'd joined the Muslims learning the Qur'án, being instructed in the teachings of the Prophet Muhammad. The ideology seemed airtight, seamless and it made sense. The idea that anyone wouldn't see the simplicity and elegance of it was strange to him. "I had so many questions about Christianity that my teachers were never able to answer. Every time I found something that would explain everything, if I could get an answer, I was just told that 'It's a mystery.' Then I started learning the Qur'án and what Muhammad taught and it makes sense and there's no mysteries. I think if there's too many mysteries, maybe what you believe isn't really the truth."

His answer infuriated Tamara. She fought to control her response and keep it calm and level, but her anger and frustration still was clear in her tone. "Are you serious? You've joined this group for some lofty religious reason to explain obscure questions about God that you didn't have answers for?" She gaped, searching for words. He opened his mouth to respond, but she cut him off. "Look around you. These men are killing – murdering – their way across the land. They're stealing everything that's not nailed down and raping every woman they find! What does that have to do with your religious theories? How can you ally yourself with anyone who would do such things?" She struggled to keep her voice down. She was so upset, she wanted to yell at him, but she dared not draw attention from outside the tent to what they were saying.

Bashour had considered these things himself and had voiced his doubts to Rashad, so he was prepared. He spoke quietly, slowly, making sure he was selecting the right words to express what he was trying to say. "We don't fight anyone who does not fight us. We're carrying the word of Allâh for everyone to hear. We invite everyone we meet to accept Islam. Even if they choose not to, they may remain under Allâh's protection, if they pay the Jizyah. We don't violate anyone's conscience. The only ones we fight are the unbelievers who attack us because we profess Allâh."

"Oh, and that gives you the right to steal everything you see?"

"Allâh has granted us the reward of booty for our Jihad. It's a punishment to the unbeliever, to take what is his and give it to the faithful. All things belong to Allâh. If it were not his will that we do these things, he wouldn't grant us victory. Allâh in His wisdom has withheld our enemy's hand from us and rewarded us with booty. Listen, this isn't a war of conquest. A fifth of everything that's taken is given to the temple, where it's distributed to the widows and orphans. We don't want anything but for people to accept Islam, or to pay their poll tax if not. We're not overthrowing governments, unless they fight against Allâh. Is that so wrong?"

"And that includes forcing people into marriage against their will? Does that include beating women for the fun of it? Is that some sort of punishment, too?"

Bashour didn't know how to respond, he vaguely remembered something about hitting a disobedient wife, but there was so much he hadn't memorized yet. If they would only write the Qur'án down!

Satisfied he had no answer, she went on, "Did you know that a Muslim can divorce his wife just by saying 'divorce' three times? But a wife cannot divorce her husband for any reason? That a Muslim man can have four wives? These Muslims have destroyed the sanctity of marriage. Is that another punishment for the infidels, or just for women in general?"

"Islam exalts women."

She snorted, "Yes, like a prize camel to be bought and sold and bred, and to work as a slave to the whims of the men."

She was afraid he might start to get angry, so she changed the subject. "You say this isn't a war of conquest. What was this battle you fought last week? I didn't see any attempt to persuade anyone to join Islam. You fought for two days and killed thousands."

"They were invited to join Islam. I was there, I translated the invitation. They declined."

"And so what then? You had to kill them?"

"That army was going to attack us. We were defending ourselves."

"If the Muslims had stayed in Arabia, there would be no need to defend against anybody. How is anybody fighting you? You invade this land, bringing a foreign god and demanding we bow down to him. How do you see that as attacking you or fighting you? It's you who brought this fight. Go back to your desert and take your Allâh with you and no one will fight you there!"

"No, the Muslims are right. How can you deny the messenger of God when what he tells you is the truth? Allâh has commanded all Muslims to fight until the unbelievers accept Allâh or be subdued."

Tamara sat quietly. Her head was lowered so he couldn't see her eyes. He felt satisfied that he'd made his point and was proud of himself for doing so. He waited for her response, for her to admit she was wrong. Instead, after a long silence she said, her head still lowered, "So they killed my father. They cut off the head of my best friend right in front of me. They took me from my home by force and raped me every night for weeks and sold me as a piece of property. They did all this because your Allâh thinks I need to be punished for not believing the way you do? I think your Allâh is a sick, sadistic son of a bitch. I think you should take your Allâh back into the southern deserts where he belongs and leave the rest of the world alone. You deserve your Allâh and he deserves you."

Bashour was shaken. He was sure she'd misunderstood everything he'd said. He felt sympathy for what she'd told him. He reached out his hand to touch her knee, saying "Allâh is merciful. . ."

She slapped his hand away. "Don't touch me!" She turned her back to him as usual and lay down to sleep. "Good night. . . Master!"

The words stabbed Bashour like a knife. "Tamara, it's not like that."

She turned back to him. "Isn't it? You own me. I was given to you as a reward. You order me around like a slave, tell me to do this and that. What would you do if I said no?" She turned away and pointedly ignored him.

Sleep was a long time coming for Bashour. He stared at the tent above him and tried for hours to reconcile what she'd said with what he knew. He was upset, because it was the first time she'd said more than a word or two to him, and it had gone so badly. He wanted so much for her to believe, to understand.

Tamara also lay awake. As the silence fell and her anger subsided, she realized that she'd said too much, that getting angry was dangerous. She began to be afraid. What if he decided she was too contentious, decided he didn't want her? Her lot wouldn't change, and she couldn't imagine any Muslim who would be better to her than Bashour.

The next morning they were brought awake by the call to prayers. Bashour wearily pulled himself erect and started to arrange his cloak. "You need to pack everything and. . ." He stopped, check himself and started again. "I'd greatly appreciate it, if you would please start packing the tent and make ready to travel. I'll be back to help you as soon as morning prayers are done."

Tamara rolled over and regarded him, noting his choice of words. "I'd be delighted to start packing things and I look forward to your help," she said in a careful monotone. Then, as he opened the tent flap, she caught his arm. Looking up at him she said in Greek, "Please don't do that in front of them." Her eyes shifted towards where his companions were rousing themselves. Bashour looked at her quizzically and was gone before she could elaborate.

She folded the extra cloaks they used for sleeping. Bashour's pack had room for one of them. The pack was made to be carried by a man, but she was sure it would be loaded on the camel. As she shifted the contents to make room for it, she felt something heavy and hard. She pulled it out. It was a cross, apparently made of lead. It must have some kind of sentimental value to Bashour, because it wasn't very pretty and couldn't have been worth much. She was about to return it to the pack, when a small flash on a corner caught her eye. She examined it closely, then took a corner of her shawl and rubbed it vigorously. The spot yielded reluctantly, but with a lot of effort she made it a bit larger. The disguise was clever, but underneath the lead patina the cross appeared to be made of fine gold! Bashour had a secret! She quickly and carefully wrapped the cross in a tunic and returned it to the bottom of the pack.

She gathered the cooking utensils from around the small camp they'd made and bundled them all in a bag. Then she collapsed the tent and was just finishing when Bashour and his companions returned from their prayers and started gathering their goods. There was a flurry of activity as the army broke camp.

"Tamara! Come here, please!" called Bashour. He handed her a wooden switch. "We're going to load Shai-tan. Take this and stand in front of her. If she starts to turn her head, smack her face with this, hard, to keep her looking at you. Don't get too close, or she'll try to bite you, and be ready to dodge if she spits."

"What? Why don't you just tie her head?"

"You want to try to put a harness on her? I like my fingers right where they are."

"You men are babies." She did as she was asked and had to keep from laughing as they danced around the camel. It was still kneeling when they approached it and Rashad grabbed its tail to try to keep it from standing. Shai-tan let out a groan and stood anyway, scattering the men. She aimed a vicious kick at Rashad for his efforts, which he narrowly avoided. She was staked to the ground by a rope around her neck, but it didn't seem to inhibit her as she danced sideways when the men approached. They backed off and consulted each other. She stood there chewing her cud sleepily and didn't seem to notice when Jabir tentatively approached her. He cautiously touched her flank, ready to leap away if she so much as flinched. She didn't seem to notice. He rubbed her side with his hand, talking softly and she ignored him. He placed both hands on her with more confidence. Satisfied that she was ready to play nice, he turned his head and jerked it to signal they bring the pack saddle. As his attention wavered for an instant, the camel snapped a back foot forward to stomp on him. His hands told him she was moving and he leaped out of the way, only to have to leap again as she sidestepped and tried to stomp him with a front foot. His legs tangled and he fell on his back. Tamara aimed a sharp strike across the camel's cheek to get its attention and keep Jabir from being trampled to death. He scrambled out of range on all fours as his friends laughed.

As they stood there contemplating their next move, Tamara dropped the switch and picked up the rope that tied the camel. She started a slow approach, making sure that Shai-tan was looking at her and spoke quietly and firmly. "There, girl. Easy. It's okay, no one is going to hurt you."

Bashour took a step towards her. “Tamara, don’t! That camel will kill you!” She cut him off with a sharp motion of her hand, while keeping her eyes on Shai-tan’s

The camel regarded her steadily, its long, elegant eyelashes waving in the early-morning breeze. She stopped a foot or so away, in easy reach of the camel and the two regarded each other. She felt no fear; she made sure she stayed relaxed and calm. After a long moment, the camel stretched its neck and snuffled at her. It sniffed her belly, then slowly upwards until it was at her shoulder. She felt the hot, wet breath on her neck. The long elegant lips played with a fold of her tunic. Never breaking eye contact, she reached up with her free hand and rubbed the camel along its chin. Shai-tan gently tossed her head and Tamara smiled at her and talked a little louder, with a little more authority. The camel lowered its head and gently nudged her. She brought up the hand with the rope and threw a loop around the camel’s nose. It didn’t object and just continued to bump her with its head. She chucked at it a couple of times, saying, “Down! Down! Kneel!” The camel slowly and obediently sank to its knees, then folded its legs and laid down. Tamara removed the rope from the peg in the ground and returned to the animal’s head.

She looked at the men standing there in dumbfounded amazement. “Well, what are you waiting for?” She motioned at the camel’s back, then started scratching it behind the ears.

Bashour and Rashad brought the saddle pack. “How did you. . .?” Bashour started.

Tamara looked at him with contempt. “All of you have a lot to learn about how to talk to a lady.”

With Tamara holding Shai-tan, the loading went quickly and easily. At her urging, the camel rose obediently to its feet without complaint and didn’t try to stomp or kill anybody as they tightened the saddle straps.

“I’ve never seen anything like it,” said Qutayba, “That camel has never passed up a chance to try to kill me since before we entered Persia.”

Jabir pointed at Tamara and said to Bashour, “You can do whatever you want, but she stays!”

Bashour was proud of Tamara, but at the same time felt a little disgruntled that she upstaged them all so easily.

The army set off to the northeast along the main road and Bashour, Tamara and their companions fell in with the column when they were ready.

Tamara led Shai-tan, talking to her softly all the time. The men followed at a respectful distance, still not trusting the hooves of the animal. The camel regarded Tamara with her huge, beautiful eyes that seemed full of compassion. Before long Tamara found herself quietly unburdening her soul to the animal. It felt good to finally talk to somebody who seemed sympathetic, even if it was just a camel.

The column marched back the way they'd come, northeast towards Jerusalem. Bashour fell in with Rashad. He was troubled from his conversation the previous night and was thinking of what questions he could ask Rashad to clear away his confusion.

"What does Allâh say about women?"

Rashad smiled. "Ah, an excellent question." He then looked serious, "Before Allâh spoke to the Prophet, Peace be upon him, women had no rights except those which came from the men in their family. They are not warriors, so they cannot defend themselves. Without a man, they had no way to stop anyone from taking what they wanted.

"Bashour, we were a destitute people. There's little food in Mecca. The merchants who trade during the Hajj have gold and silver, but you cannot eat gold. A family will frequently have a child and pay a Bedouin family to raise it in the desert. The Bedouins have herds and always travel. They can always use an extra set of hands. Even a child can herd sheep. But what Bedouins will take a girl-child? So many times a girl baby was just buried after birth, because there will be no food for her. But Allâh in his mercy has prohibited this act.

"If a man dies and has no sons, or his sons are still young, his wife could lose everything. People could take anything from her and how could she stop them? If another man wanted her, he'd ask the town elders to marry her to him and often her children would be killed or left to starve. But Muhammad, may Allâh be pleased with him, required that the temple tax be used to support the widows and orphans. Islam has greatly improved the life of women."

"And what of marriage? Why do men get to marry more than one woman?".

Rashad gave him a strange look. “And why not? Doesn’t a rich man marry as many women as he wants? Didn’t King Solomon have thousands of wives? But Allâh prohibits a man from having more than four wives, and only then if he can afford them, because no man can give more than four women the attention they deserve. This is another way that Islam protects women,” he said brightly.

Bashour had grown up never knowing anyone who had more than one wife. Questions sprang to mind that he chose not to voice. What was the relationship of the wives to each other? Did the man sleep with them all at once, or did they have separate rooms? How did this work? He was embarrassed to ask about such things.

Another thing had been troubling him. Bashour grew up on the edge of two empires. The Persians practiced slavery, but Tadmur had been such an isolated outpost from the rest of the Persian empire that little Persian culture had found its way into the town during the seven years it had been occupied. Slavery had become almost non-existent in the Byzantine empire since the plague had swept the empire forty years previously. Millions of people had died and the huge demand for manpower in its wake had all but extinguished slavery. Bashour had no particular antipathy towards the idea of slavery, but had no direct experience of it. Last night Tamara had painfully reminded him that she was effectively his slave; she’d been awarded to him as if she were property. He had no idea how to react to that.

“And what about slaves?” he asked Rashad. “What rights does a slave have?”

“Ah, very good. Such practical questions you have today. The Prophet, blessed be His name, instructed us that the slave is your brother and Allâh has placed them under our command. If you have a brother under your command, you should feed him what you eat and clothe him the way you’re clothed. You should not overwork him and if you give him something difficult to do you should help him.”

“And what of female slaves?”

Rashad winked at him. “Of course, your slave girl is part of your household, not of your blood, and is therefore permitted for you. But you must not make her a whore for others, if she desires chastity. As her master, it is your responsibility to teach her manners and educate her in the ways of Islam. Then when she accepts Islam, you should manumit her and marry her.”

Bashour was relieved. Islam seemed to have an answer for everything. It made sense and he was pleased that now he had something to work towards.

They stopped for noon prayers and a light meal, which Tamara prepared. They were soon on the march again, with the sun moving to be at their backs. Bashour fell in with Tamara, who was leading Shai-tan. He kept the girl between him and the camel, still not trusting the animal.

"You have an impressive way with our camel," he said.

"I've been thinking about it, and all I can think of is that she was abused by a man and has never forgotten it. She may never let a man near her again."

"Well, you're most definitely not a man." said Bashour, as he admired her curves, visible despite her cloak. He regretted his words as soon as they passed his lips. He really needed to learn to quit saying what he was thinking.

She gave him a look, then turned her gaze ahead. "You would know best. . . Master."

"Hey, look, about that. I'm not. . . I mean, I don't want it to be like that."

They walked in silence for a few minutes. Tamara's mind was racing. She remembered her panic last night after they'd quarreled. She knew of far worse men to be with than Bashour. She mustn't do anything to spoil her position. "I'm sorry for what I said last night."

Bashour hadn't been expecting this. He'd been trying to think of something to say that wouldn't lead to a fight. "Huh?"

"I said I'm sorry. What I said. . .I didn't mean that you were like them. You're different." She felt she was betraying herself with the next words, but buttering him up wouldn't hurt. "You're kind of sweet."

Bashour's chest felt like it expanded two inches. "Look," he said, "I was offered a reward for something I did for Khalid and I knew you were having a hard time. I thought if I asked for you, I could protect you. I don't want to be your master."

She reached out and tugged his cloak gently and looked reprovingly at him. "Don't let them hear you say that!" she hissed in Greek. He looked taken aback and she went on, in a low voice. "Bashour, you have no idea how dangerous these people can be and how deeply suspicious they are. You have to fit in with them in every way. If you don't they'll become suspicious of you and you may become a slave or worse before you know it."

He started to say they weren't like that but checked himself. She was right, he knew. These Muslims were intolerant of anyone not like them.

After they'd walked some distance, he broke the silence. "You know, if you're my slave girl, you're permitted to me."

"I know. I know better than you can imagine," she said bitterly. She tried not to think of the nights with Mus'ad, or the beatings she took to thrill Nu'man. Thank God they were dead. But she was wary of the turn this conversation was taking. What did Bashour intend?

He placed his hand on her shoulder, gently. She closed her eyes and willed herself not to stiffen or flinch away. When, to his surprise, she didn't react, he squeezed her gently. "It won't be like that. I don't want from you anything you won't give me."

He didn't notice the tears that leaked from her eyes and went on, thinking out loud. "They say that if I have a slave, I'm supposed to teach her to be a Muslim and when she becomes a Muslim, I can manumit her and marry her."

She gave him an incredulous look, dumbfounded that he'd even suggest such a thing.

He caught the look and felt ashamed for making the suggestion. He lowered his voice, adding hastily, "You wouldn't have to really become a Muslim. Just act like you are. Think about it, if anything happened to me, you wouldn't be given to another man if I manumitted you."

Her eyes narrowed suspiciously. "Why not just manumit me now, if you think so much of the idea?"

"Come on, didn't you just tell me not to do anything that would stand out? They told me you have to accept Islam first."

"I'll think about it," she lied.

They walked in silence for a time. Bashour felt good that they were talking without fighting. Something she'd said the night before troubled him. She'd referred to a 'foreign god.' "Allâh isn't a foreign god, you know."

Tamara was caught off guard and had no idea what he was talking about. "What?"

"Last night you said the Arabs invaded with their foreign god. That's wrong. Allâh is the one and only God that Abraham and Jesus and Moses worshiped."

"No, I think you're wrong."

"Why?"

She struggled to put words to her feelings. How could she say that it just felt wrong? After some thought, she hit on something she could express. "Look, you know how these people hate the Jews. You've heard them speak."

Bashour thought about a conversation where his friends had expressed a desire to kill Jews in Jerusalem. "Yes."

"Well, what of God's promise to Moses that 'You shall be my people and I shall be your God?' Does God renege on promises? The Jews are God's chosen people, they always were. Yet Allâh wants them dead."

"Well, Allâh isn't alone. You know what Heraclius did to the Jews of Jerusalem when they sided with the Sassanids to overthrow the city?"

"Oh, that was insignificant compared to the entire Jewish people. Look, it's been five hundred years since the Romans extinguished Israel, yet we still have Jews today. Where are the Philistines, the Babylonians, Alexander's Greeks, the Edomites, the Pharaohs? All gone. All the nations contemporary with Israel have been absorbed into other, greater empires, or scattered to the winds, but we still have Jews! God may chastise his people, but he will never forsake them or turn on them the way your Allâh wants to do."

Tamara had a point, Bashour admitted himself. He never could understand the bloodthirsty obsession his companions had towards the Jews.

"Bashour! If you talk to your woman too much, we may not be able to tell you apart!" laughed Qutayba from behind them.

Tamara looked at him gently. "Laugh at their joke and go," she said in Greek, with an imperceptible jerk of her head.

That night they camped on the hills around Jerusalem. Torches lined the walls of the city and they could see the guards moving about the battlements, preparing for a siege. But the word had been passed not to engage the city, nor to enter into any type of communication with its inhabitants. The air wasn't quite as humid as it was in Elah, where they'd spent the last week. Bashour and Tamara chose not to erect the tent that night. They stayed up late and made their way away from the encampment to a hill where they could see most of the city. They talked softly, exchanged wonder at the size of the city, the likes of which neither of them had experienced.

"I've tried to imagine it from the stories, but I never dreamed it could be this big," said Tamara. "Can you imagine how it must be to live so close together like that?"

"I'm amazed at the walls. How many men, how long would it have taken to build them so high, all the way around the city?" said Bashour. "Tamara, can you imagine all that this city has seen? That flat area way over there, I bet that's where the temple was. And look there, that big building on the knob there, do you think that's the church of the Holy Sepulcher? Right there, that's where Jesus was crucified."

Tamara enjoyed his enthusiasm and shared it. She let him go on, giving her a guided tour of the city. She was sure he knew as little about it as she did, but he sounded so authoritative. It was so peaceful on this hill, beholding a city that overwhelmed all their preconceived notions. Bashour didn't feel like a stranger. The world seemed to fall away and it was just the two of them and no expectations. Tamara allowed herself to live in the moment and was surprised to find that the moment wasn't all that bad. She shivered in the chill night air blowing out of the desert and moved a little closer to him. He felt it and threw his cloak over both of them. She huddled to him, soaking up his warmth, and for a few minutes she forgot her situation and felt safe.

After they'd finished discussing Jerusalem, Bashour quietly and earnestly began to tell her about all that he'd learned about Islam. He wasn't insistent, it sounded like he was thinking out loud, trying to rationalize what he'd learned and associate with Christianity. She listened quietly for the most part. She knew he was wrong, Islam was wrong, but had decided to learn as much about it as possible, so she could argue against it.

47. Tiberias, Near the Sea of Galilee
August 11, 634

The morning sun sparkled off the Sea of Galilee. A cool breeze cleansed the air of the portico where Taticus gathered his centurions. Once they'd assembled and were looking expectantly at him, he invited them to be seated.

When they'd marched into Tiberias, the local governor had been horrified. He'd made it abundantly clear to Taticus that their presence was unwelcome. There simply weren't enough supplies in the city to maintain a garrison, let alone a force such as Taticus led. He hadn't been hostile, but was eager to do whatever it took to get Taticus to take his column and move on.

"Gentlemen, I'd planned that we'd rest for a couple days before we begin a concentrated training syllabus." Several days ago this announcement would have been met with rolling eyes and looks of disdain, but Taticus had marched them relentlessly from Jerusalem to Tiberias. In the process he'd pruned his officer corps. His centurions were now seasoned combat veterans and accomplished leaders of men. Gone were the political appointees and sons of politicians. These men knew the value of hard training.

Taticus continued, "But that's not going to be possible." The assembled men looked at each other questioningly, but said nothing. "Word is that the Arab army has bypassed Jerusalem and is heading this way, following our tracks. I've been given discretion of command from the local governor. Without orders from Basileus Heraclius, I have the authority to act independently." He stopped and swept his gaze across the men. "I've served under Heraclius. He wouldn't order us to retreat further from this enemy. Neither would he order us into battle to our certain deaths.

"The power of this Arab army is its mobility. They achieve this advantage because they move across the land unopposed. We're going to end that. We'll use hit-and-run tactics. We'll lay ambushes for them and allow their combat echelons to pass, then hit their baggage train. Scouts are reporting that a large column of camp followers has joined them. They'll have no choice but to slow to protect the non-combatants. We haven't the strength to meet them toe to toe, but we can sow confusion in their ranks and buy time for Heraclius to act.

"The governor has opened his armory to us. Make sure your cohorts are fully equipped. We march in two days. I plan to position the main body of our force at the headwaters of the Jordan river and see which way their army turns. We'll travel light and we'll be moving day and night. Centuries will operate independently. This will give us the mobility to leapfrog ahead of them, but it'll require initiative from each of you. Don't look to higher command for direction. We're going to be scattered along their line of march and communications will be difficult. I'm confident you men can handle it. Avoid a static engagement at all costs. No one will rescue you if you get in trouble.

"Stratopedarches, you will arrange a supply line running from settlements here in Galilee. We will have no baggage train. Every century will detail an individual to coordinate supply and ensure the supply line stays up to date on your whereabouts.

"Questions?"

Questions were plentiful. The foot army hadn't been trained to operate like this. These men weren't used to operating independently and the task of maintaining a supply line in such a fluid situation had never been attempted. The discussion lasted most of the afternoon. Tactics were argued over, problems were presented and solved. They finally decided that the centuries would operate in groups of three, with one making a harassing attack and withdrawing and the other two providing an ambush to halt any attempt of the Arabs to use their cavalry to pursue their tormentors. This was to be repeated all along the Arab line of advance.

As the discussion went on, ideas flowed more easily. One that Taticus endorsed and immediately ordered put into action was to dam parts of the Jordan River. A series of locks and diversions were already used to send irrigation water across the valley's northern fields. A little creative water management would turn much of the valley into a swampy morass, difficult for a large army to pass through quickly.

Taticus was pleased with the way the discussion had gone as he retired that night. Initially reluctant to think tactically beyond their immediate orders, the men he'd chosen had valuable insights once they relaxed and realized they weren't endangering their careers for voicing an opinion. He felt his small army was stronger as a result, as each leader could lay claim to part of the resulting plan.

48. Damascus
August 12, 634

Thomas had spent the morning ensconced in a small office in the back of the warehouse, reviewing inventories, examining offers and contracts and writing instruction letters to his agents spread across the Levant. He'd worked through lunch and was grateful for the interruption when Nicetas stuck his head in the office. "Visitors, Thomas. Governor Azrail is here to see us."

Thomas raised his eyebrows in question and Nicetas shrugged. As he followed Nicetas into the warehouse , Nicetas called for chilled wine and grapes to be served.

"Governor! This is a surprise! What brings you here?" Thomas asked as the two men grasped hands.

"Ill news, I'm afraid," said Azrail. He looked pointedly at the laborers in the warehouse who went about their work, but all ears were turned toward their conversation.

"Of course, Governor. This way." He herded Azrail into one of the larger offices in the back. The men waited while a third chair was fetched and the wine served. When the door had closed behind the departing servant, they turned expectantly to Azrail.

"Several messengers have confirmed that our army in Palestine was defeated by the Arabs southwest of Jerusalem. Casualties were horrendous and the remnants are scattered across the countryside."

"And the Arab army?" asked Thomas.

"Intact, I'm afraid. They licked their wounds for nearly a week near the battlefield, but they're on the move again and it looks like they're headed this way. Thomas, I need to know the state of your preparations."

"Right now we could hold out for three or four months. That will improve dramatically if we have enough time to get the wheat crop in. The harvest will begin in about a week."

Azrail looked thoughtful. "That would get us to midwinter. If they laid siege to us, that might be enough to starve them into leaving."

"Only if we burn the fields," said Nicetas, "and leave them nothing to forage."

"Yes, excellent idea. We'll do that when they get close. Unfortunately there's another complication. Heraclius is sending five thousand heavy cavalry to reinforce our garrison. How will that affect your preparations?"

Thomas shrugged. "It might shorten our endurance by a couple weeks. Five thousand isn't much against the population here already. Do you know who the commander will be?"

"Yes, a Merarch named Caloiis. Do you know him?"

Thomas nodded. "Mostly by reputation. He's a right arrogant bastard, but an excellent commander of the cavalry. Fearless, by all counts, but his experience was fighting Persians. It will be interesting to see how he fares against the Arabs, with their cavalry skills."

"Interesting isn't quite the word I'd use," said Azrail drily. "Thomas, I'm considering evacuating the non-combatants and civilians from the city. If we cut non-essential mouths to feed, we could easily last the winter."

Thomas and Nicetas looked at each other. "Governor, the decision is yours, of course. But consider the effect on the morale of the men who stay."

"Some city guards would desert to evacuate with their families," said Nicetas.

"And consider this," said Thomas, leaning forward. "Basileus Heraclius would be far more inclined to send a relief force to break a siege if civilians were involved."

"Well, perhaps we could issue a warning, advise people what's happening and leave it up to them if they want to leave," suggested Azrail.

Thomas shook his head. "No, that could end up worse than an organized evacuation. Everyone would look to each other to see what everyone else was going to do. All it would take is for one person to panic and run and you'd have a panicked mob on your hands. The resulting riot could do a lot of damage. They might even break into the warehouses to steal food for their trip."

"Hm. Yes, I see your point. I appreciate your experience, Thomas. I never considered that I'd have to deal with such things when I received this appointment." He rose to his feet. "My thanks for the wine. So I can confidently report to the city fathers that we can hold a siege until midwinter?"

The other two rose and shook his proffered hand. “Of course, Governor. We can easily support that. Longer if we went on half-rations.”

“I trust that won’t be necessary. Very well. It is what it is, then. Nicetas, that’s an excellent idea about burning the fields before we’re besieged. I’ll put that to the council. Good day, Gentlemen. Thank you for your efforts.” He turned and left.

Nicetas dropped heavily into his seat and poured another cup of wine. “Thomas, do you think we should send our families north?”

“Epiphina wouldn’t go. She sees herself as an extension of the Emperor, and she’s right. If word got that she was leaving it would cause just the sort of panic we warned Azrail about.”

“I’ve been thinking about sending the girls away. That would be a fight. My wife was born and raised here and doesn’t like travel; and Eudocia is all aflutter about Jonas.”

“Word is out that you’re planning the wedding event of the year. If you call that off, people will talk.”

“Hmph. Talk is cheap. I’m beginning to have second thoughts about that boy, Thomas. I can’t put my finger on it, but there’s something about him. He’s too smooth, too quick with an answer, but he speaks with the assurance of a horse seller, not a person who has the confidence of experience. You know what I mean?”

“I wasn’t going to mention it, but he doesn’t seem comfortable leading men. The workers here in the warehouse do what he says, but I don’t think they respect him.”

“Yes, I noticed that, too. Thomas, what will I do? How would I explain this to Eudocia if I forbid the marriage to go forward?”

“You could plant a seed of doubt and see if it takes root and grows. Eudocia is an intelligent girl. Hopefully love hasn’t blinded her too much.”

“I’m afraid that’s exactly what’s happened, but not like you mean. All I hear about is plans for the wedding. I don’t know if she’s in love with Jonas, but she’s definitely in love with the idea of a grand wedding.”

Thomas shrugged. “Well, you know that any problem, if ignored long enough, will eventually go away.” He smiled at his friend.

Nicetas laughed and toasted him. “Let’s pray that philosophy works with the Arabs, eh?”

49. The Jordan River
August 12, 634

The column had left the desert east of Jerusalem and descended again into the Jordan River valley. Both Bashour and Tamara were grateful to escape the unaccustomed humidity they'd experienced further west. They marveled at the endless, wide swath of green along the river. The land was flat along the road they walked. They weren't so far from the river that they couldn't wash the dust out of their clothes at the end of the day.

The past two days on the road had been monotonous, despite the breathtaking vistas they'd encountered. Bashour had abandoned his Muslim friends whenever he could and spent his time walking beside Tamara as she led Shai-tan, who was as docile as a lamb towards her. Bashour still kept Tamara between him and the camel.

You can only walk so many miles without saying anything and eventually Bashour's attempts at conversation elicited a response. They talked about nothing, telling stories, carefully avoiding discussion of religion, or their situation, where they were going or where they came from. Slowly, Tamara began to relax towards Bashour.

That night as they prepared for bed, instead of lying down with his back to her, Bashour sat, quietly watching her brush her hair out of a loose braid. Her beauty made him ache in his stomach. She reached for the loose gown she used for sleep and stopped and looked at him expectantly. He turned away, reseating himself with his back to her as she undressed and changed in the soft lamplight.

"You can turn around, I'm done," she said. He did so and she did a double-take on him. Smiling, she picked up the lamp and leaned close. "You're blushing!" she exclaimed.

He started to say something and caught himself, and just rolled his eyes instead. She giggled, "It's all right. It's cute. My little brothers would blush like that when I caught them staring at me."

He smiled as she settled herself, sitting in front of him. "Tell me about your family."

She looked pensive, collecting her thoughts. “My father raised cattle. We were four. My older brother, me and two little brothers. My older brother joined the army and went west. I haven’t seen him in a couple of years. My little brothers would play games and try to trick me. Sometimes they put a lizard in my bed. I played along a couple of times and acted like they’d surprised me. Then it got old, but they never stopped trying.

“I’m glad it was just lizards. If it had been spiders, I don’t know what I’d have done. I hate spiders and they know it. I wonder why they never put a spider in my bed?”

“Maybe they’re just as afraid of spiders as you are?”

She looked at him and smiled. “I never thought of that. You’re probably right. Those two always seem so fearless. Once they found a frog near the irrigation ditch, just a small one, but Mother refused to let them in the house with it. She made them take it back to the water and let it go.”

She paused and thought briefly. “I always had to take my clothes with me into the washroom when I went to bathe. Those two would egg each other on and try to steal my clothes if I didn’t. They were always spying on me, trying to catch me naked.”

Bashour smiled, remembering similar antics he and Marid had played, but remained quiet, desperate not to break the spell of the moment.

“If I’d been Mother, I would have beaten them at least once a day, but she let them get away with murder. It’s funny, they know exactly what they can do around her, but they’re really terrified of making her mad, because when she beats them, she’s not like Father. He holds back, because he’s afraid of hurting them, but Mother, she’s got no such concerns. She uses every ounce of strength when she beats us. Once I hid for three days because she was angry with me for breaking a milk jug!”

Bashour laughed. “You’re joking. Where did you stay? With a relative?”

“No, my aunt would have marched me home straight away. She’d no sympathy for me. No, I hid in the shed where we kept the goats.”

“How did you eat?”

Tamara giggled. “My Father had sympathy on me and sneaked meals out to me. It was our secret.”

“Your Father sounds like a great man.”

"Oh he is. . .he used to play with us, get down on his hands and knees. . . He'd be a camel and we'd sway as he walked like a camel, both feet on each side at once. Then he'd be our horse, but it was hard to ride him because he'd move sideways as we tried to get on. Sometimes he was a monster and my brothers would defeat him with wooden swords, while I played the maiden that he'd captured. He'd always give them a good fight, but eventually lose and be beaten into the ground and they'd stand on him in victory. Then we'd all laugh and it would be time for bed. . . ." Her voice trailed off and she turned her head away, hiding her eyes. She closed her eyes tight to hold back the tears.

He reached for her arm. "Tamara?"

"Now. . . . now he's gone. They killed him!" She lost the battle with her grief and her shoulders were wracked by sobs and she seemed to crumple.

Bashour moved closer and gathered her into his arms and held her head on his shoulder. She let go of her control and poured out her grief. For the first time in all these weeks, her self-control was shattered. She wrapped her arms around him and clung to him. Gone was the beautiful woman whose reserve he'd been trying so unsuccessfully to defeat. In her place was a frightened, grief-stricken girl, looking for some sanctuary, some safe place where she could escape the horrors that she'd witnessed.

He didn't know how long he held her like that, softly rocking her, whispering soothing noises in her ear. Her face was buried in the folds of his cloak on his shoulder, which muffled her cries, so she wouldn't be heard from any distance. He stroked her hair and comforted her. For the first time he didn't feel awkward around her, afraid he might do something foolish. She was completely vulnerable and he was prepared to hold her like this for the rest of the night, if she needed it. His heart was heavy with the grief he was absorbing from her.

After a long time, her sobs subsided and her breathing evened out. She still clung to him and when he shifted position she tightened her grip. "It's okay. I'm here. I'm always here for you." He nuzzled her ear and kissed her hair softly. She relaxed slightly and raised her head and looked at him. He shushed her softly and kissed her forehead gently. In the light of the waxing moon and the flickering of distant campfires through the tent, he could see her tear streaked face and he used the back of his finger to brush the tears away. "I'm sorry for everything that's happened. I'll never let anything like that happen to you again."

He kissed her forehead again and this time as he withdrew, she turned her face to him and thrust her chin towards him slightly. Their lips met. Gently, almost barely touching, they kissed. He didn't force the contact, content to let her control the moment. After several hesitant brushes of their lips, she pulled him tight and kissed him properly.

When they broke for air, he looked at her with surprise. She lowered her eyes and smiled shyly, embarrassed. He wrapped his arms around her and held her close and together they slowly toppled over and were lying down.

Tamara felt emotionally drained, but cleansed. She knew it wouldn't last, but for the moment she felt at peace. It had felt good to cry like that. She knew there would be more tears to come, but for now she was content to burrow into the protective warmth of Bashour's arms and pretend it was a refuge. She willed herself not to think about anything but the moment and soon relaxed into a deep, healing sleep.

Bashour didn't sleep. He felt every slightest motion, every breath she took. He savored the moment, the closeness he'd sought since the first time he'd seen her. He was afraid that if he slept, he'd miss a moment of this precious gift that he'd stumbled on.

The morning call to prayers found them curled together, his arms forming a protective shield over her. Before he leapt to answer the call, he contemplated the relaxed beauty of her face, serene in sleep. He was sorry to break the spell. She awoke as he shifted his weight. He kissed her forehead and shushed her. She smiled slightly and closed her eyes again as he left the tent.

50. Damascus
August 13, 634

Nicetas stuck his head in the office. “Thomas, messenger for you from the governor.”

Thomas raised his head and waved him in without saying anything. The boy entered, breathless. “A large column of cavalry is coming down the road to the east, sir. Governor Azrail requests your presence at the Citadel.”

That got Thomas’ attention. “Ours or theirs?”

The boy’s eyes widened and he stuttered for a second, as if afraid to answer incorrectly. Then he processed the question and relaxed. “Ours, sir.”

Thomas was visibly relieved. “Run ahead and tell the Governor I’m on my way, thank you.”

The boy bowed and backed out of the room. Nicetas entered with a question on his face. “News?” he asked.

“I believe we’re being reinforced. Care to join me?” Thomas reached for his cloak.

“I wouldn’t miss it.”

They were waiting with the Governor on the steps of the citadel at the center of the city when Merarch Caloiis entered the square at the head of huge column of men. He was wearing burnished armor and sat astride a giant of a horse. He reined the animal to a halt in front of Azrail’s group and saluted. “I am Caloiis, sent by Basileus Heraclius with five thousand heavy cavalry.”

“Your presence is welcome, Merarch,” Azrail said, returning the salute. “I am Azrail, Governor of Damascus. These are my advisors.” He waved his hand at the rest of his group.

Caloiis did not smile or acknowledge the others. He dismounted heavily and handed the reins of his horse to a mounted aide at his side. He turned towards Azrail. “My men are weary and the horses need tending. Detail someone to lead them to their billet and stable the horses. I’ll meet with you in your offices directly. Now, show me a washroom, so I can get some of this dust off my skin.”

Azrail looked stone faced and gestured for an aide to take care of the soldiers, then stepped aside for Caloiis. “My servant

Justin will see to your comfort and bring you to my office at your leisure."

Caloiis stepped off after the servant without another word or look at the group. Azrail turned to Thomas with an irritated look on his face. "Stiff bastard, isn't he?" he muttered, careful not to be heard by the passing column of cavalry.

"I was thinking that he lives up to his reputation for arrogance."

"You know of this man then?"

"I've encountered him in passing but never actually interacted with him. They say he's fearless in battle. He thinks he's brilliant, but hasn't done anything to prove it."

"Hmm. Well, it wouldn't do to keep the man waiting. We'd better summon the city fathers."

They'd assembled in the large portico that formed a wing of the Governor's mansion and were waiting when Caloiis arrived. He seemed a touch less stiff and acknowledged the city fathers individually as they were introduced. He brightened when Thomas was introduced. "Ah yes. Son-in-law to Basileus Heraclius. He sends his regards. I thought you were shunning public service?"

Thomas smiled as they shook hands. "Indeed, that was the plan, Merarch, but the governor asked for my assistance in the current emergency."

"Of course, there's no finer logistician. Good to have you."

Once the introductions were complete, Caloiis took control. "Now, to business. How many men have we currently under arms?"

Governor Azrail responded, "We have fifteen thousand foot soldiers and I can muster about three thousand light horse."

Caloiis looked surprised. "So few?

Thomas spoke up, "All the reserves were diverted to Palestine for the buildup there."

Caloiis looked unhappy and pursed his lips. "What is the state of your defenses? Your supply situation?"

"The walls are in good repair," said Azrail. "As you've seen, they're ten cubits high or more. The gates have been reinforced. We've got wells in the north side of the city that can supply us with adequate water. The city had grown past the wall to the south and east, but over the last few months we've cleared the land out to two hundred paces from the walls, to allow a killing zone for the archers." He stopped and looked at Thomas.

"We've been accumulating supplies since early summer. With the current population, counting your detachment, I think we could hold out for a six-month siege. That will be improved if we have a chance to bring in the harvest before they invest the city."

Caloiis nodded and turned to Azrail. "What is the battle readiness of your garrison, Governor? Are the men trained and drilled?"

Azrail bridled. "Of course they are, Merarch. I'll put my men against any in the Empire."

Caloiis looked skeptical. "Your soldiers are regulars? How many more men can we get if we levy a draft of able-bodied men? Are there enough weapons for such a draft?"

Azrail took a breath to answer. The implication that his men were less than ready had angered him. Thomas touched his arm and answered for him. "We could conceivably conscript thirty to forty thousand men. We could probably arm twenty-five thousand of those with the arms on hand."

The men watched as Caloiis paced the room thoughtfully. After a moment he turned and addressed them. "I would like to inspect the garrison first thing tomorrow morning. Be ready.

"Issue orders for a training draft of all men between sixteen and fifty. I want them drilled in combat and ready to take orders. I don't want to be handed untrained conscripts in the heat of battle. Train them, and then release them back to their civilian tasks.

"On my way in, I noticed structures built right up to the wall. Remove them. I want a cleared street ten paces wide all the way around the inside of the wall, to support rapid troop movements."

Azrail's face grew hard as he stood up. "Excuse me, Merarch, but I am the governor here. I'll give the orders if a military draft is to be implemented."

One of the city elders also stood and supported Azrail. "Merarch, by what authority do you come to our city and begin issuing orders like this?"

"I was sent here under orders of Basileus Heraclius to take command of this fortress and the surrounding district." replied Caloiis hotly.

"Then you have a dispatch for me that relieves me of command?" demanded Azrail.

Caloiis looked uncomfortably angry. "I have no such dispatch," he admitted sourly.

The elder who'd challenged him pressed him further. "We did not ask for a military commander, we requested reinforcements. We have a governor appointed by Basileus Heraclius already." He indicated Azrail.

"I command a meros of cataphracts. This is a major maneuver unit of the imperial army. It's not a mere reinforcement."

The old man shook his head wearily. "I'm sorry Merarch, but these military subtleties elude me. What is a 'maneuver unit' and how is it not a reinforcement?"

"My heavy cavalry is the hammer to be used on the enemy, once he's against the anvil of the regular infantry. We move much more quickly, can react to the enemy's movement, are more highly trained and better equipped than the standard line unit. Using them for garrison and siege defense would be like using your prize racing stallion as a plow horse."

"Well, why did the Basileus send a maneuver unit when we asked for more men to man our defenses?" demanded Azrail. "And I fail to see the logic behind the idea that your command of a maneuver unit places this city under your orders. Show me your authority, Merarch."

Caloiis took an angry step forward and opened his mouth to answer when Thomas stepped up and raised his hands. "Gentlemen! Gentlemen, calm yourselves." When he had everyone's attention, he went on, addressing Azrail. "Governor, no one is questioning your authority over the city. Basileus Heraclius sent one of his elite units to assist with the defense. The heavy cavalry gives us a great deal more flexibility than a turma of infantry would have." He turned to Caloiis. "Merarch, your presence here is welcome and your suggestions are noteworthy. We'd be grateful to hear any other ideas you have to strengthen our defenses. You as a military commander have too many duties associated with your command to worry about the details of the civilian part of this garrison. I think Governor Azrail is far more suited to such mundane tasks, and he already knows our defenses. May I suggest you two work together as a joint command? Hand-in-hand, as it were? There's no reason one of you should be subordinate to the other."

Azrail and Caloiis regarded each other silently. One of the elders spoke up. "There's wisdom in what Thomas proposes. I move we adopt his proposal of a joint command." The assembly voiced their approval.

Azrail smiled and raised an eyebrow to Caloiis and extended his hand. After a moment, Caloiis accepted it and they shook.

Plans were made, lines of authority were drawn. Despite some lingering friction, they got down to the business of dealing with the Arab threat. Reality soon set in and they warmed to the idea of a joint command.

Later that evening, Azrail pulled Thomas aside from the dinner they hosted for Caloiis. "You know, Thomas, I don't like this idea of a joint command. I'm the governor of the Damascus region. All military control should come through me."

Thomas placed his hand on the other man's shoulder reassuringly. "Don't forget that Caloiis has the ear of Heraclius. He's too close to the court for it not to have rubbed off on him. That makes him feel independent, not subordinate to local government. In his mind, he's an extension of Heraclius himself. If we press the issue and force him to subordinate himself to you, he's likely as not to take his meros and return to Emessa, with a bad word for you to Heraclius."

Azrail shook his head. "I don't like politics like this, Thomas. This kind of thing has you constantly looking behind to see who's about to plunge a knife in your back."

"This is nothing. Think of how court must have been under Emperor Phocas."

Azrail regarded him with respect. "And you, Thomas? Does this sort of intrigue come naturally to you? Are you a political animal?"

Thomas laughed. "It's a matter of survival for me. How can I be married to the daughter of the Basileus and not be aware of the politics? But I loathe it, Governor. People playing petty power games. They forget what's real, where the source of that power derives. God help me if I ever forget that."

Azrail grasped his hand and shook it. "You're an exceptional man, Thomas. Would that our leaders were all like you."

"We're blessed. Heraclius hasn't forgotten the common touch, and isn't afraid to do what it takes to stamp out corruption and malfeasance in government. He's truly one of the people. It's the power-mad crowd around him I don't have any time for. But Heraclius, he's a gift from God."

"And the Arabs? Are they a scourge from God? Rumors are flying that this is God's punishment for Heraclius marrying his niece."

Thomas pulled back slightly. "I'm in no position to judge what does and doesn't come from God. As to the choice of my Father-in-law's wife, I'm in no position to speak on the matter," he said coolly.

"Yes, yes, of course. I presume too much to even bring the matter up with you. Come, let's rejoin our guest of honor and toast a victory against the Arab barbarians."

51. Jordan River
August 13, 634

Tamara still couldn't get over the endless green that characterized the Jordan River valley. On either side of them, in the distance to the west and closer to the east, the dun-colored hills reminded them that they were in the greatest oasis she'd ever seen, but were still in a desert. They were marching through farmland, irrigated from the nearby river. As usual, she was leading Shai-tan.

Bashour and Tamara had spent the nights in mutual companionship. The kiss of several nights ago hadn't been repeated. They both felt a little shy and embarrassed about that. But at night she felt safe when he shielded her with his arms around her. She felt protected, and it was a welcome feeling. In her mind she knew it was an illusion, but it helped her sleep, so she didn't dwell on it.

She was ashamed to admit it to herself, but her body was developing a growing desire. She couldn't help but notice how sensitive her breasts became sometimes, or the thrill she got when Bashour's arm would accidentally brush them as they cuddled.

She'd never been with a man on her terms. All she knew of sex was pain, humiliation and a total helplessness. She knew it wasn't supposed to be like this. She'd occasionally awakened as a child and heard the muted sounds of passion from her parents' bed. It meant nothing to her as a child, but when she got older she began to have an idea of what was happening. Her parents loved each other and the sounds comforted her. She used to listen when they thought she was asleep and dream about what it would be like when she had a husband of her own.

Would she ever be able to live like that now? Would she ever know the joy of unreserved love for a man like that? The way Bashour acted made her think it might be possible. He never made a demand of her, never suggested anything inappropriate. As precarious as her situation was, she was learning to feel safe when he wrapped his arms over her at night. The previous night she'd slept soundly for the first time in weeks.

They'd been walking north along the east bank of the river since morning prayers. The going had been slow. Someone had flooded the fields, and they frequently found themselves having to backtrack and pick their way around inundated plots of land. The column had been forced to the east, where the land was a little higher at the edge of the wide valley and they could move unimpeded. Now it was the time for noon prayers. Tamara sheltered herself in the meager shade of Shai-tan's bulk until the men were finished. She smiled to herself at how silly they looked, kneeling and bowing over and over, chanting mindless verses that she recognized as part of this "Qur'án" that they'd memorized.

Once they'd finished, Bashour rejoined her and they started north again. As usual, Bashour kept Tamara between him and Shai-tan.

"Why do you do that?" she asked in Greek.

"Because I don't trust that camel!"

Tamara looked puzzled for a moment, then laughed lightly. "No, I mean why do you bow down and recite like that?"

"That's how Muhammad, peace be upon him, instructed us to pray to Allâh."

"Do you really think that's praying?"

He looked nonplussed for a moment. "Of course, what would you call it?"

"I'm not sure what I'd call it, but it doesn't look like prayer. Look, I know you were a Christian. You must not have been taught much about Christianity, though."

"I was a student of Imad bin Najib!" He retorted hotly.

"I've heard of him. My father spoke well of him. I can't believe you would ignore what he taught you about prayer, then."

"And what is that?"

"Remember what Jesus taught in Matthew? Don't pray loudly in public. Those who do have received their reward. You're to lock yourself in your room and pray in secret and the Lord will reward you in secret. You're not to pray with mindless repetition, like the pagans do. You're to pray like Jesus taught us in the 'Our Father.'"

"You don't understand," said Bashour, weakly, "They say that prayer offered in congregation is twenty-five times more superior than the prayer offered alone. For such prayer Allâh upgrades him a degree in reward, and crosses out one sin."

"So you're telling me that Allâh is keeping score? How many degrees do you need to get into heaven? What does that even mean? What is it you're repeating over and over? It's some sort of poem, isn't it?"

"We recite parts of the Qur'án, the holy message given to Muhammad, may Allâh be pleased with him. They are the words of Allâh."

Tamara snorted, "And why does Allâh want to hear his words repeated back to him? He sounds awfully impressed with himself. Some birds can be taught words, like the raven. If he wants to hear his words like that, why didn't Allâh just teach them to repeat his Qur'án and leave us alone? Really, Bashour, don't you find this a bit odd?"

"By praying the Qur'án, we're demonstrating our obedience, our submission and thus gaining his blessings."

"And where did you learn to do this? Where did this Qur'án come from?"

"You know that the Qur'án was delivered by Allâh's messenger, Muhammad, peace be upon him. He taught everyone to pray five times a day."

"And by what authority does he teach this?"

"He is God's messenger. He wouldn't tell a lie."

Tamara shook her head. "Don't you see the problem with that, Bashour? You say he wouldn't lie, but if he were lying, how would you know?"

"Why would he lie? For what reason?"

"Oh, come on, Bashour, think. Money, sex, power!"

"No, Allâh's Messenger wasn't a wealthy man. He lived a modestly. He was a very quiet man."

"Oh, really? Come on, Bashour, I hear your companions talking about him, how many wives he had and how he would service them all in one night. Just look at the power he had. I'm telling you Bashour, whatever this man was, he was no prophet."

Bashour felt his anger rising and he willed it away. Getting angry with Tamara was counterproductive. He knew that if he showed any anger, she would shut up and speak to him no more. He didn't want that. He wanted to convince her, to show her the truth, to lead her to Islam of her own free will, so he could marry her under the law. "He was the last and greatest of prophets! Allâh gave him the Qur'án to confirm all the previous books Allâh has given. Allâh has grown tired of waiting for people to listen to his word. Under the teaching of Muhammad, peace be upon him, the word of Allâh will be heard by every soul in the world."

"Greater than the Son of God? Why would Allâh send another prophet after he'd sent his Son?"

"Ah," said Bashour knowingly, as if he'd caught her in a trap, "that's a mistake. How could Allâh have a son, when he has no consort? That's in the Qur'án. The Gospel is mistaken."

Tamara was speechless. She couldn't believe he'd said this. It challenged the core of her faith, claimed that a fundamental tenet was a lie. His statement was so monstrously preposterous that she had no idea where to start to challenge it.

They walked in silence for a minute and Bashour gloated, "You see, you're thinking about it and you know I'm right."

"No, on the contrary. You're so wrong I don't know where to begin. Like at Jesus' baptism – what part of 'This is my Son, in whom I am well pleased' don't you understand?"

"Oh, come on, that was a misrepresentation. Many of the people who were there just said they heard thunder, not words. The person who told that story was just imagining it."

"And all the apostles, all the letters of the apostles that identified Jesus as the Son of God, they were all wrong, too? How could they have possibly arrived at such an incorrect conclusion? You think Jesus would have said something, wouldn't you?"

"That's why Muhammad had to come, to set the record straight."

"Well why didn't the Holy Spirit correct the mistake? If you're a student of Imad, you're familiar with the Acts of the Apostles. Why didn't the Holy Spirit maintain the truth? Why did it take six hundred years and an Arab from a thousand millarium away to set the record straight? Why didn't Jesus himself make the clarification?"

"Who am I, to speak for Allâh? Every message he ever sent to earth has either been lost, misinterpreted or corrupted. Look at how Jesus came to set the law straight from the Pharisees. Thus Muhammad has come to set the law in its rightful place for all time, and for all people to accept Islam and live under Allâh's Law."

"Or die if they refuse? What good is a profession of faith if it's extracted at the end of a sword?"

"Allâh commands us to fight the unbelievers until they submit."

"Who says? Muhammad? He's not a prophet, Bashour! He must be a madman. He has none of the attributes of the prophets."

Again, Bashour swallowed his anger. "What do you mean?" he asked tightly.

"Look, he's not of Israel. . ."

"That means nothing. Balaam was not of Israel, but he was a prophet."

"Yeah and he died, too, when his nation fought Israel. Look the great prophets, Isaiah, Elijah, they weren't sent to make new laws, or start a new following. They came to call people back to God when they'd strayed. Your man says to forget everything and start a new religion."

"Well, isn't that what Jesus did?"

"No!" Tamara felt she was on firm ground with her argument here. "Jesus said himself that he didn't come to replace the law, but to fulfill it. He taught that the law was for man, not man for the law. It sounds to me like your prophet missed that lesson. How can you be a prophet if you contradict the law, or what other prophets have said? Isn't that one of the tests of a true prophet?"

"It's not a test if what the other prophets have said has been corrupted, misinterpreted or just forgotten."

Tamara was dumbfounded. "I don't believe you have the gall to say that. How far will you go, what truths are you willing to twist to justify your belief in what this man says? Why can't you just look around at what's happening and ask if this is really something God would ask for?"

"What, you think Allâh is all about peace? Do I have to remind you about the wars fought to conquer the land of Israel? This is no different."

"Yes it is different! Those were to return the land that God had promised to Abraham to his descendants. That was about the land that rightfully had been bequeathed to Israel."

"Well, are we not the children of Ishmael and have a stake in that inheritance as well? This land should belong to us."

"Even if I granted you that – and I do not – how does that explain the wars in Persia? How about our current direction? We're heading back into Syria again. That was never part of God's promise to Abraham."

"It's no longer about land, it's about humanity. Just as Jesus sent the apostles out to preach the Gospel to all people, so do we take the Qur'án to all people. They had their chance to accept the Gospel and many haven't. So we will give them the Qur'án."

"You know what? Never mind. I'm sorry I asked. I had no idea that you were willing to rewrite thousands of years of scripture to justify your strange beliefs. You have to make incredible leaps of reasoning to arrive at your conclusions, and it escapes you that a far simpler explanation is just that your prophet was a madman."

"You don't understand! I . . ."

Tamara cut him off. "I said drop it!" Her voice had acquired an edge to it.

They marched in an uncomfortable silence for some time before Bashour spoke up. "Tamara?" He had an apologetic tone to his voice.

"Yes?" Tamara was worried that she'd pushed too hard.

"Don't let them hear you talk like that about Muhammad, even if you speak in Greek. These are dangerous people and they tend to get violently irrational if they think you're insulting him."

She smiled coyly at him and patted his shoulder. "Don't worry, my young hero. I'll mind my tongue."

Bashour was thrilled. She'd called him her hero!

52. The Jordan River
August 14, 634

The Yarmouk and Jordan rivers cut deep channels into the flat, high desert plains of Syria. Where they meet, just south of where the River Jordan spills from the Sea of Galilee, they leave a broad flat promontory some 500 meters high that overlooks the entire northern Jordan River valley. Taticus had the bulk of his forces assembled there, waiting to see if the approaching Arab army would go north along the eastern shore of the Sea of Galilee, or follow the Yarmouk river to the east. This excellent tactical position allowed him to strike at the enemy's flank whichever path they took, and it was nearly impregnable to attack itself.

The flooding of the fields had been partially successful. The Arab army had been moving up the farmlands of the valley rapidly, moving in a broad front that helped avoid traffic jams and bottlenecks. The soggy ground they encountered forced them to work their way to the east side of the valley and proceed with a much narrower, slower moving column. Taticus guessed that the tactic had bought him a day to prepare.

He really wanted to arrange to have his forces strike the column from both sides at once, but that was impractical. If they took the coastal route, their left flank would be secured by the Sea of Galilee. If he set up such an ambush on the Yarmouk, that would put a huge chunk of his forces hopelessly out of position if they went north. Instead, he'd decided to wait for the Arabs to bivouac for the night, then strike them in the dark. The moon was full, so it would be light enough to move his forces into position. Hopefully they'd have the element of surprise on a sleeping camp. The shoreline route would offer such a chance at any point. If the enemy moved up the Yarmouk, Taticus was sure they wouldn't camp in the narrow confines of the canyon. Directly below his current position was a smallish flat valley, just big enough to hold the Arab camp before the Yarmouk entered the Jordan River plain. It was a day's march to where an army would arrive at the flat, high lake country of Syria. The Arabs would camp there for a night, then force-march up the winding river road the next day.

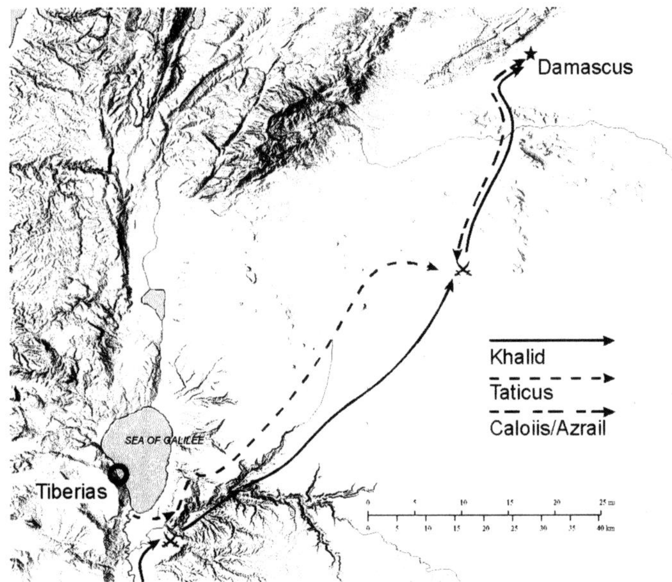

Khalid's advance on Damascus

Taticus was just below the top of the steep slope of the canyon with a soldier named Annius, known for his keen eyesight. Near noon, Annius called out, "There!" and pointed down the valley to the south.

Taticus squinted. "I don't see anything."

"Mounted horsemen, moving fast. They're not carrying anything to be moving that fast. They must be scouts. There! Four of them have split off and are moving this way along the Yarmouk."

Taticus turned to a runner. "Pass the word. Douse all the fires and order everyone to stay off the skyline." The young man scrabbled up the slope, staying low until he was well clear of the edge of the canyon.

Khalid ordered Raafe bin Umeira brought forward. The man had requested to return to Medina after the great battle that the soldiers were calling Ajnadeyn, but Khalid had refused his request. Blind as Raafe was after the desert crossing, he still had knowledge of the terrain locked in his head.

"Raafe, we've been following the eastern side of this valley, but our way is blocked by a river coming out of a canyon to our east. Scouts tell me we're not far from a large body of water at the head of the valley."

"Yes, yes, that would be the sea they call Galilee, same as the entire hill country around here. This river you speak of, that would be the Yarmouk."

"Which way do I go to get to Damascus, Raafe? Cross the river or follow it up the canyon?"

"If you cross and then follow the sea, you'll have a reasonably good road north. If you follow the canyon, you'll have a narrow road for about a day's march, before you reach flat country."

"Which way gets us there faster?"

Raafe scratched his beard. It bothered Khalid to see the way he cast his head about, sightlessly. He had a cloth wrapped around his eyes, but it still looked eerily like the man was looking for something that no one could see but him. "I don't think either one is any faster than the other, Sahib."

Khalid dismounted and called his commanders into a circle and explained the situation to them. After some discussion, Ubaidah spoke for the group. "We should follow the shore of the sea. It's wide and would give us room to maneuver if attacked. We could make good time if we don't have to squeeze into a single column." The others nodded their assent.

Khalid sat silently, considering the crude map he'd drawn in the dust at his feet. Then he said, "No. That's what they expect us to do. The boggy terrain we almost walked into wasn't an accident. Someone deliberately flooded those fields to slow us down. There may be an army nearby that we don't know about. The seashore route would allow them to choose when and where to attack our flank and would prevent a retreat. No, they're counting on us to do that. We'll go up the canyon."

"The main body is assembling on the riverbank," said Annius. "They're beginning to move along the river, this way."

Taticus couldn't tell for sure, but the ground seemed alive where the river canyon opened into the wide valley to the west. The river bent sharply to the right before looping back to the south when it reached the valley. His eyes couldn't make out detail at this distance, but a darkish mass was funneling up the left bank of the river into the broad canyon, directly towards them. They were definitely coming up the river and not crossing it.

"Shall we move the men to intercept?" asked one of his lieutenants.

Taticus studied the terrain before replying. "No, it's afternoon." He gestured to their left, at the small, square valley below them, where the river valley widened at a bend. "They'll either cross the river and encamp there early, or they'll be forced to camp in the narrow canyon further upstream. Either way, they'll be vulnerable. We'll wait until sundown and move on them after we know their intentions."

The scout galloped up to Khalid and pulled to a halt, "Sahib!"

"What do you see, Abu Fatin?"

"In about an hour, the valley widens out and offers an excellent place to camp. There's a small village, with an inn for travelers. Beyond that it will take a day to get to any open ground."

Khalid eyed the bluffs a thousand feet above the narrowing defile. He'd have preferred to be up there, instead of at the bottom of a narrow valley. But it would be too challenging to move the army up that slope before sundown. Foot soldiers could do it, but the camels and the horsemen would have a difficult time. A well-traveled road followed the river, evidently a main road to Damascus.

"I don't want to encamp strung out along a road at sundown. Issue orders to set up camp in the valley. We'll stop early today."

Taticus wiped the sweat out of his eyes and fanned the cloth he'd pulled over his head to protect him from the sun. At least the humidity wasn't as bad once you got some altitude. He didn't need the eagle-like eyes of Annius to see the Arab army crossing the river and gathering in the valley below. They were only a stadia away, literally at the base of the slope on which he was perched.

"They're going to camp there for the night," he said. "We'll make a direct attack right down this slope, then withdraw downstream when they react. If they follow, they'll lose time."

A runner came quickly over the edge of the bluff and skidded down the slope to a stop in a cloud of dust. "Idiot!"

hissed Taticus. “Move slowly and don’t do anything that would draw attention! Everybody be still. Pretend you’re a rock.”

“Sorry, sir. Enemy scouts came up the west side of the bluff and contacted our picket there. They escaped downhill before we could stop them.”

“Damn. Okay. We have to assume they know we’re here.” He clapped Annius on the shoulder. “Stay here and stay still. Send a runner if they make a demonstration up the hill.”

He waited some moments, then slowly and carefully worked his way up the slope, being careful not to dislodge any rocks or make any sudden moves. He crawled over the skyline on his belly to avoid being seen.

Once out of sight of the valley below, he quickly found some soldiers and gave them orders to set up assembly markers that would tell others how close they could get to the edge of the bluff and still be out of sight of the valley. He didn’t want to give away the size of his force just yet. Let the Arab wonder if anyone was up here and how many. Then he went to organize the rest of his small army.

The tail of the Arab column was crossing the river into the small flat valley where they were setting up camp. Khalid had made a circuit of the encampment before leading his horse to the river for a drink. He watched the remaining men cross the river, stopping to play and splash. Growing up in the deserts of Arabia, they were unused to clear, fresh water in any large quantities.

Ubaidah was at his side, his smile revealing the huge hole where his front teeth had been, “By Allâh, the men consider it a blessing to be given an afternoon off, with plentiful water at hand. They will be washing their clothes free of weeks of dust.”

Khalid thought about that and considered the implications. He realized that his men were unused to running water. “Old friend, issue an order that no one is to use the river for their latrine except from this point downstream. Laundry is only to be done from that bend there,” he pointed upstream to the southeast. “Only above that may water be taken for cooking. And all water should be boiled.”

If Ubaidah was disappointed that he hadn’t thought of such commonsense precautions first, he didn’t show it. He reached down and cupped his hands to scoop up some water. “As you say, sahib. But why boil the water? It looks clean enough.”

Khalid looked sideways at him. "How many camels are urinating in the water upstream from us? Do you know?"

Ubaidah wrinkled his nose and dropped the water he'd scooped up and wiped his hand unconsciously on his cloak. "Of course. How thoughtful of you."

A rider approached them and hailed Khalid. "Sahib, scouts have made contact with enemy forces on the west slope of this bluff!" He gestured up the slope north of the river.

"How many? What happened?"

"They were ascending the slope on foot, leading their horses. Once on the top, they were to be outriders on our left flank. About three-quarters of the way up the hill, they were attacked with arrows and stones. They retreated quickly and didn't see enough of the enemy to estimate numbers. They said it wasn't many."

"Stones? Are you sure it was an army and not some angry farmer?"

"Yes, sir. Several arrows were recovered. Roman army."

"Very well. Locate Yazeed, Shurahbil and Amr, and have them meet me at my tent." He turned to Ubaidah. "An outpost, local garrison, or the picket for a major army? I'm blind, Ubaidah. Get me some eyes on top of that bluff and tell me what's there."

"I'll dispatch a foot contingent immediately to scout the bluff."

Annius raised his head slowly from the bush where he was concealed, watching the enemy movements. His eyes widened and he called for the runner. "Get back to Taticus and tell him several hundred Arabs are coming up the hill on foot."

Taticus took the news calmly. "Who was it that said the finest plans never survive contact with the enemy?"

"What will we do, Commander?" asked one of his lieutenants with alarm. The man was terrified of the Arabs after what he'd seen at the battle at Elah.

"Calm down, Lysas. We're five thousand strong and hold the high ground. They'll have to come at us on foot; their mounts can't make that slope easily. This is just a reconnaissance in force. They'll be tired when they get to the top. We'll meet them as they crest the slope and send them to hell."

They had more than an hour to wait. Taticus pulled Annius back from his observation post. He ordered his men to conceal themselves back from the bluff and to stay that way until he gave the signal. He watched as the vanguard of the Arab force reached the top and stopped to catch their breath, then slowly spread out. They were alert, but unaware of the presence of the Byzantine soldiers. Taticus waited until several dozen Arabs were standing on the flat ground, milling about and encouraging their fellows below to hurry up. They acted unconcerned that there might be any enemy close by. Taticus could almost touch one when he roared, "Now!" His voice was pitched to carry a long distance. A meager hail of arrows led the way as the front rank of his men rose and rushed the Arabs. They were caught completely by surprise. Instead of standing to fight, they ran away, plunging headlong down the hill. The Byzantine soldiers pulled up at the edge of the drop-off and shouted challenges down to the Arabs below.

The Arabs rallied quickly and attempted a push up the hill, but were quickly repulsed. They took up defensive positions down the slope, piling rocks against the occasional opportunistic arrow and held there. For his part, Taticus was willing to hold them in position and wait for dark, when he could execute a flanking maneuver and assault the base camp without being seen.

Khalid and his commanders had watched the debacle on the bluff from the valley floor. "Well, that answers our question about what's up there," said Ubaidah drily.

Khalid paced angrily. "This valley is a trap. I don't like camping here. The enemy will assault us from the high ground under cover of night."

"We still don't know how big their force is," said Yazeed, "Why did they not continue their attack and drive us off the slope?"

"This commander knows what he's doing," said Khalid. "He's keeping his strength concealed until he can strike a telling blow. He gives up nothing until he has to."

"Suppose he has nothing left to give up?"

"I'm not going to take that chance. I have to assume there's a major force up there and we have a disadvantage of terrain. No, we can expect an attack tonight and we'll get bloody."

"We'll be ready for them!" exclaimed Shurahbil.

"No," said Khalid, "I'm not ready to fight a battle here. The terrain is bad, there's no room to maneuver. They have the high ground. A victory will gain us nothing." He smiled at Shurahbil. "I have no doubt we'd win, my friend, but it would squander our force. It wouldn't be overwhelming. The best way to win a war is to know which battles not to fight."

They watched him in respectful silence as he thought for some time. Then he said, "Allâh has given us a full moon tonight. It will be quite bright. . . ." He straightened with renewed resolve and issued orders. "Detail a thousand cavalry to ascend the slope on foot. Leave their horses here in the valley. Get as close to the top of the bluff as possible and engage the infidels. Hold their noses, but don't make a committed assault. The rest of the army will strike camp and continue marching. We'll march through the night until we reach the high desert. The remnant we leave behind will engage the infidels until dawn. Then they'll withdraw, retrieve their horses and catch up to us."

"More coming up, sir!"

Taticus hurried to the precipice of the bluff and looked over. He could pick out several columns of Arabs moving up the slope. There were about four or five times as many as had originally ascended, perhaps a thousand. They threaded their way through the scrub in several columns, moving quickly up the slope with purpose.

It took nearly forty-five minutes before the advancing Arabs came close enough for Taticus' forces to start harassing them. Taticus had passed the word for the archers not to shoot. The Arabs had spread out as they advanced, forming a loose, broad front. Taticus didn't want to waste arrows unless he could bring the enemy under a withering barrage. He already had enough of an advantage. He encouraged his soldiers to make a sport of throwing rocks, however. It gave them something to do, raised their spirits and kept the Arabs below nervous. Soon bets were made and money was exchanged among the soldiers about who could land a telling blow on one of the Muslim attackers, who had no way of retaliating in kind.

As for the Muslims, the hail of stones raised their ire and they were in a murderous mood. They advanced methodically up the slope, dodging falling rocks and swearing to Allâh to make the infidel taste steel when they closed with them. They were at the height of their fury when they finally came to blows with the first Byzantines near the top of the slope. Fighting like crazed madmen, they plunged ahead into the ranks of the Byzantines, ignoring their disadvantage of assaulting uphill, oblivious to any fatigue they felt from the climb.

The Muslim commanders did their best to check the assault, mindful of Khalid's order to engage the enemy and hold him. It was little use. The Byzantines, shocked by the ferocity of the attack and remembering the stunning loss against these same mujahideen at Elah, fell back. Taticus moved quickly among the ranks, restoring order with the flat of his blade. Well-placed kicks and sharp words stopped panic from spreading and causing a general rout.

The Muslims gained a purchase above the lip of the bluff and established a defensive perimeter, facing the more numerous Byzantines. The fighting settled into a static duel, both sides trading desultory blows but unable to connect. The edge of the bluff prevented flanking maneuvers by either side, negating the numerical advantage of the Byzantines, who couldn't engage any more men than they could fit into the line.

Meanwhile, in the valley below the lengthening shadows of the setting sun fell across an army on the move. The camp had been struck and the army began moving up the river road to the northeast. By the time the last rays of the sun faded from the sky, the valley was empty. The rising moon in their faces provided enough light for the night march. Small fires were built where visibility was considered important. Moving along the narrow prepared road allowed the escaping Muslims to move far more quickly than Taticus could have along the top of the bluff, which followed the river unevenly at best. Even if Taticus hadn't been engaged, or if he'd split his forces and pursued the Muslims, his chase would have been at a disadvantage.

The fighting between the two armies remained in a stalemate and fell off raggedly after the sun went down. The Byzantines rallied briefly at sundown when half the Muslim contingent inexplicably abandoned the line briefly and proceeded to pray. When they were through, they relieved their comrades, who then prayed in their turn. By the time the moon had climbed halfway up the eastern sky, the armies had disengaged by a few paces and an uneasy no-man's land had formed between them. The Muslims periodically disturbed the equilibrium by mounting shouting charges into the Byzantine line and then retreating. Neither side slept.

The sky was beginning to brighten slightly in the east when the moon finally set. Under cover of renewed assaults in the darkness, the bulk of the Muslim forces began pulling off the bluff. By the time the brightening eastern sky provided enough light to see, the Byzantines were bewildered to find their enemy had faded from the field. Taticus approached the edge of the drop-off and examined the empty valley below him. He cursed at the lost opportunity as he realized that the Muslim army had escaped in the night.

53. Southeast of the Sea of Galilee
August 15, 634

The bright full moon provided an eerie light for the march up the narrow Yaqusa River valley. Bashour didn't understand why the haste, or why they'd avoided a fight. He'd started the evening walking with his Muslim companions, who were unusually quiet after the evening prayers. They talked of djinns who prowled the night, preying on travelers who didn't stop and wait for the sun. Bashour thought they were trying to scare each other, or scare him. He eventually became concerned for Tamara in the dark, and fell back to walk with her.

At one point he took her hand to guide her where a small landslide had littered the road. After that he hadn't let go, nor had she withdrawn it. The whole column was quieter than usual and they walked much of the night in silence.

The sky was brightening when the river split. They stayed on the east side and followed the smaller tributary. The small valley they followed became much narrower. The nearer side of the valley sloped gently above from them to the south, but across the stream the walls rose much more abruptly. Bashour eyed them and was thankful they wouldn't be asked to ascend there.

The column stopped at dawn for prayers, then pressed on. They'd been marching nearly round the clock now and everyone was exhausted. The stream and valley turned sharply to the right and became wider. Bashour and Tamara rounded the small promontory formed by the turn, and saw the column crossing the stream and ascending a landslide which had carved an exit on the steep northern wall of the valley. As they approached the stream, a man directing traffic told them to water their camel and fill their water bags.

Bashour was grateful that the ascent out of the river valley was done in the cool morning and not the brutal heat that would come later. When they reached the top, they saw a broad plain rising gently to the north. Word came to move away from the canyon edge and encamp. The army would stay here for a day and a night to recover from the nighttime force-march.

54. Damascus
August 18, 634

"My cavalry will be far more effective in the field against these barbarians if we march and meet them on the road," declared Caloiis to the assembled council of Damascus.

"I suppose you'll want the city's mounted guard to reinforce you," said Azrail. "Surely you don't intend to meet these Arabs with only your five thousand men?"

"Yes, if you could add your five thousand to mine and another ten thousand foot soldiers with pikes, that would be a substantial force."

Harbis looked unhappy at this. "Merarch, I object to stripping our defenses like this. What would happen to Damascus if by some chance you were defeated in the field, or if the enemy outmaneuvered you? I can give you four or five thousand men, no more."

Caloiis glared at him, but said nothing. As the regional commander, Harbis wasn't technically under Caloiis' command. "Merarch," Thomas asked, "You're facing an army that defeated a force three times its size. And you're proposing to do it with a force that's either equivalent or smaller than theirs?"

"I don't pretend to know what happened in Palestine, Thomas, but the reports my scouts bring is that a column of some twenty to twenty-five thousand is approaching this city from the south. You know as well as I do the amount of support necessary to keep an army like that in the field. Why, I'd be surprised if there are as many as fifteen thousand actual sword-swingers in the whole lot."

Azrail addressed Thomas. "Certainly their army must have split up and sent a contingent up the coast, or left it to besiege Jerusalem. There's no way that a force this small could have defeated the army Heraclius had assembled in Palestine."

Thomas looked skeptical. "I think it might be prudent to locate the rest of this army, then, before we commit to an attack."

"Nonsense!" Caloiis responded, "You're thinking like an infantry man, Thomas. My cavalry will move swiftly, strike them and bloody their nose and send them in flight to the south.

We'll have plenty of time to regroup and engage any other contingents that show themselves. If we stay and wait for them, we cede the initiative and lose control of the battle space. For all we know, the rest of their army is slowly starving outside the walls of Jerusalem."

"I agree with Caloiis," said Azrail, "But my men march under my banner. Since you wouldn't place your troops under my command inside these city walls, neither shall I place mine under yours in the field. We'll march together and command together."

Taticus knew he was walking a fine line with his men. They'd been demoralized two weeks previously in the stunning defeat at Elah, marched 140 millaria, then had the Arab army slip out of a trap and escape under cover of night. They were tired and had nothing to show for their effort but worn footwear. Taticus knew that if he said the wrong thing, pushed a little too hard, he'd have a mutiny on his hands.

He'd pushed the men as hard as he dared after the Muslims broke contact. He guessed that the Arab army was heading for Damascus. If he'd led them down from the high plain and crossed the Yaqusa, they would have been committed to a fruitless tail chase. The Arab commander also could have slowed them with rear screen units. Instead, for the last five days he'd stuck to the heights on the west side of the Yaqusa river valley and followed the plain north. He'd lost contact with the Muslim army, but didn't lose time negotiating steep terrain. He planned to forge ahead until the canyon country was behind them, then try to intercept the Muslims in the flat agricultural country south of Damascus.

If he could keep his men moving and not outrun his supply line, it might just be possible.

Khalid surveyed the plain before him. The land was rich and fertile. He'd seen large-scale agriculture before, but only near rivers. But this land was criss-crossed with small streams. They were mostly dry this time of year, but they clearly held water every year, something rare where he grew up in the desert wastes of Arabia. The farmland and cultivated fields seemed to go as far as the eye could see, broken only by the occasional low cinder cone that hinted at a volcanic past.

He'd broken the armies into several columns, the more quickly to advance across this plain. Amr and Yazeed's armies were advancing on his left, Ubaidah and Shurahbil were on his right. He formed the anchor and the spearhead of the advance.

Ubaidah rode up to join him. "Scouts have reported a large mounted force ahead, coming directly at us."

Khalid looked around. They were in flat, cultivated land. As good a place as any, he decided. "How many?"

"They have no clear estimate. We're just getting the first contact reports. Thousands, at least."

"Very well, deploy the columns line abreast and keep advancing once deployed. Let me know when you have a size estimate on the enemy."

The armies had drawn up to a halt a short distance from one another. Caloiis was furious. The reports that he'd received suggested that, at most, fifteen thousand Arabs were advancing through Syria. Arrayed before him were at least twice, perhaps three times that many.

Azrail regarded him silently. It was too late to withdraw, but they had little choice, in the face of such an overwhelming force. Azrail's horse sensed his tension and pranced nervously.

Azrail had been skeptical about marching forward in force without a complete reconnaissance and a clear idea of where the enemy was or the size of the force they faced. But Caloiis had disdained the idea, stating that audacity would more than compensate for incomplete intelligence. These were only barbarian Arabs after all. Caloiis was sure they'd never encountered a modern cavalry army and would break themselves against the iron discipline of his trained soldiers.

Now Caloiis didn't seem so sure. They faced a force of staggering size. He masked his lack of confidence in anger, cursing the reports that had failed to tell him the true strength of the enemy. He felt fear stab through his bowels, realizing that if he didn't do everything just right, his army could easily be destroyed in the next few hours. He'd made a serious mistake, one that Psellus would gloat over for years to come.

"Well, Merarch?" asked Azrail in a sardonic tone.

"Let's wait for them to send emissaries to negotiate. Perhaps they're running short on supplies. They have to be tired."

Azrail snorted and studied the position of the sun, halfway from its zenith in the west. Perhaps if they could forestall a battle this day, they could escape under cover of darkness. . .

Ubaidah regarded Khalid and asked with a smile, “Shall we send an emissary to ask for their surrender?”

Khalid regarded him steadily, wondering if he was being tested. Ubaidah’s level, patient gaze told him nothing. “Yes,” he said, “Send for Dhiraar.”

When Dhiraar arrived he charged him, “Now is the time, Dhiraar Ibn al Azwar, to show yourself a man and emulate the deeds of your father and other illustrious soldiers of the faith. Take twenty men, go forth in the righteous cause and Allâh will protect you."

Dhiraar said nothing. He grinned broadly, turned back to the baggage train and retrieved his lance and with whistles summoned riders to join him.

The two lines of cavalry had drawn up with a wide gap between them, beyond accurate bowshot range. Dhiraar and his troop broke the ranks of the Muslims and trotted confidently across the emptiness between the two armies. The Byzantines, stirred restlessly, wondering if this was a negotiation party.

When they were only 20 yards away, Dhiraar lowered his lance and shouted, “Allâhu Akhbar!” and kicked his horse into a full gallop. The others did likewise and they penetrated the enemy lines in a flying wedge. The Byzantine cavalry was surprised and unprepared for the ferocity of the assault. He unseated four horsemen with his lance as his attack crashed through the line of cavalry into the back rank of pikemen. The foot soldiers had no time or warning to prepare and his men caused tremendous confusion, milling around, trampling and laying about with their swords and lances. Dhiraar cast away his lance as the impetus of his charge dissipated and he was left at close quarters with the enemy surrounding him. He circled his horse in a tight spiral to the left, freeing him to lay about with his curved scimitar. He ran down and killed at least a half-dozen more infidels, shifting his weight to urge his horse into kicking and trampling even more. He whooped in exultation at the excitement of the battle and the ease with which he dispatched his foes.

It didn’t take long for the Byzantines to recover from the initial shock of the assault and they quickly rallied. Soon Dhiraar was facing a wall of pikes arrayed at him from every direction, and the circle of carnage he and his men were in was getting smaller. With a cry of victory, he wheeled his horse and led the charge in reverse, galloping headlong back to the safety of his own lines, where he was greeted with hoots and cheers of acclaim from the other Muslims.

Not to be outdone, Abdul Rahman quickly gathered a troop and made his own assault on the Byzantine lines. The enemy was ready this time and he failed to penetrate the front rank, drawing up short when faced with a forest of pikes arrayed against him. He and his men rode a short way along the lines before returning to the Muslim ranks to the jeers of his comrades.

Taticus was at the head of his weary command when he thought he heard something carried on the wind from the east. He halted the men and ordered silence. He cocked an ear and waited for the sound to repeat. The lieutenant at his side looked at him questioningly. He concentrated for a time, then, "There! Do you hear it?"

The other man closed his eyes and a moment later, they opened again, wide. "Yes."

"Cheers? A Battle?"

"Maybe both."

"Organize the column on an assault line facing east. Tell the men to prepare for battle. They can't be far away."

Azrail and Caloiis watched as a single rider detached from the Arab lines and rode back and forth between the two armies. He was a huge man, clad in heavy black armor with a red turban over a leather headpiece. He was shouting something towards them in Arabic. "What's he saying?" asked Caloiis.

"He says he's the leader of the army and he challenges anyone to single combat with him."

Caloiis silently studied the man. Azrail shifted his weight in the saddle. "Well?"

"Well, what?"

"The Emperor sent you to protect our country in this hour of danger. Aren't you going to accept the challenge and dispatch this scum?"

Caloiis glared at him and was rewarded with a sly smile. He cursed under his breath and kicked his horse into motion.

Reaching the front of his line, he waited until the Arab had passed, then hesitantly urged his horse out into the open. Khalid noticed him and spun his horse and kicked it into a gallop, moving to cut Caloiis off from the Byzantine line. Caloiis limbered his sword and was shocked by the ferocity of the attack when Khalid came close enough for the two to engage. He was immediately on the defensive, parrying a flurry of devastating blows from the big man. He only got a glimpse of the other man's face, obscured by a huge, bushy black beard with tiny pig-like eyes that blazed fiercely from under heavy eyebrows and a nut-brown, sun-battered skin. The man looked and fought like a demon.

Fending off the merciless barrage from the big man's sword was all he could do. Caloiis was completely on the defensive. He reeled and barely recovered from a blow that slipped past his parry. His horse sidestepped away, giving him a momentary respite. He looked down to see a spreading bloodstain on the tunic that covered his armor. He had been so busy trying to counter the heavy blows from the other man that he hadn't landed a single blow or had any time to even swing at the mad Arab. The sight of his blood shattered his confidence and he spurred his horse towards the safety of his lines.

Khalid saw what he was doing and raced after him, easily catching him before he'd reached safety. He reached out and grabbed the back plate of Caloiis' armor and hauled him off his horse to crash heavily on the ground, stunned. Khalid pulled his horse up short and turned quickly towards the fallen Caloiis. Khalid sheathed his sword and slowed the horse to a trot. He leaned low from his saddle and grabbed a huge handful of the man's hair as Caloiis struggled to his feet. With Caloiis twisting in his iron grip, he trotted triumphantly to the Arab lines and threw him unceremoniously into the waiting arms of his cheering men.

Khalid dismounted and called for a fresh horse and his translator. It took several minutes for them to locate Bashour and even more for him to hurry to where Khalid was. He found the big man regarding a bound prisoner.

Caloiis was trying to think of a way to survive this encounter. He realized that if he admitted that he commanded this force, they'd kill him to demoralize his force. The young man who'd been summoned asked him, "Who are you?"

“My name is Caloiis. I’m just a cavalry officer from the imperial guard.”

Bashour translated this and added, “I think he’s lying.”

“Of course he’s lying.” replied Khalid, “Ask him who his commander is.”

Caloiis was angry with himself for allowing Azrail to goad him into challenging Khalid. He now saw a way to not only exact revenge, but increase the chance that he might escape this with his skin. “The commander of our force is the military governor of Damascus, named Azrail. He’s the one you want.” At the mention of the name, a cloud seemed to pass over the faces of the Arabs around him. He wondered what that was about.

Khalid experienced a moment of doubt when he heard the name Azrail, the Arabic name for the Angel of Death. Then he recalled that his life was forfeit to Allâh and he’d win or die by Allâh’s will. If today was his day to die in battle, then he’d rest in paradise this night. He rode forward on a fresh horse and pulled up short of the Byzantine lines and called for Azrail by name. It took a few minutes for a rider to appear. “You are the commander of this force?” demanded Khalid.

“I am!” Azrail limbered his sword and kicked his horse to approach the big Arab slowly. The two men instantly began trading deliberate blows. Azrail was older, but still made of hard muscle. Khalid was fatigued from his fight with Caloiis. The horses danced in a circle as each man sought to crush the defenses of the other.

They fought for several minutes before Khalid kicked his horse to put some distance between them. Azrail allowed him to retreat several steps and the two men sat on their mounts and regarded each other, panting and gasping for breath in the sweltering heat.

Khalid fought to calm his heart and expel the bad breath from his lungs, taking deep, cleansing breaths. “Your name is Azrail?”

“That is my name,” panted Azrail.

Khalid took a deep breath and hefted his sword to renew the fight. “Then, by Allâh!" he cried, "Your namesake is at hand, waiting to carry your soul to the fire of Jehennam!"

Again they matched blow for blow, unable to inflict more than superficial wounds. Azrail sensed a stalemate. The bigger man lacked a finesse to his technique, but made up for it in ferocity and strength. Azrail wouldn't have wanted to meet him when he was fresh. He pulled his horse in close, colliding with Khalid's horse, who stumbled momentarily. Seizing the opportunity, Azrail made a break for the lines, making it look as if he was trying to escape the way Caloiis had done. As he fled, he sheathed his sword and limbered a short lance from his saddle.

He'd traveled far enough to establish the race, then suddenly pulled up short and wheeled his horse, lowering his lance to point straight at Khalid's chest in a classic charge. Khalid's eyes widened when he realized how he'd been duped, but he didn't hesitate. He threw himself headlong sideways from his horse and rolled to his feet in the dust, snatching his fallen sword an instant before Azrail was upon him. He lightly ducked under the lowered lance and aimed a mighty blow with his sword at the back of the leg of the charging horse. The animal screamed in pain as muscle and tendon parted, then collapsed in a dusty cloud of shrieking, kicking flesh. Khalid grimly strode forward and landed a knee on the chest of the fallen Azrail. He held the point of his sword at Azrail's eye, found the discarded sword by feel and threw it away. He hauled Azrail to his feet.

Both sides had surged forward at the dismounting of their heroes, but the Arabs reacted more quickly. Lightly armored riders quickly snatched Azrail and Khalid from the battle and spirited them to the Muslim lines.

Caloiis and Azrail were on their knees, hands bound behind their backs when Khalid had finished his ablutions and afternoon prayers and rejoined them. The young man Bashour was on hand to translate for the one who spoke no Arabic. "I don't know nor much care which of you is the real commander of this force," he said. "You have three choices: Accept Islam and follow us, pay the Jizyah tax for your protection, or die."

The two men glared at him, their lips white with fury, but said nothing. He considered whether to press them for an immediate response or to give them time to think about it, perhaps to confer with one another. If either of them valued life more than the other, perhaps he could turn them and this army without wasting time with a pointless fight.

His thoughts were interrupted by a messenger galloping up. "Sahib! Yazeed reports a large force of infantry is engaging him from the west. He can no longer hold the line to the north."

Khalid whirled on his two prisoners. "How many are out there? What is the size of your forces?" Azrail looked confused, but Caloiis had time to think while Bashour translated. He simply smiled.

Khalid turned to Ubaidah who'd been quietly observing. "We've been lured into a trap. Issue orders to withdraw. Pull the left flank back and assume a defensive position for the night. Get scouts out. I want to know what's out there, how many and what their composition is."

He turned back to his prisoners and grabbed Caloiis by the hair, jerking his head back savagely. "You have until dawn tomorrow to decide! Accept Islam, pay the Jizyah, or die!"

55. South of Damascus
August 20, 634

The encampment stayed in battle readiness throughout the night after they disengaged from the Byzantine trap. Instead of the usual sentry watches, the army was split into two watches. Bashour and his companions had the first watch, waiting for a surprise Roman strike to materialize out of the darkness. The half moon rose three hours after sunset, and was a third of the way up the sky when the watch was relieved and Bashour turned in. Tamara was awakened as he entered the tent. She pushed into him as he lay down and he was grateful for her warmth. As hot as the days were, the nights could still be chilly.

"I heard we captured the enemy general."

"Yes. I was there. I translated."

"And? What will happen to him?"

"Nothing, if he accepts Islam or submits."

"And if he doesn't"

"I suspect they will kill him."

After a long silence, she asked, "And how do you feel about that?"

Bashour thought about it quietly. "This is war. In a regular war, he'd have already been killed."

"You make it sound so magnanimous."

"Allâh gives everyone the choice. He rewards those who follow him and punishes those who don't."

"Reward? Punishment? I thought those were for the afterlife. What of atonement, forgiveness, reconciliation?"

"I don't think man is in any situation to negotiate with Allâh."

"Yes, that's right. Man is just a slave of Allâh. Like I'm your slave."

Bashour's heart sank. He hated when she brought that up. "Tamara, you know it's not like that."

"Bashour, I'd rather be your slave than anyone else's. You've been kind and gentle with me and not forced me to do anything. But I'd rather not be a slave at all. How can you not see that?"

"I told you before. . ."

"No, stop. I'm not going to bow to your false god and earn my freedom with a lie. I'll be your slave and do your work and even bear your children before I turn my back on Jesus."

"You're stubborn. And you're wrong. But I love you."

She lay there in silence, finding it difficult to return to sleep. He'd never said that before and it bothered her. In another time, another place, she'd have been flattered and perhaps interested. Now, it scared her a little bit; yet it was also oddly reassuring.

After breakfast, Thomas ascended the city battlements on the southern wall and walked along the parapet. The wall was crowded with archers. The city was on edge since the expeditionary force returned the night before without their commanders. Thomas was unsure of what happened, but from what he could piece together, they'd encountered a far superior Arab force. The commanders had been captured in single combat, which Thomas thought was a foolish thing to have done. Then a small force of some five thousand friendly infantry had appeared out of nowhere and apparently panicked the Arabs, who'd inexplicably quit the battlefield. The Byzantine cavalry had joined the new force and took advantage of the opportunity to run like scared rabbits back to the sanctuary of Damascus. Now it was only a matter of time before the Arabs appeared over the horizon.

He didn't recognize an older soldier on the parapet, studying the half moon in the western sky. Thomas approached him. "You seem fascinated by the moon."

The man roused from his reverie and turned. "Do you think it produces its own light? The brightness always seems to face the sun, whether it's in the morning sky or the evening. I wonder if it's just reflecting the sunlight?"

Thomas regarded the moon and admitted that the man had a point. He wasn't sure what that meant. "I couldn't tell you. That's a question for philosophers." He held out his hand. "I'm Thomas, merchant and trader."

The old soldier took his hand in a powerful grip. Thomas could feel the thorny calluses of a hard life as they shook. "Taticus of Antioch." He smiled. "My rank may be a matter of speculation. Officially a komes, but I suppose a brevet drungus."

Thomas smiled back. "War does strange things to one's career."

"Did you serve, sir?"

"I marched with Heraclius at Nineveh."

"Then this isn't the first time we've been comrades."

"Really?"

"The army is a small world."

A voice rang out down the wall. "Rider coming in!"

Taticus turned and peered. "Just one?" he called.

"I only see one!" responded the soldier.

The rider was unarmed and riding at a full gallop on a bareback horse. As he approached the city gates, he showed no signs of slowing. "Don't shoot!" shouted Taticus to his archers.

The rider pulled to a stop several paces from the guard detachment at the city gate, all of whom had drawn their swords. He produced a pair of bags tied with a rope, each the size of a large melon. He swung them around his head and threw them at the feet of the guards at the gate, then shouted, "Allâhu Akhbar!" and rode off the way he'd come.

Thomas followed Taticus down the stairway to the gate and watched as he undid the knots and peered inside the bags, then wrinkled his nose in disgust. Thomas looked in one.

Peering up at him were lifeless eyes gazing out of the head of Azrail.

Thomas invited Taticus to the emergency council meeting that was called that morning. Bishop Peter prayed an invocation when the meeting was called to order. The meeting hall was crowded. Priests, military officers, businessmen and the regular council were all present, concerned about the events of the last few days. After the Bishop wound up his opening prayer, Harbis took control of the meeting.

"As you're all aware, the heads of Azrail and Caloiis were delivered to the Small Gate this morning. According to what I've heard from the soldiers who returned last night, they met an army at least twice their size two days ago. Azrail and Caloiis were captured in single combat." He nodded at Taticus. "Fortunately, a detachment from Palestine which had been shadowing the Arab army struck them by surprise from the west. The Arabs withdrew, allowing our army the chance to escape.

"I expect them to arrive anytime now. We must consider this city in a state of siege. If you haven't done so already, call your workers and farmers into the city. Burn whatever crops remain in the field. Abbot," he said to Lecanepus. "I urge you one last time to bring your monks into the city."

The monk bowed his head slightly and smiled. "Thank you, Commander, but we will do God's work among the heathens, if you please."

One of the city council members spoke up, "Commander Harbis, are you taking command of the city, then?"

Harbis looked uncomfortable. "My commission is the military chief of staff of the region. Technically, I suppose I now command all the troops in this city. But I'm a soldier, not a governor. I suggest you choose a new governor from among yourselves to replace Azrail. I'll coordinate with him."

The assembly quickly grew noisy as the council members began conferring with one another. With nothing more to say, Harbis ceded the floor and strode over to Thomas. "Thomas, how are we set for a siege?"

"The arrival of five thousand new troops that came with Taticus required us to recalculate the reserve. My colleague, Nicetas, also pointed out a problem with the horses that I hadn't considered."

"Problem with the horses? This is the first I've heard of it."

"Well, yes. You see, we only have a limited amount of fodder and when that's gone the horses will starve. Nicetas pointed out that the horses themselves are a valuable source of meat that would help us extend our rations. The problem is that if we run out of fodder, they'll all die and we'll be unable to capitalize on that resource. Nicetas is drawing up a schedule of slaughter of the horses that will both feed the people and maximize the fodder resources. Ideally, the last batch of horses will be slaughtered right as the fodder runs out. That way none of the horses will go to waste."

Harbis raised an eyebrow. "Yes, quite brilliant. I hope we don't run into too much resistance with the cavalry about your idea. They tend to be quite attached to their animals, you know." He winked at Thomas, who laughed quietly.

One of the city councilmen banged a table for attention. "I've conferred with my colleagues and we've agreed. There's only one person of the proper stature and experience in Damascus who's above petty politics and can lead the city in this time." He turned to where Thomas and Harbis were standing. "Thomas, will you accept our invitation to be the emergency governor of Damascus, until Basileus Heraclius appoints a successor?"

Thomas felt the room press in on him as everyone turned their gaze to him. He steeled himself not to take a step backward. “Ah, gentlemen, I fear you’ve made a mistake. I’m just a merchant, I have no desire to govern.”

“Precisely the attitude that makes you the obvious choice, my boy,” said Bishop Peter.

Harbis turned his back on the assembly so his words were for Thomas alone. “You’ve made the obligatory protest, my friend. Now accept the inevitable.”

Thomas shot him a dirty look, then turned back to the assembly. “I came to Damascus to avoid public service. I reluctantly accept your commission, but only until a successor has been appointed.”

Everyone cheered. Thomas wondered if they’d be cheering in a month or two, when he was drafting their youth, cutting their rations and butchering their animals.

56. South of Damascus
August 20, 634

Bashour was unusually quiet when he went to bed that night. He didn't say much around the fire at dinner and turned away Rashad's overture to teach him the next part of the sura they were working on, saying he didn't feel well. Tamara sensed he was troubled about something, but didn't ask. She figured he'd talk to her about it when he was ready. As they lay down, she gave him a tight hug and a fleeting kiss on the lips before turning away. He was surprised and gratified by this overture, but unsure what to make of it.

The truth was, he was shocked by the executions of Azrail and Caloiis that he'd seen that day. The men had been bound with their hands behind their backs and made to kneel. Khalid had arrived and had addressed the two while casually swinging his sword. He first asked Caloiis if he accepted Islam. When the man said he did not, Khalid offered him the chance to surrender his forces and pay tribute. Caloiis again declined.

So fast that Bashour had no time to prepare for it, Khalid cried, "Allâhu Akhbar!" His sword sang through a mighty arc and Caloiis' head went flying. Blood fountained from the body as it fell forward, twitching and contorting in a paroxysm of death.

Looking back, Bashour was grateful that Azrail spoke Arabic and didn't need his service as a translator. He was too stunned, too speechless to have provided a translation. His eyes were fixed on the growing puddle of blood, pooling and soaking into the dust. The nightmare replayed itself with Azrail, except the man didn't speak, he just spat at Khalid's feet.

Bashour had seen death in the heat of battle, he'd seen Andrew's head cut off at Elah, and the prisoners that he'd tried to convince to convert. But Andrew had been a situation of kill or be killed, when anger ran high and men acted without thinking. He realized he hadn't thought much about the other prisoners because Khalid had rewarded him with Tamara the same day. He recalled the men at the well the day they'd left Huwareen. But Khalid had been angry then, had killed them in a fit of bad temper. Who knows what stress he'd been under that those men had provoked him so? This . . . this was cold-blooded. Premeditated. These men were helpless prisoners, like the ones at Elah. It was murder, plain and simple. Bashour struggled to find a way to justify the act, but all the while his brain replayed the execution over and over, enough to drive him mad. He lay awake in the tent, listening to the sounds of the slumbering camp around him. Whenever he closed his eyes and shut out the sounds, the vision returned of a body falling, blood spraying in a huge, pulsing arc from the neck. He simply couldn't get it out of his head.

Tamara feigned sleep, but she knew that Bashour was troubled. He slept fitfully through the night and woke often. He trembled and sometimes called softly in his sleep. She felt sorry for him, and hoped that he'd tell her what was on his mind in due time. She had too many demons of her own to begin asking questions, too many dark things that she struggled to keep locked away, afraid of what she might do if they managed to escape and take control of her mind.

"How can you pray if you don't memorize the Qur'án?" asked Rashad.

Bashour was tired. What little sleep he'd gotten the night before wasn't enough. When he had slept, he'd dreamed of trying to go to sleep, with visions of men's heads coming off and blood everywhere. "Can we take a break today, Rashad? I'm really not up to it today."

"What's wrong with him?" asked Jabir, "He's been moping around since yesterday morning. Is it that time of the month for you, Bashour?" The others smiled at the jab, but Bashour ignored him and just stayed quiet.

Qutayba spoke up, "He's been like that ever since he came back from translating for Khalid with those two infidel commanders. I heard their heads were cut off. Maybe he's upset that his friends were killed."

"They weren't my friends!" snapped Bashour.

"Then what's the matter? Haven't you ever seen someone executed before?"

"I've seen people killed, but what crime did they commit? Why did they have to die?"

"They were given a choice. They chose death."

"Doesn't it say in Al Baqarah that there be no compulsion in religion?"

"Yes, of course," said Rashad and he began to recite. "Let there be no compulsion in religion. Truth stands out clear from error; whoever rejects evil and believes in Allâh has grasped the most trustworthy handhold, that never breaks. And Allâh hears and knows all things!"

"Well, don't you think killing someone for not accepting Islam is compulsion?"

"But they were not only given the choice of accepting Islam," said Qutayba. 'They were also allowed to submit to Islam and pay the Jizyah. They could have stayed Christian if they'd just accepted the authority of Allâh."

Sameer spoke up, "They were given the choice and they chose hellfire. They fight until they die or are subdued. They must pay the Jizyah with willing submission and until they do, we fight them. It says in Al Tawba, 'Fight those who believe not in Allâh nor the Last Day, nor hold that forbidden which has been forbidden by Allâh and His Messenger, nor acknowledge the religion of truth, even if they're of the People of the Book, until they pay the Jizyah with willing submission and feel themselves subdued."

"But they were prisoners. How much more subdued could they be?" protested Bashour.

"They weren't prisoners," replied Jabir. "Just because they'd been captured, they still resisted Islam. Their men still fight even now and the Prophet, peace be upon him, said it's not fitting to have prisoners of war until we've thoroughly subdued the land. They resisted us even when bound, so they were still combatants."

"You should have been with us after we fought at Ullais earlier this year," said Qutayba. "The enemy broke and fled. We chased down and captured thousands of prisoners. Khalid was so angry that they refused to accept Islam that he had us cutting their throats for three days beside the water. He wanted to make the Euphrates run red with blood."

"That was a big river," observed Sameer.

"And what if the religion of a man prevents him from submitting himself to Islam?" asked Bashour.

"That's an affair between him and Allâh!" Jabir said angrily. "It's of no concern to us!"

"Bashour, you ask too many questions," said Qutayba. "You haven't learned the entire Qur'án yet; you've hardly even begun. All the answers to your questions are in the Qur'án. That's the perfect word that Allâh passed to his Messenger, peace be upon him. Other people questioned the Prophet; and in Al Ma'idah it was revealed, 'O you who believe! Ask not questions about things which, if made plain to you, may cause you trouble. But if you ask about things when the Qur'án is being revealed, they will be made plain to you: Allâh will forgive those: for Allâh is Oft-Forgiving, Most Forebearing! Some people before you did ask such questions and on that account lost their faith!'"

Rashad elaborated. "Questions like that come from Shai-tan to test your faith. You should shun such questions and accept the truth of the Qur'án in a spirit of obedience. Allâh has revealed what he wanted to reveal and has kept secret what he didn't want us to know. Who are you to question Allâh?"

Bashour felt angry with the response. Why couldn't you ask questions? What good was faith if it couldn't be explained? But he saw that their thinking was inflexible. How could you question a revelation that specifically forbade questioning? He sullenly kept his silence. The argument was soon forgotten by his comrades when the walls of a large city were spotted ahead, and they looked forward to what the news would bring.

Khalid rode ahead of the army with his commanders, flanked by a small bodyguard under the command of Dhiraar. They skirted a small bluff on their right and saw the city in the distance. Khalid sent a scout up the hill to see if there was a better view, but the answer had returned negative. Just beyond Damascus was a line of mountains, but from the south the valley floor was flat as a plate. Khalid wished he could get high so he could survey the layout of the city, but that didn't look like it would be possible.

They were in clear sight of the walls when he pulled his entourage up and dismounted. He crouched in the dust and made a rough oval, representing the city. "Yazeed, you set up your army on the south wall. Ubaidah, you'll be on his left, covering the west. Amr, go to the left and tie into Ubaidah's left flank and cover the north. Shurahbil, go to the right and meet Amr on the other side. I'll cover the east side and establish a reserve for reaction, should they try to force any of the gates.

"Tell your men to keep their distance from the walls. I want time to examine this fortress before we decide to attack it."

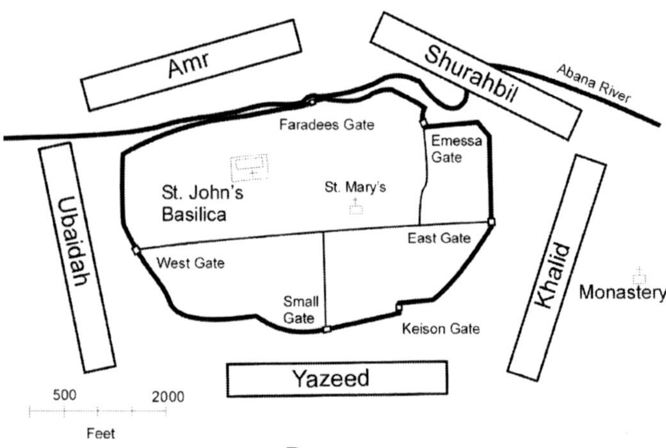

Damascus

Bashour and his companions were detailed to encamp east of the city in a secluded olive plantation, not far from a monastery. Tamara helped him erect the tent and the work went quickly and efficiently. Bashour went forward to inspect the fortifications. They stood well back from the walls, wary of archers. Jabir whistled softly at the height of the walls, taller than three or four men standing on each other's shoulders. The area around the walls was level and showed signs of recently having had houses and outbuildings on it, which had been razed or burned to deprive any attackers of cover if they approached the fortress.

"There's no way to attack such a place," moaned Sameer.

Wahid glowered at him and Jabir said, "Trust Khalid! If there's a way to take such a place, he'll find it."

"We could just stay here until they starve," said Qutayba.

"Assuming we don't starve first, and another army doesn't attack us while we're committed to holding this city under siege," said Sameer.

"What do you think, Bashour? You're a member of Khalid's staff," asked Jabir.

Bashour raised his hands. "I'm just an interpreter, I don't know anything."

"Truer words have never been said," Qutayba said wryly.

Jabir poked Sameer. "You're just worried that if we stay still for long that Dimah will find you!"

Sameer looked horrified. "Do you think that would happen? Oh, by Allâh, I will take the city by myself, just to get us moving again!" He turned toward Wahid. "You'll help me, Wahid, won't you? You can have my share of the booty. Please don't let us stand still long enough for Dimah to find us!"

Rashad looked at the sky. "I don't know, Sameer. If I were Khalid, I'd stay here for months. Maybe send messengers to Medina and request my household be sent here." He kicked at the rich brown soil. "It's a nice place; it wouldn't take many slaves to make a decent farm."

"A farm?" cried Sameer.

"Imagine, Sameer, you could have a plot of land and a dozen slaves to work it and be home every night to fulfill Dimah's every desire."

"No!" cried Sameer, "I will become a Bedouin, and chase my animals across the desert. Qutayba, if you were a real friend, you would tell her family that I was killed and went to paradise, and let me fade into obscurity."

"Now, Sameer," said Qutayba, "you would trade a dowry such as Dimah for the houris of paradise? I think you're mad, my friend. Your woman has depths that have yet to be plumbed."

Jabir couldn't resist. "Rumor has it that Sameer isn't equipped to plumb such depths."

The jesting continued. It was amusing in a way; but Bashour wondered if it would ever end, as they heaped good-natured abuse on Sameer's plight. At times like this, Bashour felt most like an outsider. The weeks they'd spent together still hadn't given him the right to join in the jesting about Sameer and his wife. Bashour was convinced she was an ogress by the way they talked, but if he so much as said a word to join in the jest, he was sure they'd all turn on him and attack him.

That night he was still silent, as he and Tamara prepared for bed. Tamara worried that he was upset with her. As they lay down, she looked him in the eye and reached up and pushed a lock of hair off his forehead. He smiled weakly at her and she felt relieved. Whatever was bothering him, it apparently didn't have to do with her. "What's wrong, Bashour?"

He was silent for a time, then quietly said, "I just can't get the vision of them cutting off those heads out of my mind."

Tamara's thoughts immediately went to Jamila and the horrifying scene that played in her mind's eye in an unending loop – Jamila's head hitting the ground, the fountain of blood, her endless screaming. She moved to embrace him. "Oh, Bashour!"

She held him and they rocked together. Tears streamed down her face. One fell and hit him. He reached up in the darkness to feel the wetness on her cheek. "You're crying!" he said.

"Look, um, you're upset about those men. How would you feel if you'd seen the same thing happen to your best friend?"

Bashour was speechless. He realized how little he knew about this woman. "You. . ..?" He had no idea how to form the question.

She sat up and wiped the tears off her face. Her voice grew firmer, as an adult would speak to a child. "Yes. I've told you this before, but you weren't listening. Her name was Jamila and we grew up together. The day they entered - the day *you* entered Qaryateyn, they cut her head off in the village square. Right in front of me. And there isn't a night that passes when I don't see that a hundred times or more."

"But. . ..why? What did she do?"

"She resisted her rapist!" she hissed. "She fought against him, gouged an eye out and they chose to make an example of her."

"Oh, my God, Tamara, I'm so sorry." He gathered her to him and held her. Tears flowed for both of them.

After some time she pushed back from him and wiped her nose and face. "I just don't see how you could follow anyone who could do such things."

The implications of what Tamara was saying struck into Bashour's heart. He thought about it before saying, "What people do in spite of their teachings doesn't invalidate the teachings. You can't condemn Islam because of the excesses of a few Muslims."

Tamara was stunned and nearly speechless. "Oh my God. Look around. Do you hear anybody here condemning what's happening, speaking out against it, or even upset about it like you are? This is *normal* for them! Surely you've seen this enough to know better!"

Bashour was silent. He thought about the men he'd watched die the day before, the two penitents he'd seen Khalid kill who'd professed incorrectly. He remembered how his companions had laughed about beheading Persian prisoners. He realized that

Tamara was right. But that couldn't be. He couldn't believe that any religion condoned such brutality. Deep down he was sure that such excesses would be disapproved of by the Prophet. No man of God would find that acceptable.

After a long silence Tamara spoke again. "Bashour? I know you like me and you want me to like you. I think maybe I could, too. You're nice. But I'll never give myself to someone who worships with these animals. Never."

Bashour had no answer to that.

57. Damascus
August 22, 634

Thomas met with Harbis after breakfast and they began a tour of the city walls. The farmlands around Damascus were filled with encampments. Harbis told him, "Right at dawn they did the most peculiar thing. Here and there someone started yelling, then they got into a loose formation, faced south and did a series of standing and kneeling bows, while chanting some sort of poem. Strangest behavior I've ever seen."

"And then?"

Harbis shrugged. "Then, nothing. They broke it up and returned to what looks like normal camp life.

Thomas greeted Taticus, who was waiting for them on the wall. Together they surveyed the Muslim camps that encircled the city. "What do you think of our situation, Taticus?"

"Were it a different enemy, I'd say grim. But I don't know about this lot. I've never seen a more brilliant field commander, nor a more fanatic group of soldiers. Do they have the stomach for a long siege? Can they sit there and wait and do nothing? I have no idea."

"Tell us about your experiences with them, Drungus," said Harbis.

"I fought under Andrew at Elah, southwest of Jerusalem. This commander of theirs, he's thoughtful and prudent. We outnumbered them three to one, but the terrain prevented lateral maneuver, so we could only meet them along a battlefront that prevented us from using our numbers directly. He made them suffer an archery barrage without attacking until late in the afternoon, when he could fight and then withdraw as it got dark, before his soldiers grew too tired and we could press them with fresh reserves.

"Then he orchestrated a negotiation that was actually a decapitation strike and killed Andrew just before dawn. They attacked at dawn, and he maneuvered us into a trap that could have been lifted straight from the history books, exactly like Hannibal did at Cannae. We took the bait and he destroyed a good third of our army right there.

"I evaded to Jerusalem and was ordered to take charge of the remnants and march north. I refitted at Tiberias and set up an over-watch to ambush them east of the Sea of Galilee. This commander, he's a mind-reader. Our position was discovered, and he slipped out of reach in the night, marching under the full moon. We trailed his flank until we met your army."

Thomas asked, "You say these fighters are fanatics?"

"They don't appear to be well-drilled, but they more than make up for it in ferocity. Their war cry is, 'Allâhu Akhbar!' They seem to enjoy fighting and have no fear of death. Do you know how hard it is to kill someone who doesn't flinch at the thought of dying?"

Nearby an archer took a hard pull on his bow and loosed an arrow. It fell short of the enemy positions.

"Tell me about their dispositions," said Harbis.

"I figure between twenty-five and thirty thousand soldiers. We've seen some camp followers among them. Women. No children. About half are mounted. They have the city surrounded, but more than half their force is on the south and west. They apparently aren't worried about us breaking out and then having to cross the river."

"That works both ways," said Harbis.

"Yes. There also appears to be a large reserve force encamped near the monastery. From the banners, I think there are six armies. One in front of the West gate, one to the south guarding St. Paul's and Small gates, one across the creek facing the eastern gate, one north in front of the Orchards gate, one straddling the river in front of the Emessa gate and one that seems to roam and patrol."

"I don't see any sign of siege engines," observed Harbis.

"Hmm. I wouldn't expect it," said Thomas. "These are nomads. I don't think they have a mechanical mindset. I think if they're serious, we may be facing a waiting siege. We have the advantage of time, because Heraclius is probably even now arranging a relief force."

58. Antioch
August 22, 634

Libanius ordered his men and their horses into the barracks area in Antioch and set out alone to report to Heraclius. He'd been alarmed when he discovered that Heraclius had moved the court from Emessa. It was unlike Heraclius to move away from a fight.

When Libanius appeared in his chamber, Heraclius struggled to his feet from the recliner. "Libanius! Welcome back! Very good! You made quick time! What news?"

Libanius ignored the informal cloak that Heraclius wore and the grimace that crossed his face as he rose. "The Avars and the Bulgars have reached an uneasy peace, Basileus. The front is quiet. The tribes are hunkering down and preparing for the winter. I felt comfortable returning with ten thousand cavalry."

"Excellent." A servant appeared with a pitcher of steaming warm wine, which he poured for Heraclius. "Merarch, I'm afraid I can't afford to rest your men after their march. I need you to move on Damascus. The city is under siege by an army of some twenty or thirty thousand Arabs. I need you to lift that siege. I sent Caloiis from Emessa with five thousand men. With your army and the garrison in the city, that should be plenty to send those Arabs back to the desert."

Libanius pursed his lips. "Basileus, if such a plan is to work, the attack from within the city will have to be coordinated with my attack."

"Send a spy into the city, if you can, and arrange a signal from the hills north of the city. Caloiis is no doubt expecting a relief force, so he'll be ready for you. Go by way of Emessa. I left an additional two thousand cavalry there for you to add to your force. See Psellus, he's already arranged your supply train."

Libanius left with his orders. He couldn't shake his sense of unease that Heraclius was still in the court, instead of marching at the head of an army. Of course, the man's health obviously wouldn't allow it. Libanius had been out of the communication loop for nearly two months because of his trip to Thrace. He was dismayed at what had happened during his absence. Somehow the Arabs had defeated a force three times their size in Palestine.

Heraclius appeared off balance and reacting to their moves, instead of making them react. Libanius felt he was violating his own principle of concentration of force, and trying to meet the Arabs in too many places at once. Despite his orders, Libanius wasn't going to charge headlong into battle with this enemy until he'd learned the secret of their inexplicable success.

59. Damascus
August 22, 634

Just off the street, Jonas was lounging in the shade with some chilled wine on the porch of a small restaurant. He had more time to himself since the shipments into the city had stopped, and he was pleased to be out from under the constant scrutiny of Nicetas. He'd been paid for his efforts. It wasn't much, but the down payment on his debts to Kostas had given him some breathing space. The city was under siege and he was quietly trying to figure out how to turn that to his advantage. If he could somehow denounce Kostas as a collaborator, he could have him imprisoned, and his threat removed permanently.

The porch was a popular place for young men to gather in the early afternoon. It wasn't particularly crowded today, but neither was it empty. Jonas sipped his wine and closed his eyes, enjoying the atmosphere and the momentary lack of demands on his time.

He heard a commotion down the street that was drawing closer. Jonas disregarded it. He was unperturbed that the porch quickly emptied and no one was left but him and the serving girl. Everyone was probably heading to see what the fuss was about.

Then several squads of soldiers hove into view, marching down the street with a hard looking officer at their head. He locked eyes with Jonas and pointed at him with a short baton he was carrying. Three soldiers split away and came at him. Jonas realized this was one of the conscription patrols they'd been talking about. He'd thought they were just evil rumors! He looked around in panic, but since he'd been spotted he had no way to go. He decided to brazen it out. He stood and smiled as they reached his tiny table.

"Gentlemen, how can I help you?"

Two of the soldiers looked at each other with smirks. The third said, "By order of the governor, all able-bodied men are to report for defense training." He studied Jonas and added, "I don't see any infirmities." Jonas silently cursed himself for not affecting a limp or something that would disqualify him. He decided to continue his bluff.

"I'm sorry, Tetrarch, you must not be aware of who I am."

The officer looked disgusted and glanced over his shoulder at the officer, who'd overheard the exchange and was striding over. "And just who might that be?" he demanded.

Jonas drew himself up and said as haughtily as he could muster, "I am Jonas Tournikes, of one of the wealthiest households in the city. Further, I am the assistant quartermaster of the city, reporting directly to the Governor's assistant, and therefore exempt from military service."

The grizzled officer gave him a level gaze that went on far too long to be comfortable. He worked his jaw silently for several moments, then turned his head slightly and spat contemptuously. Then he returned the deadpan stare to Jonas. After a measured pause designed to intimidate, he finally said, "Well, if you'll excuse me, that's the biggest load of bullshit I've heard all day!" Directing his gaze to the other soldiers as he strode away, he said, "Seize him and put him in ranks."

Jonas refused to accept the inevitable and continued to protest as they grabbed his arms. "You're making a big mistake. My father. . . ."

"If he says one more word, gag him," ordered the officer.

The Tetrarch gave him an evil grin. "Please keep talking," he quietly said, "I'd love to hear you."

Jonas resisted slightly as they started to march him along, but their hands closed painfully around his arms like a vise. He was thrust into a small group of other civilians who'd also been press-ganged, and they spent the rest of the morning marching through the city, sweeping up what stragglers they could. Occasional talking among his fellow conscripts was swiftly and sometimes violently crushed by the no-nonsense officer in charge.

60. Medina, Arabia
August 23, 634

Aisha, the youngest wife of the Prophet and long considered his favorite, sat by the bedside and held the hand of her father, Abu Bakr, Caliph of the faithful followers of Muhammad. She was shocked by how much weight he'd lost. He was scarcely more than a skeleton. They'd tried feeding him, but he lacked any interest in eating and eventually was too weak to get out of bed; at first to say prayers and finally to even relieve himself.

The old man was tired. He'd requested that Ali come and perform the ritual purification of his body this day, as Ali had done for Muhammad two years previously. The day before, he'd appointed Umar bin al Khattab to be his successor. He'd instructed Aisha to use three pieces of cloth for his burial shroud, in the manner of Muhammad. All of this had physically worn him out.

The pain came and went, leaving him breathless, in agony, drenched in sweat and doing his best not to cry out. The other women never stayed long, couldn't tolerate the sight of the pain or the nearness of death. Aisha stayed. The Prophet, peace be always upon Him, had died with his head in her lap. She'd seen death up close, and calmly waited for it to come to her father.

For a woman of twenty, it was a huge responsibility. Perhaps her youth gave her the strength to meet death so close to her.

"Aisha?" It was barely a whisper, a croak.

"I'm here, father." She gripped his hand, still strong, still powerful. "My sheik, my Caliph! I'm here for you."

Another wave of pain racked his body and he gripped her hand painfully. When it passed, he moved his lips. He was gasping for breath and lacked the strength to make a sound, but his lips moved, "Ta'hab beki." *I love you.*

"I love you too, Father!" His eyes were unfocused, staring into space and his chest heaved for air. Another wave of pain came, he gripped her hand tightly. Then his grip loosened. His breath quieted. He breathed no more.

Aisha waited. After a minute he heaved a shuddering breath, but only one. She closed his eyes and announced, "He's gone."

His senior wife, Qutaylah, and Aisha's mother, Um Ruman, peeked into the room, then entered. Together they began to chant. "O Allâh! Pardon my sins which are many, and accept my deeds which are very little. There is no God except Allâh the Generous and Patient. There is no God except Allâh the Almighty and All-Wise. Pure is that Allâh Who is Creator of the seven heavens and the seven earths and all that is in them and between them; He is the Lord of all these things and the throne and all praise is due to Allâh, Who is the Lord of all the worlds." She could hear women sobbing elsewhere. The words, the ritual, calmed her, kept her from releasing her grief.

Umar had prepared the letter before Abu Bakr was even dead. Immediately upon hearing that the Caliph was dead, he sent a rider to find Abu 'Ubaidah ibn al- Jarrah and deliver it. Khalid's power on the battlefield was a great temptation for any man and Khalid had ambition. He wouldn't allow a successful general to return in triumph and challenge his seat as Caliph. Khalid must be removed of his command and Ubaidah put in his place. Ubaidah had no ambition; he'd be content to be a high-ranking servant.

61. Damascus
August 31, 634

Thomas walked along the parapet, quietly exhorting his archers, "Easy does it, lads. Half draws, suck them in. Give them some confidence. Don't give away your range."

The arrows from his archers lofted in lazy arcs off the wall. Below, the Arabs had formed a cheering line just beyond where the arrows were falling. Periodically a group of them would step off in a ragged line and walk slowly towards the walls, their eyes on the sky. The men behind would cheer on their favorites. They would stop occasionally to avoid an arrow. If one stepped to the side to avoid an arrow, he was apparently disqualified and returned in shame to the line amid hoots from his fellows. The game went on until they came dangerously close to the wall and avoiding the arrows became more difficult. Occasionally one of the archers would ignore Thomas' orders when they got close and would loose a hard, deadly shot in the hopes of felling one of the barbarians. Despite some close calls, no real blood had been drawn yet.

Thomas noted the infractions but said nothing. He knew how frustrating his orders must be. But by deliberately concealing the true range of his archers, the line of cheering Arabs slowly edged forward, thinking they were safely out of range. If one or two of the enemy got skewered in the process? He shrugged.

Bashour eyed the walls nervously. They seemed awfully close. No one else was paying much attention. They were calling out to their favorites, urging them to stay steady, jeering and insulting the others, trying to distract them. Bashour was pretty sure that gambling was forbidden by the Prophet, peace be upon him, but every time the field of advancing heroes was reduced to one, he was sure he saw gold changing hands.

Bashour was sure they were too close to the walls; that if the archers wanted to, they could rain death right into the crowd, instead of harassing the heroes. He tugged on Rashad's cloak. "Rashad, let's back up. We're too close." His friend ignored him, so he tapped on his shoulder and put his mouth close so the other could hear him in the din of shouts and cheers. "We're too close! Let's back up a bit!"

Rashad took a moment from cheering his favorite to look at Bashour. "Don't worry so much! If we were in range, they would have hit us by now." He turned away again.

Thomas decided they'd advanced far enough. He stopped at one archer and tapped his shoulder. "Your bow, if you don't mind." The man handed over his bow and stepped back. Thomas gave it a couple of test pulls pointed down, then nocked an arrow. He gave it a full draw and centered in on the chest of one of the men in the line, then raised his aim to compensate for the distance. He drew a deep breath, let half of it out and let fly. Before it found its mark, he bellowed, "full draws, men! Hit them hard!"

A ragged cheer erupted along the wall as his arrow was followed by a cloud of others.

Rashad was in mid cheer when he abruptly gasped and sagged backward into Bashour. Startled, Bashour instinctively grabbed him. "What's wrong?" he asked, then he saw the arrow deeply embedded in the right side of Rashad's chest, just below the shoulder. His friend's eyes were wide with surprise and his mouth was working without making a sound.

Time was frozen for a long minute, then there were other shouts of surprise as arrows rained into the crowd and the festive atmosphere turned into panic. Bashour struggled to get under Rashad's good arm, then half-dragged, half-carried him away from the wall. He got far enough to be sure he was out of range of the archers, then kept going a little further for good measure. He eased Rashad to the ground as Wahid and Qutayba ran up to him. By this time Rashad had recovered his voice, and was cursing loudly and with great scatological eloquence.

Bashour grabbed the shaft of the arrow as if to pull it out and was immediately cuffed aside by Wahid. "Are you trying to kill him? Leave it alone," said the huge man. Then Wahid lifted Rashad as if he were a rag doll and rolled him on his left side and felt his back. "Hmm. It didn't go through. That's too bad." Laying Rashad back down he swiftly grasped the arrow and before Bashour could say anything, he snapped it off about two hand spans from the body. He scooped up Rashad under the arms and instructed Bashour and Qutayba to each take a leg, and they started carrying him back to their campsite.

They hadn't gone far when Dhiraar rode by them then stopped. "Serves you right for playing stupid games," he said. "There's a monastery past the orchards over there," he motioned to the east. "They've set up a hospital there under the care of the local priests. Take him there."

Several others wounded in the surprise were already there when they reached it. The priests in their robes were bustling with quiet efficiency, conducting triage. One of them took a quick look at the wound. "Are you able to speak?" he asked in Greek.

Bashour didn't translate but said, "Yes, he's talking."

"The priest gave him a quizzical look, then examined Rashad's mouth. "Good. You had the sense to leave the arrow in. Has he coughed up any blood? Any pink froth?"

"No," said Bashour confidently.

"Okay, he can wait. Lay him over there and see that he gets lots of liquid. There's wine in those flasks."

"We are followers of Allâh. We do not drink wine," said Qutayba haughtily.

A look of disgust flashed across the priest's face. "Fine, then. Make him drink a lot of water. Don't let him move around."

They lay him down where they were told and stood around awkwardly. Bashour asked, "How are you feeling?"

Rashad's face was pale, but he managed a weak smile. "It hurts like a bitch!"

"Think of the scar you're going to get," said Wahid. Bashour was surprised and realized how worried the big man must be to joke with them. He was usually silent and kept his thoughts to himself.

Bashour busied himself trying to keep Rashad drinking and waving flies off the wound, while they told jokes and stories of other injuries to keep his spirits up. A priest eventually came over and pulled aside the cloak to look at the damage. "Bring him this way," he ordered, indicating a raised table in the courtyard. A small fire was burning hotly in a nearby brazier.

The priest dipped into a pouch and with two fingers scooped out a black, tarry paste. He rolled it around into a ball. Then he eyed Rashad and pinched the ball in two and discarded one-half. He handed the other half to Bashour with a cup of water. "Make him swallow this. It tastes foul, so best he wash it right down."

Rashad tried to refuse the pill. He turned his head away, but Wahid grasped his head and pried his mouth open. Bashour dropped the little black ball in and poured some water. Rashad choked, but Wahid had slammed his jaw shut and was holding it closed. He finally swallowed and grabbed at the cup Bashour was holding.

"By Allâh, that's the foulest thing I've ever tasted!" he exclaimed.

The priest took a sponge and dipped it in wine and started cleaning around the wound. Bashour watched Rashad's face as he did so and was amazed as the young man's features relaxed and a sleepy smile spread across his face. "Oh, that's nice," he whispered.

"What's happening?" asked Bashour, puzzled.

"That's the opium taking effect. He won't feel the surgery now, and even if he could he wouldn't care," said the priest. "Here, you. Wash your hands in this wine."

Moving quickly the priest took a small, sharp knife and washed it with wine, then made an incision across the hole the arrow had made, lengthening the wound. Then he wiped the skin dry with a clean linen towel and staunched the fresh blood. He stuck a finger into the newly opened wound and felt around. "Okay, place your hands on either side of the cut. I need you to hold this open. Yes, just like so. Hold that."

"That tickles," said Rashad thickly.

"Tell your friends to hold him still!" barked the priest.

He reentered the wound with the knife and deepened the cut. Then he placed his finger in and experimentally rocked the arrow shaft. It moved freely and he slipped it to the side and out. Dark blood welled up from the newly excavated wound. The priest raised the gore-covered arrowhead for all to see, then cast it aside. He poured water over the wound, flushing it clean, then poured wine into it. He picked up a bone needle with a silk thread and expertly sewed the wound closed.

"If he avoids an infection, he should be fine. He'll be dopey the rest of the day from the opium. Then he'll be in pain. I want to keep him in the infirmary here so we can watch for an infection."

"What's he saying? He talks funny. Make him talk right, Bashour!" said Rashad, then giggled. His laughter subsided and he stared into the distance. "Ooooh!" he said with a sense of wonder.

Bashour translated what the priest had said for his Arab companions. Qutayba squeezed Rashad's good shoulder. "Insha'Allâh, get well quickly."

Rashad looked at him and giggled. "You look better with those horns. You should grow them more often!" Then he dissolved into a fit of laughter that dwindled to a stupid grin. Wahid and Qutayba looked at each other with puzzled expressions and started to leave.

"Are you coming, Bashour?"

"I'll catch up." He turned to the priest as the others left. "He said something about horns on my friend? What's he talking about?"

"That's the opium talking. He's hallucinating. It'll wear off, then he'll be in a black pit of depression for a while."

"Why are you doing this, even when we attack your city?"

The priest was busy washing the blood off his hands as he answered. "We're all God's children in the end. Jesus charged us to heal the sick. He didn't qualify it and say we should only heal our friends. Jesus healed the Centurion's servant. He forgave those who crucified him even as he died."

Bashour thought of the things he'd learned from his study of the Qur'án. "The prophet, peace be upon him, says that Jesus wasn't crucified. Allâh cast an illusion and they crucified someone else, thinking it was Jesus."

The priest looked at him and smiled. "Is that so? Tell me, do you know who St. John the Evangelist was?"

"Of course. I studied the Gospels before I became a Muslim."

"Well, then you're aware that St. John was there and witnessed the crucifixion. Christ charged him to take Mary as his own mother. Would an imposter have done that?"

"Well, I. . . "

But the priest cut him off. "As he hung there dying, he spoke of forgiveness. He invited the good thief Dismas to join him in paradise. Would a man wrongly identified and punished have done that?"

Bashour remained silent, thinking of a response, so the priest went on. "St. John was the first to enter the tomb on the third day and see the resurrection. Now think of these men, the twelve who followed Jesus. They were terrified, they were sure they'd be the next to be captured and denounced. They thought the High Priest would stop at nothing to crush the teachings of

Christ. Even St. Peter, the most faithful, had denied even knowing Christ. The movement should have died with Him, if he were really dead. But something happened to convince these men beyond all shadow of a doubt, convince them so thoroughly that they spread the Gospel across the world and suffered hideous deaths for their belief. Deaths which they accepted happily. The accounts are clear; Christ rose from the dead, and they walked with him, ate with him and saw the holes in his hands and feet.

"Your prophet can say what he wants, but the man closest to Christ, who called himself the most beloved, who cared for Christ's mother, says he watched the man die on a cross then rise from the dead. He was there and your prophet wasn't. Believe what you want."

"The prophet only repeated the words of Allâh. It's Allâh, the mighty, the merciful, who repudiates the Christian belief."

The priest looked at him levelly. "I don't know your Allâh, boy. But you need to ask yourself who stands to gain the most by denying the crucifixion and the resurrection."

"What do you mean by that?"

"You're a bright boy. Figure it out for yourself. Now get out of here. There are more wounded, and I haven't time right now for your catechism."

Bashour made his way slowly back to the camp, deep in thought. He felt like he'd taken the worst in the exchange with the priest, and resolved to learn more about what the Prophet taught so he could acquit himself better in any similar debates in the future.

62. Damascus
August 27, 634

Sweat burned in his eyes as Jonas hefted the unfamiliar weight of the wooden training sword. He wore an ill-fitting set of body armor without a cloak over it. The sun raised the temperature of the iron plates to where they were painful to the touch. His body ached from days of endless drilling, marching and combat practice. He'd quit wondering why his father hadn't interceded to get him out of this duty. The young man facing him in the sword practice drills looked as exhausted as he felt, but refused to acknowledge it.

Today they were being drilled by Taticus. The man's reputation had grown to almost legendary status among the soldiers who'd marched with him since Jerusalem, but Jonas was unimpressed. He was a martinet, demanding instant and unyielding discipline. Jonas was sure that a soldier would be more effective if he could think for himself, to be able to react with independence in a battle.

"Lunge!" Jonas' opponent drove forward with his sword.

"Parry!" Jonas swatted at the advancing sword, but not enough to deflect it. It banged into his armor.

"Take it easy!" he hissed, "We need to pace ourselves!"

"Thrust!" Jonas' timing was off because he'd missed the parry, and he half-heartedly stepped into the riposte. His opponent easily batted it aside and leveled his wooden sword straight between Jonas' eyes, inches away. He glared at him over the training weapon.

"Again!" The trainees separated and resumed their opening position, just out of reach of each other. Jones stood lazily, taking a casual stance as if he wasn't serious about the drill. "Lunge!" Jonas' opponent thrust deeply, aiming with intent at his breastplate.

"Parry!" Jonas hacked at the oncoming sword with an ineffective roundhouse. The momentum of his opponent's lunge carried through, barely deflected, and again smashed into his breastplate, making him stumble. He completely ignored the command to thrust as he tried to regain his balance.

His clumsiness attracted the attention of Taticus, who moved to get a better view of him as he restarted the drill. "Thrust!"

Jonas performed no better than the previous drill. He made an indifferent attempt to follow the motions, but was clearly making no real effort at mastering the movements. Veterans of Taticus' training methods smiled knowingly when they saw his face darken. Jonas had already developed a reputation in the unit, and he wasn't well liked.

Taticus ripped the training sword from Jonas' opponent and faced Jonas with the weapon held loosely at his side. "Switch roles! Ready! Lunge!"

Jonas stood there, stupefied, as his comrades began the drill. Those who'd been on the lunge now parried. Jonas was unsure what to do. Taticus stood in a relaxed stance, unprepared, nor did he wear any armor.

"Soldier, I said lunge!" yelled Taticus.

Jonas bit his lip and aimed for the heart and drove his sword forward. With catlike speed, Taticus smashed the sword aside with a blow that made Jonas' hand sting, then he moved in and body checked Jonas so hard on the breastplate that he was lifted from his feet. He fell backward and landed heavily on his back, nearly knocking the wind out of him.

Taticus loomed above him, blocking the sun. He tapped Jonas' breastplate with the training sword. "You can pretend this is a game if you like, but I assure you the Arabs out there are serious. And so am I. You slack off on the battlefield and they might kill you. You slack off here and I will kill you! You train hard here, now. Then you might survive out there."

Jonas couldn't see the smiles around him, but he heard a snicker. He vowed revenge on this low-class barbarian of a soldier for humiliating him so. Taticus left and his training partner took his arm to help him up. He angrily shook off the assistance.

63. South of Emessa
September 3, 634

Libanius led his twelve thousand cavalry down the main road from Emessa to Damascus. The flat desert gradually gave way to a deepening depression as they approached the mountains from the north. The Anti-Lebanon Mountains ran northeast to southwest at this point and the road turned to the southwest in their shadow. For several days they would have a steadily increasing slope to their left. The tan landscape was broken by scrub bushes and the occasional outcrop of darker rock. It was a harsh, arid, inhospitable place to be.

Libanius had delayed the march this morning to give his scouts time to get well ahead. Twelve thousand horsemen riding through a desert could be seen from a long way off. He wanted the hills in front of him cleared of spying eyes before his main force came close enough to be detected.

A cloud of dust ahead resolved itself into one of his scouts, galloping towards them at full speed. This could not be good news. A contact report would be the only reason a scout rode in such haste. His suspicion was confirmed when the young man reported.

"We encountered a pair of riders. They fled as soon as they saw us. We gave chase, but their horses were far too fast."

"Which way did they go?"

"East, initially, off the back side of the ridge. As soon as they made the desert floor they went south."

"Were they close enough to have seen the army?"

"I don't think so, sir."

"Very well. Thank you." Hopefully his scouts would keep the enemy patrols far enough away to conceal the main body of his force. He turned to his second-in-command, "Order the column into a combat formation. Flankers out in both directions. It's safe to say that we can expect to be attacked at any time from this point forward." He was taking no chances until his scouts could locate the main body of an enemy force, even if it slowed his advance. Damascus wasn't going anywhere.

Outside the city, Tamara and Bashour had retired to his tent for the night. “How is Rashad?” asked Tamara.

“Hm? Oh, he’s got a slight fever, but the wound is draining. The priests are quite satisfied with his progress.”

“You’ve been awfully quiet all day. What’s on your mind?” Bashour was usually trying to engage her in conversation. Sometimes, when she felt lonely, she responded. She’d learned long ago that she couldn’t maintain the painful silent routine; it just wasn’t in her. It wasn’t like he was cruel or mistreated her. Considering the circumstances, she honestly couldn’t ask to be treated better.

“I don’t know. I’ve been thinking about what happened to Rashad. It really drives home how close death can be. I’m wondering if I’m ready to be a martyr for Allâh.”

“Martyr? What do you mean, martyr?” Tamara had never seen any Muslim act in the way she’d expect of a true martyr.

“They told me that the Prophet said: ‘The person who participates in Jihad in Allâh's cause, for no reason except belief in Allâh, will be admitted to Paradise if he is killed in the battle as a martyr.’”

Tamara was dumbfounded. Every time she thought she’d found a limit to how far these people would twist the truth, twist meanings, she was proved wrong.

“Do I understand this? If you die in battle fighting to force Islam on others, you’re a ‘martyr’?”

Bashour had the same reaction when he’d first encountered the definition, but his companions had assured him that it was so, that fighting in Jihad in Allâh’s cause was almost the best deed, second only to believing in Allâh and his Apostle. “Oh, yes,” he said brightly. “For a Muslim it’s the best way to die. The Prophet himself said that had he not found it difficult for his followers, then he would have loved to be martyred in Allâh's cause and then made alive, and then martyred and then made alive, and then again martyred in His cause."

“So let me see if I understand this. To a Muslim, being a martyr is dying in a fight to try to force someone else to believe the way you do?”

Bashour looked uncomfortable. “Well, I don’t know if I’d put it like that. . .”

“I would. Tell me, isn’t it true that you Muslims must fight until us non-Muslims accept Islam, or feel ourselves subdued? I’m sure I heard your Qur’án say that.”

"Yes," he said, weakly.

"Congratulations. I feel subdued."

Bashour looked exasperated. How could she twist his words, his ideas so easily? "Tamara, look. . ."

"No, you look! A martyr is someone who's persecuted for their faith and dies for it. Martyrs don't fight back. A martyr dies because they're given the choice to die or renounce their belief in Jesus. A martyr goes to his death gladly with praise of God on his lips and forgiveness for his persecutors. He dies for what he believes in, not because he wants to force others to believe the same thing. That's how Christianity spread, because people were so impressed that the followers of Christ would sooner die than deny him."

"Allâh commanded us to fight those who believe not in Allâh nor the Last Day, nor hold that forbidden which hath been forbidden by Allâh and His Messenger, nor acknowledge the religion of truth, even if they are of the People of the Book, until they pay the Jizyah with willing submission and feel themselves subdued."

"Yes, I'm sure Allâh does command that. But Allâh is not God, Bashour. If you had eyes, you would see that. God never said anything like that to anyone in history."

Bashour bit back an angry response and they sat in silence. Tamara regretted her outburst. She just wanted to know why Bashour was so quiet, it was so unlike him. And however innocent they started, the moment their conversations turned to beliefs, they fought. She realized that Islam would always be a barrier between them that could never be crossed.

After some time, she reached out and laid a hand on his arm. "Bashour, don't be a martyr. I don't know what I would do if you did. I'm afraid of what would happen to me if that happened."

Bashour was still and silent for a while. He was angry with her, the way she always attacked Allâh and the Prophet. But she was trying to make amends and he didn't want to be at odds with her. He laid a hand on hers. "It's all right, Tamara. I'm sorry."

64. Damascus
September 4, 634

Thomas prowled the parapets of the city wall in the dark, studying the fires of the Muslim camp that encircled the city. Tiny pinpricks of light, too many to count, spread across the landscape. The waxing moon cast a feeble light, making it too dark to make out details outside the circles of the fires.

He'd ordered all lights to be extinguished on the wall. Glowing braziers smoldered here and there, next to bundles of pitch-tipped arrows. These would provide light if anyone detected an advance on the wall in the dark. Thomas paced close to one of the archers standing guard and placed a hand on his shoulder. "Don't focus on their lights, you'll ruin your night vision. Look at the sky and scan the ground in your sector. Keep your ears as well as your eyes open." The man quietly nodded in acknowledgment.

Thomas moved on and heard the gentle mumble of a pair of guards chatting. He approached them and quietly admonished them, "You can't hear anyone approaching if you're talking to each other. Save the gossip for off-duty. Your ears are as important as your eyes at night."

He stopped over the Small gate and leaned forward against the wall. The night was quiet. A cool breeze blew through his hair, bringing the acrid smell of smoke from thousands of small fires. He thought about how beautiful it would look if those fires didn't indicate the presence of his enemies. A hand on his arm startled him.

"I knew I'd find you here," said Epiphina, his wife. She looked out at the sea of campfires. "There's so many of them!"

"Yes. In a way, that works in our favor. We haven't seen any siege engines, so we're safe in the city. They have to feed all those soldiers and winter is coming. Hopefully we can hold out until they get too hungry and withdraw for lack of supplies."

"Do you think my father will attack them, lift the siege?"

"I know he wants to, but with the defeat of the army in Palestine, I don't know if he can muster the force to do it. Hopefully the situation in Thrace is quiet and he can divert some forces from there. But, my love, we've got to deal with the prospect that there's no relief force coming."

"Isn't there anything else we can do?"

"We might be able to break out, meet their armies piecemeal. If a concentration of force at one point in their line could deliver a devastating blow, we could fall back to the city before they could bring their superior numbers against us. If we did it repeatedly we might be able to whittle them down to size and encourage them to leave."

"Is such a thing possible?"

He smiled, "I doubt it. It's impractical."

They studied the enemy encampment again and after a while he said, "If they don't leave, we may have to surrender the city to avoid bloodshed. If they capture it by force, I shudder to think what they'd do to the general population."

"Would you live as a slave rather than die free?"

"Do I have the authority to make that choice for everyone here in Damascus?"

She looked at him in admiration. "I love you Thomas. You're a great man."

"I love you too, m'love." He hoped he could live up to the expectations of the Emperor's daughter.

The Decharch walked past the nine men lined in front of the gate. He stopped at each and poked and prodded their leather armor and accessories, looking for anything that would clank or make noise. The men had wrapped metal fittings in soft cloth and blackened their faces with ash. When he came to Jonas, he shook the scabbard of the sword and was satisfied there was no sound. Then he looked Jonas in the eye. "Silence is golden. If you make one sound out there, you're a dead man. If the enemy doesn't alert to our presence and kill us, I'll kill you myself the moment we're back through the gate. Do you understand, recruit?"

Jonas swallowed. "Yes, sir."

"I'm fucking serious, recruit. You've been taking it easy for too long and this is life and death. You get lost, you lose contact, you make a noise, and your life is forfeit. I've been looking for a way to get rid of you since the moment you were assigned to me."

Jonas held his eyes forward and bit back his response. The Decharch finally moved on to the front of the line and ordered the torches at the gate be extinguished. They waited for their eyes to adjust in the darkness for nearly ten minutes before he was satisfied. He drew the bolt back from the Judas gate and touched the shoulder of the lead man. "Go."

Jonas filed out with the rest of the men. They crept to the left along the wall after they were clear of the gate. They'd left the Emessa gate and the walls kept them in the shadow of the weak moon. Jonas could hear nothing except the pounding of blood through his ears and his heavy breath. His eyes were wide in the dark and he was sure that enemy soldiers were lurking in the shadows behind every rock, their eyes on him.

After seeing the last one out, the Decharch brought up the rear. He glided past Jonas noiselessly, touching each man in turn with a reassuring hand. Once in the lead, he made a chopping motion with his hand to move out. Their objective was to scout the outer wall and make sure no one was sneaking up in the darkness with grapples and rope. The north side of the city wall was of particular concern, because the banks of the small river could offer defilades where soldiers could hide from the archers on the wall.

Jonas didn't look around, he just concentrated on the dark shape of the man in front of him. He stifled a curse when he stubbed his toe on an unseen rock and nearly stumbled. The man behind him grabbed him roughly and steadied him, then shook him before letting go. They made their way away from the wall to where the steep bank of the small river descended, then turned left along it. The walls of the city loomed black to his left, and the pinpricks of hundreds of campfires and torches from the Arab camp spread to the north. He felt the enemy could see him clearly, though his mind told him that wasn't possible.

Someone shouted a challenge from the top of the wall and a trio of lighted arrows landed near their position. The soldiers around him dropped to the ground. Jonas stood wondering what to do, when the man behind him roughly shoved him down. Jonas suddenly realized that they were in as much danger of being killed by their own archers in the dark. Ahead of him he heard someone mutter, "There's always one dumb son of a bitch that didn't get the word."

They stayed crouched, waiting for the torches of the arrows to sputter out. Above them they heard a sharp exchange as a sergeant disciplined the watchman who ordered the flight of illumination arrows. Jonas studied the Arab camp, but it didn't look like anyone had taken notice. He felt sick to his stomach when he realized that their scouting route took them well within bowshot range of the Arab archers.

Being conscripted was a mixed blessing. Kostas seemed to leave him alone since he'd been pressed into service, which was a plus; but the hours, the food and the constant discipline rankled him. He was gathering a list of the low-class soldiers and sergeants who would feel his wrath when he regained his rightful position on the social ladder. These people had no idea who they were dealing with. The indignities he'd suffered at their hands would be repaid with interest.

He thought of Eudocia. His military obligations left him little time or energy for women. In his loneliness, his mind returned to Eudocia and how much she loved him. He missed her terribly, realized that he'd been wrong to treat her so casually. He decided he needed to pressure her to get married as soon as possible, but he could only send the occasional message to her since he'd been pressed into service. The sergeants wouldn't give liberty to any of the pressed soldiers, afraid they'd never return.

This dark reflection returned his thoughts to those of revenge. He lost himself in thought for the rest of the patrol, dreaming of various sorts of punishments he could get away with. With his father's resources, he could someday have all of these men working for him and he'd make their lives hell when they did. The time passed quickly and he was surprised when they arrived at a gate and the Decharch rapped a pattern on the door. A challenge was made and the password given, and the gate opened to allow them in.

Bashour and his companions were on guard duty in the dark, watching the city battlements for infiltrators. Tamara was alone in their small camp. She lit an oil lamp in their tent and unwrapped the heavy bundle from Bashour's belongings. She'd been working discreetly for some days now, polishing his cross, slowly removing the gray patina and revealing the fine beautiful gold underneath. She normally had no more than a few minutes at a time. Whenever she unwrapped it, she did so fearfully, anxious that Bashour might come unexpectedly and catch her. She didn't know how he'd react, but she was sure it wouldn't be good.

But now he was sure to be gone for some hours, and she could work in peace. She took a coarse linen rag and began working the surface, wearing away the gray. The effort was rewarding, she could see the slow progress, the gradual transformation to beauty. It calmed her and she began to pray as her fingers worked. She made a prayer of thanks for the strength she'd been given thus far, thanked God that he'd provided a protector in the person of Bashour and prayed that she could be the instrument of God's word to turn his heart and return him to Jesus. Eventually she ran out of words and felt as if she was in God's presence, that the symbol of the cross she worked in her hands was connecting to her heart and bringing her peace. She felt peaceful for the first time since that awful day that the Muslims had come to Qaryateyn.

The lamp flickered and dimmed, breaking her out of her reverie. Rather than fill it, she realized she'd lost track of time and had no idea how long it would be before Bashour returned. She rewrapped the cross and returned it to the bottom of his bag, then arranged herself to get some sleep.

Bashour had drawn away from his companions during the watch. They hadn't been ordered to pay strict attention to what was happening along the walls. Sameer had tried to engage him in further instruction on the Qur'án, but he'd begged off. He just wanted some quiet time to think.

They were watching along the river, in full view of the east wall of the city, with a line of sight along the north wall. At one point a flurry of two or three fire arrows were shot from the north wall. He wondered what was going on, but nothing further happened and he soon forgot it.

Bashour wrapped his cloak tighter against the chill of the night and tried to put distracting ideas out of his mind, so he could concentrate on the ones which troubled him.

When he'd accepted Islam, it had seemed such an easy thing to do. The philosophy had simplified all the questions, paradoxes and controversies that seemed to surround Christianity. The message was new, clear and fresh. It allowed him to discard the laborious teachings of the priests and open his heart to a message that came right from the mouth of God. He'd been accepted into a brotherhood, and began learning the details of the Qur'án and the Prophet. He was highly regarded by the commanding general and he even had this beautiful girl. He avoided dwelling on his relationship with Tamara; he didn't want to ponder the fact that he actually owned her, that she was his slave. He wanted it to be much more than that.

What bothered him was that every time he discussed it with someone who wasn't a Muslim, he got the worst of the discussion. He'd decided that Tamara was so close to him that she knew how to manipulate his emotions, make him feel guilty. He normally didn't dwell too much on the things she said. After all, she was only a woman. But the priest at the monastery had easily and thoroughly demolished his position. Now he actually thought about what Tamara had said about martyrs, and had to admit she had a point.

So what did it mean? Well, the problem boiled down to two choices. Either the Prophet Muhammad was authentic and spoke for Allâh, or he wasn't. If he was, then Bashour had to find a way to account for the massive disparities he was starting to find between what the scripture and the priests taught and what he was learning from the Qur'án. He couldn't talk to his companions about it, they knew nothing of scripture and they always seemed to grow very angry whenever he started asking uncomfortable questions.

If Muhammad wasn't the messenger of Allâh, then how to explain the victories the Muslims were enjoying against all odds? Surely someone was looking out for them, guiding them to victory. They were all so devout. They seemed to pray constantly, and every event was attributed as a celebration of Allâh's might and mercy. Their faith had made them fearless in battle. Could a false teaching inspire such devotion? Where would such a teaching come from? It baffled Bashour.

Since it was beyond him to determine whether Muhammad was legitimate at the moment, he turned his thoughts to Christ. Could he have been the Son of God, or God himself, as Imad had taught them? Or was he just another prophet as the Muslims claimed? He did great works and miracles, but then so did Moses and Elijah the Prophet, so that wasn't conclusive. Bashour wished he had access to a lectionary so he could research the scripture. He regretted not having paid better attention at his studies at the knee of Imad. He'd always assumed he'd be able to refer to scripture as needed.

The Monastery surely had a copy of the scriptures. Perhaps he could inquire there to see if he could read them and remind himself of exactly what had been said by and about Jesus.

Bashour sat under the stars, staring at the dark bulk of the Damascus city wall. He felt as if he'd awakened from a long dream, where he'd been content to let others do his thinking for him. He resolved to find the truth about who Muhammad was, wherever it led. He allowed that Muhammad could indeed be the messenger of Allâh, but Bashour felt as if he needed more substantial proof than he had before. The holy sounding words of his Muslim companions didn't seem to fit the actions he'd seen in the army. Yes, it was war, but these people seemed to equate the war as a holy obligation, not the regrettable necessity that sometimes comes of living in an imperfect world.

65. Damascus
September 5, 634

"By Allâh, I sent you out to learn about enemy movements, not to turn and run at the first sight of an infidel!" The messenger cringed at Khalid's wrath. He'd reported the contact with the forces to the north and regretted that he had no accurate count of the men coming towards them. "What good is a scouting party if they won't scout?"

The huge general turned toward Ubaidah. "Do you have that dispatch I dictated for Abu Bakr this morning? Is it ready?" Ubaidah disappeared and hurried back, bearing a scroll. Khalid took it and thrust it into the hands of the messenger. "Take this and get out of my army! Deliver it to the Caliph in person, then stay in Medina. There's no place here for scouts who cannot scout!"

The messenger maintained his stoic silence, bowed quickly and disappeared. Ubaidah caught the eye of one of his aides and motioned him to follow and detain the messenger with a slight twitch of his head. Khalid was reacting in anger. He knew full well that the messenger had nothing to do with the failure of the scouting mission to survey the enemy. The man had no reason to be chastised. By the time he returned from Medina, Khalid would have long forgotten his face.

"Dhiraar," said Khalid, "take five thousand cavalry up the pass and intercept that column. There's a regiment at the village of Bait Lihya at the top of the pass. Take command of them as you pass through. Take Abu Abdullah Bin Umar as your second-in-command."

"Yes Sahib. Insha'Allâh, we will send the infidel running."

Khalid caught him as he turned to leave. "Dhiraar, don't be rash. If you're outnumbered, don't engage. Send for reinforcements if the enemy force is too large."

Dhiraar smiled sardonically. "Of course, Sahib."

As he left, Ubaidah murmured, "Your words are wasted. Dhiraar is a man of many fine qualities, but caution isn't among them."

"He's a great fighter," said Khalid, "and he's no fool. Allâh will guide him rightly."

Libanius led his column of cavalry slowly down the desert valley towards the low mountains that separated him from Damascus. To their left the ground rose steeply to a smooth ridge running northeast to southwest. The road followed the base of this ridge, but he had his forces spread wider than the road in a modified battle formation designed to allow him to bring the bulk of his force forward if necessary, yet still keep some of the advantages of a marching column. It slowed them, as they couldn't move at full road speed across the desert, but he thought it worth the trade-off. He squinted his eyes at the bright sky, looking at the beige ridge to see if he could spot the flankers that he'd sent up there to prevent any spying eyes from looking down on him.

One of his forward scouts galloped up and reported. "Sir, the road continues like this for another two or three millaria, then takes a sharp turn to the left and enters a gap in the hills."

"Show me," said Libanius. He motioned his bodyguard contingent with his head and spurred his horse into a canter.

They topped a small rise and joined a small scout patrol that had gathered to study the terrain below. Ahead the road dipped and turned in to a narrow defile through the mountains. The slope rose steeply on the left. A small sheer bluff formed the right, with a slope above it. The hillsides on either side of the road were covered in a sparse forest of conifers.

"Has anyone scouted that defile yet?" asked Libanius.

"No, sir. We wanted your opinion"

"Your job is to scout, but in this case, I'll forgive your caution. I've never seen a more perfect place to set a trap." He looked around. The road through the defile was the only route through the hills to their left. The crest curved from their left across their front. To the right and straight ahead, the ground rose more gradually to the top of the ridge line. He gestured in that direction. "Is there another way to the top of the pass?"

"Yes, sir. It's a few millaria farther, but this slope leads to the crest, then drops more steeply to the road again, right where it starts down the pass."

"Very good. That's the route we'll take." He surveyed the rise. It was wide and relatively smooth. He could keep his forces deployed in a combat formation against an unexpected encounter. That would save valuable time in the event. He eyed the defile through the hill again, "Position a blocking force on the left flank, in case any hornets swarm out of that nest down there."

Dhiraar cursed under his breath as he watched the Byzantine army bypass his carefully laid trap. Had they spotted his position? He'd been very careful to conceal his men among the trees. He didn't think anyone would have seen them until it was too late. He estimated the size of the force passing from his right to left. Easily twice as many as he had. They weren't deployed for a road march, they were moving in a slow line abreast, almost an assault-in-depth formation. A rolling screen of flankers stayed between him and the main force. They didn't seem particularly focused on his position, but were more like a just-in-case sort of compromise. Someone feared an assault from where he was, but didn't seem to think it too likely.

He backed away carefully to where his sub-commanders waited on the backside of the slope. He began taking off his tunic. "Mount up," he commanded. "We will strike their flank. I want to punch through that screen and get in among their main force before the commander knows what's happening. Allâh will deliver our enemies to us this day."

Libanius was at the head of his army some distance up the slope when he heard a commotion to the left. Turning, he saw a cloud of dust and immediately surmised what was happening. "Order the left flank to assume lead. Box formation, assault left. Rear echelons break and perform flanking maneuvers. Go!"

Such an evolution would have resulted in chaos for an untrained army. The line of horsemen in the leftmost column became the head of the column as the army turned left. Instead of a time-consuming wheel that would bring the lead platoons and their commanders into the line, the lower-ranked individuals assumed responsibility for the charge. The right flank now became the rear and began to slide sideways to move in two directions to form pincers against the enemy force. These were the trained veterans of the Sassanid wars and the ongoing conflicts with the Avars in Bulgaria. They executed the change quickly and without confusion, just the grim preparation of seasoned soldiers readying for the blood they were about to spill.

Libanius galloped down the front of his line as the Arabs approached in an arrowhead formation, then waved them into a slow advance towards the wildly attacking enemy. Libanius understood cavalry and believed that a kinetic engagement would give his men more ability to maneuver and react than if he stood his ground and waited for the assault to reach them.

At the point of the Arab arrowhead was a man with no shirt on, yelling something unintelligible to Libanius' ears. He pointed the man out to an aide. "Take that man alive, if possible!"

The Muslim arrowhead formation impacted the Byzantine line. Instead of collapsing in disarray, the Byzantines received the assault and almost invited it in. The point of impact gave way to the left and right, not impeding the momentum of the assault, allowing them to be drawn deep into the ranks. The Muslims unexpectedly found themselves surrounded from three sides and under disciplined attack. Instead of penetrating the ranks and being able to lay about with impunity the way Dhiraar liked to fight, he found himself surrounded by a forest of lances. He was cut off from his companions and couldn't get close enough to any of the enemy surrounding him to get in a decent blow. An arrow punched his horse, causing it to rear. He dropped his sword to hang on, and rough hands pulled him from the saddle.

The flying wedge of the Muslims flattened and spread along the front of the Byzantine lines. The flankers coming from behind the enemy force began to make themselves felt. Abdullah Bin Umar stood in his saddle to look for Dhiraar. He spotted him across a sea of heads and flailing weapons, just as the other man disappeared off his horse. "Dhiraar!" he shouted. He turned and gathered the men around him and pointed them where he'd last seen Dhiraar. They made some headway, but were stalled. He backed off to gain some room for an assault and tried again several times, but couldn't break through to where they were holding Dhiraar. No doubt they were hustling him to the rear as a prisoner. Abdullah Bin Umar ultimately quit trying to reach him and looked around to see how the battle was developing. He saw fighting on three sides of him and it looked like a circle was starting to close in their rear. He bit his lip, considered what Khalid might say about a retreat, then decided that it would be better than what he'd say if they all ended the day in Allâh's bosom. Dying as a martyr was good, but it wasn't fair to leave your comrades in a difficult position when you did so. He ordered his men to break the engagement and retreat up to the higher ground.

The Byzantines pursued them for a short distance, then reformed their lines and continued on. Abdullah Bin Umar ordered his men to quickly pull back to the top of the pass and set up a blocking position and wait for reinforcements.

The red sun was on the horizon when the messenger reached Khalid with the news of the battle and the loss of Dhiraar. His face darkened as the messenger delivered the news. Before the man was done, Khalid backhanded him with a massive blow that sent him sprawling. He stepped forward reaching for his sword, but Ubaidah's hand closed around his wrist with an iron grip. The messenger scrambled away from his fury. Khalid turned to Ubaidah, who released him. "I told that young fool! I told him to avoid an engagement against a superior force! By Allâh and his Prophet! Am I a toothless old woman lacking in wisdom, that people ignore me?"

"Easy, my young friend. You know it's Dhiraar's nature. You're angry because he's too much like you."

Khalid breathed hard and fought to control his temper. He turned away and paced in thought for a few moments. "Mount your army. Notify Amr to bring his men. We will meet these Romans at the top of the pass and send them to hell."

"And when we return we find that the garrison here has taken advantage of the weakened army, staged a breakout and destroyed the force you leave here? If you split our forces, you tempt our enemy to defeat them individually. I'm not sure Shurahbil could contain a breakout with the weakened forces you leave here."

Khalid paced restlessly, then sat and put his head in his hands to think. Ubaidah made tea, waiting for him to develop a solution.

"Yazeed and Shurahbil will stay here with their armies. Of those going, one man in five will stay and maintain the appearance of a much larger army. The camp followers will remain and help with the charade. Fires will be kept burning for the entire army. Every man remaining will pray five times instead of once tomorrow, in large groups, making it look like we have the same number of men. Withdraw to the south and circle around. Exit quietly, alert no one. And make sure those damned monks aren't allowed to enter the city while we're gone."

"Well, that's easy," said Jabir. "Bashour's obviously the one to stay."

"They're giving everyone that's going a camel or a horse for the battle." Sameer said, as he finished packing a small road pack and shouldered his weapons and armor. "Khalid must really want us to move fast."

Bashour wasn't unhappy at the idea of missing a battle. He was more chagrined that it was such a matter of course that he'd be the one to be left out. He knew it made sense, but he didn't like being reminded of it like this.

Qutayba saw his look and misinterpreted it. He slapped Bashour on the back. "Don't be so upset. It's not like you can fight or anything, right?"

Wahid said, "Leave the boy alone. He's proven his worth as much as anyone."

"Well, don't spend all your days and nights in the tent with your lady friend," said Qutayba. "Keep the camp looking alive for all five of us, okay?"

They took their leave quickly, sliding into the darkness, leaving Bashour and Tamara alone. Bashour picked up a stick and prodded the fire morosely.

"They don't act like your friends, you know," said Tamara on the other side of the fire.

"They've been together forever. No matter what, I'll always be an outsider to them."

Tamara watched him poke at the fire. At last, they were alone for a while. She'd looked forward to getting him away from his friends for an extended length of time. She had so many things to say to him, to try to show him why he was wrong, to get him to admit that Islam worshipped a false, satanic god. But now she had no idea how to bring it up, no idea how to approach it that wouldn't turn into a fight. She couldn't stand another fight with him. She was so worried what he might do every time they disagreed. She eventually retired to their tent.

66. Bait Lihya, 25 miles east of Damascus September 7, 634

Libanius had beaten the Arabs to the top of the pass, since the Muslims under Abu Abdullah Bin Umar had retreated away from the summit to the northeast when they broke contact from their disastrous assault. But the setting sun left Libanius with a dilemma. To continue down the pass would leave a significant enemy force at his rear, with a height advantage. If he pursued Umar they could fall back east into the desert, drawing him away from Damascus. He loathed the idea of dividing his force. Leaving a screen strong enough to deal with Umar's army would weaken his main body too much to lift the siege around Damascus. He arrayed his army to face the immediate threat of Abdullah Bin Umar's horsemen.

He began making plans after sunset as his army settled for the night. He'd detach half his force to return the way they came, cross the ridge some miles north. They'd form an anvil behind the enemy forces, trapping them between his divisions, then defeat them in detail. He called his commanders and they worked well into the night, planning the movement and preparing the orders.

Sunrise found Khalid nearing the top of the pass at the head of fifteen thousand horse and camel cavalry. He went forward with his scouts, leaving the road and going east up a steeper incline to reconnoiter the ground ahead. They eased over the ridgeline and found themselves looking over the right flank of an army nearly as big as their own.

"Sahib, they're breaking camp. See the formations?"

Khalid saw, indeed. They were mounting up and forming echelons. And they were all facing away from the pass, to the northeast! Khalid realized that this must be the direction of Abdullah Bin Umar's force. The Romans must be unaware of his presence!

"Quickly! We have no time to lose!" he said, scrambling down the slope for their horses. They reunited with the army and Khalid led them in morning prayer, then commanded them to ride for the glory of Allâh.

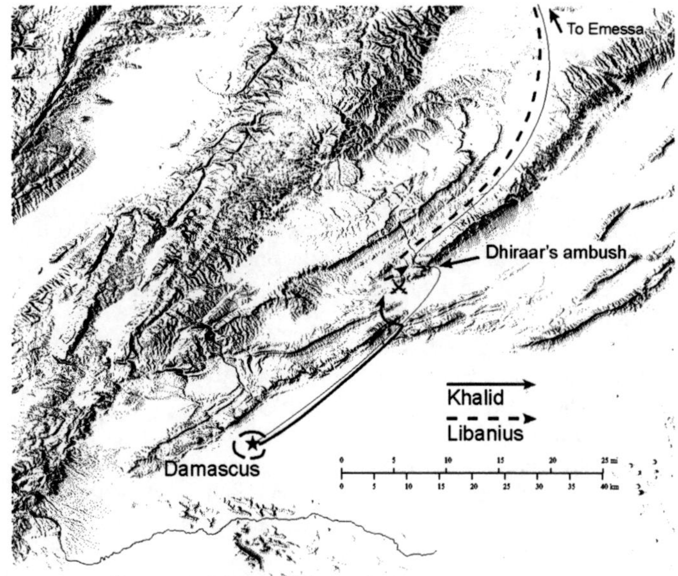

Battle of Bait Lihya

Libanius had arrayed his forces to face Abdullah Bin Umar's army and had just given the word for the flanking force to begin moving when Khalid's army rose over the pass and deployed behind him. Before he'd realized what was happening, fifteen thousand horse and camels had slammed into his rear. Panicked soldiers began to flee. He had no time to redirect his army to the south; the battle was developing too rapidly. By the time his unit commanders received his orders, they would be obsolete. When the third messenger reached him to report details of the attack, he made his decision.

"Order all units to retreat north up the road to Emessa! Rally at one millaria past where the road turns to go through the mountain!"

He turned to the north. Thankfully the enemy there hadn't coordinated with this new threat. He still had room to maneuver.

The initial shock against the Romans had been devastating. Khalid was satisfied with the damage they'd done before the enemy commander had extricated himself from the fight and escaped up the road. As the army had dissolved its position in front of him, he'd pressed his men hard and inflicted tremendous casualties. The few prisoners were demoralized from the surprise he'd achieved. By noon, he and his commanders took their prayers, then stood to watch what was left of the battle. The remnants of the enemy was operating an effective rear guard action, giving way without losing too many more men in the process. Khalid knew he'd have to keep the pressure on to prevent them from catching their breath and reorganizing.

"Brilliant! Allâh be well pleased with you!" called out Abdullah Bin Umar, arriving from the north.

"Abdullah Bin Umar! How many men do you have yet?" asked Khalid.

"All five thousand, sahib. We disengaged from the fight almost as soon as it started and pulled back to await your relief. I honestly didn't expect you to arrive so quickly."

"And what of Dhiraar? Does he live?"

"I saw him unhorsed, Sahib. I have not seen a body. Last night some local goatherds came to me and told me that they saw a large group of men riding up the road to Emessa with a half-naked man being held bound in their midst."

"That can only be Dhiraar! Take two hundred men and pursue them. Try to get ahead of them and lay an ambush. Rescue Dhiraar." He turned to Yazeed, "Instruct Samt bin Al Aswad to take a regiment and hound these infidels all the way back from whence they came. Don't stop harassing them until they're dead.

"Only a regiment, Sahib?"

Khalid squinted at the dust cloud where the skirmishers continued to press the remaining enemies. "They're running scared. If you don't give them a chance to stop and think about who's chasing them, they'll keep running. I need every man I can for the siege of the city." He took the horse's reins from the groom who'd been holding them and twisted himself up into the saddle. "Recall the rest of the army. We march back to Damascus tonight."

"Hundreds of prisoners are on foot, Sahib," said Yazeed. "Shall I detail a detachment to escort them behind us?"

"We have no time or manpower for prisoners right now. Kill them all." He turned and trotted his horse towards the head of the pass.

67. Outside of Damascus September 7, 634

Sharjeel ibn Hassana received the exhausted messenger and escorted him into the open-sided tent where Ubaidah and Shurahbil were having tea, having just come from afternoon prayers. He fell to his knees and pronounced, "In the name of Allâh, I have traveled half a month from Medina to bring you the news. The Caliph Abu Bakr is dead and Umar is now the Caliph."

The two men rose in surprise and Ubaidah intoned, "Surely we belong to Allâh and to Him shall we return."

"Allâhu Akhbar!" pronounced Shurahbil, echoed by those around him.

"Rise, young messenger," said Ubaidah, pouring another cup of tea. "Refresh yourself and tell us what you will. How is it that Umar is the Caliph?"

The man gratefully accepted the tea and slurped it noisily in appreciation. "Abu Bakr knew his time was at hand and dictated his last testament to Uthman Ibn Affan. He nominated Umar bin al Khattab as his successor. He commanded us to hear and obey him and confirm his actions if he acts rightly."

Ubaidah and Shurahbil sat back and looked at each other. Shurahbil spoke first. "By Allâh, if Uthman supports this claim, it must be true. There's no love lost between those two."

Ubaidah nodded in agreement. "Umar is a harsh man. Very different from Abu Bakr. I find it unusual, such a nomination, but perhaps Allâh was speaking through Abu Bakr's dying wish."

The messenger put his tea down and spoke again to Ubaidah. "Forgive me, Sahib, but I have a sealed message for you from the new Caliph."

"For me? Not Khalid? How odd." He took the scroll and broke the seal. He held the sheet at arm's length and scrutinized the writing, slowly deciphering it. A cloud crossed his face and he put the scroll down in his lap. He reached out and placed his hand on Shurahbil's arm. "Leave us, all of you."

When the others had left, Shurahbil raised an eyebrow. "What is it?"

"Umar has ordered that I relieve Khalid of his command and take over command of the army."

"Well, there's no surprise there. There's always been bad blood between Umar and Khalid. Remember that it was Khalid that routed him in the Battle of Badr. Khalid has always been the better military commander, and they both know it."

"Yes, Umar fears Khalid. He doesn't want him to grow in popularity or power."

"Really, can you blame him? It's good that Abu Bakr chose a successor. A fight for the caliphate could easily lead to another civil war."

"Do you remember when Muhammad, peace be upon him, died and Umar refused to accept it? How he declared that Muhammad would return and cut off the hands and feet of those who said he was dead?"

"I do, but he was in denial. I saw him fall from his feet when Abu Bakr told him that Allâh would not have Muhammad die twice, that he was just a messenger that he was indeed dead and that Allâh still lived."

"Umar runs hot or cold. I remember just before he accepted Islam, he was actually on his way to kill Muhammad."

"Hmm, yes. He's very passionate, but he's fair and thoughtful, if he has time to think. What do you think of his proposal to Abu Bakr that the Qur'án be compiled into a book?"

Ubaidah looked very thoughtful. "I have mixed feelings. The words of Allâh should never be consigned to a dead thing like a book. It's a living word, which should be written on the hearts of the faithful, and pronounced from their lips in its beauty. If you write it down, scholars will begin to analyze it. Infidels may acquire it and twist it to their own purposes. That's not right for the word of Allâh. But, on the other hand, I am afraid that no one person has the whole Qur'án memorized. Not even Muhammad could do it; he admitted to forgetting certain passages. When a sahaba is killed, who knows what part of the Qur'án may die with him? And what of someone who recited a sura incorrectly, or just makes one up? Who'll contradict that person, now that the Messenger of God is gone? We need an objective source, where all that's known of the Qur'án is written."

"Yes, you make a very good argument for both positions." Shurahbil motioned at the message. "What will you do about that?"

"I don't think it's good to relieve a commander in the middle of a campaign. It's bad to replace a commander when he is buckle-to-buckle with the enemy. I'll wait until the city is captured. If Khalid still lives, I'll deliver this scroll to him then."

68. Damascus
September 8, 634

Bashour didn't find Rashad in the infirmary of the monastery when he went to visit him. The monk tending the wounded there suggested he might look in the chapel, and gave him directions. When he found it, he entered quietly. He found the holy water in shallow bowls at the entrance and quickly blessed himself without thinking about it, as he was accustomed to doing.

Near the altar he spied Rashad sitting with one of the monks, deep in conversation. He must have made some sound, because they looked up at him. The monk said something to Rashad and blessed him with the sign of the cross as he bowed his head, then got up and left through a side door near the altar, carrying a large book.

Bashour walked up the aisle and smiled awkwardly at Rashad. "You seem to be doing better."

Rashad raised his wounded arm slightly in its sling. "There's no infection and it's healing well. The monks don't want me moving it at all for a few more days, then they say they have some exercises they want me to do if I eventually want to get full motion back. They want the muscle to heal more before I start pulling it, though."

Bashour turned a questioning eye towards where the monk had disappeared. Rashad followed his eyes. After an uncomfortable moment, Rashad asked, "You were raised a Christian, right?"

Bashour sat beside him. "Yes."

"Did you ever read the Gospel of John?"

Bashour tried to explain how the scripture was taught. "We don't actually read it like a lesser book. They normally don't give lay people access to the scriptures, because they're so valuable. But there are daily readings from the Gospels and from the letters and Acts of the Apostles and the Old Testament. If you attend mass every day for three years, I suppose you hear the entire scripture read to you."

Rashad nodded towards the door to the sacristy where the monk had gone. "Brother Stephan has been reading the Gospel of John to me. He reads the Greek and tries to translate it into Arabic for me. I was expecting it to be like the Qur'án, but it's nothing like that at all."

"How so?"

Rashad thought about it for a moment. "Well," he said, "the way Muhammad taught it, I understood that the injeel was the word of Allâh that he gave to Jesus. But Brother Stephan says that the injeel in Greek is 'evangelion' and means 'good news'. It wasn't the word of Allâh at all, but the story of Jesus the way John saw it."

Bashour shrugged. "Yes, I knew that."

"But Bashour, don't you see? We have the Qur'án, but it's a very high language, sometimes hard to understand. It uses holy words that only Allâh knows the meaning. But John is very easy to understand. He just tells you what he saw and how he understood it. It's simple, but it's also deep. I'm still trying to understand what he meant when he said that Allâh was the word."

"Perhaps that means that the Qur'án is Allâh?"

"That's an interesting point, but let me tell you something. I tried to correct Brother Stephan when he mentioned Jesus being crucified. I told him that Allâh had told Muhammad that the people were deceived. He laughed at me."

Bashour sat a little straighter and looked suspiciously at Rashad. "What do you mean?"

"Well, he kind of laughed at me, then he got a book and he read the story of the crucifixion to me. He went on and on, told details of the trial and how they tortured Jesus, almost killed him, then talked about all the things he said while he was dying. Bashour, if it didn't happen like that, how come John has so many details? I never heard Muhammad, peace be upon him, tell a story like that, about what people said back and forth, and what they were thinking. And it wasn't just John. Brother Stephan showed me books by Luke, Mark and the other fellow. . ."

"Matthew."

"Yes. They told the same story, but slightly different, like you would expect from different people who were actually there."

"I don't think Luke was there. He was a Greek and a gentile."

"Well, he told the story very nicely then." Rashad was silent for a time and stared down at the floor. Then, "Bashour? If

Muhammad got that wrong, then there's something wrong with the Qur'án."

"What do you mean?"

"Look, it's the Qur'án, the literal word of Allâh. How could a single word be wrong? It tells us to look to the people of the book, for the message that Allâh gave to them. But that book, it's not a message, but a history. And that history is different from what the Qur'án says. And it's older. Brother Stephan said that all of these things happened six hundred years ago."

"Well, Allâh sent Muhammad as his messenger to add to the message he already gave through Jesus."

Rashad looked up at him, with a steady gaze. "Bashour, I'm not sure I accept that anymore. I knew Muhammad. I saw him. I heard him recite the Qur'án. He was a fantastic poet, brilliant. He'd hypnotize you with his voice when he recited. But how could he lie about Jesus the way he did? I'm starting to wonder if he made it all up."

Bashour recoiled in surprise. How could this man, his friend who'd been instructing him in the Qur'án, voice such a thing? Didn't Muhammad say that anyone who said such a thing should die? "Rashad, that's a dangerous thing to say."

Rashad waved his hand. "I know, I know, and Muhammad admonished us not to question the messenger, that if I choose disbelief then I've gone astray." He shook his head. "But wouldn't he say that if he wasn't telling the truth but still wanted us to follow him?" He pointed at the sacristy. "That, in there, makes more sense without poetry than anything Muhammad said. Why didn't Muhammad tell us about the miracles that Jesus did? He told us that Jesus gave signs, but he never told us that Jesus healed people, raised the dead, walked on water, fed thousands with almost nothing. How could a mere prophet do all of this? Muhammad says he was the greatest prophet, but when I hear about Jesus from Brother Stephan, he was so much more than Muhammad. He spoke to the devil in the desert and refused what he was offered. I never saw Muhammad refuse anything he wanted."

"It makes sense the way they speak it, brother," said Bashour. "But be careful. When you start thinking about it, it wraps you in contradictions, stops making sense."

"What do you mean?"

"Well, like the Trinity. If you accept that Jesus and God were one, then you have a problem. Was Jesus God? Then he couldn't die. Was he a man? Then how could he be God? Was he some fusion of the two? Then what part is man and what part is God? The Christians themselves are fighting over this question. And it's stupid. Muhammad's explanation is easier. He was a man, nothing more. Problem solved."

"Well, I said that to Brother Stephan and he showed me many places where the apostles of Jesus believed he was God incarnate. He said they didn't understand it and Christians still don't really understand it, but that's what they believed and Jesus never corrected them. We had a long discussion about the opening of the Gospel of John. John was pretty clear that Jesus was God."

Bashour thought about it. He knew the passage, something about the Logos in the beginning and the Logos was God. Logos could mean a lot of different things: word, logic, essence. It didn't make sense, so Bashour had assumed the philosophy was above his head and hadn't thought about it much. Now he was confused. Muhammad's teaching was easy and made sense, but it somehow seemed too easy. Are things ever as simple as they seem? "If what you say is true, then everything you've taught me. . ."

Rashad slapped Bashour's thigh and smiled. "Don't worry about it! I'll still teach you! I'm not sure myself. Surely if Allâh was lying to Muhammad, we couldn't have been as victorious as we have, right? Allâh guides us rightly. I need to study what Brother Stephan is teaching and figure out what's wrong with it."

Bashour laughed nervously. "Rashad, if Khalid thinks you're a Christian, he'll surely kill you."

Rashad's face grew serious. "Bashour, you mustn't say anything to anybody. Not just Khalid, but Qutayba and Jabir would kill me for this. And this bothers me, too. Why is it necessary to kill someone if they change their religion? Shouldn't you listen to them and persuade them that they're wrong? All of us have changed our religion to become Muslims. Even the Messenger."

"But Allâh hates an infidel. How can a person praise Allâh and commit to being his servant, then turn his back on him? Allâh's wrath cannot be contained. Better to kill that person for his sin, rather than everyone suffer the consequences of Allâh's wrath."

Rashad squeezed his shoulder with his good hand. "You're right, of course. How silly that I forget that. You should go now and tell the others I'm all right."

"I will when they return. They've marched with Khalid to intercept a relief force at the top of the pass. I was left here to make it look like no one left."

Thomas attended the Mass celebrated for the feast of St. Eupsychios and was pleased to see Abbot Lecanepus assisting with the service. The monks had been barred by the invaders from entering the city for several days. Thomas was anxious to find out why. He sought the priest out in the sacristy after the Mass.

"Abbot, I'm glad to see you. Tell me, is there any news?"

The abbot kissed his peritrachelion and placed it reverently in a narrow drawer then turned gravely to Thomas. "Yes, I'm afraid I have some bad news for you. The reason we were stopped from coming and going from the city was because the Arab general had taken two-thirds of his force over the mountains in the night and they didn't want you to realize it."

Thomas looked puzzled, then angry. Yes, he'd noticed a definite decline in activity outside the walls, but had attributed it to the enemy's lethargy. Laying siege was a boring business. There had still been campfires and when they prayed it seemed as if he could see just as many Arabs as before.

Lecanepus continued, "As far as I gather from listening to talk in our hospital, they met a rather large force of cavalry at the top of the pass and emerged victorious. I suspect that would be the relief force from Emessa you were hoping for."

A cold hand gripped Thomas' guts. No relief would come. "Abbot, can you please attend a council meeting and relate what you've just told me?"

Lecanepus finished his account in the grim silence around the table. Thomas stood as the councilmen looked at each other. "I think it's safe to say that we can't rely on a relief force from Heraclius anytime soon."

Taticus was present, at the request of Thomas. "If Heraclius has any spare forces," he said, "he's probably reinforcing Emessa and other metropolitan centers. I doubt he'll strike directly at the Arabs, the way so many generals want to. He'll try to bypass them, flank them and threaten their lines of communication."

"You mean he won't try to rescue us?" asked one of the councilmen.

Thomas suppressed a look of disgust. "Strange as it may seem to you, there are larger considerations than the fate of one city."

"Then we're on our own, is that it?" asked another.

"That's precisely the case."

The assembly murmured in alarm. Most councilmen were local citizens, with little or no military experience. Thomas sought to reassure them, "Gentlemen, have no fear. We've been preparing for two months and we have plenty of supplies to outlast any siege this Arab hoard can lay against us." It was a white lie, but Thomas needed them to be calm and confident, not making decisions in a panic.

"How can you say that?" asked one. "They have our fields, our orchards. We have only what you've managed to put into storage. They can last forever off the land around the city."

Lecanepus spoke up, "That's not precisely true. These men are herdsmen when they're not warriors. They seem to know nothing of tending a crop. They don't seem to have any interest in harvesting what's left of the dates, olives and figs. Besides, the harvest is nearly over, we're going into winter. What will they eat then?"

One of the older, more senior councilmen, a well-known citizen named Dositheos, said, "It doesn't matter. A siege will prove an extreme hardship for our people. And it's unnecessary. We're Damascans, not Greeks or Romans. It doesn't matter to what foreign capital we pay our taxes. We've lived under the Byzantines and the Sassanids. We can live under the Arabs just as easily." The sentiment reflected what many locals felt, that Damascus was an unwilling pawn in a game between competing foreign powers and owed little allegiance to any of them.

Lecanepus stood, commanding the attention of the room. "With all due respect, my Lord Dositheos, it's not as simple as that." He began walking slowly around the room, addressing each man as an individual. "For more than two weeks I've been dealing with these people in the monastery. Our hospital is tending to their wounded." He raised a hand at the muttering that this provoked. "We're Christians, gentlemen, we will assist anyone in need, no matter what their creed, as our Savior taught us to do. But I've been studying these people and I assure you that capitulation will not be as easy as changing the address of where we send our taxes."

He held up a finger for all to see. "In the first place, this isn't a professional army, answering to the rule of a general or a statesman. This is an army of brigands, all volunteers, and their motive is treasure. If we give up this city, I assure you they will loot it. They'll steal everything that's not nailed down. They'll take your women and either keep them or sell them into slavery. Yes, these people trade heavily in slaves. From what I gather it's one of the prime sources of income for their leaders." Slavery had been all but eradicated in the Christian world. Most present never considered that it was still in practice elsewhere in the world.

"In the second place, these people are religious fanatics. They consider you and me as infidels and worthy of the punishment of their God. They practice a certain amount of tolerance, the way a man tolerates the curs that slink in the corner waiting for a scrap of meat. But these people have no code of justice, no laws that define their civilization that aren't informed by their sense of religious superiority. Under their domination you will have no real rights, no recourse. The lowest of them can do unto you whatever he wants and any complaint you make on the matter will only give them a reason to remove your tongue, if you're lucky. They can forbid anything you wish to do on a whim, and you won't be able to do anything about it except comply. They can tell you what you may or may not buy or sell, they can forbid you to practice any trade they wish, to eliminate competition.

"Third, surrendering to these people will mean the end of Christianity in this city. They've already instructed me that I am to make no repairs on the monastery and that no new churches may be built under their rule. We may not practice our faith in the open where anyone can see. The big bastard who leads them, Khalid, was very firm in this regard.

"Now think, gentlemen. Christians under these people will be reduced to second-class citizens, virtual slaves to any that profess the faith of their prophet. They will enact laws to guarantee the impoverishment of Christians. They will put a boot on our neck from which we will simply not be able to raise ourselves. And the real kicker is that we can quite literally become one of them and throw off our chains of servitude by merely renouncing Christianity and professing the faith of their prophet."

"That's absurd!" exclaimed Dositheos. "Abbot, you have a very poor opinion of the strength of the faith of our citizens. Why, this is one of the oldest Christian communities in the world. Right here is where Saint Paul was baptized, and we have the head of John the Baptist in our crypt."

"Is it absurd? Think, gentlemen. You're all well-bred. How many of your children have the fiber to be martyrs? How many of them just pay lip service to the church as part of the status that's their birthright? Are your children soldiers of the Lord, or do they believe because it's the culturally acceptable fashion?" He looked around the room and no one would meet his eyes. They all thought about their children: rich, spoiled, used to finery and the good life and realized the truth in what he said.

"Enough," said Thomas. "We won't be surrendering to the enemy. This council is advisory, but I am the governor. We will resist this siege and in so doing buy time for Heraclius to prepare his next move against these invaders. It's much easier to rescue a city than it is to recapture it. But we're not going to sit here quietly. We're going to sting these bastards, keep them on their toes, make them nervous. We have the advantage of inside lines and can strike at them from any of our gates without warning. We'll strike and inflict damage and retreat before they can rally to overwhelm us, then do it again elsewhere. I will not allow this to be a comfortable time for them."

Khalid railed at Dhiraar for the negligence that got him captured. "Next time you might not be lucky enough to be rescued!" Dhiraar looked contrite, but Khalid knew it was an act. The brave young fool felt he was invincible. His heroics had made him a legend among the men, and that had intoxicated him. Khalid gave up. No amount of scolding would change his behavior. "I'm glad you're back. We'll need you to attack this city."

Ubaidah sipped his tea calmly. "Insha'Allâh, we can sit here for a year and take the city when they have all starved. There's no reason to fight for it."

"No, by Allâh!" exclaimed Khalid, "I have no stomach to sit around growing old like an old woman. Every day we waste here, waiting for them to get hungry, is a day that we could be moving northward, conquering more territory for Allâh. I want an end to this siege!"

"Khalid, the men having been constantly marching and fighting for nearly two months. You have to give them a rest, or you'll wear them out. You can't continue the pace you've been setting indefinitely."

Khalid knew he spoke the truth. The men were tired, many of them wounded. They were all growing thin, lean and hard. Except for the battle at the top of the pass, they'd welcomed the last two weeks of sitting around the walls of the city. Some families from Arabia had caught up with the army, and men were enjoying the company of their wives and servants again.

"You're correct, old friend, but we need winter quarters. The monks tell me a rainy season is coming, nothing like what we see in the desert, and it will grow cold. They even tell me at times that it's so cold that the rain falls as white ice; they call it 'snow'. Can you believe that? I can't ask the men to live in the open or in a tent under those conditions."

Ubaidah smiled. "White ice as rain? I'd love to see that, it sounds very beautiful. But I think that's a tall tale. The men will be fine. The nights are cold enough for frost in the desert, too."

They sat awhile in silence, sipping tea. Khalid was thinking, weighing his options. "If we leave this city, they'll learn that a show of force on the defense will be enough to turn us away. We dare not do that. We must show determination of purpose."

"Perhaps if we had catapults, like we used at Taif?"

Khalid shook his head. "I've sent the word to search through the army, but we have nobody from the Banu Daws tribe. They're the only ones who know how to build a catapult."

"Those walls are going to be a problem."

"We need somebody on the inside, someone who can either tell us what's going on in the city, or to open the way for us to enter."

"You allow the priests from the monastery to come and go from the city. Why don't you ask them?"

"Bah!" spat Khalid. "They would tell me nothing."

"Maybe you shouldn't be so nice when you ask? Properly motivated, a man would tell almost anything you want to know."

Khalid reflected silently, then rose and retrieved his helmet. "You're right, I will speak to these priests now. I won't torture them for information; any man of God can withstand torture. But will they stay silent while we torture one of their own?"

69. Damascus
September 9, 634

As Khalid and Dhiraar arrived at the monastery, he realized he'd forgotten something, "By Allâh, we forgot to bring our interpreter. That boy from Tadmur. How will we speak to these priests?"

"You want me to fetch him, Sahib?"

Khalid looked disgusted. "No. I won't be seen waiting here like an errand boy. Let's see what we can make of this situation." He threw open the door to the courtyard that served as an infirmary. Wounded men lined the covered porticoes on cots.

"Does anyone here speak Greek?" bellowed Khalid.

The wounded cheered raggedly as they recognized him. One of the men close to him said, "Oh, Allâh's Sword, if you're looking for an interpreter, ask for Brother Stephan," he repeated the name in Greek. "He speaks fluent Arabic and will be able to translate for you."

The two commanders strode purposefully through the garden area and entered the labyrinth of passages and rooms in search of their man. They repeated the name to several monks that they encountered, until they were directed to a chapel.

Rashad and Brother Stephan had been discussing scripture and were concluding with a prayer and a blessing when Khalid and Dhiraar burst into the room. "Shto ónoma tou Patrós kai tou Yioú kai tou Agíou Pnévmatosh" intoned Brother Stephan, as Rashad crossed himself.

"Are you the priest called Brother Stephan?" demanded Khalid.

The two men turned and stood. Khalid's eyes widened as he saw how the other man was dressed, the bandage across his shoulder and slung arm. "What's going on here?"

"Sahib, I. . ." Rashad was speechless.

"We were just praying," said Brother Stephan calmly. "Surely you appreciate the power of prayer, commander? What can I do for you?" He started towards Khalid, who brushed him aside as he descended upon Rashad, who stood rooted to the spot.

"Did I see you accept a Christian blessing?" Khalid towered over Rashad, who fought to keep from cowering in the face of his wrath.

"Sahib, you don't understand! I. . . I. . ." He looked at Brother Stephan.

"What is your name?" demanded Khalid.

"I am Rashad al-Hamza al-Ansari, Sahib, I. . ."

"Infidel!" shouted Khalid. His sword leapt from its scabbard and plunged through Rashad just below the sternum, coming out his back. He looked into Rashad's surprised eyes. "If any Muslim turns away from Islam, kill him!" The young man's eyes widened as he gasped for air. He collapsed on the floor in a pool of gore when Khalid roughly shoved him off the sword. The big man whirled on the monk. "By Allâh, I gave you leave to heal my men, not to fill their ears with your loathsome heresy!" The sword flashed again, neatly removing the monk's head from his shoulders. Khalid wiped the blood off the sword on the monk's cassock and resheathed it. "Round up all the priests in this cesspool of polytheism and kill them," he said to Dhiraar.

"Sahib, if I may, if none of the others speak Arabic, there's no worry that they'll corrupt any more of our men. They're necessary to heal the wounded. Let this one be an example to them, to strike fear into their hearts."

Khalid looked about. No one was present to hear him rescind his order. Dhiraar was right. These priests were useful. "Question the other priests and if you find others who speak Arabic, cut their tongues out." He strode angrily from the room and left the compound, forgetting the original reason he'd come there.

"We will sally from the Jabiya gate at first light. Move quickly while they're off balance. There's a large tent to the left, some hundred paces past the gate," Taticus indicated the position on a map spread before him. "We think it houses supplies, or a headquarters. Either way, that's the objective. We sally, we strike deep, seize the objective, inflict as much damage and injury as possible, then return to the walls before they have a chance to organize a counterattack."

The officers around the table craned their necks to see the map. Thomas stood back and allowed Taticus to conduct the briefing. “We will sally under an arrow barrage. As soon as the gates open, get through them and establish a perimeter in your designated areas. At the sound of a single horn, the strike force will move toward the objective. Three blasts of the horn will sound the recovery.” He deliberately avoided the word retreat. “Fall back by section and collapse the perimeter in an orderly fashion.”

He continued assigning sectors to the individual units. When he’d finished and answered the inevitable questions, Thomas took a step forward and spoke for the first time. “Above all, don’t move past your designated areas and don’t get engaged in a fight from which you can’t withdraw. We’re not trying to make a breakout; if we wait too long outside the gate the entire weight of the Arab army will fall on us and crush us. There won’t be any reinforcements, so stay in contact with your chain of command.”

“Dismissed,” said Taticus. “Get some sleep. Rally your men at the gate beginning on the third watch.”

As the men filed out, Taticus took Thomas aside. “Have you heard the rumor that the Arabs are offering fifteen dirhams of gold to any soldier who defects and joins their side?” Thomas’ eyebrows went up in surprise and Taticus nodded grimly.

“Do you think it’s something to concern us?”

“It’s a pretty steep price for a mercenary, even if it’s for propaganda purposes. I worry that someone who has information about the city might be tempted to help them.”

“Do we have holes in our security that we should be concerned about?”

‘I can’t think of any. I suggest we change the passwords on a frequent basis.”

“Agreed. Make it so. And thank you, Taticus.”

Bashour had brought Shai-tan back from the grazing area south of the city and was staking her for the night when they brought Rashad’s body into the camp. Tamara cried out in surprise and he ran to see what was wrong.

“Oh, Allâh, what happened?” he asked.

Jabir and Qutayba unceremoniously dropped the body. “He fooled us all, is what happened. Turns out Rashad was an infidel.”

Tamara disappeared into their tent. "What are you talking about?" Bashour asked. "Rashad is a Muslim like the rest of us."

Jabir said dismissively, "Khalid found him praying with a Christian priest and blessing himself with the Christian Trinity, which the Prophet, may Allâh be pleased with him, told us specifically not to do."

"So is that any reason to kill a man?"

"Of course," said Qutayba, "if someone turns his back on Islam, he should be considered a kaffir and be killed."

"But what about the prophet's teaching that there be no compulsion in religion?"

"Yes, he said that," said Sameer, "but he was talking about those who hadn't accepted Islam. You cannot force someone to become a Muslim. They must do that willingly. But once they've done so, if they become apostates and turn from Islam, that is a great offense to Allâh. That person must die."

Bashour looked to Wahid to see what he would say, but the big man simply sat near Rashad's body, staring at it silently. His face was devoid of emotion, a mask, but in the fading light, Bashour thought he could see a tear at the corner of the big man's eye.

Bashour sank to the ground next to Rashad and placed his hand on Rashad's shoulder. He knew what had caused this, he'd discussed it with Rashad. He started to become very afraid, deep in his stomach. What they said made no sense. What good was no compulsion in religion if a man's conscience couldn't question a decision made without information? He gradually realized that he may have made a huge mistake when he became a Muslim. He didn't know everything that it entailed. What they'd said had made sense at first, but as he'd learned the details – mostly from this young man lying here dead – many questions arose. He'd rationalized these questions by telling himself that he just hadn't learned enough about Islam; that the answers were there and he would learn them. But now, now Rashad was dead, because he'd found those answers, and they weren't in Islam.

He deliberately avoided looking at the others. Could they tell what he was thinking? Would something he said or did give him away, tell them that he had begin to doubt Islam, that he was wondering if Rashad was right? Would he be the next to die?

He looked at the tent and saw Tamara looking at him through the flaps. They locked eyes and she mouthed the word "martyr," then looked pointedly at Rashad. The idea came crashing in on Bashour. Rashad had professed his belief in Jesus Christ and had died for it. He didn't fight back. Bashour suddenly realized that he was braver than any man who died in battle. To die fighting those trying to kill you was easy, but how hard to stand and die because of what you believe? Bashour had read about the many martyrs of the early church, but had never really appreciated their sacrifice until now, sitting by the body of a real martyr. Would they name a feast day after Rashad? Would his name be remembered with the other Christians of history?

"Let's bury him in the morning. I'm hungry," said Qutayba.

"Why bother burying him? Give him back to the Christians and let them bury him. He's one of theirs anyway," said Jabir.

Wahid spoke up for the first time. "Bashour and I will bury him tomorrow," he said simply. He locked eyes with Bashour, who gave a slight nod, then glared at the others as if to challenge them. No one wanted to cross the huge man.

70. Damascus
September 9, 634

Bashour couldn't will himself to sleep. Rashad's death had turned his world upside down. As he lay awake, he tried to rationalize his thinking and decisions, tried to discern the truth among all he'd been told. For three months he'd been marching and living with these Muslims, praying with them and learning the words of the Prophet Muhammad. He realized that he'd joined them because they offered an elegant solution to the perplexing problem of the nature of Christ and a fresh view of the nature of God. Bashour liked the idea of turning conventional wisdom on its head, looking at things with fresh perspectives that questioned everything that had been taught before. He felt that was the only way to see if his beliefs stood up to the test of criticism.

But that wasn't what these Muslims were about. He decided that Allâh reflected the ancient God of Moses, intolerant, angry, pedantic. But that wasn't right, because God had appeared to Moses and instructed him to do things. Bashour realized that in everything he'd learned about Muhammad and the Qur'án, Allâh had never told Muhammad to do anything, just how things should be done. Bashour thought about other biblical prophets. Moses and Jonah came to mind, and he realized that God had told them both to do things they didn't want to do, but they did them anyway. Nothing he'd heard of Muhammad fit that model; apparently Muhammad did what he wanted, then Allâh would endorse it.

Bashour noticed that any time he questioned the logic presented by his companions, they grew angry. That bothered him. Were they angry with him, or themselves? He dared not think how they'd react if he had the audacity to say something critical of Muhammad. He thought about it and realized he'd heard Wahid say some unflattering things about Muhammad and no one said anything. He thought they probably didn't object because they were simply afraid of the huge man. He'd also been one of the original Ansari who'd followed the Prophet since he arrived at Medina, so who would know him better?

Bashour couldn't reconcile the claim of no compulsion in religion to what he was seeing happening around him. What did "no compulsion" mean? To Bashour, it meant that one would be free to evaluate the claims of the belief system and choose the one he thought best, with no repercussions for having done so. It was a tolerant view of religion. But that's not what the Muslims did. They belittled those who didn't believe, forced them to pay gold for the privilege of not believing. A Muslim could take a non-believer as a slave. And if a Muslim chose to follow a different belief, he was killed. That wasn't hypothetical; Rashad's body was wrapped right outside the tent, attesting to that. Wasn't that compulsion? Didn't the Muslims enforce a real system of penalties for not choosing to believe as they did? How is that not compulsion? Bashour's community had opened their gates to the Muslim army and they'd impressed him with their piety, their moral standards and the consistency of their belief. But what if they'd resisted, as Tamara's town had done? Would his parents have been killed, the girls taken as slaves? Bashour shuddered at the idea of Imad bin Najib being tortured, as they'd told him that Muhammad had done to Kinana bin Al-Rabi at Khaybar. He knew that Imad would never have submitted to Islam.

So where did that leave him? He was back to the question of the nature of Christ, which seemed to have no answer. The Muslim solution was so elegant; just dismiss the idea that Christ was divine. But what had the priest said, who stood to gain by denying the resurrection? He thought about that. He could easily see how people might gain from claiming that Christ had risen. Just look at the whole structure of the church, built on that premise. But who would benefit by denying it? It made no sense.

"Tamara?" he said softly. "Are you asleep?"

She rolled to face him. "No."

"A priest asked me who benefited by denying that Jesus had died on the cross and was resurrected. I can't think of anyone. Can you?"

She raised herself to an elbow. "Are you serious? You can't think of anyone?"

"No," he said abashedly.

"Think about it. Christ died to fulfill the covenant that Abraham made when he was going to sacrifice Isaac. God had to show that nothing – no sin – was greater than his love for us, just as Abraham did for God. He had to sacrifice his son. If you accept this, then Satan's power over you is broken, you realize that God has been calling to us since Adam and Eve. Remember how they hid themselves from God? They separated themselves because of their shame for their sin. That was never what God intended. Satan's only recourse after the crucifixion was to try to convince people that it never happened."

Bashour thought about this for some time. "You can't convince the Christian world that it never happened, because it was too well documented. Satan had to start elsewhere, on the edge of Christianity, with people who weren't Christians and had no other religion."

"Yeah," She didn't elaborate and Bashour didn't bother her anymore. He finally slept, fitfully.

71. Damascus
September 10, 634

They crept close to the walls in the pre-dawn darkness. Torches along the walls cast strange shadows, and if one moved slowly enough, they could approach without notice. The idea was to get close enough so that when the light of the day came they could loose an arrow and maybe pick off a guard or two along the wall, then run like hell to get out of range of return fire.

Others watched from beyond range. They waited for the first arrows to fly after the morning prayers had been said, but none came. The wall was empty of archers. No one could see anything, and the ones who'd crept close to the wall became bold. Their cover of darkness removed, they stood, still searching. Then, with growing confidence, they moved slowly closer to the walls. Those from beyond arrow range saw this and they, too, started edging closer to the city walls. Still no arrows came.

The bravest began approaching the walls warily, followed by others. For some reason, this section of wall was unguarded. A runner was sent to inform Ubaidah.

Veterans stayed back, sensing a trap. But every army includes the foolhardy who are unable to think things through, to weigh risks against consequences. The no-man's land near the wall had filled with these sorts, when the ramparts suddenly came alive with archers. The walls were black with them, and they loosed their deadly barrage into the mass of men who'd gathered below them. The Arabs scrambled out of range in panic. As they did so, the gate opened and men poured forth with a shout. Soldiers flooded through the gate and efficiently deployed in an ever-expanding semicircle anchored against the walls. Taticus stood at the gate, exhorting men to speed as they came through.

When the perimeter had been established, Thomas trotted through the gate at the front of a thousand soldiers. The battle horns blew once and the army surged forward into the surprised Arabs.

Ubaidah emerged from his tent amid the scrambling and shouting and immediately assessed the situation. He called his archers forward and sent a runner to inform Khalid that the garrison had attacked out the west gate. He then grabbed his sword and strode purposefully towards the fighting, gathering fighters and organizing them as he went. A spearhead of enemy soldiers were advancing directly towards him in a flying wedge. He directed his men in a heavy line to meet them head-on. As the two armies collided, the advance of the Christians halted and degenerated into chaotic fighting. Those behind the vanguard sought another way through and the line of fighting spread in both directions as more Muslims rallied to stop their advance.

Thomas was in the front of the wave that collided with the Muslims. He fought fiercely and had dropped two of the enemy when he managed to fade back and let another man take his place. He surveyed the scene, trying to make sense of what was happening. The Arabs in front of him were holding firm, but he could see their ranks were thinner to each side and his men were stretching those lines even thinner as they maneuvered, trying to find a weakness they could break through.

Behind the enemy, he could see a banner and a tall, thin man standing beside it with several others. By the carriage and the way he saw the man talking to the others, he guessed this would be the commander. He cast about left and right, but could find no way to punch through towards that man.

Ubaidah studied the development of the battle and grew concerned. He didn't have the men to contain the enemy, and as they flowed behind the line of battle they were stretching his forces more and more thinly. Soon they may succeed in turning his flank and forcing him to give ground. The left was particularly thin. "Over there!" he directed his guards and strode ahead of them to where reinforcements were needed.

Thomas saw the enemy commander's banner start to move towards his right and began working his way in the same direction. He sensed his men were holding firm. He felt an indefinable air of victory that he couldn't put a finger on, but he knew it was there. The enemy was reacting to him. That was good. He started gathering soldiers as he went, pushing them, pointing, moving them in the same direction he was going. Then he heard a gasp behind him and turned. His flag bearer had collapsed, an arrow sticking out of his neck. Thomas grabbed the banner and thrust it into the hands of a passing soldier, then pulled the man by the shoulder to guide him along.

He turned and his head was slammed to the side. Pain blinded him and he fell to avoid any further blows. An arrow had hit him in the side of the head, shattering the orbit around his left eye and burying itself in his eye socket. He buried his face in the dirt, trying to assess the limits of the pain. For a moment, he wondered if he were dead and hadn't realized it yet. The battlefield closed in on him and became a personal battle between him and the shaft that ran through his eye, causing him such excruciating pain.

Taticus saw the banner go down, then raise, then drop again, this time not to rise. The movement of men in that area developed into a knot and he saw ripples in the line expand out from that spot. He sensed that something dreadful had happened. Grabbing several bodyguards, he ran towards where he'd last seen the banner.

He met several men carrying Thomas back towards the gate, a short Arab arrow gruesomely sticking out of the side of the man's head. The side of his face was covered in gore. "Does he live?"

"Yes, sir." said one of the men.

"Go on, then. Get him into the city, don't stop!" He found the fallen standard and had it raised and told the trumpeter, "Sound the retreat!"

The man gave three mighty blasts on the horn and Taticus began directing the disengagement. The vanguard that had formed the spearhead collapsed in reverse, the flanks falling in and the center covering the retreat. Once inside the perimeter, the army efficiently folded itself back through the gate almost as quickly as it had come. Archers on the walls kept the Arabs at bay, making the final withdrawal orderly.

By the time Khalid led his forces to the scene, it was all over. "What happened, Ubaidah?"

"They attacked out of the gate just before sunrise. It looked as if they were attacking towards my headquarters. I managed to stop their advance, then as quickly as they'd started, they pulled back and went back inside their city. There's a rumor that their commander was killed."

"Were they trying to break out?"

"No, if they'd been trying to do that I would have expected cavalry. They were all on foot. And break out to where? If they leave, then, Insha'Allâh, we get the city."

"I agree, I think this was a harassing attack, trying to inflict casualties. Nothing more."

"Nevertheless, it was very effective. They nearly turned the flank, which would have given them the casualties they were after."

Khalid eyed him coldly. "By Allâh, it's not like you to admit weakness, Ubaidah."

"I'm not admitting weakness at all, Sahib. It obvious that we're spread too thin, that we have no way of defending against a dedicated sortie from any one gate."

Khalid snorted, "The proper way to fight is to make the enemy be the one to react to our attack."

Ubaidah looked pointedly at the walls of the city, "There's a matter of a fourteen cubit high stone wall that gets in the way of that idea. The defenders have the initiative, Khalid. They can come out whenever and wherever they choose, and we can't touch them until they do."

"What do you suggest?"

"We need a reserve, which can be deployed at a moment's notice wherever they come out of the gates."

Khalid's lips grew tight with frustration. "And how do I know that any sally they make isn't just a feint, to get us to commit the reserve before they make a real attack through a different gate?"

Dhiraar had been silently observing the exchange, but finally spoke up. "Ubaidah is right, Sahib. Give me two thousand men on horseback and I will form two mobile reserves, capable of quickly reinforcing any two battles!"

Khalid looked at them. "It's against my better judgment, but all right. If they come out again, try to cut off their retreat. Don't meet them directly."

Taticus and Eudocia waited anxiously for the surgeon to finish working on Thomas. He finally came out, cleaning blood off his hands with a wet linen towel. "I had to remove the eye, but he'll be fine. The outside of the eye socket is damaged, but I managed to stitch it up. It looks gruesome and no doubt hurt like hell, but once the eye is removed there's relatively little pain."

Eudocia's shoulders sagged in relief. "Can we see him now?"

"Of course. We gave him some wine laced with herbs to dull the pain, but he's lucid."

Thomas was sitting up when they entered the room. He shook Taticus' hand firmly and hugged his wife. The left side of his face was bandaged and she burst into tears when she saw him. He hugged her firmly for a long time. He turned to Taticus, his remaining eye furious. "By the blood of Christ, Taticus, before I'm through I'll have a thousand Arab eyes to pay for this one! I'll pursue these animals into Arabia and I'll do whatever it takes to render that desert uninhabitable."

"Yes, sir." replied Taticus.

"The attack, how did it go after I fell?"

"Once you'd fallen, I felt we'd done all we could be expected to do and called the retreat."

"Damn. You should have pressed on. We nearly had them flanked. Did you see that commander commit his personal guard to the right flank?"

"I missed that, Governor."

Thomas struggled to his feet. "Prepare an attack as soon as it's dark. We will feint out the West gate again, but put the bulk of the forces out the Emessa gate. Order feints of several hundred out the East and Small gates, I don't want anyone thinking they can spare forces to reinforce. We strike quickly, tonight, while they think we're still licking our wounds. They won't expect anything so quickly." He wavered and grabbed the bedside. "Move swiftly, count on surprise, keep moving, don't bother to form up. Take no prisoners. Kill any Arab you see. Oh, my God. . . !" He turned and threw up violently on the floor.

The doctor came in and made him sit down. "You're suffering from vertigo. That's normal after losing an eye. Sit down and don't move so quickly."

They'd been told to get some sleep in the day, that there would be another attack outside the city after sundown. Jonas found a shaded spot against a wall and tried to force himself to sleep. The others in his unit did the same. He heard a quiet conversation not far off. He wasn't sure if he slept; time stretched and tormented him.

Without warning, a hand clamped over his mouth, and a knee pinned him to the ground. He couldn't see his assailant, but a hot breath at his ear said, "Don't forget your debts. Kostas hasn't forgotten. We know where you are. Be a pity if you got hurt in battle."

Then the assailant pulled his cloak over his head and wrapped it a couple of times. By the time Jonas untangled it, the man was gone. His heart beat fast for some time as he lay down again, and sleep refused to come.

Immediately after morning prayers, the army in the city had attacked out of the west gate, but had been beaten back before a counterattack could be fully mobilized. After a breakfast of boiled wheat and dates, Wahid and Bashour carried Rashad's corpse outside the siege encampment, into an olive grove not far from the monastery. Bashour was thankful for the shade as he attacked the ground with a shovel. Wahid was his usual taciturn self, not given to conversation, and they worked in silence. Bashour watched him. Sometimes the man's face looked angry and other times sorrowful.

Wahid's mood infected the rest of the camp when they returned. The others said nothing and avoided Wahid and Bashour. Bashour for his part was thankful. He stayed quiet, lest he reveal that he was disturbed about Islam. Normally in quiet times like this, Rashad would instruct him in the Qur'án. Bashour didn't know if that would continue; Wahid never said anything, Qutayba was disdainful of him, Jabir was sometimes openly hostile and Sameer seemed too lazy to rise to the challenge. He was relieved to leave the camp when he and Tamara took the camel to the stream north of the city to get water. He prolonged the chore for as long as he could. They said nothing of consequence, not sure if anyone would overhear them, and Bashour realized he didn't like the looks he got from strange Muslims when they heard his northern accent.

The moon had just risen in the east when a gong sounded in the city, followed by horns at the gates. Arabs roused themselves out of their beds at the commotion and reached for their swords. Gates opened and soldiers came pouring out. The Muslim commanders frantically roused their men with calls to battle. Northeast of the city Shurahbil immediately sent out calls for reinforcements and joined his men on the line.

Thomas was the first out the Emessa gate, with Taticus at his side. He ran with his left hand on Taticus' shoulder, still not used to the loss of vision on his left side. They made the stream that ran along the north side of the walls and crossed it, clambering up the slope. By torchlight Thomas saw Shurahbil shouting orders to his flanks and indicated to Taticus, "There! That one is the commander!" and they made for him. Thomas heard the animal shout of the men behind him, reassuring him that he wasn't entering the lion's jaws alone.

Taticus sidestepped to deal with one of Shurahbil's bodyguards and Thomas met the Muslim with a clash of steel. The two men fought furiously in the semi-darkness, lit from fires, torches and the moon's light filtering through olive trees on the horizon. Thomas turned a vicious roundhouse slash that ended with Shurahbil's sword smacking flatly against his breastplate. Thomas trapped the blade with his forearm and twisted his body savagely, snapping the blade at the pommel. Shurahbil gaped in surprise and took a step back. His place was immediately filled from either side with other Arab fighters, as he went in search of another sword.

Thomas also backed away from the fray and took stock in the battle. They were fighting uphill from the riverbed and had very little room to maneuver for a flank. The Muslim lines were firm and holding. He decided to fall back and see if the attacks out of the other gates had met with more success. He grabbed Taticus out of the line and together the two men loped back to the gate.

"Report!" he demanded when he was inside.

"Yes, sir. We've just got runners in from the other areas. The small gate attack went very well, until a thousand horses appeared out of the dark and drove them back. The East gate attack ran directly into a huge force and collapsed almost immediately. We lost thousands of men there, sir. I've heard no report from the west gate yet."

"Very well." He turned to Taticus with a questioning look.

Taticus shrugged. "We're getting nowhere at this gate, sir, and we're vulnerable if they strike us from the right, where they defeated the East Gate force."

"I agree. Sound the retreat."

As the horns blew and his men flowed back through the gate, Thomas slumped to sit on the ground against the wall with his head down.

72. Damascus
September 10, 634

They'd begun to prepare for sleep as the moon rose, when an alarm went up. The city defenders were attacking again. Bashour grabbed his sword and followed the others in the dark towards the city walls, dodging tents and campfires left unmanned in the alarm. He could hear the roar of battle beyond the crush of fighters. He made his way along the mass of humanity, looking for some way to contribute, some way to get into the line, but the enemy pulled back before he could find anyone to fight. He followed the surge forward until arrows from the walls began to rain among them, then turned back with the rest. Men milled around beyond the range of the arrows. They saw the doors of the east gate had closed. It took some time, but the fighters eventually realized that no further attack was coming, so they calmed down and began to filter back to their campfires.

Bashour had spent the day thinking about Islam and Christianity. He'd decided that while Christianity raised some questions, they were obscure issues, difficult to understand and they had no real impact on how a Christian practiced his belief. But Islam, while at first it had seemed to make sense in a direct sort of way, raised fundamental questions in its day-to-day practices. It contradicted itself and contradicted what he'd been taught as a Christian. He decided that he'd been deceived.

That night as they laid out their blankets for sleep, he asked Tamara, "When Jesus called his disciples, how did he do it?"

"He just said 'Follow me.'"

"And if they refused?"

She shrugged. "Nothing. Some people did refuse. Some people asked to follow him and he turned them away. Remember the rich man who wouldn't give away his wealth to follow Jesus?"

He nodded and they laid down. She blew out the oil lamp. He laid on his back staring at the top of the tent. Finally, he said, quietly so no one outside the tent would hear even though he spoke in Greek, "Tamara? I was wrong. I'm not a Muslim. I can never be a Muslim."

She turned towards him intently. “What do you mean? What are you talking about?”

“Oh, there’s a lot of things. Things that just don’t seem right. I don’t like the idea that someone can be killed if they convert to Christianity. That’s wrong. God would never command such a thing. You’ve been right all along, and I’ve been stupid.”

“Do you know what you’re saying? They’ll kill you if they know.”

“I know. It scares me. How can I pretend to listen to their nonsense if they start teaching me the Qur’án again? How can I recite their prayers? How long before they realize I’m pretending and kill me like Rashad? What if I make a mistake?”

At first, Tamara had been relieved, joyful that he’d finally come to his senses. Then she realized how precarious her own existence was, how it was tied to his position with these people and she became very afraid. “Bashour, you have to pretend. You have to be convincing.” Her breath started to quicken, she felt the panic begin to rise in her throat.

He reached out and patted her shoulder. “Don’t worry. I won’t give myself away.”

She thought about it a little while and became uneasy. He’d changed his religion before. Perhaps he was just naturally inconstant? “Why the sudden change of heart?” she asked. “Is it because of Rashad?”

“Partly. I’ve just been frustrated at how much everything revolves around blind faith in what Muhammad said. I’ve been waiting for them to give me some reason to believe him, but it all comes back to believing him because he said so.”

“I think you’re just confused and don’t know what you believe. Next week, you’ll be a Muslim again.”

“That’s not true. I’ve been thinking about this a lot, trying to make sense of it. I told you before, I studied Christianity extensively under Imad bin Najib, as well as mathematics, history and philosophy.”

“Was he the one who gave you the cross?”

“What? What are you talking about?” Bashour was confused for a moment, then remembered the lead cross Imad had pressed upon him as he’d left Tadmur. “Oh, that old thing. Yeah, he gave me that. I don’t understand why.”

Tamara raised her eyebrows. Was it possible he didn’t know? “‘That old thing?’ I think you’d better see this.”

“What are you doing?” he asked as she turned and dug into the pack containing his belongings. She turned back, holding an object wrapped in cloth.

She placed it on the ground. “I’ll be right back.” She left the tent quickly and returned with a glowing brand from the fire that she used to relight the oil lamp. Then she carefully unwrapped the cross she’d placed between them, revealing the lustrous glow of gold. Bashour sucked in his breath at the sight and picked it up, examining it, then looked questioningly at her.

“I’ve been polishing it for days, cleaning the paint off it.”

“Of course,” he said in wonderment. Then he remembered what Imad had said to him. “Things aren’t always as they seem,” he whispered to himself.

He looked at her, her eyebrows furrowed at his odd response. “It’s wonderful, Tamara! Thank you, I had no idea!” He put down the cross and gave her a huge hug. Then he looked into her eyes. “I promise you, I’ll find a way for us to escape, to get away from these people safely.”

She looked up at him, at the earnestness in his eyes and believed him. She closed her eyes and kissed him, accepting his promise.

Outside the tent, the others were asleep, except Wahid, who sat and stared into the fire. They were very quiet, he could barely hear snatches of what was said and couldn’t understand their language. But he heard the tone, and could guess at what they might be saying. A small smile crept across the big man’s face as he stirred the embers of the fire with a stick.

Later that night, Tamara roused herself and left the tent to answer a call of nature. When she returned, instead of covering herself with her blanket, she crawled under Bashour’s. He woke with a start, surprised, but she quieted him with a kiss. After a moment, he relaxed and returned the kiss. They lay there kissing softly for some time. Then they began to kiss more urgently. He held back, afraid of crossing a line of propriety, but she took his hand and guided him. In the night they surrendered to an imperative far more ancient and urgent than any religion.

“That was an utter waste of resources!” proclaimed Jonas to the rest of his squad. They sat in a circle near the East gate, eating their afternoon ration of bread. “The attack was done all wrong. We should have concentrated our forces at one gate and made a breakout.”

"Tell us about it, general Jonas," said one man sarcastically.

"Well, if I'd been in charge, things would have gone differently. There's no control here, no one knows what's going on. That's no way to run a battle."

The other members of the squad just looked at each other in disgust. "Yeah," spat one of the men, "you be sure to take that up with the Governor when he comes to ask your advice."

"I will! I used to work directly for Thomas, you know. I'm engaged to the daughter of his partner."

"Sure you are."

"Say, Jonas, how's this for an idea? Why don't you shut the hell up?"

"You going to make me?" retorted Jonas.

One of the men used the butt end of his spear and shoved Jonas in the chest with it, knocking him off balance. Jonas leapt to his feet angrily. The other men did the same and the one who pushed him stepped forward so they were nose to nose. "Let's settle this right now, rich boy!" he said, "Come on, do something!"

Jonas glared at him, then stepped away, grabbed his remaining loaf of bread and his weapons and slunk away down the street. The others laughed behind him.

73. Damascus
September 15, 634

The group that Marid was with was camped several hundred yards away. Bashour found him at work mending a sandal. One of Marid's companions was snoring heavily on a bed roll, the rest were nowhere in sight. Marid's face lit up when he saw Bashour, then fell when he saw the expression on his face.

"What's wrong?" he asked.

Bashour sat down heavily by the fire, was silent for a moment then, without looking directly at Marid, said, "Rashad's dead."

"What? How? What happened? I thought he was getting better?"

"Khalid was in the monastery and found him praying with a monk and killed him for being an infidel."

Marid was stunned into silence. Together, they sat quietly for some time.

"Was it true? Was he an infidel?"

"I think so. When I talked with him, he was telling me what he'd learned from the priests."

"Well, then, it's only just."

Bashour looked at him incredulously. "How can you say that? He was your friend too."

Marid shrugged. "He was an apostate. 'Whoever changes his Islamic religion, then kill him.'"

Bashour switched to Greek. "Don't you remember what Imad taught us? 'Question everything,' he used to say. What if we question Islam and don't like the answers we get?"

"As I recall we weren't too happy with the answers we were getting about Christianity."

Bashour squeezed his forehead with his hands. "It doesn't mean the answers were right. Maybe no one understands? Who can understand the mind of God?"

"That's why the message was given to Muhammad, peace be upon him," said Marid brightly. "He was given the Qur'án to remove questions."

"By rewriting history? Do you think God revises his word?"

Marid was pensive for a moment, then said slowly, "How are you sure that the message from before wasn't altered?"

"How? Why? Wouldn't someone have objected? Come on, Marid. How could that have happened? It would have caused a war."

"Well then, why did Allâh give Muhammad the Qur'án?"

Bashour knew the answer. He wanted to say that the Qur'án wasn't from God, that it couldn't be, but he realized that he could no longer trust his friend. Marid was apparently infected with the same fanaticism as the rest of the Arabs they'd been living with. Would Marid tell someone, or attack Bashour himself? With a shock, Bashour realized that he wasn't sure. Once, Marid had been like a brother. Now, he was a potential enemy and should be treated as such.

Bashour nodded, acknowledging defeat at Marid's logic. They made small talk, discussed the state of the siege. Then Marid asked, "How is that girl of yours, Tamara? She's a beauty, Bashour."

The memory of the previous night, the ecstasy they'd shared welled up in Bashour's chest. "She's fine," he said guardedly.

"Is she as fine in bed as she looks?" Marid leered. Bashour said nothing, but his face turned beet red and Marid laughed. "Say no more!"

Bashour remembered something that had been on his mind. "Say, did Imad give you anything when we left Tadmur?"

Marid looked at him quizzically, as if wondering what this question was about, then he brightened in a flash. "Yes. Yes, he gave me some old leaden cross. You too?"

Bashour nodded. "Yeah. Do you still have it?"

"No, I threw it away. It weighed too much and was just a symbol of infidel teachings. You still have yours?"

Bashour hid his surprise and shock and nodded nonchalantly. He studied Marid out of the corner of his eye to see if there was any reaction, if his old friend would see through his masquerade and start asking more uncomfortable questions.

Marid stood. "You'd better go back to your woman and take good care of her. You need to enjoy every moment of that in case you're martyred."

Bashour rose and they clasped hands. Unexpectedly, instead of letting go Marid drew him near. "You learn the Qur'án and keep your faith. If I hear you left Islam, by Allâh I'll kill you myself, and take your woman for my own!"

74. Damascus
September 19, 634

"Patrols of twelve will secure the perimeter overnight and ensure no infiltrators are approaching in the dark. The first patrol will exit the West Gate as soon as it's dark and make their way around the south to the East gate. Stay close to the wall. If you're spotted, the archers can cover you. If problems arise, you can retreat to the nearest gate.

"The second patrol will leave two hours after dark, again from the West gate, this time going north and around to the Emessa gate. Keep an eye on the riverbank; make sure no one is hiding in the water.

"The third patrol will leave at midnight, from the small south gate and go east and again, return through the Emessa gate.

"The challenge tonight will be 'John.' Your response will be 'Baptist'. Don't forget it; you won't get in the gate without it.

"If you have a chance to take a prisoner, it would be helpful. But don't cause a commotion, and try to stay out of sight. Don't evoke a response, okay?"

The officer giving the briefing looked across the room full of soldiers. "Any questions?"

One of the squad leaders raised his hand. "The moon will be rising shortly after midnight. Won't that make it difficult for the third patrol?"

The briefing officer held a hurried, whispered conference with the senior officers in the room. He turned back and said, "Very good point. There's still enough of a moon to give adequate illumination. The third patrol is canceled." This prompted some good-natured jeers and catcalls between the men who would be able to sleep and the ones who still had to patrol.

Jonas' shoulders sagged in relief. He'd been assigned to the third patrol. He feared any chance of contact with the enemy since the warning he'd received by the unknown assailant the previous week.

Dressed in a night cloak against the coming cold, Jonas waited until it was dark, then mounted the battlement on the wall. He carried his sword and a bundle of rope under the cloak.

He greeted the odd watch standers he encountered and passed without question. A soldier on the wall was nothing worth noticing.

He walked the wall slowly, monitoring the watchmen around him. He was nervous and unsure about what he was about to do. He could see no other way to solve his debt with Kostas. He was sure that his life was forfeit if he didn't do something. He couldn't ask his father for more money; that well was dry. Eudocia wouldn't marry him while the city was besieged. Until she did, he had no access to her dowry. He had to find a way to neutralize Kostas. He'd heard the rumors of a reward by the Muslims for defectors, they were common knowledge among the ranks.

He paused near a wooden shelter built on the parapet. He was hidden from sight by the shelter in one direction. In the other direction he saw some sort of conference with three soldiers some way down the wall. No one was looking at him. It only took a moment. He produced the rope and shook it out down the wall, looping it double around the kneeler. He looked around a second time, convinced himself no one was looking and quickly went over the wall. Hitting the ground below, he shook the rope free, coiled it up and hid it under a nearby bush. Then he ran like the wind away from the wall, hoping no archer spotted his movement in the dark.

"Sahib, we've captured a deserter. I think he has information for you. He seems very agitated, but we can't understand a word he says."

Khalid looked up at the news. He motioned at an aide. "Find that interpreter of mine. And bring Dhiraar. Maybe we have work for him."

Bashour was confused why he should be summoned so late in the night. When he arrived at Khalid's spacious tent, he found an uncomfortable looking man, a few years older than himself, in a Roman army cloak. Dhiraar was there, as were some of Khalid's other aides that Bashour didn't know. Khalid gestured at the Roman soldier. "This man came from the city on his own. Find out what he wants."

Bashour turned to the man and spoke in Greek. "This is Khalid, the commander of this army. Why are you here?"

"I am Jonas Tournikes. I have urgent information that could give you the city." Khalid sat forward with great interest when

Bashour translated this. Jonas told about the patrol schedule and the passwords to be used this night. Bashour translated nervously. He eyed the other aides, wondering how much, if any, they understood of what this traitor was saying. He desperately wanted to ask the man why he was doing this, why he was betraying the city, but Khalid was hanging on his every word now. No dialogue was possible without Khalid demanding a full accounting.

Dhiraar saved him the trouble. "Why should we believe him? What if he's leading us into a trap?"

Jonas explained it to Bashour. "I have. . . obligations that I'm unable to meet. My life is in danger while this siege continues. All I ask is that I be allowed to marry my fiancée when this is done and that I be allowed to point out some criminals who'll cause problems for you when you take the city, so you may dispose of them."

Khalid and Dhiraar conferred on this piece of information. Khalid addressed Bashour. "What do you think? Is he telling the truth? Can we trust him?"

Bashour turned to Jonas. "What sort of obligations? Tell me true. They think you're setting a trap for them."

Jonas' eyes went wide as he realized the precarious nature of his situation. Then he looked down and admitted, "I have gambling debts. I lost too much money on the horses."

When they heard this, the Arabs howled with laughter. "Horses! These Romans haven't got a clue about fast horses! And I suppose that these undesirables he'd like to point out are those who hold his debt? No, don't ask him that, I'm already sure that's the case.

"Very well, but to be sure, this man must first accept Islam."

Bashour translated this and explained to Jonas what it meant and how to say the shahada. He felt ill at conveying such a requirement that he himself no longer believed in, but he kept a stoic face and translated accurately, again not sure if others could understand the exchange.

Jonas didn't hesitate for a second. He recited the shahada, first in Greek, then with Bashour's prompting in guttural Arabic.

Khalid acted swiftly. "Dhiraar, this is your sort of task. Take the men you need and go. You get that gate open and I'll be right behind you with thousands of soldiers." He turned to Bashour. "Fetch your armor and weapons and return here quickly. I'll have you at my side this night." Bashour fought to keep the disappointment out of his face. A plan had started to form that involved running away in the confusion of a major battle.

An aide stepped forward. "Shall I send runners to alert the other commanders, Sahib?"

"No, there's no time. With surprise we can take the city with my army alone. I will be there to open the gates for Ubaidah in the morning."

75. Damascus
September 20, 634 Just after midnight

The attack happened so quickly no one had a chance to raise an alarm. The patrol never saw the assailants, had mistaken them in the darkness for rocks piled against the city wall. Dhiraar had originally planned to cut their throats quickly, but had been reminded that they didn't want to get a lot of blood on the cloaks, since they planned to use them. If a single victim managed to shout, they would have been in trouble. They'd risen as one and assaulted the patrol as it had passed them. Dhiraar had brought thirty men, to be sure that the patrol would be overwhelmed from the beginning. They hit their targets amid grunts of surprise, muffled by arms locked around windpipes and covering mouths.

Dhiraar removed the helmet of the last man and clubbed him over the head. The body went limp and the Arabs all crouched, looking expectantly at the wall above them. They heard no shouts or alarms, no questioning voices. After some seconds, they relaxed and quietly stripped the cloaks off their victims. Once that was done, they slit the throats of the patrol, ensuring their silence.

Dhiraar and selected men donned the captured cloaks and left their comrades at the base of the wall, where they would stay to avoid detection. They continued the patrol, moving silently and unhurriedly. It wouldn't do to arrive at the gate before they were expected. Dhiraar kept repeating the unfamiliar word "Baptist" to himself, trying to erase any hint of an accent. Would he whisper it? Say it? He wasn't sure.

They left the wall near the northeast corner, where rocks descending towards the stream made the path difficult. A narrow trail led around the obstruction. Then they were facing a small gate, recessed where the wall was indented at the corner, before it turned south towards the larger East gate. This must be the one the traitor called the Emessa gate. Dhiraar approached it and thumped the wood with the butt of his sword.

A voice called down from above, "John!"

Dhiraar avoided looking up. His beard was much heavier than anything he'd seen on the soldiers they'd killed. "Baptist!" he called out, quietly but clearly.

A muffled command from above and the gate creaked open. Dhiraar and his men pulled their chins down and turned their heads, avoiding eye contact as they shuffled through the gate. They were bathed in torchlight. An officer approached him, saying something in Greek. Dhiraar raised his head and responded by shouting, "Allâhu Akhbar!" and thrusting his sword through the man's belly.

His men threw off their cloaks and attacked the guards at the gate. Two men ran up the nearest rampart and engaged the ones above. Men began shouting and an alarm went up. The immediate threat was removed, but several had been too far away and had run when they saw what was happening. Dhiraar could hear them shouting down the streets. He motioned his men to open the gate, quickly. He grabbed two torches and slipped through the gate the moment it cracked open and waved them over his head. He was rewarded by the throaty roar of thousands of voices as the army that had gathered in the darkness rose and rushed the gate.

Taticus intended to meet the second patrol when they returned through the Emessa gate, to debrief them in case they'd encountered anything unusual. Chances are they hadn't. The Muslims generally stayed away from the north wall because of the steep slope to the river.

He was puzzled by the sounds of commotion as he and the few men with him neared the vicinity of the gate. "Come on!" he said and broke into a trot. As he rounded the last corner, his heart stopped. The gate was open and the enemy was flooding through it.

He skidded to a halt so quickly that one of the men behind him collided with him. "Go raise the alarm! I need the entire garrison turned out now!" He shoved the man back down the street to get him moving, then turned his attention to the fighting in front of him. The guards at the gate were spread thin and couldn't hope to hold the tide surging through the gate. Taticus pointed at several men and directed them at the porch of a market stand along the street. "You! Take whatever you can there, barrels, tables! Make a barricade here on the street! Slow them down so you can stand back and kill them as they cross!

Hold fast here until reinforcements arrive!" He slapped one of the soldiers on the shoulder. "You're with me!" As the two backed away down the street, the others began tearing down the supports of a porch overhang. *Good men,* thought Taticus, *that would yield enough lumber to build a formidable barricade.*

He turned at the first cross street and ran sideways to the onslaught, trying to gauge how far the enemy had penetrated already into the city. He ran into squads of sleepy and disoriented soldiers responding to the alarm. He quickly directed them to streets and alleys with the same instructions to build barricades and funnel the attackers into kill zones. He occasionally found an officer and paused to give more detailed instructions. He kept moving, knowing that time was working against him.

He wasn't far from the east wall when he gave the centurion with him instructions to carry on. "Okay, you see what we're doing! Continue on to the wall, grab everyone you can and finish making barricades at choke points. If they get through the barricades and can exploit the side streets, you have to fall back to the next street. Keep your lateral lines of communication open and don't let them get behind you. I have to organize the northern sector."

He left the man with a quick salute and started retracing his steps. The streets were coming alive with soldiers responding in small groups. He could hear horns and bells in the distance further in the city. He grabbed one young soldier. "You there! Run to the headquarters and tell them that Taticus has established a defense from the Emessa road to the east wall, and that I'll attempt to do the same to the north wall. Got that? Go!"

As he passed the soldiers crossing his path, he directed them down the streets to the forming barricades. Would it be enough? Did they have time? He glanced down one of the wider streets as he passed and saw his men fighting at the barricade there. Some men were on the ground, others crawling away to the shelter of doors in the street. The sounds of battle, shouts and screams were echoing down the street. He could clearly hear the battle cry of the Arab's "Allâhu Akbar!" through the din. He fought back the urge to lend his sword to the fray; he needed to complete organizing the defenses before he could start helping kill the invaders.

The traffic in the streets was picking up. Occasional squads of soldiers were turning into a steady stream of reinforcements heading for the battle line. At the same time, civilian refugees were starting to clog the streets, running in panic from the battle, many in their nightclothes. At intersections he grabbed passing soldiers and detailed them to direct traffic, making sure that the flow of soldiers was evenly distributed across the line. It wouldn't do to have overwhelming force in one spot, only to be surrounded when they broke through elsewhere.

The Arabs had penetrated further into the city on his left flank. No one had taken control of the defenses and the soldiers fighting there were disorganized. He intercepted a few running from the battle and turned them around with angry commands. Then he detailed groups of soldiers to start barricades behind the lines, hoping to have a defensible redoubt before the main body of Arabs fought their way through the streets to his positions.

He located a team of archers and directed their aim at the ramparts of the wall, with instructions to sweep the top of the walls clear of any Arabs who tried to flank their positions that way. Then he returned to the center of the line, intending to pull them back to secondary positions and shorten the line.

His direction was unnecessary. The Arabs had already overwhelmed his original defense and had pushed several blocks deeper into the city. Those soldiers who'd survived had fallen back and rapidly formed new barricades. The initial panic was over and the line was holding. The fighting at the barricades was desperate, but the Arabs had been funneled into alleyways where the weight of their numbers was felt less by the defenders.

Left with breathing room for a moment, Taticus set about establishing a command structure. He couldn't keep track of the entire battle line in the city, he needed competent sub-commanders and constant updates so he could coordinate the big picture. Where was Harbis? He realized he'd been in constant motion and was probably difficult to keep track of, so he sent a runner to headquarters to notify them where he'd established his command post and to find out if anyone was coordinating the defenses at a higher level.

The main street leading to the Emessa gate was his biggest concern. The width of the boulevard made it harder to defend. He approached the fighting at the barricade and stopped an officer who was shouting commands and directing reinforcements into the gaps. "Kentarch! Report!"

The man glanced at him and took his arm and led them a few steps back from the fighting. He had to shout to make himself heard over the roar of fighting nearby. "Sir! We've fallen back twice! They've been using long lances to fight through the barricades, and it's difficult to keep them at bay! I've lost several centuries already! I have to commit men directly into the line to plug holes as they arrive. I don't have time to form a solid defensive line!"

Taticus shook his head. "I can't help you on that score; the men are arriving as fast as they're being alerted, but it's taking too long to turn out the whole garrison."

The centurion was sweating and dirty from the fighting, but Taticus was relieved to see that he wasn't wild-eyed with panic. The man was holding up well, considering his report that he'd already fed hundreds to their deaths in their desperate attempt to stop the tide of the advance. "Can you hold?" he asked.

The man examined the line and nodded. "I'd feel better if you could put up another barricade behind us to fall back to."

"Done!" Taticus rose to leave, when the man he was talking to choked and collapsed, an arrow piercing his throat at an odd angle. Taticus looked up and saw Arab archers on the roofs above him. Men were running along the roofs and he could see fighters dropping into the alley behind their position.

"They're on the roofs!" he bellowed above the din. "Fall back!" Unsheathing his sword, he lent his arm to the fighting as the Muslims swept over the barricade. He fought to keep himself from becoming too focused on the killing at the end of his sword. If he lost touch with what his men were doing, he was no longer a commander, but just another swordsman. The Arab in front of him raised his sword for an overhand strike and Taticus stabbed hard, straight at the man's ribs. He felt the blade meet armor, but the blow was enough to cause the man to fold with a chuff, falling back into those behind him.

He stepped back off the line and yelled left and right, coordinating an orderly retreat. Once the cadence of thrust, parry and step back was established, he turned command over to the nearest officer and worked his way back down the street. The Arabs from the rooftops were creating chaos; the line was rapidly dissolving into a general melee in the streets. He realized he had to trade space for time. He ran across a wider cross street and started intercepting approaching men from the rear and forming them up along the cross street, safe from being flanked by men on rooftops.

Damascus was divided into neighborhoods by wide thoroughfares. Inside each neighborhood was a rabbit's warren of side streets and alleys. Taticus had hoped he could slow the enemy and make them pay for every step in the maze of small streets, but with them on the roofs he realized that he'd have to sacrifice whole neighborhoods as they became untenable. He started directing some of his own men onto the rooftops themselves. He sent all the archers up, with instructions to cut down anyone they saw on the roofs across the boulevards.

He didn't know if it was enough. He didn't know what was going on elsewhere in the city. He still hadn't heard from Harbis. He had no idea if his dispatches had even gotten through. How many men had he already lost? Thousands, surely. How many were left? Would he keep feeding men into the meat grinder until no one was left to send? He needed answers!

Thomas was awakened by someone pounding on his door. He could hear bells ringing and people shouting as he hurried to see what was happening. He didn't recognize the runner who'd awakened him, "Sir! The Arabs have somehow gotten through the East gate and are in the city!"

He hurriedly got dressed and ran to the city hall. Harbis and Bishop Peter were already there, looking worried. Runners were running in and out in a scene of mass confusion. "What's happening?" he asked.

Harbis turned to him, looking haggard. "Somehow they got into one of the gates on the east wall. We think it was the Emessa Gate. They have several thousand men in the city now and we think more are entering. We've been trying to stabilize a line, but we can't muster the men fast enough. I've been putting men into the line as they've reported, but it's been piecemeal and they're being ground up as I commit them. I can't do anything else. If we give them breathing room to allow ourselves time to form up, they'll overrun the city."

"Archers from the wall?"

Harbis shook his head. "They're on the walls and have cleared them as they've advanced."

"Make way! Make a hole!" the bustle of activity at the door parted and Taticus stormed through with a quick stride. He didn't waste time with pleasantries, just nodded at Thomas and reported to Harbis, "We can't hold them. I thought we had a decent roadblock set up that would give us a defensive position, but the bastards just used the rooftops and went around us. They're like ants, they're everywhere."

Harbis looked grim. He looked up at Thomas. "Governor, there's a possibility. We set fire to the city in their path, channel them into kill zones. We sacrifice part of the city to save the rest."

Thomas shook his head. "No. I will not destroy this city to save it. We light fires and then what? That'll stop them, but unless we can eject them from the city and get those gates closed, we're no better than we are now in the long run."

"Then the city is lost."

The four men looked at each other in silence. Bishop Peter broke the tension. "Thomas, the decision is yours. If we continue to fight, a terrible price will be extracted from this city by an army with the taste of blood."

Thomas looked at Taticus, who said, "It will make Nineveh look like a picnic." The veterans had seen the Byzantine army sack Nineveh when they captured it. Atrocities were committed, despite the efforts of the commanders to control the men. Heraclius had paid lip service to controlling his men; nonetheless, he knew retribution would be extracted by the angry soldiers. From what they'd heard about these Arabs, the commander wouldn't try to restrain his men. For all they knew, he'd be at the front of the raping and looting.

"How do we do it?" Thomas asked. "Waving a flag will do no good at night in the city."

Taticus agreed. "If you go near the combat line, you'll be cut down, no doubt. I don't think they have any interest in negotiation."

"The reports I've heard," said Harbis, "are that the other gates are all calm, there's no attack anywhere else."

Peter said, "I understand their general in the southwest sector is said to be a reasonable man. Ubaidah is his name, or something like that. Perhaps we can negotiate terms with him."

Thomas looked at them, all watching him, waiting for a decision. "Okay, let's go. Taticus, can you manage the battle from here, stall the attack as long as possible?"

"Yes, sir."

Thomas took the other two by the arm and they headed for the West Gate. "Let's go, then. We'll discuss the terms we seek on the way. Find someone who can interpret for us."

Ubaidah was awake, watching the city. They could hear a commotion, but no one had any idea what was going on. He'd sent runners to find out from Khalid if something noteworthy was happening, but none had returned yet.

"Sahib! The gate is opening!"

The main gate in the west was indeed open and a small group of men with torches strode out. Ubaidah's first impulse was to sound the alarm, prepare for an attack, but no additional soldiers were coming out of the gate. "It appears someone wants to talk. I will go meet this delegation."

They stopped at the edge of the archers range from the wall. Arab fighters formed a silent ring around them. The light from their torches caught the occasional gleam of metal from armor and weapons. The two groups regarded each other in silence for some time. Thomas' interpreter finally called out, "We seek to speak with your commander!"

"I command these men," a quiet voice said. A tall man strode through the ring of men and approached them, several bodyguards on his flanks. He stopped before them. "I am Abū 'Ubaidah ibn al-Jarrāh," he said and smiled, showing a huge gap where his front teeth should have been.

Thomas took a step forward. "I am Thomas, the acting governor of Damascus. I wish to discuss terms of surrender of the city to you."

Ubaidah smiled paternally and inclined his head in agreement. "That is certainly welcome news. Perhaps you would like to discuss this over a cup of tea?"

"I beg your pardon, but the tea will have to wait. Time is of the essence. I'd like to conclude the surrender as quickly as possible. Your army even now is destroying our city and killing our people."

Thomas was surprised at the reaction this caused from the tall man. He seemed unaware of what was happening on the other side of the city. "Is that so? Well, then we shouldn't delay. Of course, I shall require you lay down your weapons. Shall I accompany you into your city and accept your surrender? We can discuss details on the way."

Ubaidah realized that the man was negotiating from a position of weakness. Khalid had obviously found a way into the city and exploited it without telling anyone. That was typical of the way he often monopolized the glory. He no doubt wished to punish the city for daring to resist him. Well, that was his prerogative as the commander of the army, but Ubaidah knew Khalid no longer commanded, although he hadn't been notified.

Ubaidah was pleased at the developments this night and was in a magnanimous mood. The city would be given generous terms of surrender. They'd been wise to come to him.

The sun had just cleared the horizon when Khalid's men broke the enemy line and entered the city center square in front of the church of St. Mary. The resistance had mysteriously grown less as the sky had become lighter. Bashour followed Khalid as he entered the square. Throughout the night he'd cowered in the big man's shadow, sometimes in the rear issuing orders and ordering units to and fro, but all too often in the very thick of the fighting. The man actually enjoyed the fight and laughed when he killed someone. Bashour had stayed quick on his feet and never actually had to wield his sword. He just fought to stay in sight of Khalid as he'd been instructed. He didn't know why. There'd been no attempt to talk to anyone. His skill as an interpreter was completely wasted this night and he admitted that he had no stomach as a fighter.

The square was free of fighting as they entered it, but to his surprise several official looking men and officers were standing on the bottom steps of the church. Beside them were Ubaidah and several other Muslims. Looking at the crowds at the edge of the square, Bashour realized that many were Arab soldiers.

Khalid caught his eye and drew him forward. Together, they strode up to the officers in front of the church. They were well dressed in contrast to Khalid, drenched in sweat and liberally covered in welter and gore from the fighting. The one standing in front had a patch covering his left eye and an air of authority about him. Khalid ignored the Muslims and addressed this man, obviously the head of the city, directly. "I claim this city by right of conquest!"

Before Bashour could translate, Ubaidah stepped forward. "Greetings, son of Waleed. I'm afraid that this city has already surrendered. You cannot claim the conquest," he said calmly.

"No, by Allâh!" cried Khalid. "I've been fighting in this city for seven hours now and have defeated it. It's conquered and we shall loot it. Everything in this city is forfeit, the women will be sold into slavery and I shall have the men slaughtered."

"You would be fighting still, had the governor not sought surrender on terms that I have found very acceptable. The city has capitulated. You must accept the surrender."

"Pah!" Khalid spat. "The only reason he offered terms was because we'd shattered his defense. Were it not for my fighters, there would be no surrender, and you and I would still be scratching fleas outside this wall."

"Be that as it may, a surrender was offered and I have accepted it. You must comply with that."

"By what authority do you accept any surrender? Why did you not consult me first?" Khalid was furious and it was disconcerting to have Ubaidah standing up to him like this instead of acquiescing to his command.

"For the same reason, no doubt, that you failed to consult me before you assaulted the city." Ubaidah produced a small towel and handed it to Khalid and indicated he should wipe his face with it.

"Obviously, I would have if you'd made yourself available for consultation."

Ubaidah felt it wasn't the right time to tell Khalid that he'd been relieved. To reveal that the command wasn't unified would be poor form and would reveal weakness to the Romans. He took Khalid by the arm and drew him aside. "You are the Sword of Allâh, but there's a time when the sword need not leave its sheath for its power to be felt. You have won this battle. The enemy has surrendered. If you disregard this surrender and pillage the city anyway, word will get out and no city will ever surrender to us again. Be lenient now, and things will be far easier for us in the future."

The battle fury that had fueled Khalid began to fade and he suddenly felt very weary. He waved dismissively at Ubaidah and told him, "Do whatever you want."

Ubaidah turned to the men on the steps and declared, "The terms of surrender are agreed. No slaves will be taken from among you. No harm shall come to your places of worship and we will take no booty. The city will pay one dirham of gold for every citizen as tribute. Those citizens who do not choose to live under Islam are free to leave unharmed."

This statement caught Khalid's attention. He stopped Ubaidah and had a tense confrontation with him that Bashour couldn't overhear. Ubaidah turned back and reluctantly announced, "Anyone who leaves shall do so under a guarantee of three days of peace. If, after three days, a Muslim conquers any place they are residing, they will not then be under a guarantee of peace."

This caused a look of consternation from Thomas. This wasn't what they'd agreed on. He stepped forward to protest. Ubaidah cut him off. "I have altered your terms of surrender. If you dislike those terms, you can negotiate with him," he gestured at Khalid. "I suggest you keep your peace, lest I alter them more."

76. Damascus
September 20, 634

The council chamber was full of military officers, clergy, city officials and prominent citizens of Damascus. The babble of conversation ceased as Thomas called them to silence. He spoke quickly, with a tone of authority that brooked no discussion, no argument. "Okay, people, we don't have much time. I want to be on the road by noon. Please hold your questions. We need to put as much distance as we can between us and this city in three days.

"Here's the situation: We surrendered the city on the condition that the Arabs don't plunder it. The Arab general that took our surrender agreed to this, but his commander disagrees with the conditions. He's not happy, but somehow the general convinced him to settle for it. They've offered that anyone who doesn't want to stay here and live under their rule will be free to leave, under a three-day peace pact. I have no idea what will happen after three days is up, but I'm certain that it won't be good.

"I intend to march out of here with my family and what's left of the army this afternoon, and make my way to Antioch. I know that Emessa's closer, but we have no guarantee of safety in Emessa. For all we know, it may be under siege as we speak. We're going west over the pass to the Bekaa valley, then north from there.

"Harbis, assemble what's left of your men. Detail teams to quickly canvas the city and round up anyone who wants to join us. Everyone will meet on Gate Road. We'll form the caravan there. People are to bring the bare minimum, we'll be traveling fast and I won't tolerate anyone with a large baggage load slowing us down.

"Taticus, you take a team to Gate Road and organize the caravan as people show up. Inspect the loads, throw out anything excessive.

"Nicetas, I'll need you to round up every wagon and cart you can lay hands on and load them with the supplies from the warehouse. We need at least two weeks of rations. Sorry, but I have no idea how many people there will be, so take whatever you can. If necessary, we can discard any excess as we go."

He addressed Bishop Peter. "Your Grace, I understand the monks have already stated they'll stay here. I suggest you assemble whatever relics and finery you can carry. It's up to you how many priests you leave here. These barbarians have said they'll respect our places of worship, but I wouldn't count on that."

The bishop replied, "The head? I'm not comfortable with that." He was referring to the head of John the Baptist, interred in the Cathedral of St. John.

"That's your decision. Leave it here, if you trust these Arabs. I wouldn't."

One of the businessmen called out, "Governor, I can't possibly assemble my household in the time you've given us."

Thomas shook his head. "Not my problem. The caravan will leave on schedule. If you can't make it, then stay here, or take your chances on your own." He held up his hand to silence the rising mutters of protest. "People, there are times when you need to leave everything you hold dear, drop everything and run for your life. This is one of those times. These things you need time to gather are just things. They can be replaced. Get your gold, get your small valuables, get a warm cloak, a good set of shoes, a pack animal if you have one and leave the rest.

"That's all I have to say. I have to get my household in motion. Please hold your questions and solve your problems yourselves." He ignored the cacophony of shouts and questions on his way out, accompanied by Taticus and Harbis.

"There he is!" said Sameer. The four had been working their way through the crowds at the edge of the central square for an hour since sunrise, looking for Bashour. They saw him with Dhiraar, translating a conversation with someone from the city. They caught his eye and he acknowledged their presence with a nod. Soon he was done and after a quick nod of permission from Dhiraar he joined them."

"Come on, Bashour, tell us what's happening," urged Qutayba. Sameer and Jabir pressed in to hear him over the surrounding hubbub. Wahid stayed back slightly, aloof as always.

Bashour adopted an air of importance. He realized that his position made him something of an insider. "The city surrendered to Ubaidah before we finished taking it. Under the terms of surrender, Ubaidah convinced Khalid to accept the surrender and not to sack the city."

At this news, Jabir's face fell. "No women?" he said. Bashour hid his disgust and shook his head.

Sameer slapped Jabir's shoulder. "You're still a rich man, Jabir. You'll be able to afford a mahr for Mut'ah. I'm sure there're needy women here who'll marry you for a contract."

Qutayba agreed. "Yes, I'm sure we made many widows last night, didn't we? You can pick from any of them."

Jabir ignored their banter and jerked a thumb at the activity in the center of the square. A crowd was forming with packs and baggage, while people were loading carts pulled by mules. "What's happening here?"

Bashour looked wistfully at the forming caravan. He desperately wanted to join that crowd, to disappear and escape with them. He could easily slip out of sight, change his cloak and mix with the gathering refugees, but he couldn't leave Tamara. He didn't notice Wahid studying him. "Ubaidah agreed that anyone who wanted to leave the city could do so. Khalid gave them a three-day peace pact to get as far away as they can."

Jabir rolled his eyes again. "By Allâh, we don't get to sack the city and now we let all their gold and silver just walk out of here? This is madness!"

Bashour noticed Khalid talking to Dhiraar, who turned and pointed at him. Khalid came over. "Translator, take a few minutes, get some breakfast and meet me back here. We have a lot of work to do to organize this city, and I need to talk to them."

Bashour ducked his head and had a sudden inspiration. "Sahib, if I may, we'll need a lot of translators. I have a woman who speaks Greek and Arabic almost as well as I do. If you give me some time to fetch her from our camp outside. . ."

A flash of irritation crossed Khalid's face. "Absolutely not. You stay close. When I need you, I don't want to have to look for you."

He turned and left and Jabir chided him, "Bashour, what in Allâh's name were you thinking? A woman as a translator?"

Bashour pursed his lips in anger and embarrassment, but said nothing as the others enjoyed a laugh at his expense; he then went with them to find someone who could sell them some bread and dates. Wahid studied Bashour thoughtfully, saying nothing.

Tamara had prepared a pot of crushed grain gruel sweetened with dates, expecting the men would return demanding food. But by mid-morning the camp was still mostly deserted except for other women and camp followers. She'd settled with a full bowl for herself when Wahid unexpectedly appeared, startling her.

She looked up at the dark visage of the big man, but couldn't read his mood behind the thick beard. He usually ignored her, but this time he came right up to her. Her heart palpitated with fear. Had something happened to Bashour?

"What's wrong? What's happening?" she stammered.

Wahid said in his deep voice, "We don't have time. Bashour is fine. Gather everything you have that you can carry on a long trip." He threw a cloak at her that he'd purchased from an old woman in the city. "Change into this."

Tamara was confused. "What's going on? Where am I going?"

Wahid gave her a look that froze her into silence. He really was a very large, frightening man. "Just do as you're told and hold your tongue, woman," he said tightly.

She gathered the blankets and Bashour's pack out of the tent. Wahid had disappeared, so she wasn't sure if he meant the tent as well. She went ahead and collapsed it and folded it as tightly as she could. It wasn't as pretty as when the men did it for her, but it would suffice. She couldn't carry it, though, it was too heavy. What was going on? She had no idea. The others near her camp ignored the activity. Minding one's business was a way of life among people who'd been enslaved by the Muslims.

Wahid returned with a small mule in tow. She didn't ask where it had come from. He nodded approvingly at her work and threw the tent over the animal's back and added the pack to it. They set off together for the nearest city gate.

Wahid's huge bulk opened a path for them in the crowds that teemed in the main thoroughfare that ran the length of Damascus from the East gate to the West gate. The crowd was milling around, unorganized. Wahid made their way down the wide boulevard until he came to where the crowd was being whipped into line by soldiers. Tamara was confused, but she recognized the signs of a caravan being formed. Wahid led her to the middle of the line, where she was crowded by refugees from both sides. He stopped her and put his face right up to hers and told her sternly, “Stay right here.” Then he disappeared into the crowd.

“You’ve got everything with wheels that I can find, Thomas,” said Nicetas. “Just get out of here and put as much distance as you can between you and this place.”

“You’re not coming?” asked Thomas.

Nicetas shook his head. “Are you kidding? This is the opportunity of a lifetime. Do you know what an occupation does to prices?” He smiled, but the mercenary jest was belied by the worried look in his eyes.

“Come with us, Nicetas. We can rebuild the business farther north, set up a trade treaty with the Avars.”

“No, I was born here. I lived here through the Sassanid occupation and I expect I can survive this, too. Just come back with enough force that you don’t have to destroy the city to retake it.”

“How about your family?”

“I told the wife she should go, but she chose to stay with me. Eudocia is evacuating. She should be along any minute. Can you keep an eye on her?”

“Of course. What about that fiancée of hers?”

“Jonas?” Nicetas looked disgusted. “Haven’t seen much of him since he was drafted. He may have been killed in the attack last night, for all I know. Doesn’t really bother me; he’d turned out to be a great disappointment.”

Thomas looked surprised. “Then why did you agree to let him marry Eudocia?”

“He came from a good family. I didn’t know how useless he was until I tried to put him to work in the warehouse.” He dropped his voice and leaned in so only Thomas could hear him. “Rumor has it that he has a bit of a gambling problem. I think he may have been counting on the dowry to settle some debts.”

“How does Eudocia feel about this? Have you talked to her about it?”

“Oh, we’ve discussed it. I think she’s having second thoughts, but hasn’t done anything about it since the whole situation has been so chaotic. With any luck, these Arab bastards have solved the problem for us already.”

They clasped hands and embraced. “I’ll be back as soon as I can, at the head of an army,” promised Thomas.

Bashour shadowed Khalid, who was issuing instructions to a team of Arabs concerning the confiscation of buildings to house the army. Without warning, Wahid appeared at his side. He looked at the big man questioningly and Wahid just avoided his gaze stoically. When Khalid paused, Wahid excused himself, "Sahib, we have wounded and I need a translator for the physician."

Khalid glanced at Bashour and waved them away with a dismissive air. Bashour followed Wahid into the crowd as they entered the main boulevard and started working their way toward the west gate.

Bashour saw no other Arabs around and was tempted to ask Wahid why they were going this way, but kept quiet. Wahid probably wouldn't answer anyway. He spoke so infrequently that it was hard to tell what he was thinking.

They were in the middle of the street and Wahid had stopped and pushed him ahead. They'd gone just a little way when Bashour was surprised by a blow from behind that pitched him forward off his feet. He fell clumsily, confused by what had happened. Wahid blocked the light from the morning sun as he bent over him. Instead of helping him up, the big man held him down and said into his ear, "Be quiet and do as you're told!" He pulled Bashour's keffiyah off and tossed it aside and threw a nondescript brown cloak over him, then took him by the arm and lifted him to his feet.

Bashour was shocked, confused and speechless. He opened his mouth to ask Wahid what the hell he was doing, but the big man just pressed a finger to his lips, then took him by the shoulder and turned him around.

And there, facing him in surprise, was Tamara; covered in a light tan cloak with Byzantine embroidery on the edge. The two were frozen in shock and surprise for a moment, then collided in an embrace.

Bashour turned to Wahid. "Why?"

The big man took the rope for the mule and shoved it into his hand. "Go. You're no Muslim, Bashour." The two men locked eyes for a long moment. For the first time, Bashour saw a glint of tenderness in the dark orbs above the big man's beard.

"God bless you, my friend."

Wahid just blinked. "As-Salāmu `Alaykum," he muttered, then turned and disappeared into the crowd.

They were pushed and jostled and moved forward in fits and starts. Soldiers worked their way through the crowd. A big man with officer's insignia on his cloak was harassing the family in front of them. "You're carrying far too much!" He gestured at the donkey, loaded down with a gigantic pack. "This animal won't make it two days with that load. Remove everything that's not absolutely necessary."

"But sir, this is. . ."

The big officer looked exasperated and got close to the man's face. "Look, you. I don't have time to explain. We'll be moving at a force-march for more than a week. If you don't take at least half the load off that animal, it'll die by tomorrow night. If you can't keep up, you'll be left behind – it's your decision. . Now either shut up and do as I say, or fall out and stay here." The man he was speaking to became red in the face, but he turned away before the man could answer. He approached Bashour and Tamara. He grabbed the pack on the mule and shook it to ensure it was secure and nodded approvingly. "Just the two of you? Yes? Can the lady walk?"

Bashour stammered an affirmative. Another officer approached. "Taticus, we have a problem over here." They disappeared without another word to Bashour. He looked at Tamara and squeezed her tightly against him.

The hot sun was high in the sky when the west gate opened and the column began moving through it. Bashour's heart raced, fearful that they might be spotted. They kept their faces down and shuffled through the gate under the gaze of the Arabs lining the wall and road. Once free of the city, the column spread out and picked up its pace.

Bashour looked back at Damascus. They were free!

77. West of Damascus
September 21, 634

The Abana river cut a deep canyon into the mountains due west of Damascus from its source on the high plateau of Zabadani. Thomas stood on a promontory above the narrow valley formed by the river and strained to catch any sign of motion further east in the predawn brightness. Due to the late start the previous day and the winding, narrow canyon they'd entered to cross the mountains not three miles from the gates of the city, they were a mere six miles as the crow flies from Damascus.

"Do you think they'll follow us?" asked Harbis.

"Under the terms of the peace agreement, they shouldn't, not yet. But when that big bastard figures out how much gold we're carrying, he'll follow. I'm not sure how well that Ubaidah fellow can control him."

"It's Sunday, the bishop wants to say mass before we start moving this morning."

"Tell him to make it quick. Did you get an estimate of how many people we have?"

"I figure about ten thousand. Maybe three thousand remaining military. The rest are civilian."

Thomas whistled softly in surprise. "I hadn't expected so many."

The Eucharist service was short. The liturgy of the word was dispensed with because of the situation; only a fraction of the huge crowd could hear the reading. Bishop Peter was determined to organize things better for the following week. He considered how he'd divide the gigantic caravan into "parishes" to be managed by individual priests. For today, this was sufficient. He consecrated the Eucharist and sent a small army of priests into the crowd to distribute it.

Bashour and Tamara had joined the service. They couldn't hear what the bishop was saying, but the familiar responses rippled through the crowd, so they knew what was happening. When a priest came through, everyone knelt to receive communion. He looked familiar to Bashour, but he couldn't place where he'd seen him before. When the priest came to them, Bashour declined, placing his fingers over his mouth. Tamara had thought about it and decided she should also decline. The priest raised his eyebrows, but said nothing more and moved on.

Before long they were moving again, the long column snaking its way up the old Roman road through the canyon. Soldiers had been positioned along the march to keep things moving quickly. On their left the basin of the small river made a deep green swath through the dun-colored hills. The sides of the valley were more gentle here than they were further downstream. The edge of the road was littered with cast-off belongings that the more optimistic travelers had decided weren't worth carrying after all. Bashour was thankful that the temperature seemed a few degrees cooler as they slowly ascended into the mountains.

Ahead, a priest with a small pack on his back was standing by the road, studying people as they crowded by. He spied Bashour and Tamara and fell in with them. Bashour recognized him as the priest who'd offered him communion earlier that morning. "Good morning," the priest said cheerfully. "I'm Father Marcian." He looked at Bashour strangely, as if he were trying to place him.

Bashour introduced himself and Tamara. "I am Bashour bin Ghalib and this is Tamara . . ." He realized that in all the time they'd spent together, he never thought to ask Tamara's patronymic. The sentence hung awkwardly, unfinished.

"Tamara bint Waqar," she said with a small smile.

"Bashour. . . Bashour. . ." He examined Bashour thoughtfully. "Have we met?"

"I was wondering the very same thing."

"Your Greek is very good, but with just a trace of an accent from the east." He snapped his fingers. "You're Imad's student!"

Bashour remembered the dinner in his teacher's house. It seemed like a lifetime ago. "Yes! Father Kalekas! I remember you now!"

The priest turned towards Tamara. "You two are traveling together? You're not married? Cousins?"

"Yes," said Bashour. "Ah, no, we're not related," he continued uncomfortably. Tamara had a mischievous idea and wondered what the priest would say if she announced that she was Bashour's slave? She smiled at the thought of it, despite herself.

"Ah, married, then? Betrothed, perhaps?" The priest was admittedly ignorant of the customs of Arabs. Perhaps they kept their names after marriage?

"Uh, no. Well . . . no, not exactly," said Bashour uncomfortably. He looked at Tamara, who pointedly studied the landscape across the river. *Let him talk his way out of this on his own*, she thought. She'd done nothing to be ashamed of. Well, nothing compared to what had happened to her.

The priest had encountered a variety of improprieties in his career and knew when to push and when to back off. He changed the subject to relieve Bashour of further discomfort. "What brings you here from the high desert?"

Tamara looked at Bashour, interested in how he would answer this question. "Well, to tell the truth," said Bashour, "we came with the Muslim army."

The priest was intrigued. This sounded like an interesting story. "Well, if you're spies, you're very poor ones. So how is it that you're traveling with us?"

"Well, Father," Bashour paused, unsure how to go on. Tamara just looked at him expectantly with raised eyebrows. She was so beautiful, he thought. "I was a Muslim," he finally blurted.

The priest raised an eyebrow. "Really? That is a surprise, from one of Imad's students." He looked at Tamara. "And you, too?" he asked.

Tamara shook her head emphatically. "Oh, no, never! I would die first!"

"She was taken captive," offered Bashour. He didn't elaborate when Tamara gave him a look full of daggers.

"So you were a . . . a Muslim? But you're not anymore?" The priest was aware that the invading Arabs professed the cult of Muhammad that he'd heard about.

"When they came into our town, they taught us. It made so much sense that I joined them. But it was wrong, Father, it's a false doctrine. So I left; and I helped Tamara escape with me." He felt the white lie explained why they were together.

"Why are you here with us? Why didn't you just go home?"

"Oh, I can't do that, Father. The Muslims control that area now."

"Bashour has left Islam," Tamara interjected. "If a Muslim catches him, he'll be killed."

The priest was sure they were exaggerating now. "Really?" he said skeptically.

"It's the truth. The penalty for apostasy is death. One of my companions became a Christian while he was in the hospital at the monastery. They killed him for it. I helped bury him."

Father Marcian had heard about brother Stephan's execution. He saw they were serious and realized there was probably much more to this tragedy than met the eye. "So you left Islam and helped Tamara escape as well; and now the two of you are traveling together. Since you're not married, that's a bit of scandal, you know."

Tamara felt a wave of panic rising. This priest had the power to take her away from Bashour, to make her journey with the maidens in the caravan, protected with them. Bashour was the only person she trusted. She realized with a jolt of surprise that the idea of being separated from him terrified her. She instantly decided to speak up, lie, explain that they were really married. Before she could formulate the lie, Bashour spoke. "We're not married, Father, but we'd like to be."

The priest looked inquiringly at her and she nodded mutely. She couldn't say anything; she was too busy fighting off the sudden wave of panic.

"Well, let me consult with the Bishop. Until then, may God bless us all on our journey." He picked up his pace and pulled ahead, leaving them alone.

Tamara gave Bashour a sideways look. "Thanks for consulting me!" she scolded, but her tone told him she wasn't angry.

"Tamara, I've known what I wanted for a long time. Will you marry me?"

"Hmph. You're such a romantic. I'll have to think about it." She waited with a straight face until his expression fell, then laughed. "Okay!"

78. Damascus
September 21, 634

Dhiraar had found Jonas after the battle and located a group of Muslim fighters who understood a patois of Arabic and Syriac. He made it clear that Jonas' first job was to learn Arabic, so he could start learning to recite the Qur'án. Jonas' new companions were solicitous. Once they realized he was a native of the city, they'd made him their tour guide. They'd never been in a city as large as Damascus and they wanted to see everything. They had endless questions and the communication barrier rapidly fell as they learned how to talk to each other. They were awed by the open spaces of the Basilica of St. John the Baptist. The call to prayer created some confusion, as they tried to convey to Jonas how to perform ablutions and arrange himself for prayer.

It wasn't until the following morning that he made excuses and managed to get away from them. He went in search of Eudocia. The house of Nicetas was in the northwest quarter, so he was confident that it had escaped damage in the assault on the city. A servant answered his call to the door and bade him to wait when he asked for Eudocia. Instead, Nicetas came to greet him. "So, you survived the fight?"

"Yes, sir," he said, craning to see over the man's shoulder, trying to see if Eudocia was there.

"You must have missed your orders, then. The army was ordered out of the city with the refugee column." Nicetas was in a foul mood and Jonas couldn't understand why.

"Oh, uh, I was a draftee. That order didn't apply to natives. I was discharged yesterday morning." He felt safe in the lie; with the army gone there would be no one to contradict him.

Bullshit, thought Nicetas, *you're a deserter*. But he didn't press the issue. "If you're looking for Eudocia, she's not here. She left with the refugees yesterday."

Jonas was speechless. Nicetas watched with some satisfaction while he struggled for something to say, then closed the interview. "I have no further need of your services in the warehouse. Best you go now." He closed the door in Jonas' face.

Jonas remembered his other problem. He had to find out if Kostas was still in town. But how could he find Kostas without being found out himself? Then he recalled his newfound Muslim companions, with their razor-sharp swords at their sides. That would give Kostas pause. He could find him, denounce him as a spy and a troublemaker and they'd make life very hard on him. Yes, that would work!

79. Bekaa Valley
September 22, 634

By the time they stopped on the third night, they were clear of the mountains and in the flat Bekaa valley of Lebanon. As night fell across the camp, Thomas met with Harbis and Bishop Peter. People were exhausted, and talked very little as they tended their animals and made a light dinner.

"We have to pick up the pace," insisted Harbis, "We're not making good enough time."

"Harbis, we can't drive the civilians any harder, or we'll start losing them. We're making excellent time. I've seen armies do worse."

Harbis looked unconvinced. "Where are we headed?" "We can't go south, Jerusalem is probably dealing with their own siege at the moment. We can't continue to the coast. There're no ports that can handle this many people. We'd spend weeks waiting for enough shipping to be assembled to evacuate everybody. I don't think we have any choice but to head north, for Emessa or Antioch."

"Antioch is too far away. It has to be Emessa."

Thomas shook his head. "We're taking the long way to get to Emessa. The Arabs can go straight there, cut three days off us and be waiting when we get there. Or we could arrive there only to find ourselves under siege again a day later. We need to go far enough to make these people secure."

"I see your point. Antioch it is, then. Now, about the order of march; should the soldiers be at the front of the column, the way we've been doing?"

"No, I've been thinking about that. The peace pact ends after tonight. I think we should keep a millennia forward and put the rest in the rear, with the civilians between them. That'll give a buffer if we're overtaken and attacked from the rear."

"They're not going to like that," warned Harbis. Being in the rear of such a huge column meant wading through copious amounts of animal waste.

"Now that we're in the valley we can spread the column out. Form five or six parallel columns. That should alleviate the problem."

Bishop Peter spoke up. “Won’t that cause problems with the local farmers, tramping through their fields, instead of sticking to the roads?”

Thomas shook his head. “I imagine most of the harvest is either done or under way. They’ll be happy for the fertilizer we’ll leave in our wake.” The men laughed. Thomas went on, “We haven’t many horses for cavalry, but I’d like to take what we have and put out scouts both ahead and behind us. From tomorrow on, we should treat this like hostile territory.”

“I’ll see to it,” promised Harbis.

80. Damascus
September 22, 634

"By the throne of Allâh, it's your fault, Ubaidah, for agreeing to let them run away! You never should have allowed that. Naturally the entire government went, leaving us with no one in authority to coordinate governing the city." Khalid paced back and forth in the large council chambers where they'd set up their headquarters, waving his hands in anger, his voice building up to a full-throated yell. "And even if we did have anyone with any authority to coordinate with, it wouldn't matter, because they also took all the gold with them!"

Ubaidah had been sitting placidly and letting him rant. "It's only a matter of convenience, Khalid. We'll simply draw up a schedule of exchange and they can pay their Jizyah in goods instead of gold. The winter is coming and the army will need to be reequipped in the next couple of months anyway. I'm told that they sometimes even have snow in the heights around here. The men will need heavier blankets, cloaks and winter footwear."

"How are you going to get an accurate accounting, Ubaidah? With no infidel to hold responsible and make sure the census is correct? How will we know how much Jizyah is owed?"

Ubaidah waved his hand in dismissal. "Relax, we'll give the problem to men with merchant experience and let them figure it out. It's just an inventory problem writ large. You're worrying too much about petty details. Relax and delegate the problem, then watch how someone else solves it."

Khalid threw himself into a chair and proclaimed, "The three days is over, Ubaidah. By Allâh, I'm going after that gold!"

"They have a three-day head start on you, and no doubt they're still moving. It would take you two weeks to catch up to them, even if you force-marched. Forget it, Khalid, they're gone."

"Maybe, maybe not. Where's Raafe?" He pointed at one of the men standing near the door. "You, go find Raafe and bring him here."

The man soon returned, leading Raafe by the arm. “Son of Waleed, you sent for me?” His eyes cast about sightlessly.

“Raafe, As-Salāmu `Alaykum old friend. Still no vision?”

“`Alaykum As-Salāmu, oh Sword of Allâh. Oh, I see light and dark and vague shadows in the light. Insha'Allâh, someday, maybe.”

“Raafe, where do you think the refugee column went?

“They left out the west gate, did they not?”

“Yes.”

“If they were going to Emessa they would have left out the east gate, or the one they call the Emessa gate. But they will go west, into the mountains. If they go far enough, they will hit the sea. Then they’ll have to turn north.”

“Is there a shortcut we could use to cut them off?”

Raafe shook his head. “I don’t know, Sahib. I’ve never been north of Damascus.”

“We need someone familiar with the area who can help us,” said Ubaidah. “Perhaps the man who helped you enter the city can help?”

Khalid nodded to one of the men. “Go and get Jonas Tournikes. And fetch my interpreter.” He poured a cup of aromatic tea and pressed it into Raafe’s hands. “Drink tea while we wait.”

It was nearly an hour before the messenger returned with Jonas and a strange young man. “Who are you?” demanded Khalid. “Where’s my interpreter?”

The soldier who’d fetched them spoke for him. “Sahib, your interpreter is missing. They haven’t seen him for days. They say this one is his friend and can interpret just as well.”

“What is your name, boy?”

The young man looked uncomfortable with the attention, but said in a firm voice, “Marid bin al-Asad!”

“A fine name. Speak to him for me,” he nodded at Jonas. “Tell him the refugee column has gone west. Ask him where he thinks it’s going and if there’s any way we can head it off.”

Marid fell into a lengthy discussion with Jonas, then reported, “He says the Bekaa Valley is three days from here. It’s a long valley that runs north and south through Lebanon. He says they probably won’t go to the sea, because there are no large ports nearby. He thinks they’ll follow the valley north and either go to Emessa or maybe try for Antioch, which is even farther north and closer to the coast.

"There's a shorter route. If you go up the Emessa road and turn west at Emessa, it would take a day or two off the trip. He says he can guide you there. His betrothed is in the caravan and he wants her back."

Khalid leapt to his feet. "Excellent! Assemble my horsemen. We'll leave tomorrow at first light. Horsemen only, I have no time for foot soldiers on this trip. You," he pointed at Marid. "Can you ride? Find a horse; I need an interpreter I can trust."

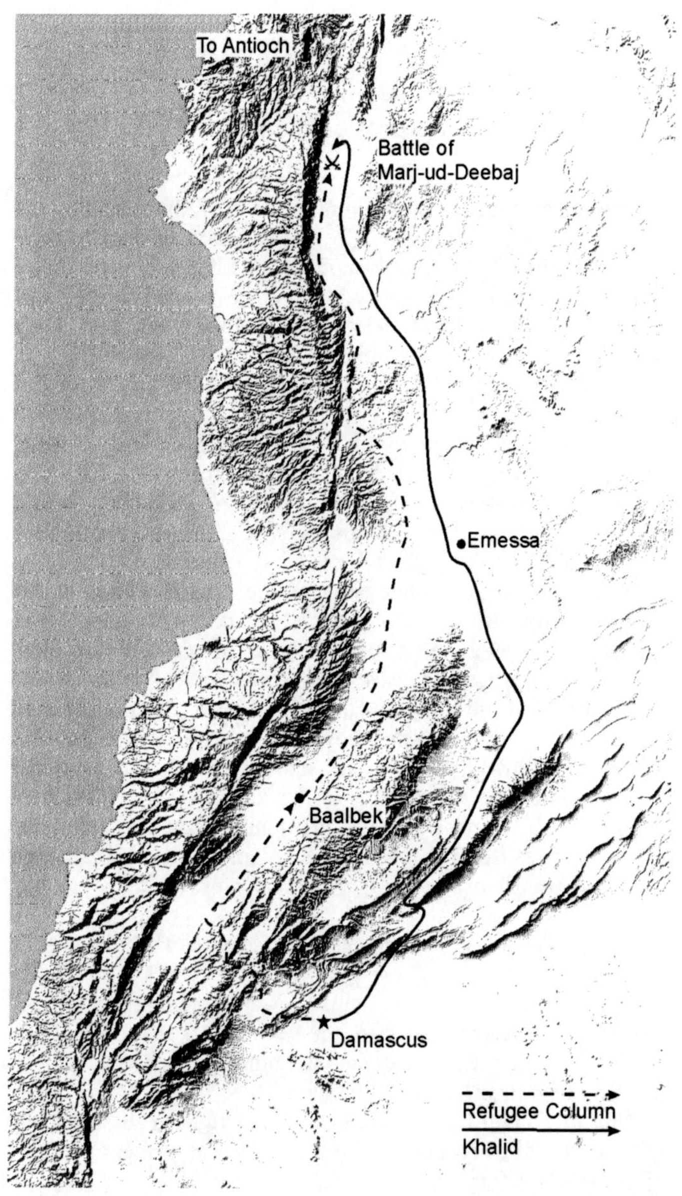

Khalid's Pursuit of the Refugees

81. Bekaa Valley
September 24, 634

They were walking in the morning sun, Tamara leading the mule, when they were joined by Father Marcian and, to their surprise, Bishop Peter. The bishop was leading a horse with an ornate saddle on it. After introductions, he handed the reins of the horse to the priest and bade Bashour to walk with him. They moved out of earshot of the others.

"Father Marcian tells me you professed the beliefs of our recent attackers."

Bashour took a deep breath. "Yes, Your Excellency. I made a terrible mistake. I've sinned and I'm sorry for it."

Bishop Peter put a fatherly hand on the young man's shoulder. "You can drop the formality. It's just you and me for the moment. Why don't you tell me what happened?"

Bashour told him about how the Muslims had come to his town and how he and Marid were persuaded to adopt their ideology and joined their army. He spoke of battles and endless days of walking with the army, of learning the Qur'án, which seemed to be infinite. He told how he'd been awarded Tamara for an act of bravery and how she'd resisted the Muslim ideology and slowly nurtured the seed of doubt in his own mind. He related how he'd lost faith in the idea of Islam when they killed Rashad for converting to Christianity, and how Wahid had helped them escape for reasons unknown. The Bishop listened attentively in silence, asking questions only to keep the boy talking.

When the story was finished, he asked, "The girl, she is your slave then?"

"No, father, it's not like that. I never treated her as a slave. I've been in love with her from the start. I wanted to rescue her. You have no idea what the captured women go through."

"But technically, she's your slave."

Bashour hung his head in shame, but refused to accept the full import of the accusation. "By their law, yes, I guess so. But I reject their law. She's free."

The Bishop chose to let it go. "Tell me about this 'Islam'. I've heard very little about it. They say it's like Christianity."

"Oh, no. No, nothing like Christianity. Oh, it seems like it at first glance, but the way they believe, the things they believe, the way they worship; no, it's nothing like Christianity."

"How so?"

Bashour was at a loss for words. Where to begin? "They deny that Christ was crucified and that he was resurrected. They deny the Trinity, or that Christ was anything more than a prophet. I'm kind of confused whether if they think he was even the greatest of prophets. Their words say they do, but they act like Muhammad was a greater prophet."

"What do you know about this Muhammad?" asked the Bishop.

"I'm not sure. They call him the messenger of Allâh. They speak reverently about him, as if they adore him. They can't even say his name without adding 'peace be upon him.' Everything they do, whether it's good or bad, they seem to do because someone remembers that Muhammad did it. The way they pray, the way they eat, even the way they use the toilet. Someone will always tell you the 'proper' way to do something and if you ask why they say, 'because that's how the prophet did it,' or 'that's what the prophet did.' They even fight about it if someone saw him doing something else."

"Well, what do you think? Was he a prophet?"

"I thought he was, at first. His teachings appeared to sidestep a lot of the questions I've heard about Christianity. But now it seems that everything he taught was just to satisfy his whims. The Arabs believed him, because it seems as if he used a lot of biblical stories and turned them into poetry. That got them believing he was speaking for Allâh. Once they believed that, anything he wanted he claimed that Allâh commanded it."

"Oh, surely it wasn't that easy. I'm sure someone called him a liar when he did that."

"Some did, and I was told they were killed. The Muslims brag about it, say they were doing Allâh's will. I even heard they sneaked into one lady's house and pinned her and her baby to the ground with a spear for making fun of Muhammad."

"So the critics learned to keep quiet."

"Exactly. And if they kept quiet and paid lip service, even if they didn't believe it, they were rewarded."

"Rewarded? How?"

"With loot." Bashour waved his hand behind them. "That back there, that was just the latest in a long series of fights and conquests. These people have been raiding and stealing in the name of Allâh for years. If you fight them, they'll steal everything you have and take slaves. If you don't fight them, they make you pay tribute. And they tell you they're doing you a favor, that you're paying them for protection."

"Protection from whom?"

"From them!"

"I'm disturbed that you cast your lot with such people."

"Oh, you don't see this at first. They act very holy, very devout. You have to admire their devotion to Allâh. It isn't until you spend a lot of time with them and realize that what you're doing is wrong, that you see that it's all a sham. They make a big show of praying five times a day, but all they're doing is reciting the memorized verses of the Qur'án. They're not petitioning God, or thanking him, they're just repeating a poem. I think they have a superstitious fear of Allâh and that he'll send them to hell if they don't do everything exactly right. And if you do it right, it doesn't matter what else you do, what you think or believe. You can kill a non-believer or rape a woman slave, because Allâh never forbade that, so it's all right and besides, Muhammad did it."

"And you realized it was wrong when your friend was killed?"

"No, not really. I was having trouble with it before then. I was rationalizing it to myself, I told myself that I didn't understand, that I just didn't know enough, that I was misunderstanding things. But Tamara kept arguing with me about things, and I would never have an answer for her that didn't seem hollow. It disturbed me. She never wavered, never conceded that I might be right; she just kept trying to teach me what I already knew in my heart. When they killed Rashad, I just admitted what I knew all along."

The Bishop changed his stride and took Bashour by the arm and led him out of the column of refugees, off the path, where he bade him to kneel. Placing his hands on Bashour's head he intoned, "Bashour, you have sinned grievously. You have dishonored your parents, you have turned your back on the church, turned your back on Christ and sinned against God. The Holy Spirit has encouraged you to return to God. Bashour, do you truly repent your actions and your sins?"

The answer was almost a sob. "I do, your Eminence."

"God, the Father of mercies, through the death and resurrection of his Son has reconciled the world to himself and sent the Holy Spirit among us for the forgiveness of sins; through the ministry of the Church, may God give you pardon and peace. I absolve you from your sins in the name of the Father, and of the Son, and of the Holy Spirit." He made the sign of the cross above Bashour, who felt as if a heavy load had been lifted from his shoulders.

They returned to the march and quickly overtook Tamara and Father Marcian. Bishop Peter took the reins of the horse from the priest and said to Bashour, "Please walk with the good Father for awhile."

The two men walked ahead. The Bishop walked quietly with Tamara for a bit, then suddenly excused himself. "Dear me, how long have you been walking, child? You must be exhausted. Here, climb on my horse for a spell and rest your feet."

Tamara protested weakly, but allowed him to help her into the small saddle. The bulk of the animal seemed strange to her, and a little frightening. Many years had passed since she'd ridden an animal as a child. Such things were frowned upon for a young lady. The Bishop put a fatherly hand on her knee as he walked beside the horse. He looked up at her. "Tell me what you will, child."

Not sure what to say, she was silent for a long, long time. The Bishop didn't press her, didn't ask any questions. He walked beside her and waited for her to speak.

She started tentatively, told how the Muslims had fought to capture her town, about the auction of the women who'd been taken slaves. Once she started, the words poured from her in a flood that she couldn't control. She spoke of how Jamila had been executed, about the screaming that seemed to never end and the way Mus'ad had raped her that night. She told how she watched her father killed at a distance and how Khalid executed people on the side of the road for no apparent reason. She talked of the long days on the march and the nights of being repeatedly raped by her captor. She told of the death of Mus'ad and how she exulted when it happened; then of her next captor Nu'man, his brutality, the beatings, and the farce of a marriage she'd been subjected to. Her long story ended when Nu'man was killed and she'd been awarded to Bashour.

Tears were rolling down her face and she saw that the Bishop had been crying, too, as he listened to her horror story.

"And Bashour, he treated you like the others?"

"Oh, no. I was afraid he would. I was so scared, but he's always behaved properly. I think he had a crush on me." She smiled at the thought, slightly embarrassed.

"Tell me about Bashour."

She thought about it. How to describe him? "He's headstrong and inexperienced and brave and honest and passionate about his beliefs. He kept trying to convince me to accept Islam and we'd argue when I wouldn't. I was so afraid he'd get angry and send me away, but he never did. He cared for me and protected me and even defended me against his friends. I know he loves me, but so long as he was a Muslim, I could never love him."

"And now? Now that he's left Islam, do you love him?"

She looked at Bashour walking ahead with the priest, well out of earshot. She thought of how she'd panicked when she thought the priest might break them apart. "Yes," she whispered. "Yes, I love him."

The bishop granted her absolution, then apologized and lifted her off the horse. He led the horse ahead to Bashour and Father Marcian. He bade Bashour to return to Tamara. Once he was gone, he said to the priest, "Do you think those two young people are in love?"

"I do, your Excellence."

"As do I. I just hope it's not a love born of circumstance, but that circumstance has placed them together as part of God's greater plan. What of the girl's family?"

"All dead, I believe."

"I don't know, I think her mother still lives. But these two, they're living in sin. They must not be tempted to further sin. We must sanctify their marriage as soon as possible."

"A wedding on the march?"

"We will be staying near Baalbek tomorrow night. That will be a good opportunity. Extraordinary circumstances mitigate the need for a conventional betrothal period this time, Father."

Thomas called a short council meeting as they made camp that night. Harbis, Taticus and Bishop Peter were there. Thomas started the meeting. "I'm very concerned that we're driving the civilians too hard," he said, rubbing at the eye patch he was wearing.

"I've been walking back and forth among the people," said the Bishop. "They're holding up well and spirits are high, considering the circumstances."

"I wonder if spirits would be so high if they thought we were being pursued," grumbled Harbis.

"Do you think we are?" asked Thomas.

"That Khalid, that bastard is a demon from Hell. He'll pursue us, no doubt," said Harbis.

"I have to agree," said the Bishop. "I've heard some pretty horrific stories about that one."

"Really? From where?" inquired Thomas.

"There's a young man with us who used to be one of them. He marched with them through Bosra and fought at Elah. Now he's escaped them and is running with us."

"That's fascinating. Can you find this young man? I'd like to speak with him," said Thomas. Father Marcian was called and instructed to find Bashour.

As tired as everyone was, people were nevertheless excited at the prospect of a wedding. A group of women had adopted Tamara and were busy outfitting her with dresses and jewelry for the wedding. One woman insisted on washing and styling her hair, though Tamara objected that it would be ruined in the following day's march. She soon realized that it wasn't about her at all, these women were thankful for something to take their minds off their immediate plight. She was little more than a doll to be pampered for their satisfaction. She smiled and resigned herself to it, though she'd have preferred to spend the time with Bashour.

One girl, about the same age as Tamara, introduced herself as Eudocia and presented her with a beautiful dress to wear. "I was betrothed to marry back in Damascus, but I have no idea where my man has gone. My father insisted I go with the column. I think my dress will fit you, and I'd be happy if you wore it for your wedding."

"Oh, thank you!" Tamara was overcome by her generosity. Very few women were their age and the two formed an instant bond. Eudocia asked about Tamara's experiences. Tamara tried to make light of it, but as the older women fretted over hair and other details, then slowly dispersed to deal with the rigors of making camp on the march, Eudocia persisted with penetrating questions. Tamara told her about the brutality of the Muslims.

She explained that she felt nothing but hate and loathing for them, because of what she'd experienced. Eudocia's sympathetic ear prompted her to spill her feelings. She didn't go into details of what had happened to her, but she related to Eudocia her conviction that Islam was nothing but evil. Eudocia listened with wide eyes that grew fearful as Tamara went on.

Bashour was bone-tired from the day's walk, but was understandably feeling left out when Father Marcian located him. When they arrived in Thomas' tent, Bashour was surprised to see the man with the eye patch who'd negotiated the surrender of the city. Thomas also recognized him after a moment. "Aren't you the interpreter?" he asked.

"Yes sir," replied Bashour.

"Bishop Peter tells me a lot about you. I'd like to hear your story in detail some day, but we haven't time right now." He leaned forward towards Bashour. "What I urgently need to know is whether Khalid will follow us now that the peace period has expired. Will he pursue us?"

Bashour didn't hesitate for a second. "Yes, sir. No doubt about it."

Thomas leaned back and cast a worried look at Harbis and Bishop Peter. "Thank you Bashour. That will be all. Please return to your encampment." As Bashour was leaving the tent, Thomas stopped him. "Oh, Bashour?"

"Sir?"

"Congratulations on your wedding tomorrow night."

"Yes, sir. Thank you!"

The others examined Thomas curiously. Bishop Peter hadn't discussed that aspect of Bashour with him. He looked around. "What? Come on, the whole camp is buzzing with the news. Do you think I'm blind and deaf? I can put two and two together."

82. South of Emessa
September 25, 634

Jonas pulled the unfamiliar keffiyah more tightly across his face in a vain attempt to keep out the dust and tried to edge his mount further to the right, to get upwind of the cloud being stirred up by those in front of him. They'd been riding constantly for two days since they left Damascus and followed the Emessa road north over the pass. His backside was sore and chafed from the constant riding. The horses and camels had been pushed on a grueling pace, and the desert had flown by. Each rider had two mounts and switched them out periodically to keep them from becoming exhausted. They stopped only for prayer and when it became too dark to travel by the light of the waning moon. Their food was dried meat, dates and flat bread.

The sense of adventure that Jonas felt when they started had given way to monotony and misery. His companions rarely spoke, even to each other. Even when they did, he usually couldn't understand them. When they stopped for sleep they acted perfunctorily towards him, neither hostile nor friendly. They laughed at him derisively the first night, when he dismounted his horse and couldn't straighten his legs. He'd gone red from the attention, but could do nothing. He spent that night in exhausted misery, too tired to stay awake and too sore to sleep.

The only thing that kept him going was the thought of Eudocia ahead of him. She must have thought him dead when she left the city. Her father had stayed, why didn't she? What would he say to her when he found her? Would she be happy to see him? He pictured her leaping into his arms, overjoyed that he was alive and promising never to let him out of her sight again. The daydreams replayed over and over, with slight variations as he embellished the scene in his imagination. It helped pass the time as the brown desert passed under the hooves of his horse.

The huge caravan they were chasing was rumored to have nearly all the gold from Damascus. He'd heard that they would all would get a share when they captured it. He hadn't encountered Kostas or his thugs since the fall of the city. With the gold he stood to share if they caught up with the refugee column, he could pay off Kostas and not have to worry about how he was going to get the money from Eudocia's dowry without her noticing. His daydreaming expanded to scenarios of how he'd pay Kostas, then have him killed by his new Muslim allies. A smile crept across his face.

83. Baalbek, Lebanon
September 25, 634

The forward riders had alerted Mayor Aspietes of Baalbek to the coming mass of humanity. He rode out to meet Thomas and familiarize himself with the situation, then the two men then rode ahead to prepare the city to receive their visitors. Baalbek was an ancient settlement perched at the base of the hills that formed the eastern edge of the Bekaa valley. A spectacular temple had been built here by the Romans to worship their gods. Some said that the size of the monument was a statement to the early Christians that the Roman gods were superior. A basilica had been erected in the main court of Jupiter in the fifth century by Theodosius. The gigantic columns of the temple were ten times the height of a man and commanded the view for miles around. As Thomas approached through the farmlands, he noted that the city was unprotected by a wall.

The sun was still high in the west when the main column arrived in the city, but Harbis reluctantly agreed to encamp there for the night. Refugees busied themselves in commerce with the city folk and many were invited into private homes to trade their stories for a home-cooked meal. Thomas and Harbis supped at the mayor's house with their wives. Bishop Peter excused himself on a matter of pressing business.

The sun was touching the western hills on the other side of the valley as they waited to be served their meal. Aspietes, Thomas and Harbis sat on the porch watching it. "We have to start moving faster," said Thomas. "The three-day peace pact has expired."

"We can make better time up the valley," observed Harbis. "We should be able to make Antioch in a week's time."

"Antioch? I would have thought you would try for Emessa, instead," said Aspietes.

Thomas shook his head. "No, for all we know Emessa is either under siege or already invested. If it's not, it soon will be. I plan to cross the valley and steer as far from Emessa as I can."

"What can you tell me of these Muslims? Will we suffer much if they come here?"

"You have no defenses to speak of, so if they come here, there's nothing you'll be able to do about it. If you resist them, they'll use it as an excuse to sack the city. That would be bad, they're a barbaric bunch, but strangely tame and well-behaved if you surrender and accept their dominion. They demand a rather heavy tribute though, a dirham of gold for each person in the city."

Aspietes whistled quietly. "That's an outrageous sum. If we can't pay?"

"We didn't ask, but my understanding is that a failure to pay would remove their protection from you and they'd feel free to sack the city. If you don't accept their cult religion then you really have no rights under their rule and they can take whatever they want, including your women, and there would be nothing for you to do."

As the first course of dinner began to be served, the women joined them without a word. Thomas took Epiphina's hand and squeezed it. He had to turn his head at an awkward angle to see her, as she was on his blind side.

"Don't be surprised if some of my citizens join your column when you leave tomorrow. There's been talk of a coming war and some people are worried enough to leave. I was wondering if I should ask you to hold some of the city's gold for me, but now I fear I should keep it on hand to pay the expected tribute."

"Your decision, Mayor. I'll support whatever you wish to do," said Thomas.

They heard a cheer and the sound of joyful singing from the Basilica. "What on earth is happening there?" asked Aspietes. "Do your people march all day and celebrate all night?"

Thomas smiled broadly, "Believe it or not, Mayor, a young couple marching with us is getting married tonight. If I'm not mistaken, the Bishop is presiding over the ceremony."

Aspietes raised his cup. "Love springs eternal! A toast to their long life and happiness!" The others raised their cups to meet the toast and Thomas again exchanged smiles with his wife.

"I'll be satisfied if they're still alive and free this time next week," he murmured quietly. She squeezed his hand reassuringly.

Bashour and Tamara were amazed and humbled by the huge number of people who attended their nuptials. The Basilica was overflowing. People were standing along the walls to watch the

Bishop bless their union. Eudocia stood by Tamara as a maid of honor. Bashour gazed at the sea of faces and didn't recognize any of them. The Bishop gave a short sermon on the sacrament of matrimony and how the most important command God gave was to be fruitful and multiply. He tied it into the current circumstances and concluded by observing that the power of love is greater than all worldly tribulations.

They recessed through the nave amid singing, cheering and a long line of well-wishers who pressed their hands and kissed Tamara. Someone produced some instruments and soon people danced to music among the columns and ruins of the old Roman temple.

The celebration was short-lived. They were still a refugee column on the march. Although the day's journey had been shorter than usual, food needed to be prepared, shoes mended and everyone desperately needed rest.

Tamara kept looking at him all night, smiling, then looking away shyly. She squeezed his hands during the ceremony and when they embraced for the kiss, he could feel her heart pounding. They felt high from the rush of excitement and the embrace of the greater community. When they finally closed the tent and were alone, Bashour was so excited he fumbled getting out of his clothes. Tamara turned her back and doused the lamp before she began to disrobe, then slid under the blanket. Bashour also got under the blanket and embraced her eagerly, leaning in and running his hands down her body. He sought her mouth and kissed her aggressively. As he did so, she stiffened and pulled back imperceptibly. The movement registered in his fogged mind and he stopped what he was doing and rested on an elbow. "What's wrong?" he asked.

"I'm sorry, it's just that you. . . It was like the others, before. . . I wanted it to be different. I'm sorry. I didn't mean to. Please. Keep going."

Bashour took his free hand and traced the outline of her jaw in the darkness. He gently caressed her cheek and explored her face with his fingertips. When he traced the outline of her ear, she turned her head to meet him, then let out a ragged sigh as his fingers traced a line down her neck. A shiver ran down her spine and she got goose bumps, which almost made her giggle.

She was aware of the warmth from his body, the brush of his skin on hers. It felt delicious. She shifted her body slightly to make more contact with his legs. As they continued kissing lightly, almost tentatively, she placed her hand on his chest, feeling the hard, flat muscles, then ran her hand over his shoulder and down his arms. She closed her eyes in the dark and lost herself to the moment, willing herself to relax, reminding herself that she was safe. A discordant voice in her head reminded her that it was only for a moment, but she willed it into silence.

His hands wandered over her shoulders and arms, leaving a trail of goose bumps wherever they went, but he seemed reluctant to explore anything more intimate. She gently guided his hand to her left breast and let out a soft gasp at his touch. She felt her nipples harden and could feel his body quivering in anticipation, tense with barely controlled desire. It delighted her that he desired her, that he desired her pleasure, not just his own. "Yes," she sighed. "I like that, that's the way it should be." She reached up and wrapped him in her embrace. They spoke no more as they guided each other carefully in celebration of their wedding.

84. West of Emessa
September 28, 634

Three day's march from Baalbek, Thomas paused from packing his tent and sleeping roll and studied the rising sun. He reflected that it didn't matter how much noise and bustle was around him, the sun coming up was always a quiet, peaceful time of the day. He idly wondered why that was. He turned and watched the golden light bathe the forest-covered slopes that rose from the valley floor to the west. They'd approached the foothills in darkness. The land of the valley floor was cultivated right to where the foothills of the coast range rose abruptly. From that point, a cedar forest dominated the hills. Small streams from the hills caused dips and rises in the otherwise relatively flat terrain they were walking on.

His reverie was interrupted by Harbis. "Still no sign of the riders you sent to Emessa?"

Thomas shook his head. "No, and I'm concerned. It's only ten or fifteen millaria from here." He waved a hand to the east, toward Emessa. "A fast rider should be back by now. What if they ran into pursuing Arabs?"

Harbis turned in the direction Thomas indicated, peering to catch sight of a rider in the early light. He laid a reassuring hand on Thomas' shoulder. "Relax, there's a dozen reasons why they haven't shown up that don't involve marauding Arabs." He turned and examined the forested hills on their left. "I feel better close to that forest. If an attack comes, we can order the civilians to disperse into the forest. It'll be much safer there."

"No!" declared Thomas. "I won't abandon any civilians in such a way. That's just what the enemy would want, to scatter the caravan and pick it off piece by piece."

Most men would have recoiled at this outburst, but Harbis had been friends with Thomas for too long to be intimidated, so he persisted. "Stop and think about it, Thomas, the Arabs are desert dwellers, and they're mounted." He gestured up the slope. "That's poor terrain for a horse and I daresay impossible for a camel. Those barbarians have no experience in trees at all. It could give us a significant defensive advantage. We could easily slow those bastards long enough to ensure the civilians have a chance to escape."

Thomas studied the forest critically. The arid climate kept the trees from being packed tightly together, but ancient fallen logs and rock outcroppings would make it very difficult to advance against any kind of organized defense; especially on foot and burdened with armor. "You have a point. Pass the word that if we're attacked that everyone should flee to the hills." He turned back and studied the rolling land to the east. "Put riders out on the flanks and in trail two or three millaria to the rear to give us some warning if the Arabs are sighted." The column was starting to move, as those who finished packing first started, anxious to avoid being in the rear of the caravan. "Disperse the military formations all along the column. It's not necessarily a tail chase anymore; they could strike anywhere if they come from the east."

He turned and examined the land ahead of them. The route narrowed ahead as it went through a defile in a small branch of the mountains that sprawled across their path. "Select a decade of fast riders to ride ahead to Antioch and tell them we need to be met with reinforcements as soon as possible."

Harbis nodded and waited for further instructions. Thomas thought for a moment, considering if he'd forgotten anything. "That's all. Let's get moving," he said. Epiphina and her maidservant were on the other side of the small cart they used to carry their goods, waiting for him to start.

Bashour was cinching down the pack on their mule when Tamara came up behind him and wrapped her arms around his waist and squeezed him tightly. He smiled and leaned back into her. Turning, he glanced around to see if anyone was paying attention, then gave her a quick kiss and they set off.

As they walked, they curiously studied the hills immediately to their left. Neither of them had ever seen so many trees in one place. The cedars covered the steep slopes as far as they could see. The hills had been dark and without detail when they'd approached them the previous night. Now they could appreciate the greenery for the first time. A light wind created a sighing sound among the branches and they could hear various birds chirping as the dawn called the world awake. Bashour fought the temptation to leave the column and explore among the mighty trunks not far from them.

Tamara had her arm through his and was in a talkative mood. "I never thought it would be like this," she reflected aloud wistfully. "I always dreamed of a long courtship and a dowry and a new house. I was going to live next to my mother and we'd cook together and take care of the little children. But Jamila and I also were planning to go to the city and meet handsome army officers and live in the finest neighborhoods in Tarsus or Constantinople."

"I'm sorry," said Bashour.

She squeezed his arm and smiled at him. "Oh, don't be like that. Those were just schoolgirl_dreams. We all knew we were bound to be farmer's wives, raising barefoot children and fighting a never-ending battle against the dust of the desert and sleeping next to dirty, sweat-covered men who snored.

"I don't want to think about what things would be like; if it wasn't for you. I'd be some Muslim's plaything, until I got too old and baby-stretched to satisfy him, and then I'd be sold off as a labor-woman, to die alone somewhere in the Arabian Desert. You saved me from a dreadful life. You're my hero."

That made him feel good and he smiled at her praise. "How many kids will we have?" she asked brightly.

He shrugged noncommittally. "I don't know. A dozen?"

"A dozen?" she squeaked in mock outrage. She smacked his arm playfully. "It would serve you right if they were all girls."

"I'll have to have to be rich to afford all the dowries, won't I?"

"Of course," she said smugly. Then with a slightly more serious tone, she asked, "What will you do, Bashour?"

"I'll find something. I'm good with numbers; I can always work as an accountant or a scribe. I can find good work somewhere in government. Maybe find something to do with teaching."

A Centurion and several centuries of soldiers were walking down the column in the opposite direction. He was repeating instructions as he passed. "If we're attacked, drop everything and make for the forest," he said loudly. "Get into the woods and go as high as you can and you'll be safe."

"Safer than we are out here in the open, anyway," grumbled a man not far from Bashour.

Bashour reflexively looked behind him, as if to see if they were being pursued, but all he could see was a mass of other refugees, trudging ahead the same as he was. He looked at the trees. They no longer fascinated him, but seemed dark and mysterious, foreboding; as if they hid secret dangers that he couldn't begin to imagine. Would they be enough to provide sanctuary against attacking Muslims? As he considered the prospect of Khalid and his army gaining on them, a stab of fear ran down his spine.

Marid was with the scouts when they returned and reported to Khalid at midday, just west of Emessa. He'd gone out with them to interpret, as they queried the farmers and villages that dotted the countryside.

The head scout pointed to the northwest. "We found signs of a large column moving north. The ground is churned and trampled in a wide swath, covered with fresh droppings. The locals say that they passed less than a day ago."

Khalid smiled. "Excellent. Draw fresh horses, then ride north and report back the instant you sight them."

As the scouts galloped off, he regarded Dhiraar beside him, who grinned. "Allâh be praised, by this time tomorrow we will be upon them."

"Allâh is great, indeed," said Khalid. He said no more as they rode on to the west.

85. North end of the Bekaa Valley
September 29, 634

The day dawned cold, with a spatter of light rain that increased as they readied the column to begin moving. The sky was dark and no one could tell when the sun actually rose, except that the gloom became brighter. A cold wind blew from the south, and after they'd walked less than two miles the rain increased to a steady torrent. Bashour and Tamara hunched their backs against the wind, pulling their cloaks tighter as huge cold drops were driven into their backs. It didn't take long before they were soaked to the skin and shivering. Neither of them was equipped for rainy weather. They slogged along silently in the rapidly deepening mud, their chins tucked into their chests against the cold.

The feet, hooves and wheels of those in the front of the column churned the ground into a quagmire, which became deeper as more and more people fought their way through it. The column started to spread out as those in the rear were progressively slowed by the mire. Where the ground was firm, the mud was slick, sending people and animals to their knees. Elsewhere, people stepped high and sank deep into the mire.

Bishop Peter found Thomas and implored him, "Governor, we must halt the column and let people seek shelter from the storm. Everyone is soaked through and we're hardly making any progress. The end of the column is getting spread out."

Thomas considered the proposal silently for several steps, then rejected it. "I'm sure that bastard Khalid won't stop for a little rain. We have to stay ahead of him."

"Thomas, you don't even know that Khalid is even following. I understand some concern, but this is bordering on paranoia."

"Excellency, I don't know that he isn't following. And I'm not prepared to accept the consequences if he is and we stop and let him catch us. We're a day away from the pass to Antioch. Once there, we can mount a defense and let people rest. Until then, we walk! You pass the word to any civilians who want to stop for the storm; the army will keep marching and they'll be without protection."

The Bishop clucked his disapproval, but acquiesced. The march went on.

The scouts returned in excitement to report to Khalid, "The trail is clear, a great churned up path of mud. They've passed this way since the rain started this morning."

Khalid smiled evilly and called for his commanders to assemble. He had to raise his voice to be heard in the deluge. "Abdur-Rahman, take a thousand men and stay behind the caravan. Stay back and don't attack until you hear the sound of battle. I'll take the rest and swing wide and strike them from the front." He peered into the driving rain. Visibility was very poor. He could use that to completely surround the enemy before they knew he was there.

He pulled his horse up and drew his sword. He raised it over his head and waited. Those around him saw the gesture and did the same. The signal propagated through the army, until four thousand swords were raised against the rain.

He dropped his sword and spurred his horse into a gallop, shouting "Allâhu Akhbar!" The army roared their echo behind him, and they charged through the rain.

Taticus squinted his eyes against the wind and peered into the rain to the south. Icy drops stung his cheeks. He couldn't tell the time without the sun, but he was sure it was midday. Visibility was barely more than a stadia, between the dark clouds and the driving rain.

A shadow moved in the gloom behind the column, then was gone. Taticus pressed his eyes closed to clear them and looked again. Nothing. Did he imagine it? He squinted again, peering harder, when a rider unexpectedly burst out of the gloom, riding as fast as he could. He slowed as he approached Taticus but didn't stop, yelling, "The Arabs are right behind me!"

Taticus waved him by, yelling in return, "Go! Go, spread the alarm!" He turned and saw that everyone around him, civilian and soldiers alike, were rooted to the ground in confusion. "To the hills!" he yelled. He grabbed the nearest civilian and pushed them towards the west. "Get into the trees! Go!" He turned to a soldier nearby and gestured to the horn at the man's side. "Blow that thing! Spread the alarm!"

Taticus moved among people milling about in the mud. "Drop everything! Run! Forget your baggage! Run for your lives!"

Soldiers were mixed into the confusion of the crowd. He grabbed each one he found. "You're with me!" Soon he had several decades of men. He formed them into a defensive line facing south. "You stay between these people and the Arabs. As the column gets into the forest, fall back with them, but keep them behind you. I'll send back more men to help you." Satisfied that the line wouldn't waver, he headed up the column, grabbing what soldiers he could find and exhorting people into the forested hills.

The sound of horns behind them pierced the noise of the storm and Bashour's blood ran cold. People began shouting in confusion, asking what was going on, but Bashour didn't wait. He took his knife and quickly cut the ropes that secured their small pack and tent on the mule. Pushing the tent aside into the mud, he fished the sword out of the bundle, then grabbed Tamara to run. Tamara pulled out of his grip. "Wait!" she said and grabbed his backpack.

"No time!" he shouted, but she already had it and it wasn't worth arguing about. They fought their way west through the sea of confused humanity. A rider rode by, yelling, "Arabs! Run for the hills!" Bashour and Tamara were ahead of most of the people as they began to drop their baggage and run.

Thomas heard the horns blowing behind them. Epiphina turned to him with a questioning look. A rider galloped up and shouted that the Arab army had been spotted. Thomas grabbed two of his aides and told them, "Get the civilians into the forest. Tell them to drop everything and go!"

Thomas cast about, looking for Harbis. He spotted him through the driving rain and started making his way towards him when another rider came from the front of the column. "I just saw a large column of riders passing in front of us at a run, from right to left!"

Thomas said to Harbis, "They're surrounding us. Form a perimeter around the civilians and keep moving for the hills." Harbis said nothing in reply, just nodded and started issuing orders to the men close by him.

Thomas returned to where his cart was and rummaged through it to get his armor and sword. Epiphina was standing there, as if in shock. He shook her. "What are you doing? Go!"

He pointed her to the west. He buckled the weapon around his waist and grabbed his bow. Then he pulled his banner from where it had been fixed to the cart and handed it to a young page, who'd been standing there looking helpless. "Hold this high, boy!" he commanded, then raising his sword he shouted, "Archers! Rally on me!"

Jonas struggled to keep up with the charging Arabs around him. Khalid was ahead, barely visible. His heart raced from the excitement of the charge, but in truth he could see nothing but driving rain and the mass of horses and camels around him. Khalid had split off large contingents of cavalry as they'd circled the caravan, so he had them effectively surrounded. The ground started to climb ahead and Jonas could see trees looming out of the rain and fog. The riders around him never slowed, but just turned left, to the south again, to ride down the opposite side of the caravan from where they'd overtaken it.

Then he started seeing people on foot, running from left to right across their path. Khalid yelled something but he couldn't understand what. Khalid ignored a group of women who were wailing as they stumbled and ran, then he saw a man behind them and altered his course. Khalid's sword raised high and struck downward as he rode past the man, leaving him in a pile of muddy rags and blood.

Thomas had established a wedge of archers facing north and east. The Arabs had made one charge, but had retreated when they encountered a flight of arrows. Thomas fretted about his bowstrings and those of the others. They'd been coated in beeswax, but it still wasn't good if they got wet. He hoped this wouldn't develop into a stalemate in the rain and they would slowly watch their bows lose tension as the strings expanded from the moisture.

He heard screams behind him to the west and turned to see what was going on. He met Harbis' eyes, who looked at him questioningly. Thomas jerked his head toward the cries. "Take a century and go see what's happening!"

Taticus had been leading his men slowly backward as the civilians behind them thinned. He'd organized several centuries facing the threat from the south. The sounds of battle north of them made the men nervous, but Taticus kept them disciplined and focused in the direction that concerned him. He started to wonder if he shouldn't move his line left, to start facing more east and north; but then the rain and fog south of him dissolved into a mass of Arabs riding camels and horses, charging through the mire that the caravan had left in its wake.

"Kontaria!" ordered Taticus. The men on the line drew the spears off their backs and dropped to plant them in the ground, facing outward toward the charging Arabs.

The charge pulled up short as the defenders sprouted a line of spears to impale their mounts. The Arabs quickly dismounted and waded awkwardly through the mud to engage the Byzantine line on foot. Taticus moved along the line, keeping discipline, maintaining the line intact as it slowly retreated to cover the civilians behind. He looked over his shoulder and could see the tree line in sight. Once there, he could establish a defensive line that would be very costly for the attackers to breach.

Bashour and Tamara reached the trees and stumbled up the slope. Tamara had hitched her soaking cloak above her knees so she could clamber over logs and deadfalls that littered the ground between the tall cedars. Turning back, they could hear the sounds of battle below them, but they saw no sign of pursuit in the trees, just other unarmed refugees clambering up the slope behind them. Bashour turned and looked up into the fog and rain-shrouded trees. "Let's keep going," he said, taking her hand and half-lifting her up.

Thomas and Harbis had about a thousand men in a defensive circle around them. Thomas had grabbed some civilian men and placed weapons in their hands and put them on the line. In the center of the circle was a huddle of women and children, crying in the rain and mud. Arabs pressed the line from all directions. Harbis saw a tall Arab with a red turban around his helmet and recognized Khalid. He knocked the Arab attacking him backward with a wild swing then disengaged and started making his way towards Khalid. The movement and his gaze caught the big man's eye. Khalid smiled at him and swung his sword in a circle in anticipation.

Most of the Arabs were attacking a defensive circle that had formed, but many civilians were still outside the circle, trying to run to the safety of the woods. Jonas ran among them, searching for Eudocia. A bright flash of blue caught his eye. He barely recognized her face, with her limp, bedraggled hair, but he knew the cloak and called her name. She turned in surprise. Seeing him, she cried, "Jonas?" and threw herself into his arms.

He embraced her in relief, then took her hand and started leading her away from the battle, towards where he'd left his horse. She resisted, pulling at his arm. "No, this way! The hills are this way!"

He gave her a jerk that caused her to stumble to her knees. "We're not going to the hills!" he growled. She kept pulling at him and crying hysterically. He cuffed her across the face to quiet her, then wrapped her in an embrace and caressed her sopping hair. "Shhhh, quiet! You're safe now. Trust me. You're safe while you're with me. Nothing will happen to you." He turned back and, with an arm around her, continued leading her out of the battle, away from the protection of the forest.

Thomas had to keep turning his head in an exaggerated motion to make up for his missing eye. An Arab broke through a momentary gap in the line and rushed at him. He stepped back, deflecting the man's sword with his, then pulling the man further off balance with his free hand. He chopped his sword into the unprotected base of the man's neck and felt the body go limp. His head swam as he rose and surveyed the battle line to see if any adjustments needed to be made. The defense was starting to dissolve in confusion. The fight was no longer organized, but a general melee as each man fought for his immediate survival. He saw Harbis locked in combat with the giant Khalid. They swung wildly at each other. Harbis was a bull of a man, not nearly as tall as the Arab, but easily as strong. As Thomas watched, Harbis parried an attack with a half-step back, then slipped in the mud. Khalid's sword never stopped and he completed the swing with a slash that ripped out Harbis' throat. Harbis dropped his sword, clutched at his throat and pitched forward into the muck, choking and bleeding.

Thomas cried out involuntarily and Khalid saw him. He raised his sword to point at Thomas' face as he advanced on him.

Taticus was relieved when his defensive line finally backed into the tree line and started retreating up the slope. He began placing his men against the terrain, forming a final defensive position. He was satisfied that all the civilians who'd been behind him had made the shelter of the trees and that he'd only lost a couple of decades of soldiers.

He fixed his line among the trees and fallen logs, but no Arabs pursued them. Once they'd entered the trees, their attackers had broken off the attack. He briefly considered a counterattack, but decided against it, counting himself lucky to have survived at all. He was unwilling to tempt fate any longer. He sagged to the ground in exhaustion and raised his face to the abating rain. A sliver of blue sky was visible and sunlight streamed over his shoulder through the dripping trees. “I’m getting too old for this,” he said to no one.

The rain had lifted and the muddy ground was steaming. Eudocia was gasping for air, trying to breath through the convulsive crying that racked her body. Whenever she’d get a decent breath, the hysterics would return. The ground around her was littered with bodies and rivulets of blood and water ran through the mud around her. Triumphant Arabs were rounding up groups of wailing women and others were looting the discarded packs and bodies of the fallen.

Jonas held her and rocked her and told her to be quiet, to calm down. She clung to him and slowly gained control. He kept talking to her, soothing her. “It’s all right. You’re safe. You’ll be all right. We can get married now. It’s all over!”

She finally looked up at him in confusion. “How . . .? I thought you were dead! How did you get here? How did you find me? Why aren’t they attacking you?” Her eyes were wide; she remained on the edge of panic.

“I’m one of them now. I knew they were eventually going to capture the city. If they did, I knew they’d kill me and rape you, so I negotiated with them to enter the city in exchange for your safety. But I couldn’t find you after the city fell.” He’d been thinking about this lie for some time and wanted to impress her with how influential he was. He was someone to be reckoned with now. “We can get married now, Eudocia, the war is over!”

She looked puzzled. “You . . . you did what? You betrayed the city? Why?”

“For you, my love,” He explained again patiently. “I did it to protect you! Now I have the respect of the Arab chiefs and they were going to rule Syria anyway, right? You’re safe and we’re free to get married when we return to Damascus.”

“I’ll never marry you!” she cried and turned her back on him. The stories of the horrors that Tamara had told her became an imminent reality to her. She’d calmed down and felt numb, dead.

His face turned dark with anger. "You will marry me! You'll marry me and accept Islam. You have no choice!"

He stood and pulled her to her feet just as Marid and another Arab approached. "All the prisoners are to be gathered over there for an accounting."

"This one is no prisoner, she's my wife." He pushed her behind him protectively and didn't notice when she slipped his dagger out of its sheath in his belt.

Marid explained the situation to the other Arab, who shrugged and the two moved off. Jonas whirled on her and took her by the shoulders. "There! I just saved you from a lifetime of slavery and rape. Your life belongs to me. You'll do what I say and accept Islam and become my wife."

She glared up at him through the wet strands of her hair and said defiantly, "I'll never do any such thing!" With a sudden jerk she plunged the dagger right below her breastbone, angled upward to pierce her heart. Her mouth opened in surprise and she gasped breathlessly, sagging into his arms.

Jonas reflexively caught her, stunned at what she'd done. He collapsed to the ground with her, holding her in his lap. He snatched the bloody dagger from her twitching fingers, held her tight and screamed his anguish as her life drained away.

86. North end of the Bekaa Valley
September 30, 634

Several hours before sunset, the jubilant Arabs had finished looting the battlefield and marched away to the south. Those who'd made the safety of the trees spent the night there, afraid to come down until the sun had set, and then unable to move in the dark, moonless night.

Cold, hungry people crept out of the forest as dawn broke and ventured tentatively over the battlefield. The sky was clear and the air was cold. People picked their way through the bloodstained mud, plucking at a corpse here, examining the wreckage of a wagon there. Women went from body to body, looking for their husbands, and collapsing in tears if they found them. Here and there a priest walked among the devastation, administering the rites of the dead.

Taticus took command of the situation and started issuing orders to the remaining centuries of soldiers he'd managed to salvage. He sent some back into the forest to gather firewood and build bonfires to dry people out and warm them up. He detailed others to find dead animals strewn about the field and begin butchering them for much-needed food. He organized the rest into teams to gather the dead and prepare them for burial. He went with the burial crews.

One area of the battlefield was churned up where a large group had obviously made a stand. More than a thousand men-at-arms had died there. Taticus walked the area and could see where they'd formed a defensive perimeter. Once he'd established where the lines had been, he made his way to the center, turning corpses over to examine their faces.

He found Thomas near the center, easily identified by the patch over his left eye. He'd been badly cut in several places and a huge cleft had been hacked into his shoulder that went past his collarbone. His sword arm was a welter of cuts and blood. Taticus smiled grimly as he closed the man's remaining eye. "At least you went down fighting."

He found Harbis nearby. The man's throat had been cut halfway through. He directed a nearby team to give these two men special consideration when they collected the bodies. He continued to search among the dead.

Bashour led Tamara out of the forest and they surveyed the carnage of the battlefield. He wrapped his arm around her and she clung to him and tears ran down her face. A pall of smoke rose from a bonfire that some soldiers had kindled not far from where they were. They stumbled towards the warmth. Tamara kept her head down and her arms wrapped around Bashour, hiding her face from the horror that surrounded them.

Taticus walked down the line of bodies that had been gathered by mid-morning. “How many women are there?” he asked one of the Decharchs, who was counting bodies and trying to identify people.

“Very few, sir. Four or five dozen at most.”

“I’m looking for the daughter of the Emperor, wife of Thomas. Are these all of them?”

The Decharch shrugged apologetically. “I’m pretty sure we’ve found all of them. If she’s not here, then she was most likely carried off as a prisoner.”

“Riders coming in!” someone shouted. Taticus turned in alarm and was relieved to see a banner with a cross on it at the head of an orderly line of Byzantine cavalry. He stepped out and waved, attracting the attention of the lead horseman.

As they drew closer, he recognized the Turmarch that led the column. “Hail, Psellus!” he shouted.

Psellus acknowledged his greeting and dismounted as he drew close. “Taticus, by God! We came as fast as we could when we received your messenger. How the hell did you get here?”

Taticus gripped the man’s hand and smiled grimly. “That’s a long, long story, my lord.”

Psellus examined the destruction and death around them and the long lines of thousands of bodies. “My God, Taticus! What happened here?"

Bookends

To the Most Excellent Sergius, Patriarch of Constantinople
Antioch, 7th day of October, year of our Lord 634

Greetings, Sergius

May the blessings of our Lord Jesus Christ be upon you.

I have advised you in past correspondence of the invasion of Arab armies from the south into Syria. I write now with heavy heart to inform you that Damascus has fallen after a month-long siege. Jerusalem is not currently under siege as far as we can tell, but we have no coherent military forces in that part of Palestine, so the city should be considered surrounded and cut off.

The loss of Damascus had an unfortunate consequence that I wish to relate to you, to give you insight into the nature of these invaders. The conquering general agreed to allow those who wished to leave Damascus the chance to do so. My son-in-law Thomas was the acting governor and led a band of some ten thousand people out of the city.

Ten days on the road after leaving the city under a flag of truce, the Arab army caught up with the column and attacked it. Thomas was killed, as was the regional commander named Harbis. My daughter was taken prisoner. Fortunately, a numeri of cavalry that had been dispatched from Antioch pursued and caught up with the marauding Arabs and negotiated the return of my daughter, who is safe and sound with me now.

I've interviewed some witnesses to these events, including a young Arab who claimed to have been one of the invaders before he switched sides. From these interviews, I feel we're facing something far more sinister than just an occupying army.

The binding discipline of this army derives from a devotion to an Arab god named Allâh, and the belief that a man named Muhammad was the messenger of this Allâh. All of their soldiers must swear allegiance to this god. If they later renounce this allegiance, they are subject to be killed, not as traitors, but as religious heretics. They call themselves Muslims and their religion is called Islam. This army moves through the countryside and requires that towns submit; to either profess allegiance to Allâh, or to pay a tribute to him. People living in the occupied areas are segregated from the invading armies by this religious difference. If one does not covert to Islam, then they are considered a second-class citizen, with a rather capricious judicial system that favors the Muslims in all ways. Christians are not allowed to build new churches in occupied areas and are not allowed to repair their old ones without permission.

The stated goal of this cult is to subject the entire world to their belief system, by force if necessary. They've built up a whole theology around dying in battle for the purpose of furthering their cause.

My fear, Sergius, is that this system is designed to coerce populations to accept allegiance to their belief system as well as their government. I have no evidence that the two are separate. Faithful Christians will be discriminated against by the occupying Muslims, but they can end that discrimination by renouncing Christianity and becoming Muslim themselves. If this continues for more than a few decades, these peoples may completely lose their Christian identities and become enemies in name and in fact.

Sergius, you, Honorius and the other patriarchs must call to all Christians to set aside their differences and rally to this cause. We need to raise an army from all over Christendom to recapture the lands recently lost in Syria. We must then pursue this Islam into the Arabian desert where it sprang and eliminate it from the face of the earth. If we do not do so, Islam will cast a shadow across the light of civilization and we stand to be locked in battle with this ideology for thousands of years to come.

Yours in Christ,
Flavius Heraclius Augustus, Basileus of Rome

Glossary

Al-Buraq A mythological steed which carried the Prophet Muhammad from Mecca to Jerusalem and back during the fabled "Night Journey"

Allaghia A Byzantine unit of fifty troops, comprised of ten squads and commanded by a Pentecontarch

Ansari Tribe of Arabs native to Medina, and some of the first converts to Islam outside of Mecca

As-Salāmu `Alaykum Arabic - Standard greeting. Literally "peace be with you."

Ayat A single verse from the Qur'án

Cataphracts Byzantine heavy cavalry

Chiliarch Byzantine rank, roughly equivalent to a Lt. Colonel

Cubicularius Originally a title of a eunuch chamberlain, the position became a term for a trusted administrator.

Decharch Byzantine military rank, a non-commissioned officer, in charge of 10 men

Domestikos Leader of a cavalry unit of about 1000 horsemen

Drungarios Byzantine leader of a Drungus, between 2000 and 4000 soldiers

Drungus Byzantine unit between 2000 and 4000 soldiers

Ghassanid A tribe of Arabs originally from Yemen which had settled the desert of eastern Syria.

Haram Arabic – forbidden

Injeel Arabic – Gospel

Insha'Allâh Arabic: "If it is the will of Allâh"

Jehennam Arabic term for Gehenna, or Hell.

Jihad A holy war in the name of Allâh

Jizyah Tribute paid by a non-Muslim who lives in a Muslim occupied land.

Kaffir Arabic - derisive term for a non-Muslim

Keffiyah Arab head covering

Kentarch Commander of a century of infantry

Komes Byzantine military rank, leader of a Banda, a unit of two to four hundred soldiers.

Kontaria Byzantine – 6-9 foot long spear or pike that infantry could use against cavalry

Lochaghos Warrant officer

Mahr Arabic – The agreed dowry when a couple contracts Mut'ah, or temporary marriage.

Menavlatoi A specialist variant of the Skoutatoi, more lightly armored, employing a smaller shield, but armed with a much stouter type of pike (Menavlion)

Merarch Commander of a cavalry division of 4000-16000 horsemen

Meros A division of cavalry – 4000-16000 horsemen

Millarium Roman unit of distance, roughly equal to a mile.

Mudarres Arabic - Teacher

Muhajirun Arabic – "Immigrant," the term used for the Muslims of Mecca who went with Muhammad when he relocated to Medina.

Mujahideen Arabic - A soldier engaged in Jihad

Mut'ah Arabic - A contract marriage with a predefined expiration date, generally involving the payment of a dowry by the "husband."

Numeri A Byzantine infantry company, roughly 300-400 men or cavalry

Pente A shortened term for a Pentecontarch

Peritrachelion A liturgical vestment worn by priests and bishops of the Orthodox Church and Eastern Catholic Churches as the symbol of their priesthood

Qibla Arabic - The direction of prayer for a Muslim

Sahaba Arabic – A companion of Muhammad, who learned the Qur'án from his mouth.

Salah Arabic - blessing

Salat Arabic – Muslim prayer

Sariya Arabic – an army unit engaged in Jihad.

Severian A member of a Slavic tribe from the southern Russian area of the Dnieper River

Skoutatoi Byzantine heavy infantry. The name derives from the skouton, a large oval shield. They were armored with simple conical helms, kremasmata (an armored skirt), livanion (a sleeveless lamellar cuirass) typically augmented with pteruges (leather strips worn to protect the shoulders) and epilorikion (a padded leather garment worn over the cuirass). Their arms included a spatha (double-edged sword) and kontarion (two to three meter long pike)

Spatha Byzantine double-edged sword

Stadia Byzantine unit of measure, roughly 200 yards/185 meters

Strategos Byzantine commander of the army

Stratopedarches Byzantine term for quartermaster, handles supplies for the army.

Subhanahu wa Ta'ala Arabic: "may He be glorified and exalted"

Sura A chapter from the Qur'án

Tetrarch Byzantine military rank, non-commissioned officer, in command of a squad of four

Themata Army composed of multiple turma/meros.

Turma A division of soldiers – 4000-16000 troops

Turmarch Commander of an infantry division of 4000-16000 soldiers

Historical Note

Because of the relative scarcity of source material surrounding the events in question, it's both a blessing and a curse to write about this point in history. It's a blessing because it frees the author to a great extent, and a curse because you want to stay reasonably historically accurate. The only primary source we have of the campaigns of the Muslims in Syria comes from the Islamic Tabari hadiths. Theophanes barely mentions it. Edward Gibbon wrote extensively about it in the Decline and Fall of the Roman Empire, but plagiarized Tabari almost word for word. A.I. Akram's biography of Khalid bin Al Waleed, Sword of Allâh, is an excellent source, but is very recent and again draws a lot of information from Tabari. Like myself, Akram must have realized that Tabari was no military historian and had never walked the ground over which the events took place. Akram altered the timeline and sequence of events that Tabari related because Tabari's account simply didn't make sense. I ran into the same problem, and usually agreed with Akram.

The dates given in this book are approximate, and are based on the Gregorian calendar. Some dates are certain, such as the assault on Marj Rahit during the festival of the summer solstice. The actual dates were most certainly different to the people of the day, since they were still using the Julian calendar, or the Arabic lunar calendar. The partial eclipse of the moon that Bashour witnessed on his night watch really happened. The people of that time were very aware of the night sky because of the lack of light pollution. I've made every effort to make the phases of the moon as consistent with the dates as possible.

The terms Roman and Byzantine are used interchangeably in the text. The Arabs considered the Byzantines as Romans, and the Byzantines most likely did as well. All cities and towns mentioned in this book still exist. The city of Emessa is today's Homs, in Syria. The ruins of Tadmur and Baalbek, the hanging monasteries on the road west of Jericho and the great amphitheater of Bosra are part of the rich pre-Islamic heritage of the area. Bosra played a significant role in the history of early Christianity. It was also linked to the rise of Islam, when a

Nestorian monk called Bahira is said to have met the young Muhammad when his caravan stopped at Bosra, and according to Muslim tradition predicted his prophetic vocation and the faith he was going to initiate. The northeast gate of Damascus is today named the Thomas Gate because of the battle Thomas fought there. Since this name was given after the events in the book, I have chosen to refer to it as the Emessa gate.

A purist will object to the use of some modern-sounding terms by the Byzantine Greek characters, particularly swearing. Yes, some of the swear words used here didn't originate for a thousand years later, but I promise you that as long as there have been non-commissioned officers, there have been epithets used of a sexual nature, and the Greeks were perfectly capable of cussing a blue streak in terms much more colorful and descriptive than modern-day English. I've chosen to convey the intent to the modern reader within the frame of reference you would understand.

The Arabic way of speaking at the time was recorded as being far more formal and flowery than the way I've represented much of the dialogue here. I have no way of knowing if that record is representative, or was dressed up by those who made the written accounts. I chose to render it in a more modern vernacular for ease of reading. Likewise, most modern English translations of the Qur'án used archaic King James English to somehow make them sound more legitimately scriptural and holy. I have also rendered Qur'ánic recitations in the modern vernacular.

Many Muslims may object to the way Islam is portrayed in this book, through the actions of the various characters and some of the dialogue regarding Islamic teaching. I assure the reader that the scriptural references and stories told are all accurate, drawn directly from the Qur'án and hadith, except for the story of Dimah and Sameer, which is my own invention. The thing to remember about this period is that Muhammad had only been dead for two years, and none of the Qur'án had been written down anywhere. It was contained entirely in the memories of the faithful, and no single person remembered the whole Qur'án. There are records of numerous disagreements about what was and wasn't canonical, and whether any given individual remembered something correctly. Almost all the Arab faithful had some personal experience with Muhammad, and many of them followed Islam for their own reasons that may have had very little to do with religious faith. The rigid, unbending theology of Islam today is the product of the interpretations of Imams over the centuries. The Islam that Muhammad taught was very dynamic, continuously evolving to meet any situation that Muhammad encountered, and lent divine authority to the often rather capricious solutions he'd propose. In short, Islam was still a squishy sort of theology at the time, much given to individual expression, very different from the rigid canon that it is today.

In the year 634 the Byzantine Empire was recovering from a ruinous war with the Persian Sassanids. The Emperor Heraclius, who'd seized the throne by deposing the corrupt Phocas in 610, had proved himself a brilliant battlefield commander in the war against the Persians. He was intent on rebuilding the infrastructure of his empire, refilling the public coffers, and instituting numerous reforms throughout the land. He'd changed the official language from Latin to Greek, and was working on an ambitious plan for land reform. The pressing controversy of the day swirled around the nature of the human and divine character of Christ, and virtually everyone had an opinion on the subject. A substantial scandal also surrounded Heraclius for having incestuously married his niece, Marta.

The Arab incursions in the south of Syria had stalled under the command of Ubaidah, and the Caliph Abu Bakr ordered Khalid to hand over his command in Persia, where he'd won stunning victories, to lead the armies in Syria. Rather than take the long route to Syria, Khalid entered from the east in a risky and stunning surprise movement across a nearly impassable desert.

The first people he encountered in eastern Syria were Ghassanid Arabs who'd settled there from Yemen. They were Christians, but had very tenuous loyalty to the Byzantine government. The Arabs swept through with the ultimatum that communities accept Islam, submit and pay the Jizyah, or face the sword. When confronted with thousands of warriors who had a reputation of defeating armies much larger than themselves, many garrisons submitted without a fight.

Tabari states that Marj Rahit was entertaining refugees who'd fled ahead of Khalid's advance through eastern Syria during their midsummer solstice festival. I distrust this account, because the speed of Khalid's advance would have overrun any refugee columns. The Muslim seventh-century blitzkrieg literally rode on the heels of the news of their coming, and moved much faster than any refugee column would have moved. More than likely the Marj Rahit festival was simply hosting Arabs from around the area.

Gibbon states that Bosra is four day's travel from Damascus. This implies a travel rate of approximately fifteen miles a day. That's a reasonable rate for a column on foot. A force-march over a great distance might achieve twenty miles a day. That's the standard rate that I used for determining the progress of the army. Obviously an individual on a good horse could go much faster than this. A single determined rider with fresh mounts could conceivably reach Bosra from the Dead Sea overnight, as I show Ubaidah doing. No one disputes the horsemanship of the Arabs. Arab cavalry typically traveled dismounted, to save the horses for battle.

Tabari reports that Romanus betrayed the city of Bosra and led a hundred Arab soldiers through an underground passage to invest the city from within. This was a recurring theme for Tabari, who apparently didn't appreciate the implications of siege warfare. He overused the theme of a betrayer from within as the way Muslims defeated walled cities until it became a cliché. Akram disagrees with him and wrote that Bosra surrendered after an inconclusive siege, and I agree with Akram.

During the siege of Bosra, Khalid makes a reference to Caesar. Although this title for the Roman Emperors had long fallen out of fashion in the empire, Arabic writings show that the Arabs still used it.

Tamara's implied consent to marry Nu'man is correct under Islamic law. From the Bukhari hadith, Volume 7, Book 62, Number 67:

Narrated Abu Huraira:

The Prophet said, "A matron should not be given in marriage except after consulting her; and a virgin should not be given in marriage except after her permission." The people asked, "O Allâh's Apostle! How can we know her permission?" He said, "Her silence indicates her permission."

Tabari's accounts have Khalid besieging Damascus, then breaking off for the Battle of Ajnadeyn. This doesn't make sense, tactically, and puts a tremendous onus on Khalid's army to move at an almost superhuman pace to make the timeline. A.I. Akram in the *Sword of Allâh* places the battle of Ajnadeyn after the battle of Bosra, with no deviation northward to Damascus, which is more believable. I concur with Akram.

The Battle of Ajnadeyn took place in the valley of Elah, 15 miles southwest of Jerusalem. In the Arabic custom it wasn't necessarily named after a place, but the word Ajnadeyn is a descriptive of the battle, and was applied in hindsight. Tabari treats it as a place name, but no one there at the time would have considered referring to it as Ajnadeyn. The accounts of who was in charge on the Byzantine side at Ajnadeyn are confused. Some say Andrew; some say Vardan, some say both, and some say that they were one and the same person, that Vardan was an anagram of Andrew. Most accounts agree that Theodorus was there, but no one was clear on his position with regard to Andrew. I've taken the position that Andrew and Vardan were the same person, and tried to show how the uncertainty of the command structure contributed to the Byzantine's devastating defeat. The Bishop Sergius of Joppa – not to be confused with the Patriarch Sergius of Constantinople – was a controversial figure in Syria in 634. I have no historical evidence that he was actually at Ajnadeyn, but would have been surprised if he wasn't.

Tabari's account of the battle is sparse. We know that Khalid waited until later in the day to engage in general battle, and that he won a stunning victory on the second day. I've proposed a set of tactics that suggests how he may have used the terrain to accomplish this against a numerically superior force.

Tabari's account says that Andrew laid a trap for Khalid in an attempt to assassinate him, but was foiled when his emissary got cold feet and spilled the beans. Khalid then sprang a counter-trap and killed Andrew. I think this is embellished by Muslim historians who had no idea of what transpired in the Byzantine camp, and have every motivation to paint the infidels as underhanded, cowardly scoundrels who would stoop as low as a plot such as this. It's highly unlikely that a Byzantine commander would pursue such a plan if he outnumbered the enemy three to one, as Andrew did. The scenario I paint in my story is much more likely.

The executions of Caloiis and Azrail have two different accounts. One has them being bound and executed as an example in sight of the defenses of Damascus. I find this an empty gesture, since this would have had to have been done safely out of bowshot, and therefore it would be unlikely that they would be close enough to draw the kind of attention and recognition that would be desired for such an action. Another story has their heads being thrown over the wall. I find this also unlikely, because those walls were 21 feet high, and a human head is pretty heavy.

Tabari says that the daughter of Heraclius was married to Thomas, and was captured in the battle of Marj-ud-Deebaj, which is the battle at the end of the book, and subsequently released to Heraclius without a ransom. All this was highly unlikely according to western historians, and is probably a result of Muslim romantic dramatization. I've chosen to leave this part of the Muslim account intact, because it makes for a better story. The Muslim accounts say that the arrow that struck Thomas couldn't be removed and was cut off. I find this hard to swallow: such a wound would have surely been fatal, and Thomas would have been in too much pain to be functional.

In the battle of Bait Lihya, at the top of the pass against Libanius, the record states that Raafe was second-in-command, not Abdullah Bin Umar. The record is contradictory whether this is the same Raafe that led the army across the eastern Syrian desert and lost his sight. In my story Raafe never regains his sight fully, so to avoid a naming confusion I gave Dhiraar a different vice commander.

Tabari also records that the sister of Dhiraar, Khaulah, disguised herself as a warrior and fought like a demon at Bait Lihya, then volunteered to be in the force to rescue him. I chose to leave this out, as it lent nothing to my narrative.

The Tabari Hadith states that Jonas betrayed Damascus because the siege was the only impediment towards the impending marriage with Eudocia. This seems like a rather thin excuse to betray a whole city. I invented a whole back-story for Jonas to make the narrative of Tabari more believable. Tabari states that the city was having a celebration the night of the betrayal, and that the defenders were drunk and the guard was relaxed. This is unbelievable, so I altered events to something more realistic, while maintaining the general thread of the narrative. According to Tabari, after the battle of Marj-ud-Deebaj, Eudocia committed suicide. Khalid offered Epiphina to Jonas as consolation, but Jonas refused and fought bravely with the Muslim army until he was killed at the battle of Yaqusa.

The refugee column that left Damascus under the cease-fire is recorded to have been moving up the coast towards Antioch when it was intercepted by Khalid. This is impossible, since no main road ran along the coast in that part of Lebanon, and the terrain would have been prohibitive for Khalid to have executed the encircling maneuver described in the records. It makes far more sense for the column to have been following the western limit of the northern Bekaa Valley when they were intercepted. Tabari never recorded the routes that either army took, but the geography and the timing match the route I have proposed here.

Ubaidah had received orders from Umar to relieve Khalid, but did not act upon those orders until Khalid had returned from attacking the refugee column. When Khalid demanded to know why he'd held those orders for so long, Ubaidah calmly replied that it wasn't fitting to relieve a commander in the middle of battle. Khalid continued to serve with distinction under Ubaidah's command.

This book began in a debate with a Muslimah from Cairo who claimed that Islam spread peacefully. I was researching my response to her when I uncovered the details of the siege of Damascus and the subsequent slaughter of the refugee column that had been allowed to leave under a flag of truce. This story is largely unknown in the west, and I felt it was important to tell. In doing so, I concentrated on the story itself and the characters, and omitted much of the blood and butchery that Tabari recorded, because it would have seemed gratuitous in the telling of the story. The real history was far more bloody and horrific than I could convey through the eyes of some of those who may have been there. Any good historical fiction should provide a toehold for the reader to learn more about the given period, and if I have done this for you, then this book is a success.

-Sean Emerson
July 2012.

CPSIA information can be obtained at www.ICGtesting.com
Printed in the USA
LVOW05s1404020114

367742LV00030B/352/P